CONSPIRACY OF MAGIC BOOK ONE

D1541601

RUTHLESS MAGIC

MEGAN CREWE

To Lucas, the best kind of magic I know

CHAPTER ONE

Finn

When I'd rehearsed this conversation with my father in my head, I'd been a shining example of wit, passion, and the famous Lockwood composure. Unfortunately, my imagination had lied. I was on the verge of pacing a hole in his study's Persian rug, and I appeared to have lost my ability to string more than three words together. All of which was extremely bad timing, given that the course of my future as a mage might be decided in the next half hour.

I managed to partly untangle my tongue. "What I mean is, no official decisions have been made yet. For what track I'll be put on at the college. Right?"

Dad nodded. He'd shut his laptop after he'd welcomed me in, and now he stood by his broad mahogany desk. Behind him, the drapes were pulled back from the tall windows. The warm sunlight pouring in caught on the distinguished sprinkling of silver in his light brown hair.

"The placement committee won't meet until the letters have all been sent and the acceptances received," he said.

I drew in a breath. The smells of Dad's study were a mix of intimidating and comforting: all those ancient leather-bound magical texts on the shelves at my left, the lingering hint of woodsmoke from the fireplace at my right. "And Granduncle Raymond will have some say in my placement. That's what he's coming to talk to you about."

"Undoubtedly."

Dad sounded calm enough, but that impression wasn't the whole story. My right thumb spun in a rhythmic circle against my fingertips—a simple casting I'd used so often it'd become automatic. A dissonant ripple of tension sharpened amid the ever-present whisper of magic against my skin. Dad didn't think Granduncle Raymond was going to have anything inspiring to say about my abilities either. It was scarcely a secret that I was the least favorite grandnephew.

"You *will* be Chosen, Finn," Dad added. "There's no doubt about that."

"I know." The fact of it didn't settle my nerves. It was one small certainty leading to a vast unknown.

"Of course you'd like to have some say in your career. I'll try to see that you're offered a few options."

My throat constricted. What I'd *like* was to be able to conduct the magic around us as easily as I could breathe—to conjure and 'chant so well that the College of the North American Confederation of Mages would be begging for my attendance rather than squeezing me in as a token to appease my family.

I'd tried. O gods, how I'd tried. I'd memorized so much ancient Greek and Latin I dreamed in it. I'd pored over texts on technique until my eyes felt ready to bleed, and I'd performed the scales until my voice was hoarse. I'd spent years practicing the meditations and calculations that were supposed to hone the mind and attune it to the magic. So what if none of it had been quite enough? I would *keep* trying, all the way through college and every day after.

"I'm aware I'm barely ranking above the bottom quarter of my class," I said—flippantly, to offset the uncomfortable twist in my gut at the admission. "I realize I won't end up as advisor to the Director of the Joint Staff like Margo or as chief whatever-it-is-he-does-in-that-penthouse-office like Hugh. I just want to be doing something *real*. Something useful."

As Dad had done when he was little older than me, campaigning for mages to finally step out of the shadows and fully contribute to society. *We have a gift*, he often said. *It gives us a responsibility to help* everyone, *not just the magical*.

"I want to get on track to enter the National Defense division," I went on.

Dad's eyebrows rose slightly. "That work requires a significant measure of applied magic."

"Yes, and I know I'd have to settle for a minor position because of that. But I'd rather be doing what I can to preserve the country than be head inputter of tax records or secretary of office supplies."

"I don't have any direct sway. It's your granduncle who'll make the recommendation."

"Right. So I thought, when he arrives, I could perform a demonstration. Show him how I've advanced my skills in a relevant area. To help... inform his recommendation."

"Hmmm." Dad rubbed his jaw. "What sort of demonstration are you planning?"

"I'm not sure," I admitted. "I was hoping you could advise. I'm reasonably competent at locating and tracing, though I still need to work on my range. I've been building my shielding abilities, and I think I've found an enhancement to standard practice that might be useful in certain scenarios. And—"

Interest lit Dad's face. He leaned back against his desk, his hand resting beside the obsidian paperweight I'd made him when I was seven. He'd kept the damned thing all this time even though the 'chantment on it was so weak that disturbed papers would merely coast more slowly rather than holding in place—unless they were actually beneath the weight, which defeated the purpose of having 'chanted it. I could do a proper job of it now, but it seemed embarrassingly childish to offer.

"Let's see this shield of yours," Dad said. "Innovation counts for a lot."

I straightened the collar of my linen button-down, willing away my nerves. Then I inhaled deeply. The quiver of magical energy tickled over my tongue. If time hadn't been of the essence, I might have reveled in it for a moment.

With every thought trained on my intent, I rolled the words over my lips at a lilting cadence: "Qua requieverit herba, moenia..." The magic trembled through my muscles and bones as the rhythm of my voice twined with the energy's innate melody. Some shuddered away from me, as always, but I felt a significant portion resonate in harmony.

Modulating my poetic phrase at a steady volume, I directed the rising hum of magic into a shimmering barrier between Dad and me. My hands lifted with it, guiding my focus. I had to pitch the vibration perfectly so that any offensive casting would bounce off rather than shatter the shield. When I'd asked Prisha to test my last attempt, my construction had held up to a good battering.

I slid into a new phrase, calling a glinting play of light into the shield's surface—a pattern to soothe the minds of anyone observing it. The effect wasn't entirely my own invention, but I hadn't read about it being put to this use before. In the midst of an attack or a bomb scare, presumably reducing panic would be a valuable feature.

My view of Dad had blurred. A smile crossed his lips. He was *impressed*.

I sang the poetic lines again in a crescendo and pushed the conjured shield up to the ceiling and out to the walls. The energy raced through me, piercing the roots of my teeth and the bases of my fingernails, but I could carry it farther. I'd never cast a barrier much bigger than myself before, but protecting only one person was hardly the scale National Defense required. I should at least—

I pushed a little too hard, too fast, and the magic I'd managed to bend stretched too thin. A tear opened in the shield. It gaped wide before I could catch it, as swiftly as the bag of winds loosed by Odysseus's sailors. A groan escaped my mouth.

The glittering mass crashed to the floor and shivered away into the air.

Dad's face fell with it. His shoulders drooped for an instant before he suppressed his immediate reaction.

A hot burn formed behind my eyes. I blinked quickly. The only thing that could make this disaster *worse* was him witnessing me break into tears.

"Well…" I began. My voice came out a croak. I cleared my throat, my thoughts darting to Granduncle Raymond's periodic reminiscences of the city's "golden days." "Perhaps a cabaret show instead?"

Dad's lips twitched with amusement: a tiny consolation for my crushing failure.

"I'll do what I can," he said. "I know how hard you've worked." He rested his hand on my shoulder with a reassuring squeeze. The gesture only twisted me up more.

Before I could hit on some way to salvage the situation, the doorbell chimed. Granduncle Raymond had arrived early. I trailed after Dad into the hall, but I didn't quite trust my composure enough to follow him downstairs.

Dad's smooth tenor and my granduncle's dry, gravelly bass carried up the stairwell. As always, Granduncle Raymond got straight to the point.

"It's time we talked about Finnegan."

"He's right upstairs—"

"Just the two of us."

Dad couldn't argue with that laying-down-the-law tone, not when Granduncle Raymond literally did lay down the laws across all the Confederation with the other nine members of the inner Circle. There were some lines even family didn't cross.

Their footsteps approached, along with the intermittent tap of Granduncle Raymond's walking stick. Just for show—the old man's stout frame still carried him without a hitch. To spare myself being dismissed directly, I ducked into the adjoining guest room.

At the click of the study door shutting, an impulse struck me. It would be a simple thing even for me to 'chant the plaster a touch thinner, temporarily, so the voices would travel through. Normally I wouldn't have considered listening in on a private conversation, but it was *my* life they were hashing out.

I sat on the bed's goose-down duvet and pressed my pale hands to the maroon wall. After riffling through my mental compendium of memorized verses, I settled on a line from a Greek play. I murmured it to send the magic wriggling through the particles of plaster beneath the wallpaper. A chalky taste crept into my mouth.

Granduncle Raymond's voice filtered through the wall. "...certain expectations of magical performance. We don't want to put him in a position where he'll cause us embarrassment."

I winced.

"I don't believe that will be a problem," Dad said tightly.

"He's your son. I understand. But we need to be realistic. The committee will examine his Academy records and propose a career based on those, within my guidelines. And I expect that proposal to go unchallenged."

"There isn't any chance we could arrange a special curriculum for him, to see if his abilities could be further extended?"

Granduncle Raymond guffawed. "Have you denied him any opportunity in the last sixteen years? He's had his chance to shine if he were going to."

I closed my eyes as hot shame washed through me. Dad's reply was too quiet for me to distinguish the words.

"Keep in mind we have a delicate situation to maintain," Granduncle Raymond said. "The mage-averse factions within the Dull leadership are making noise again. We haven't brought any decisive victories abroad in too long. It's vital that the Confederation as a whole, and the families in the Circle in particular, appear competent to anyone looking on. Before this... intermingling, a more flexible solution might have been possible."

"We failed society much more often when we were working in secret," Dad said with the flatness of an argument he'd made too many times before.

"But at least then the Dulls couldn't hold our failures against us. Or attack us for faults they merely imagine. Your father..."

I pushed off the bed before Granduncle Raymond could finish his sentence. My grandfather was his trump card in any political argument with my father. Shortly after the Unveiling, Granduncle Raymond's younger brother Edward had been killed at a public conference turned anti-magic riot.

Dad spoke of him as a hero. Granduncle Raymond made him sound like a victim of misguided principles.

As I wandered across the room, a flash of unnatural color outside the guest bedroom window caught my eye. Frowning, I stepped up to the glass.

Partly hidden by the branches of the elm outside, a spiral of colorful sparkles gleamed against the muted blue of the sky. The image was clearly magical.

I didn't recall hearing plans for an official display. Technically, all noncommercial magic usage was legal as long as it didn't break any other laws, but large-scale, amateur public conjurings were rare. What was this?

Any excuse to leave Granduncle Raymond and his disparaging remarks behind seemed like a good one. I hurried down to the front door and out into the August heat. The intersection where 81st Street opened up to Madison Avenue would give me the best view.

I stopped on the corner amid the acrid tang of car exhaust and craned my neck. My jaw went slack, and the twisted feeling inside me was swept off by a wave of awe.

The unwinding spiral I'd observed from the window was merely the tail—the tail of an immense serpentine dragon soaring across the sky. The rich green-and-blue speckles of its scales darkened to violet along its belly and blazed orange at the tips of its wings and the crest of its head. The illusion swerved around a puff of cloud, and the hues shifted as if reflecting the sunlight.

The vibrations of the magic tingled in my ears, on my tongue, and over my skin, pulsing in time with the dragon's dance. The sensation drew an ache like homesickness into my chest.

Such a conjuring required not only power but meticulously controlled skill. Hearkening the magic, I knew I'd never cast anything even half that potent.

The Madison Avenue traffic had slowed. Astonished faces peered through windshields at the sky. If *I* found the dragon impressive, I couldn't imagine how it struck the magicless.

None of their heads turned at the flit of a smaller conjuring that streaked past me: someone's letter of evaluation. A shiver of anticipation shot down my spine, but there was no telling whom it was meant for. This segment of the Upper East Side had been an enclave for mages since well before the Unveiling, and all of us who'd turned sixteen in the last school year would receive our letter today.

After Granduncle Raymond's comments about what awaited me once I received mine, I'd rather look at the dragon.

A bright voice rang out behind me. "There you are!" Prisha slung a slim brown arm over my shoulders. "Gawping at the sky?"

I elbowed my best friend lightly. "I'd say that's worth gawping at."

Prisha tilted her head to contemplate the dragon. "Ah, I could pull that off if I really wanted to."

"I'd like to see that," I said, keeping my tone light. Prisha liked to act as if she didn't attempt major castings because she simply didn't care to, so I might have been the only person who knew she cared very much—about how people saw her, about their expectations of her. Although the Mathurs were old money, they were the newest of new magic. Prisha was the first to show any talent. Everyone else in our year at the Academy had magic intertwined through their ancestry, like I did.

Better to do a lot of little things very well, Prisha had told me in one of her rawer moments, *than to try something big and bungle it and watch them sneer as if they knew all along that I'd never measure up.* Given the number of textbooks I'd smuggled out of the Academy library to page through in secret in my bedroom— because everyone at the Academy expected a Lockwood to come by his talent effortlessly—I had no trouble sympathizing.

"Probably a Chosen, right?" I said with a nod to the sky. "That'd be one way to celebrate."

"I could think of a few better," Prisha said.

At the slight edge in her voice, I glanced over to search her face. Was she worried? She ranked in the upper half of all our classes, even if not by a large margin. The college accepted a varied number of novices each summer, but they always took about two thirds of any academy year. She was a shoo-in.

Before I could say as much, Callum Geary stalked out of the building opposite us. Long skinny legs holding up a stout torso balancing a boxy head topped with a sprinkling of russet hair—a haphazard figure that matched his erratic temperament.

"What's the big deal out here?" he demanded.

He must have noticed us from the window. The Gearys had money but not as much as some. They owned only the second floor of that divided townhouse. He wouldn't have been able to make out the dragon itself from there.

I motioned wordlessly. It was my policy not to speak to Callum unless absolutely necessary. That was easier than you might expect, considering we were classmates and near neighbors, because Callum rarely cared what anyone except him had to say about anything.

He ambled across the street toward us, crossed his arms, and purposefully-by-accident smacked his elbow into my ribs. Squinting up at the dragon, he let out a snort. "How *pretty*," he said. "It must be a girl conjuring that—or a fruit, I suppose."

Prisha's arm tensed against my shoulders. Did Callum even know he'd just insulted her twice in one go?

"Thanks for weighing in," I said, dry as dust, and remembered why I had policies about Callum when he trained his narrow stare on me. What talent he lacked in casting, he made up for with inventiveness of other sorts. The last time he'd given me that stare was in seventh year, shortly after which his hand had "slipped" to staple my sweater sleeve to the back of my hand.

I suspected he'd been restraining himself at least a little all this time, hoping that if he wasn't too blatant of a bully, he'd still be Chosen despite his terrible grades. If he was Dampered after today, which he almost certainly would be, he wouldn't have even that small motive to rein himself in.

But it *was* still today, the Day of Letters, so Callum had larger concerns than me. He swung around with a ram of his heel that would have broken toes if I hadn't yanked my foot out of the way, and sauntered back into his house. The door thudded shut behind him.

"Thank the Fates we won't have to deal with him at the college," I said under my breath. After the procedure was complete, the Dampered took on apprenticeships tailored to their remaining fragment of magical ability.

"Indeed." Prisha ruffled my hair and then started to pull me back toward my house. "Your bangs have gotten all floppy again, Finn. You need an occasional haircut if you're going to look civilized, you know."

"And trick people into believing I *am* civilized?" I said. "That seems unfair."

She rolled her eyes. "Please. You're the least boorish person I know. When was the last time you even *inconvenienced* anyone?"

My thoughts hurtled back to the conversation I'd overheard a half hour ago—to the inconvenience I was to my entire family. As we paused by my front door, I took minor comfort in seeing my granduncle's Lexus had departed.

"Whatever," I said shortly. Prisha gave me a questioning look. I might have told her about the epic failure of my conjured shield and the comments I'd overheard, but not now, not here on the street. I grasped at a change of subject. "How was the club last night?"

"The usual," she said with a shrug. "Drinks and music and lots of pretty girls. Some of them are straight, by the way. Next time I'll drag you along." Her eyes glinted with mischief. We both knew my coordination on a dance floor resembled a drunken antelope.

"Then I couldn't be your cover story for your parents."

"Oh, I'm sure we could—"

She cut herself off as a bright beam flitted into view. It hit my door and transformed into a small ivory envelope.

The twisting in my gut returned. I detached my letter of evaluation and ran my finger over the sealed flap.

"Well, open it!" Prisha said. "I know you're in."

"Of course," I said. "Because I'm a Lockwood."

"No. Because even the Confed has to know that stubborn determination is at least as good a superpower as flashy wand-waving."

She spoke with such assurance the clenching inside me relaxed. We were going to take on all of it—the college, whatever careers they threw at us—the two of us, together, as always.

I tore open the envelope and pulled out the crisp paper inside. My gaze dropped straight to the stark black lettering halfway down the page.

We are pleased to announce that Finnegan Lockwood has been chosen for admission to the College of the North American Confederation of Mages.

"Congrats," Prisha said, clapping me on the back. "All in the world is as it should be."

"Yes." I'd expected a rush of emotion reading the words, but all I felt was dull discomfort.

It occurred to me then that Prisha had never said why she'd come looking for me. "Shouldn't you be at home, waiting for *your* letter?"

"Ah, well." The grin she offered me faltered.

"Pree?" A chill jabbed through my stomach.

"I just wanted to make sure you'd gotten yours," she said. "And it arrived with good timing, because it appears my visit is over."

"Prisha!" her eldest brother called, coming into view on the other side of the street. He strode across to us. "I'm glad you're predictable. No phone again?"

Prisha made a not-entirely-believable gesture of apology. *One of the advantages of being born into a family of Dulls*, she'd said to me more than once. *Leave my phone at home, and they can't harass me.*

"Father wants to discuss preparations with you," Amardeep said. "You've had time to tell Finn by now, haven't you?"

"Tell me what?" If she'd already gotten her letter, she'd have been waving it in my face. Unless...

"It doesn't make a difference," Prisha told me. "I'm not going to be Dampered. I'm taking the Exam."

"*What?*" She turned to go, but I grabbed her wrist, waiting until she looked at me. "If you weren't Chosen, you've got to appeal. The Confed makes mistakes. This *has* to be a mistake."

She'd ranked higher than me in all our classes. She'd done everything anyone could have asked.

"An appeal will take weeks. And if I lose, then the Exam will be over and I won't have any choice in the matter," Prisha said. Then, more softly, she added, "I've already declared, Finn."

"Let's go, Prisha," Amardeep said. "There's a lot to cover."

Preparations, he'd said. How could she prepare? No one who hadn't gone through the Mages' Exam knew what the trials entailed, other than that the Confed made them brutally hard to ensure those vying for a second chance at the college deserved their spots.

The handful who made Champion each year got an excellent deal, set up with a prominent mage as a mentor to help them catch up with their Chosen peers. However, where they succeeded, dozens didn't. The penalty for rejecting the Circle's judgment unwisely was harsh. Those who failed had their magical ability not Dampered but utterly burned out of them. A few examinees didn't just fail but *died* during each year's Exam.

"Don't look at me like that," Prisha said in her more usual brisk way. "I'm sure the Exam isn't half as hard as the stories make out. I'll see you soon."

Her hug was so swift I didn't have time to return it before she hurried after her brother.

But, Pree, I thought, dread gripping me. It didn't make sense.

My hand closed around my letter, creasing the paper. I shoved it into my pocket and pushed open my front door.

The sight of the foyer with its antique furniture and molded ceiling sent acid into the back of my mouth. In that moment, I hated the house and all the old-magic history it represented. No matter what Prisha said, she knew as well as I did that the Circle's decision for me hadn't been about "determination."

"Finn?" Dad came around the curve in the staircase and halted when he saw me. "It arrived?"

"Yes," I said. "Chosen, of course. But Prisha wasn't. She's... she's going to take the Exam."

Dad's expression flickered. I thought I saw relief there alongside concern—and a certain resignation. "I'm sorry," he said, walking the rest of the way down. "But if that's what she wishes to do, it's her choice."

"She shouldn't have had to make it," I said. "She should have been Chosen! She had the talent. What in Hades's name is the point of Dampering if we're going to lose mages like her to it?"

"The Circle has always needed to make difficult decisions about who and how many they can keep proper order with," Dad said. "And now... just one generous ruling resulting in a mage gone off the rails could undo the harmony we've managed to achieve since the Unveiling."

"No one could think Prisha is going to become some sort of *criminal*."

"New-magic candidates have no established family record of behavior or loyalty. The Circle has higher requirements for skill to overcome that basic concern. If there's anything worrisome in the family history, they take that into account as well. Which isn't to say I *agree* with all of their reasoning—"

Normally Dad's calm, measured way of speaking comforted me. Now I only felt ill. "That isn't reasoning. That's... that's just prejudice."

"I understand why you're upset, but this could be a good chance for her, Finn. If she makes Champion, she'll have the opportunity to improve her abilities through individual guidance, with all the avenues that will open up for her."

She should have had that opportunity without risking all her magic. If anyone should have had to fight for it...

It should have been me.

"I want to give her my spot," I said abruptly.

Dad's eyebrows rose. "You know it doesn't work that way. What the Circle decided for Prisha is completely independent from who was Chosen."

I did know that, but how could I support it? I'd realized I hadn't fully earned my acceptance into the college, but at least my gain hadn't hurt anyone.

My heart started thudding. I'd been ready to challenge my career placement. Maybe what I ought to challenge was the foundation on which it was based. I couldn't give Prisha my spot, but I could at least show the Circle I knew what they were doing wasn't right.

"Have you accepted yet?" Dad asked, and I shook my head. "Well, don't leave them waiting. Then we should call your mother at the office. She wanted to hear as soon as the letter came."

He motioned for me to follow him down the hall, but my feet had melded to the floor.

Was I mage enough to meet the Exam's ordeals? I'd wanted to prove I was worthy of more than being shunted into a convenient spot that needed filling. I should *have* to prove myself.

Prisha shouldn't have to face the Circle's judgment alone.

"Finn?" Dad said.

I fumbled in my pocket for the slip of paper. As I raised the letter to my lips, my pulse beat hot and heavy in my head. My mouth opened.

"Finnegan Lockwood declares for the Mages' Exam."

CHAPTER TWO

Rocío

People were staring at me, but I was used to that. You'd think it was our neighbors' civic duty to keep an eye on "that witchy girl" and her witchy family. At home, they stared at me and my parents when we were going to and from school and work, when we leaned out the open windows of our apartment to catch a summer breeze. At least the people passing Brooklyn United Collegiate this Saturday afternoon had a good reason to gape.

"De colores, de colores," I murmured in the singsong tone Abuelita had cooed the lyrics to me with years ago. The hues of my dragon's scales deepened against the sky. I tipped my head, and the conjured image whirled to the left, closer to the sun.

The wrought iron fence along the school lawn pressed hard against my back, but otherwise my body was barely earthbound. The hairs on my arms were standing up, and a tingling glow filled my lungs, washing out the hot still air that hung over the street. Magic hummed through me and around me. The entire world was an instrument it was played on, and right now an awful lot of it was playing a song for me.

For me and Javier. *That'll show them*, he'd have said. *They can't ignore that.*

Three years ago on this day—the Saturday before the last week of summer vacation, the Day of Letters—my older brother and I had stood on the patchy concrete steps outside our walk-up, and he'd conjured his own dragon. He hadn't been able to cast it this high or draw it this vast, but it had been beautiful enough to take my breath away.

When I'd started conjuring today, I'd meant to make one like his. But the more magic I'd drawn through me, the faster it had rushed in, and I hadn't wanted to shut any of it out. So my dragon soared amid the clouds, more than big enough for both of us.

If some part of Javi still existed in the world, somehow, he couldn't ignore this. He'd give me a sign, wouldn't he?

I reached out through the hum of the magic for the slightest hint of his presence. All I felt was the vacant space beside me like an ache around my heart.

This is the last magic I'll get to cast freely, he'd said to me back then. *When my letter comes, it'll be the Confed deciding how I use it.*

He'd never talked that way to anyone else. I was the only one he'd known understood him completely. But even so, I'd had to say, with a thirteen-year-old's dogged optimism, *Maybe you'll be Chosen.*

Javier had laughed. *No, the mages don't want some passable-talent street-magic naco coming to their college, not unless I win that spot. But they have to take you. Even the Confed has to accept a gutter-girl who can 'chant circles around their old-magic flunkies. I'll make sure of it.* His smile had turned a little crooked then, with the kind of hope he didn't dare let out as anything other a joke.

And hey, maybe after that I can get myself named first magical advisor to the NBA.

He'd wanted to hold on to the magic just as much as I did.

I *made sure they'd take me*, I thought to him now. I'd followed the Confed's rules, learned from their books, picked up every skill they could have wanted from any novice. At the college and after I left, I'd still be answering to them, but I'd still have the magic and the full license to work with it too. That was all that really mattered.

I stretched my awareness up toward the sky. No whisper of Javi answered. The ache grew, eating at the glow inside me. Pricks of a different kind of pain pinched at my joints from the effort of the extended casting.

No matter what I tried, I couldn't find him. Which meant it was time to admit I never would.

I was on my own.

Adjusting my focus and my tone, I drew the dragon down, pulling my words tighter around it to shrink it. The resonance of the energy itched at the roots of my teeth. I cast it toward the flat brick face of the high school.

"De colores, de colores."

The scales sank partway into the bricks, leaving a shimmering impression. I let the magic rush out of me to fix the 'chantment there. Not with so much power to make it permanent but enough that it would last the week. My dragon sprawled across the front of the school from end to end, its belly resting against the lintel over the main doors.

A smile crossed my lips despite the pang in my chest. Javi had always said the Dull schools wanted us to be even smaller than the Confed did. I'd felt the truth of those words in the stuffy halls beyond those windows, watching backs turn when I passed, hearing hushed gossip behind me. The tutorial room and Mr. Jones, the Dampered mage who'd taught us novices, I would miss a little. All the required literature and math and sciences with the Dull student body, and the teachers who'd eyed me after every test as if I might have conjured my A's? Not a chance.

I wouldn't be back here, but I'd left a mark so people could see the beauty of magic when they passed by. It didn't seem fair that they'd never hearken it like I did, but maybe I could make something that evoked a little of the breathtaking feeling I loved inside them. Maybe someday they'd stare at a casting with excitement instead of apprehension, like the magic deserved.

I pushed away from the fence toward home. Mrs. Hernandez was sweeping the front step two doors down when I reached my apartment.

"Bruja-ratera!" she muttered, letting go of the broom with one hand to make the sign of the cross.

I didn't look at her. She'd called the police on Mom once for supposedly giving her the evil eye. "Witch-crook," her insult meant, translated literally. As the only magical family in the neighborhood, we got all the suspicion and hostility that came along with that.

When we were kids, Javier and I used to debate whether it would be better or worse if the Unveiling had never happened and the mages had kept their secrets to themselves. Of course, it was hard not to settle on *worse* when, without the Confed's mandatory testing, Mom and Dad might never have been identified as more than a little "sensitive," which meant they would never have ended up in the one magical tutorial class for all of Brooklyn and Queens, which meant they might never have met and we wouldn't have been around to consider the alternatives.

Once I got through the college, once I had a permit to use my talent toward employment, we'd be able to move. There weren't many new-magic families in general, but there had to be an area of the city that was a little friendlier.

As I climbed the sweltering stairwell, I pulled an elastic band from my jeans pocket and swept my dark hair into a ponytail it was only just long enough for. Our building had no air conditioning. The back of my shirt was damp by the time I reached the third floor.

A small white envelope was fixed to the outside of the apartment door. My breath caught. My letter was already here.

I peeled it off. There was nothing to be anxious about. For the last three years, I'd been heading to the Manhattan Academy of Aspiring Mages—where I was at least allowed into the library for free—every day after class to study. And even before then, Mr. Jones had said I was the strongest talent he'd ever seen in his tutorial class. Much stronger than the last student marked as Chosen by the Confed.

That former student was a magimedical consultant for the whole state now. A Harlem guy originally from the Manhattan-Bronx Tutorial had been appointed advisor to the mayor last month. The Confed made a little room for us when we proved ourselves worthy to their standards.

Still, I clutched the envelope unopened as I stepped into our cramped living room.

Mom was embroidering a blouse at the desk that doubled as a dining table when she wasn't working. Perched between the streaks of sunlight from the narrow windows, she looked worlds away from the rest of the apartment. That impression didn't totally disappear even when she raised her head and smiled at me. A sliver of distance remained in her eyes.

"Was that really necessary, cariño?" she said, nodding to the window.

She'd seen the dragon. The realization gave me an unexpected thrill.

Ages ago, Javi and I used to come back from family trips to the local library weighed down with fantastical picture books.

We'd spend the afternoon conjuring the illustrations to life while Mom and Dad applauded. Sometimes Javi had sat back with a grin, simply taking in the spectacle, but he'd never shown any resentment that he couldn't keep up. He'd always been my best audience.

"It felt like something I had to do," I said. "After what..." Javi's name caught in my throat. If Mom—and let's be honest, Dad too—lived partly somewhere else these days, it was a place called Grief. And that was already enough my fault.

"You know what I've said about showing restraint," Mom said, but the chiding was gentle.

That was why I never put on a show of my skills for her anymore. She hadn't even liked me going to the Academy so often. She'd never outright discouraged me, but she hadn't been able to completely hide her edginess either. She didn't understand why sharing the magic mattered so much to me. How could she when *she* hadn't hearkened it properly in decades?

Her gaze fixed on the envelope in my hand. She set down the blouse. "It came."

"Yeah." My grip on the envelope tightened. I wondered if she was thinking of the first time she'd seen a child of hers holding one of these.

"You haven't opened it yet."

"I will. It just... It seems so final."

Mom came over to rest her hand on my back. "Whatever they decide, it doesn't mean anything about who you are," she said firmly. "There are many paths to happiness."

I stiffened. "You don't think I've done enough to get in?"

"I think if anyone should be Chosen, it's you," she said. "But that doesn't mean you should rest all your hopes on it. You can have a good future either way."

She and Dad were both Dampered. *At first everything was... fuzzy, the way you can almost go deaf after you hear a very loud sound*, she'd said when I'd asked her how it had felt. *You know the magic is there, but you can't make it out. After a few weeks, the fuzziness, it condenses into just a single note. You can still reach the magic through that. But the rest you can't hearken at all.*

It was true that they'd always seemed happy enough. From what they'd told me, their talents had been relatively weak like most new-magic mages' were, so maybe they hadn't hoped for anything more. The magic they'd been left with was still useful.

Mom's talent had "condensed" into an affinity for thread and fabric that made her stitches stronger than any machine could manage. The custom-designed clothes she sold online brought in a better income than she'd gotten at the dry cleaners she used to work for. Dad's culinary affinity hadn't done him any professional favors, since no restaurants around here wanted to risk posting the legally mandated disclaimer for food prepared with magic— most Dulls got extra paranoid about what they put *in* their bodies—but I knew it meant a lot to him when we gushed over our family meals.

Still, I had trouble imagining only being able to see one color or taste one flavor. I wouldn't even get a choice in it. For all we knew, the Confed decided even that. *Do you* really *think it's a coincidence Mom and Dad got perfectly set up as the domestic help?* Javier had said once.

I wasn't sure if his assumption had been right, but I didn't plan to find out.

"I know," I said to Mom. "But I *have* to get in."

Mom put her arm right around me, tugging me closer. She wasn't so distant that she'd missed what I hadn't said.

"You know Javier would have been proud of you no matter what," she said. "We can't change the way they think."

I leaned into her. "He was going to change them. That was the whole reason he— If he hadn't wanted to make sure they chose me—"

I choked up too much to say the rest. Javi hadn't trusted the Confed to take me either. He'd gone into the Mages' Exam for me. If he hadn't been determined that I should keep all my ability, he'd have accepted being Dampered, but he'd thought if he could make Champion then he could advocate for me from within—carve out a space that their prejudices couldn't deny me.

When he'd died, he'd died for me.

I was twice the mage I'd been when he'd left. I could complete the most difficult exercises in the Academy's most advanced texts. I'd shown up for every assessment with a smile and all the politeness I had in me. What more could they want?

"Rocío," Mom said. I straightened up, gritted my teeth, and ripped open the envelope. The folded paper inside sprang open as I yanked it out.

We regret to convey that Rocío Lopez has not met the requirements for admittance to the College of the North American Confederation of Mages. The timing of her scheduled Dampering is recorded below.

Then a date, three days from now. A time, an address. I hardly saw them. I read the first sentence again, the paper creasing under my thumbs. *Has not met the requirements...*

"No," I said. "That's not possible. No."

Mom took the letter from me and read it with her other hand at her temple. But she didn't look surprised. She'd tried to warn me.

"Is there something you knew I needed to do that you didn't tell me?" I blurted out, my voice shaking.

Her gaze darted up. "Oh, cariño, no," she said. "It's only... The Confed seems so hesitant to accept any new-magic families. I've started to wonder if it's not just because we often have lesser talents—if maybe they reject those with great talents too, because they don't trust us enough to let us keep them. I didn't want to hold you back when I wasn't sure, but with this... I have to think it isn't that you didn't meet their requirements so much as that you exceeded them too far."

I stared at her. "They don't trust me? I've never—I *would* never hurt anyone. I've never given them one reason to worry."

"And Javier wouldn't have hurt anyone either. But there are different ways of hurting. The Confederation doesn't like differing opinions."

This was the most critically I'd ever heard her speak about the Confed. I was speechless for a second. "You think because Javi disagreed with the way they do things, they *made* it so he—"

"No," she said, "but... I don't think they appreciated his intentions. Perhaps they tested him harder than the others because of that."

"And what about me? They're going to Damper me for being good at magic, no matter how well I've followed their rules, just because I might think some of those rules are stupid? As if my opinions somehow make me dangerous?"

Even as I said the words, I thought of the dragon I'd cast at the school. It had been beautiful to me, an act of art. Would some people who walked by think it was scary? My gut clenched.

I'd be back there in ten days if I let the Confed Damper me, mixed in with the Dulls as if I were a regular student, attending only one class a week with Mr. Jones to help me adapt to my restricted talent. And then what? I'd live the rest of my life hollowed out and scraping by?

No. There was so much I'd wanted to do. A strangled noise escaped me.

"It'll be okay," Mom said, reaching for me again, but I didn't want to be comforted into acceptance.

"It will," I said. "I don't have to let them do this."

The color leached from her tan face. "Rocío, no."

"Why not?" I said. "If I'm so good that they're scared of me,

I've got to be good enough to make it through their Exam, haven't I?"

"Is it worth the risk?" she said. "After what happened to your brother—"

"You just said you think they tested him harder. I can handle that." I motioned wildly at the living room—the room where, aside from hastily eaten meals, I'd hardly spent more than five minutes in the last three years. "What have I been working so hard for if I can't handle it?"

She grasped my arm. "Please, Rocío. Nothing good ever comes from arguing with them."

"I'm not going to argue. I'll be taking the opportunity they freely offer everyone. 'A second chance'—isn't that what they say? I'll take that chance and prove they've got no reason to—"

The hum of magic that was always around me shifted, and a little tremor ran through it, a stirring of intent. My skin tightened. Neither of us was casting. Dad was off at work.

Mom's fears trickled into me. Were they, someone from the Confed, watching me to see how I'd respond to the letter?

I backed up a step. Mom's brow knit. She wouldn't be able to hearken that small shift, but she could tell something was wrong.

"I need a minute," I said. "I need—" I needed to be somewhere I could think this through without her resistance, without Javi watching me from the family photo over the couch, without whatever unknown person evaluating my reaction.

A childhood lullaby tripped onto my lips. "Quiere que lo lleven a pasear en coche." With each word, I pulled at the magic around me until the hum rose into a roar. The room around me blurred. My lungs hitched, an electric crackle stung my eardrums, and in a blink, I found myself elsewhere.

My legs swayed for a second before I caught my balance. I stood on a rocky shoreline. Water lapped at the pebbles a few inches from my sneakers.

A putrid sewage smell arrived with the humid breeze. To my left, a bridge stretched across the water to another shore maybe half a mile distant, where stark white walls rose from flat concrete.

My mouth fell open. I might have laughed if I hadn't felt so sick.

This was why you never performed a major casting when you weren't thinking straight. I hadn't told the magic where I wanted to go, only that I wanted to be *away*, so it had brought me to the place that had been on my mind right before I'd cast.

I was looking at Rikers Island, site of the Mages' Exam for the last twenty-six years. The place where my brother had died.

It used to hold a prison, Javi had told me. After the Unveiling, the Confed had wanted a place to conduct business away from non-magical society, and the government had given the island over when asked. The mages had renovated the site to meet their needs, but it still looked cold. Cruel. I wasn't sure what they used the place for other than the Exam, but *I* wouldn't want to work there.

Pebbles rasped behind me. I jerked around.

A guy was standing several feet down the shoreline, where the rocks met trees. He must have already been there when I'd arrived, but he didn't look concerned by my sudden appearance. Now he meandered toward me, his shoulders slouched in the thin gray overcoat he wore over a T-shirt and jean shorts.

At first, because of his posture and the unevenness of his gait, I thought he was at least middle-aged. Then he stopped and lifted his head, and I noticed two things at once: the little sigil like a curved X on his left temple, blacker than his dark brown skin, and the familiar shape of his features.

"Sean?" I said. He'd been part of our tutorial class—two years ahead of Javi and five ahead of me, so we'd only been in the same group for a couple years in elementary school. But he and Javi had been friendly.

Sean had declared for the Exam too, and the result was etched on his skin: Burnout. Where once he'd hearkened magic, now he'd find only a void—not even the single note Dampering would have left him with.

He looked at me, his eyes twitching as if he couldn't quite place me. "Rocío," he produced after a long silence.

"Yeah. I—" I was going to say it was good to see him, but it wasn't really, not when he looked as unsteady as he did right now. "What are you doing here?"

He shrugged and glanced toward the island. "This day, sometimes I just... I need to see it." His gaze slid back to me. "You got your letter."

I nodded, fresh pain slicing through me. "Dampered."

He grimaced. "So you're going to declare?"

I took a breath and hesitated. Looking at the island with its impenetrable blankness, I'd lost the certainty I'd felt in my living room. The Confed hadn't even been able to send back a body for Javi's funeral, whatever it was that happened to him.

"Don't!" Sean said—so abruptly I startled.

"What?" I said.

"Don't," he said again. He wasn't even looking at me. I had the weird impression he was talking to the island. "Don't. Stay away."

"Why?" I asked. "What do they do there?"

All kinds of rumors passed down from the tutorial's older students to the younger. Traps that would torture you, battles with creatures we'd been taught didn't really exist. No one actually knew, though. Except the people who'd been there.

"It's..." Sean shuddered so hard the hem of his coat flapped against his knees. "I'm not allowed to talk about it."

"If I just had some idea—"

Sean shook his head, violently enough that my voice dried up. He took a step toward the water, and his expression softened. "I was so *close*," he rasped.

His hand balled at his side. He spun on his heel and stalked away. A prickle crept up my spine as I watched him go.

Don't.

But Sean hadn't been that much more skilled than Javi, and he was warning me after five years without speaking to me, without any idea what my abilities were. If he'd been *so close*, then I had to be able to make it.

Javi had been willing to fight for me. How could I not fight for myself? I could either put myself in the Confed's hands for five days or let them destroy every hope I'd had for what the rest of my life might hold.

Is it worth it? Mom had asked.

Yes. It was worth everything.

My feet felt suddenly steady against the ground. The same lyrics that had transported me from the apartment rose to my lips. As I sang them out in a rush, the magic whipped around me. The landscape blurred. With another crackle, I was stumbling next to Mom's desk on my living room's scuffed parquet floor. Mom flinched in surprise where she was standing near the door.

"Rocío," she said, but I was looking at my letter. She'd left it lying on the desk. There was no point in talking. I'd only draw out her pain if I let her think she might change my mind.

I snatched up the paper and flipped it open.

"Rocío Lopez declares for the Mages' Exam."

CHAPTER THREE

Finn

S neaking out of one's house was not the most dignified act, but that Sunday morning, circumstances had placed dignity rather low on my list of priorities.

I crept down the stairs, foot after careful foot. "Tacerent perdidit silentium," I whispered, conducting the magic around me to mute the vibrations in the wood.

Mom's shoes tapped across the floor as she paced in her office. Dad was out, after a near twenty-four-hour marathon of arguing and cajoling and lecturing me. He was negotiating a last-minute audience with the Circle. It didn't seem to matter that I'd informed him I wasn't backing down.

He'd told me not to leave the house but hadn't taken any measures to prevent me. On one hand, I appreciated the easier escape. On the other, it rankled to think I'd questioned my parents' authority so seldom in the past sixteen years that it hadn't occurred to them that simply saying I should stay put wouldn't be enough.

On a third hand, which felt as if it were clamped

uncomfortably around my gut, he'd trusted me, and I was breaking that trust. I avoided picturing what his face would look like if he got home before I did and found me gone.

I turned the handle on the front door slowly, repeating my chant. A twinge shot through my nerves, and the magic slipped from my grasp. I exhaled, inhaled, and recited the line with all the intent I could muster, modulating it to the quiver in the air. The hinges shifted like butter; the door glided open without so much as a squeak.

At Prisha's brownstone, the housekeeper let me in. Pree's older sister was hollering across the hall to some sibling I couldn't see. "Ten more—beat that!"

I ascended the staircase through a blast of air conditioning. I was a familiar enough presence in the house that no one gave me a second glance.

Prisha's bedroom encompassed the entire front half of the top floor. The door was open. I peeked inside.

"I told you not to come," she said, striding over.

"And I told you I was coming anyway."

She huffed and crossed her arms, but her eyes darted away from me before returning. "You can't change my mind. I'm doing this. And I *really* don't want to talk about it anymore."

I hadn't expected her to be quite so defensive, not with me. I'd worked out precisely how I'd spill the news, but in the face of her glare, my plans crumpled.

"I'm not here to change your mind," I said. "I'm here to tell you I've declared too."

It appeared I'd accidentally spoken a foreign language—though I didn't know any Prisha didn't know as well. She looked at me with utter blankness. Then her eyes widened.

"Tell me you're joking," she said.

"Of course I wouldn't joke about that," I said. "I've just spent the last day listening to my parents try to talk me out of it. But it's done. I spoke the words. They can't stop me."

Her voice went ragged. "Why would you— Have you gone completely mental?" She walked away from me, her sandals rapping against the buffed hardwood, and spun back around. "Do you think you're going to *protect* me? That's the stupidest thing I've ever heard. You're an idiot, Finn."

I winced. This was a rather different reaction than any I'd imagined. Prisha had never sounded nearly this angry with me before. I sank down on the edge of her four-poster bed.

"That's not it," I said. "I mean, of course I hope we might be able to help each other, but we don't even know what the tests *are*. Maybe I'm an idiot, but I'm not that much of one. I didn't declare because of you. It's just that seeing that even you weren't Chosen made me realize..."

"Realize what?" Prisha demanded when I faltered.

"I didn't deserve it," I said, my head low. "Being Chosen. It wasn't right. Even you know that."

"You don't deserve to be burned out either!"

That statement, maybe the first kind thing she'd said to me since I'd stepped into the room and yet also the most horrible, hit me like a sucker punch. I stared at her: my best friend, the girl who'd distracted our classmates from the library books I'd lugged to and fro in my attempts to prop up my talent, who'd made excuses for my secret study sessions, who only yesterday had claimed I was Chosen material, and for more than my name.

She'd been lying.

"You don't think there's any way I could make Champion," I said.

The fire in Prisha dampened. "I didn't mean *that*, Finn," she said, but I wasn't sure I believed her. "Nobody has a guarantee in the Exam. You had one outside it. What does it matter why?"

"It matters because I don't want to spend the rest of my life tiptoeing along the edge of making my entire family ashamed of me. Audentes fortuna iuvat. If I can make Champion, maybe I'll receive a placement that'll let me truly contribute instead of going through life like a lotus-eater. And if I can't make it through the Exam, then my parents will have to accept what I am." A failure. A dud mage.

I swallowed thickly. If that was what I proved to be, then I should face it.

"You could have taken the easy course too," I added. "You could have accepted Dampering. You'd still be part of the magical community that way, even if you wouldn't be a full member of the Confed."

Prisha shook her head. "You can't possibly compare our positions."

Her second-oldest brother chose that moment to poke his head past the open door. He surveyed the bedroom.

Prisha stilled. "Yes, Daksh?"

"Don't mind me," he said. "I'm just imagining how I'll arrange my furniture when this is my room."

Because he meant to win it. Calling the Mathurs competitive was like saying a Rolex was "a bit pricy." The shouted exchange I'd heard between her siblings when I arrived was standard fare in the household. And bedrooms were reallocated biannually on the basis of net contributions to the family's holdings.

Prisha had cemented her place at the top with a prestige of unquantifiable value, but I hadn't considered the potential result if she were Dampered and her remaining ability proved impractical to the family business.

"It's not going to be yours," Prisha said to Daksh.

"We'll see," he said with a sly grin. "From what I hear, you'd better pass this 'exam' with flying colors or you'll have to work like the rest of us—and I don't think you'll catch up anytime soon."

He swaggered off. Prisha frowned at the doorway.

"Your family is going to care about you no matter what," she said. "If I lose this"—she snapped her fingers to form a spark of magical light—"then I'm worthless. I won't even bring a husband's assets into the fold. The magic is all I've got. I'm not going to lose it."

"Then we'll both have to make Champion," I said. "Shall we shake on it?"

Her smile was thin, and she didn't take my offer, but she did at least sit on the bed next to me. Her hands clenched on her lap, the curlicues of new henna tattoos flexing with the lighter brown skin beneath. She noticed my glance and rubbed her wrists. "My parents pick strange moments to go traditional," she said. "They insisted. It's for luck and strength."

The chime of a grandfather clock reverberated through the floor. It was already noon. In twenty-one hours, we were due on the Exam grounds.

"I didn't come just to tell you," I said quickly. "I came to strategize. If we're going to fly through the tests, we need all the advantages we can get."

Prisha's lips pursed. "Fine. What were you thinking?"

I leaned back against the bedpost. "I checked in with people from school. Of the thirty-three in our year, twenty-one were Chosen. Four of the others declared: you, our daredevil Paulo, Doria the know-it-all, and… Callum."

"Naturally," Prisha muttered.

"Since Angus's sister made Champion, I hit him up for the lowdown," I went on, "but he said she hasn't let any clues slip and her mentor keeps her so busy she's hardly ever home. And Shasti didn't know much either. Evidently the Confed withholds the details of deaths from even the immediate family… I guess to avoid adding to the shame."

Everyone knew Shasti's brother had died in the Exam when

we were ten, but it was the sort of thing people only murmured about when the rest of the family wasn't around, the way they might discuss someone shipped off for drug rehabilitation or fired from a placement. If his talent had been so weak he couldn't even survive the tests, I'd have expected him to know better than to try, although I'd never have said as much to Shasti, of course.

"So we've got approximately nothing," Prisha said.

"Not necessarily. It occurred to me... Margo mentioned dealing with the Exam committee via her job last year, so I invited myself over to her place for lunch." I straightened up. "We should probably get going."

"We?" Prisha said. "Did you invite me too?"

"She's not going to turn you away once we're there."

After starting her full-time work placement, my older sister had taken up residence in a Tribeca loft, somewhat to our parents' dismay. "There's a lot more to the city than the Upper East Side," she'd told them.

Indeed there was. As Prisha and I clambered out of the Mathurs' chauffeured Bentley, my eyes caught on the mismatched twin towers of the World Trade Center—the rather drab gray one beside its taller shinier companion—looming in the near distance.

"Is this where your dad gave his speech?" Prisha asked. She'd barely spoken to me during the drive over. I leapt at the chance at conversation.

"Oh, no, he took us right up to the towers." I'd been eight when the new one had been completed, and Dad had escorted me, Margo, and Hugh to visit them. *We came out of hiding so we could protect our country from threats like the one that caused the destruction here*, he'd said. *Threats the Confederation continues to combat every day on behalf of those without our talents. Mages saved thousands of lives here, but no one will forget the two hundred thirty-six who were lost because we didn't detect one plane in time to fully divert it. We must always be ready.*

If I were on hand for an attack like that, would I be of the slightest use? I dragged my gaze away. Maybe if I made Champion, maybe if I found the right mentor, then I could be ready to make a difference in the event of a next time.

We tramped up the narrow stairs. My sister opened her loft's broad steel door to greet us. Her rumpled hair, once as light as mine but now darkened to Dad's ash brown, was pulled back in a loose braid with a green gel pen and several stray tufts poking out of it. Her jean cutoffs were flecked with old wall paint. I wouldn't have believed that this time tomorrow she'd be the model of a government professional if I hadn't witnessed the transformation firsthand hundreds of times before.

Margo's dark blue eyes were as alert as ever. She looked at Prisha and then at me. I'd rubbed my thumb over my fingers in my habitual casting, and the tremor of terse anticipation that struck my skin told me she knew precisely why we were here. No doubt Mom had called her last night.

If anyone could help me convince our parents that my declaring wasn't a tragedy of the highest order, it was her. Margo was the Lockwood patron saint of justice—even when I'd been a little kid, she'd always insisted that I have a voice in family discussions. She'd always spoken to me like an equal and rebuked Hugh when he hadn't, which was often. She *had* to understand.

"Hi!" Prisha said with an awkward wave.

I gave my sister my most entreating smile. "I didn't think you'd mind Prisha coming too. I'm hoping you can help both of us."

"Well, you're here now," Margo said. "Come in. We'll eat first."

Her loft was everything a loft ought to be: worn beams stretching across a high ceiling, exposed brick walls, floor-to-ceiling windows. The scrabble of tiny claws carried from the bedroom area that was sectioned off behind sliding barn doors. Margo had kept pet rats as long as I could remember.

My sister directed us to the table and brought out cold cuts and fresh buns. We barely talked other than to say "Pass the turkey" as we constructed our sandwiches. I made it halfway through mine before the effort of pretending all was well closed my throat. I settled for nibbling at the rest until Margo had finished eating.

"You talked about overseeing discussions with the Exam committee last year," I began as she set down her napkin. "We—"

"Finn." Margo's mouth tensed but her voice stayed soft. "The negotiations I assisted with had hardly anything to do with the actual trials. And anything I *did* hear is confidential. You know that."

"You couldn't drop a couple hints for your kid brother?" I offered my most winning smile. "It's not as if I'd tell anyone I heard it from you."

"My lips are sealed," Prisha volunteered.

"It isn't that simple," Margo said.

"It kind of is," I said lightly. "Either you want to help, or you don't."

"I don't *want* you to do it at all." She pushed her plate away. "Do you think there's something glorious about making Champion, Finn? Because there isn't, and that's only the best possible outcome. You were Chosen. You should have taken that. You should still take it if you can."

My spirits sank. Not her too.

"And what's so 'glorious' about being Chosen just so the Circle doesn't have to fret that they've pissed off the rest of the family?" I said.

Margo drew in a breath as if to respond, but all she let out was a sigh. She turned to Prisha, as if it were only her going in and not both of us. "I'll say this much, because it should be obvious: Follow the rules they give you. And put everything you have into the tests, no holding back. You do that much, you'll have a decent chance."

"Thank you," Prisha said with a bob of her head.

"I'm not doing it for glory, you know," I said. "I just want it to be something *I* actually *did*."

"I know," Margo said. "I get it." As she cleared the dishes, she added over her shoulder, "Prisha, would you mind if I take a few minutes alone with my brother?"

"Of course not," Prisha said.

Margo motioned me into the enclosed bedroom at the front of the loft. Her bed was neatly made, but otherwise the space was messy. Various pieces of clothing had been flung over the armchair in the corner. News magazines scattered the top of the rosewood vanity beside the three-tiered rat cage that contained her furry companions.

My sister sang a brief verse to create a partition of silence. Then she paused, standing motionless by the closed door. "I meant what I said before. I think you should do whatever you can to get out of this."

"Then you *don't* get it," I said. "This is my last chance. I'm just a... an inconvenience right now, one that Granduncle Raymond is looking to tuck out of view. What sort of life is that?"

Margo studied me, and I stared straight back at her. If I let my resolve shake, then I'd have even less respect for myself than if I'd accepted my Chosen spot to begin with.

Finally, she looked away. "You've always been too damned stubborn," she said, sounding so hopeless that I wavered for the first time. She ran a hand through her hair, dislodging more strands from her braid. "I can't tell you anything. I don't even *know* exactly. It's just, reading between the lines... I can show you the picture I've pieced together."

She stepped past me to the vanity. Her rats—one white, one brown, and one black-and-white hooded—scrambled up the bars of their cage with a clinking of claws as Margo tugged open the vanity's top drawer. She pressed her knuckles to the front of the cage for them to nuzzle. With her other hand, she drew out a sleek silver rod about the length of her palm and as thin as her baby finger.

"If you insist on continuing even after you see this, I'm going to give you something," she said. "From what I've heard, you'll be allowed to take at least one possession with you, without restriction. If it's only one, make sure it's this. Not many of the other examinees will have access to magical tech of this caliber."

She held up the rod. "Handle it with extreme care. Never open it unless you're going to use it immediately. You push the lid like this." She touched her thumb to the small protrusion at the upper end. The lid popped up and over. A tiny needle poked a quarter of an inch from the rod's inner tip. "To activate the function, you press the other end of the rod and apply the needle to your target."

I might have cracked a joke if she hadn't looked so pained. "What is the function?"

"Like I said, I'll show you," she said. "That's your best chance of understanding." A quaver crept into her voice. "I don't want to do this, okay? But it's the best way to drive home what you're getting into. What it could require of you. I can't let you go in blindly."

She turned back to the rat cage and opened the hatch. A cluck of her tongue brought the hooded rat scampering onto the upper level. She scooped it up with a stroke over its back and set it on the pile of magazines. Her hand trembled.

"Margo," I said, and didn't know what to add. My skin was creeping.

"The 'chantment on this is drained through usage," she said, lifting the rod, "but it can make an impact very quickly. You don't need any combat skill at all."

She set her thumb against the rod's base and jabbed the needle into the rat's side.

The rat flinched, and a squeal broke from its mouth, shattered by a wet cough. Red slime dribbled over its snout. Its body shuddered and tipped, its legs twitching. Then it went still as a gush of red colored the magazine's headlines.

I was shuddering now.

Margo retracted the rod—the weapon. A pinkish wound about the size of a nickel remained in the rat's chest where its flesh had melted down to its innards. The whole demonstration had taken less than five seconds.

Margo blinked hard. "The 'chantment will dissolve any organic material in its path," she said in a scarily flat tone. "The longer it's held on target, the wider the effect will be. If it could save your life, don't hesitate."

She flipped the lid back and passed the rod to me. My fingers closed around it automatically. Nausea gripped my stomach.

Margo turned away from the ruined corpse of her rat and grasped my shoulder. Her eyes searched mine. "The Dull have a saying about not buying a gun unless you're willing to shoot it at someone. Think about that when you decide what you're going to do tomorrow. Could you use that weapon on another living being, Finn? Do you really want to become someone who has? Because if the answer is no, then you shouldn't set one foot on Rikers Island."

* * *

During the drive home, I welcomed Prisha's uncharacteristic reserve. The silence gave me space to consider my emotions. My shock edged away, leaving hollowness behind.

I peeled myself out of the Bentley with only a vague recollection of our journey. The tumble of the dying rat and the awful look on my sister's face ran on a loop through my mind.

Margo had said she barely knew anything about the trials, but she knew enough to warrant killing her beloved pet... just to frighten me into rethinking my decision? Why couldn't she have simply told me whatever it was she suspected happened on the island that would require that kind of weapon?

A few people from the Academy declared every year. Most came back Champions or Burnouts, neither looking terribly worse for wear. It took some time for the Burnouts to adjust to the total inability to hearken, so they sometimes behaved a little oddly, but nothing outrageous. The Champions were so occupied with their exhaustive studies and the intensive work placements that followed, they rarely showed up at social gatherings to be observed. Clearly they were functioning just fine, though.

I couldn't reconcile those facts with the scene my sister had laid out for me. My mind kept spinning. So when I walked into the foyer to Dad's warm "Oh, good, Finn, you're home," it took me a second to haul my awareness back to the present—and to register how strange that tone was from the man who should have been furious that I'd ventured out against his express instructions.

"Yes?" I said as he hurried over to meet me.

He clapped me on the arm. "I have great news!" There was a briskness under the warmth. "The Circle has agreed to arrange a last-minute meeting for us with the head of the Exam committee so you can rescind your declaration. We need to go right now."

I snapped fully out of my daze. "No."

"I know it's embarrassing to back down when you've already

committed," Dad barreled on. "But they understand... adolescent passion and recklessness. No one else will even be informed."

"Do you think that's what I want? Haven't you listened to anything I've said?"

"Finn..."

"What about Prisha? What about every other novice who wasn't Chosen even though they've performed better than I have?"

Dad stiffened. "You don't realize the complexities of the situation. If you'd just—"

"No." My hands balled into fists. "*You* don't realize how simple this is. I belong with them. I should have to fight for my spot. I don't care how difficult the Exam is or what it's going to take. This is what's right. You've always encouraged us to think about people other than ourselves. Why can't you let me do this?"

I felt drained, yet my body was also humming with determination as potent as any magic I'd ever hearkened.

"Even I don't know the full extent of the responsibilities that come with being made Champion," Dad said. "And there are political factors. We can't be sure how the Circle will interpret your rejection of their Choosing. You have to trust me on this, Finn."

I didn't. I'd trusted him once, and Margo too, but how could I continue to when they didn't trust *me* to know what I wanted and which consequences I'd rather face?

"I am not rescinding my declaration," I said. "This is my choice, and you have no right to take it away from me. If you try, I'll... I'll tell anyone who'll listen, as loudly as I can, that I was denied the chance to prove myself—that the entire system is a farce."

The shock on Dad's face cut me. Even after I'd declared, even after I'd snuck out this morning, he hadn't truly believed I'd defy him.

"I'm sorry," I added. "If there's fallout, I'll take all the blame. This is on me, Dad. Let me have it."

Dad's gaze held mine for a second longer. Then it slid away.

"I have to talk to your mother," he said roughly. He turned and strode down the hall.

His answer hadn't been an acceptance, but as I watched him go, I knew that I'd won.

I only wished I felt a little more victorious.

CHAPTER FOUR

Rocío

My dad parked our old Kia at the curb several feet shy of the gated entrance to the Rikers Island Bridge. Between the short stretches of trees on either side, the tall steel bars gleamed in the morning sun. The faint fizzing of a defensive 'chantment rippled off them. A man in a plain gray suit—he had to be a mage—stood guard out front.

The hum of magic in the air was nothing compared to the tension buzzing through the car. The engine turned off with a sputter, and the silence blared. Dad's shoulders sagged. Mom rubbed her mouth as if trying to work words out of it. Then they opened their doors to get out. Examinees were due at the gate by nine, and it was twenty to.

On the sidewalk, Dad pulled me to him first. He squashed me against his solid chest.

"I'm going to do whatever I have to," I said. The reediness of my voice made me cringe. I added more firmly, "Whatever it takes to come out alive and with my magic. I promise."

"It's your decision," Dad said, using the same refrain he'd

been giving me ever since I'd told him about that decision on Saturday night. "I believe in you, mija. All my love goes with you."

As he let me go, a black sedan cruised past us and glided to a stop right at the entrance. A boy—white, clean-cut—sprang out and headed straight for the gate with no time spent on goodbyes. Maybe old-magic types felt they were above dramatics.

"Don't push against them," Mom said. "You do what they ask as well as you can, and that's it."

"I know." I wasn't going to give the Confed a single reason to doubt that I fit their "requirements." I just wanted this to be over so that I could get on with the life I'd been supposed to be building.

She hugged me tight. "You know I'm proud of you and that my love goes with you as well. I want you to have this too."

She eased back and pulled a fine gold chain from her pocket. Dangling from the chain was a small, jagged sunburst charm.

"When I was eleven," she said, "and the Confed told my parents I was magical, there was a little while when it seemed I'd be able to do anything. I bought this as sort of a celebration, because it looked like the magic I felt inside me. Hold on to it, and maybe it will help you hold on to your magic too."

"Mom," I said, choking up. I took the necklace and gave them both one last look, one last watery smile. Then, before I started full-on crying, I turned and marched toward the gate.

The mage released the lock and let me through. "Proceed across the bridge and wait in the courtyard," he said. "All casting is forbidden until you're instructed otherwise."

"Okay," I said. When he added nothing more, I hurried on.

The tines of the sunburst charm bit into my palm. I raised my arms to fix the chain around my neck, and the charm settled just below the scooped neckline of my T-shirt. My sneakers slapped the asphalt in harmony with the magic in the air. That energy was always there, always with me.

The trees fell away as the bridge veered up over the East River. The boy I'd seen getting out of the sedan was walking with a jaunty stride that would have made me guess he was old magic even if I hadn't seen the car. I glanced back. Two pale figures were hustling after me: a boy with an aggressive swagger tugging a girl wearing a dress that looked a size too loose—new magic. Behind them, an East Asian girl with stiffly straight posture and a handbag that glinted silver in the sunlight meandered awkwardly, seemingly to avoid catching up—old magic.

As the bridge slanted down, the white buildings I'd seen from the shoreline came into view. They stood in a tight semicircle around a concrete courtyard. The smaller buildings flanked a huge structure that, someplace else, could have been a mall complex.

A few dozen people were already gathered between the buildings, some standing alone, some in pairs or clusters. The division between old and new magic was obvious even at a distance. Even the most modest old-magic kid had an air of nonchalance that no new-magic novice could match. Those from the established families had gathered on the left, while the scruffier, pricklier group I was a part of had taken the right side of the yard.

I came to a stop at the end of the bridge, suddenly breathless. My gaze roamed over the courtyard. Only two of the buildings had a door: A wide black rectangle gleamed on the faces of the two on either side of the large complex. The other structures offered nothing but blank white. Sunlight glared off them at me from every angle.

A prison, I found myself thinking. Shut people in and don't let them out. A shiver crawled up my arms despite the heat.

Javier had stood right here three years ago.

The swaggering boy and the girl in the baggy dress reached the end of the bridge and stopped near me. He scanned the crowd, swiping his sweat-damp hair back from his forehead. The girl stood slouched by his side, her head tipped so her mousy waves shadowed most of her face. I wondered if they were boyfriend and girlfriend, or just friends, or maybe siblings.

The boy's gaze stopped on me, the closest body. He grinned in a lazy way that didn't reach his eyes. "Is this everyone, then?"

His entire attitude put me on guard. "I don't know," I said. "I don't think so." I looked past him to the girl with the silver-beaded purse, who was just stepping off the bridge. As she drifted to the left of the courtyard, a couple more figures appeared at the peak of the bridge. Some had left their arrival to the last minute.

"Well, this bunch doesn't look like much competition. The Confed might as well make me one of the Champions now." The boy cracked his knuckles. His gaze zeroed in on me intently. "Or do you figure you can take me?"

I resisted the urge to step back. "I wasn't really thinking about it that way."

He barked a laugh. "Not thinking of it— Where are you *from*, noob?"

"Here. Brooklyn."

He shook his head, still chuckling. "Welp, you're about to get beat by a guy from the backwoods of Saskatchewan."

The mousy girl slipped her hand around his elbow. The skin of her wrist was marked with dull purple bruises—marks the shape of fingers that had grabbed too tightly.

"Axton," she said. It sounded like a plea.

"Come on, Lacey. Let's see what other dregs we'll be stepping over."

She trailed after him. "So what's *your* story?" I heard him demand of a guy with headphones looped around his neck.

An athletic-looking girl with a short afro sidled over. "Well, isn't he a darling?" she said in a dry drawl that I guessed was Southern sarcasm. "I can't wait to make his acquaintance." She held out her hand to me. "Shaleigh. Alabama. So you're a native New Yorker?"

"Yeah," I said automatically, still turning over Axton's words. He was the kind of guy my abuelo would have called "loco," but competing *was* the essence of the Exam. I was only going to make Champion if most of the people waiting with me right now didn't. If I took one of those spots at the top, it'd be because I'd earned it, but I'd also be leaving some other novice to lose their magic altogether... or die.

No, I couldn't think that way. There was a different number of Champions from year to year. If I passed, I passed. If someone failed, they'd have failed whether I was here or not.

"Living in the city," Shaleigh said, "did you hear much about what goes on in this place?"

Oh. So this wasn't just a friendly chat either. "Not any more than you'd hear in Alabama."

Javi's voice swam up in my memory. *We have to look for any edge we can get, Ro. No one's going to just hand us anything.* That was as true now as it had always been. I should be learning what I could from my competitors like they were trying to do from me.

"Did you ever meet anyone who'd been through the Exam down there?" I added.

Shaleigh grimaced. "Nah. No one else in my town was magical. The tutorial in Montgomery was pretty small, and 'cept for one kid a few years ago who got Chosen, all the novices ahead of me went for Dampering."

But she'd refused. I took in her tee and sweats: clean and neat but a cheap fabric with a plasticky sheen. Alabama was a long way to come. I'd never considered how lucky I was having been born in this city. Every complaint Javi had ever made was true, but we could have had it worse. There were only five magic academies in all of North America and only one Mages' Exam, and the Confed didn't give anyone a lift. Some of us just started with more than others.

As if on cue, a laugh rang out from the old-magic side of the courtyard. The sound was so warm and relaxed it would have caught my attention anyway, but it was also unexpectedly familiar.

My heart stuttered. My gaze darted across the crowd to snag on a lanky blond boy whose cheeks had dimpled with an easy smile.

Seeing him jarred me back through time—to my little corner in the Manhattan Academy's vast library, between the shelves of lovingly bound texts that no new-magic tutorial room had ever seen. Back to breathing in the smells of old oak and aged paper as I performed my quiet practice sessions on the hard chair-and-desk set, which the real students avoided in favor of the cushy armchairs near the fireplace on the first floor and in the discussion room on the third.

From behind the wrought iron bars of the second-floor railing, I'd been able to look down over the front entrance and the librarian's desk. And I'd seen that boy a few times a month, popping in and out, never staying for longer than it took him to pick up a book and offer a lighthearted remark to the librarian or to the librarian's assistant, who was Dampered. He'd always treated that woman as if there were no difference, while most of the other Academy students I'd seen had addressed her with a subtle dismissiveness.

He wouldn't have seen me. I'd picked my spot carefully to avoid stares and interrogation. All the Academy students lived with magic just like me, but every careless aside and arch complaint I'd overheard had driven home how separate I was from them.

But every now and then, my mind had gone wandering. I

would find myself imagining what it might be like if that boy stumbled on my corner and turned that easy smile on me. As if I could be so sure he'd accept me when the others didn't.

As if he might even have seen something special in me.

Could I call it a crush when I'd never spoken to the guy? Whatever word I used, it'd obviously been wishful thinking. I was hardly ten feet away now, and he hadn't even glanced my way. Why should any of *them* be paying attention to this side of the yard?

The boy was chatting with another guy and two girls as if they all knew each other—probably they were all from the same Academy. The other boy looked Latino, but with that uptown air he'd have stuck out on my street way worse than Axton. One of the girls, whose intricate henna tattoos wound from the backs of her hands to her forearms, was sticking close to "my" boy with a protective air. His girlfriend?

I wouldn't have expected to find him here. But then, it wasn't as if I'd seen him doing any actual studying in the library. The whole group must have had weak skills by old-magic standards if they hadn't been Chosen. None of them looked overly concerned. I wondered how much their confidence was put on and how much was earned. They'd all had the benefit of Academy training with instructors who were full mages rather than Dampered tutorial leaders.

The boy with the smile was facing the center of the courtyard. His bright green eyes lit up when a stout white guy with a midnight-blue mohawk nearly as tall as his head strode into our midst.

"*Nice*," the boy said, gesturing over his own head. "Did you have to 'chant that?"

Mohawk eyed him. His jaw twitched. "No magic involved," he said gruffly.

"Well, that's even more impressive. Is it just a matter of enough gel or whatever, then?"

"And getting the right cut." Mohawk's tone relaxed a little, even though his body stayed tense. The interest seemed honest enough.

"I have a friend who's very into, ah, extremes of style." The boy tipped his head to the rest of his group. "Right up Will's alley, don't you think?" Then, to Mohawk again, he added, "Anyway, he's never pulled off anything like that. My respects."

I hadn't noticed Axton approaching, but all at once he was shouldering the guy with the mohawk to the side. "Hmmm," he said, looking Mohawk up and down. "I gotta say, anyone trying that hard to look tough probably isn't very."

"I like the style," Mohawk said. "And I don't give a crap how some random like you feels about it."

"This could get interesting," Shaleigh murmured beside me.

I didn't think it would be interesting in any way I wanted to see. Axton was loco, all right.

"Hey, hey," the boy with the smile said. "We'll have lots of time to discover who's the toughest of the bunch in the next five days. Why start early?"

Axton cocked his head. "You really think the trials haven't started? All of this is part of it. Why else do you think they have us waiting out here like a bunch of idiots?"

The boy gazed back at him mildly. "Point," he said with just a touch of wryness. "I happily concede this round to you."

His maybe-girlfriend brought her hennaed hand to her mouth as if to hide a smirk, but Axton's attention was completely focused on the boy. He shifted on his feet in the wake of his unexpectedly easy "victory." A hint of a smile touched my own lips.

Everyone nearby had fallen silent, watching to see how the first direct clash between old magic and new would play out. The meek girl with the bruises—Lacey—wavered a few feet away, nibbling at her lip behind her veil of mousy hair.

"Good," Axton said finally. "Expect to do it again." He stalked back to our new-magic side of the yard.

"I wonder if he's right," Shaleigh said, frowning at the buildings around us. "How long are they going to leave us out here?"

Axton's comment had stirred up the examinees around us. The chatter took on a restless edge. It didn't help that the pavement was starting to bake. The courtyard shimmered with heat, and sweat trickled down my back despite the light cotton of my shirt.

The old-magic girl with the silver-beaded purse pulled out a bottle of water, and the back of my throat ached as I watched her sip from it. Why hadn't I thought to bring something to drink? The instructions for the Exam had said all necessities would be provided, but I'd had no reason to trust that statement.

"Are we supposed to do something out here?" a girl behind me asked her neighbor.

One of the old-magic kids went up to the nearest building and knocked on its slab of a door. Nothing happened. The headphones guy tried the one on our side with the same result. The muttering rose.

"We showed up on time. The least they could do is return the favor," Shaleigh was grumbling just as a tingle brushed over my neck.

A shift in the magic. I froze.

No one was supposed to be casting. Was it the examiners? Part of the first test?

None of the other examinees reacted as if they'd hearkened it, though. The tingling spread, a faint presence wrapping around me. It tugged, like a question.

My breath stopped. *Javi?* I thought. The presence didn't give me any clear answer, just another faint tug. Whatever or whoever it was, it wanted me to move.

I eased away from Shaleigh and treaded cautiously from one blank building to the next. When I passed the one with a door, the prickle of a 'chantment emanating from it left a bitter taste on my tongue. I hesitated before crossing to the left side of the courtyard, but the clusters of old-magic examinees were too busy complaining to each other to pay much attention to me. The tingling sensation nagged at me. I walked on.

The buildings on the left side of the courtyard looked identical to those on the right, down to the smooth black door and its bitter prickle. A metal circle marked the paved ground in the narrow alley stretching between that structure and its neighbor. I squeezed into the alley. Some type of manhole, I guessed as I prodded it with my toe. Did it still lead anywhere? The prison must have had underground workings—maybe the Confed made use of them too.

I slipped out of the alleyway, passed the bridge, and headed back to the new-magic side. The presence gave another tug, but there was nowhere else I could go. Maybe it wanted me inside one of those buildings?

Or maybe it was a conjured trick and meant nothing at all.

It'd been silly, imagining that feeling could somehow be Javi. But how could I not wish he were here with me? When the mages finally appeared, I'd find someone to ask directly about him. There must be records of how people died. I didn't think the examiners could fault a sister for wanting to know. At least then I'd have some kind of answer, whether anything remained of him here or not.

Several of the other old-magic kids had pulled out bottled water, and Mohawk was gulping from a canteen. Even the blond boy's smile was lopsided as he swiped at his forehead with the back of his pale arm. Two of his friends had stepped to the side in the midst of an argument, their voices harsh but too low for me to make out.

"This is ridiculous," someone snapped.

Axton clapped his hands together in the middle of our group. "All right," he said. "It's time to show the Confed one mage here can do more than sit with his thumb up his butt." He walked up to the door on our side.

My back stiffened. "What are you going to do?" I said.

He flexed his shoulders and cracked his knuckles. "Nothing's happening while we stand around. I'll bet they're waiting for us to smash our way in."

"They said not to cast," I protested.

"To cut out the people with no initiative." He raised his hand. "*I'm* not afraid to show what I can do."

Alarm jabbed through my gut. "*Don't.*" I stepped forward to grab his elbow. "I really think—"

"Get off me!" he snapped, shoving me away.

I stumbled back but avoided bumping Lacey, who was hovering nearby. Axton intoned a quick lyric under his breath and flicked his fingers. Whatever effect he'd intended, it was swallowed by the black surface with a faint sizzle. Axton flinched. Then he narrowed his eyes. Spitting out a second line, he hurled his hand toward the door.

The thrum of magic hit the door with a faint crackle and a smell like burnt plastic. The door shuddered. A triumphant grin split Axton's face just as the thrum heightened to a screech and a flare of magic rebounded straight at him.

The blaze sliced across Axton's forehead and dissolved. He stood there, still and silent, his mouth half open. A thin reddish line formed just above his eyebrows. Then a trickle of blood seeped over the line's edge and down, and his eyes rolled up. His body crumpled to the ground.

Lacey's squeak broke the silence. "What the hell?" someone shouted.

I backed up a step, my legs wobbly. My fingers found Mom's sunburst charm and clutched it against my chest.

The growing babble of frantic voices fell away. The door Axton had struck was sliding open. A woman in the gray uniform that marked her as an examiner stood on the threshold. She looked down at Axton's body, and her lips pressed tight. Then she raised her eyes to the rest of us.

"It is always regrettable when an examinee fails to heed our instructions. May this be a reminder to the fifty-six of you remaining that every action you take has consequences. I extend my congratulations to you on passing your first test. Please come in. Your fallen colleague will be attended to by the medics before his burning out."

I exhaled in a rush. He wasn't dead, just unconscious. He still lay between us and the door, blood seeping over his temple. All the arrogance had drained from his slack expression.

People shifted, but no one moved forward. I glanced around. A lot of my fellow examinees were watching me. Shaleigh was staring.

I'd spoken up and tried to stop Axton. I didn't know what they'd made of that gesture, but I'd gotten their attention. My forehead itched, as if there were a target there too.

Javi had faced all this and worse. The Confed could try to shock us all it wanted—I wasn't backing down.

I set my shoulders and walked around Axton to the doorway.

CHAPTER FIVE

Finn

Faced with the all-but-dead body of a guy I'd been arguing with just a short while ago, I felt the urge to reevaluate some of my recent life choices.

Our swarm of examinees edged toward the doorway to the Exam building. A couple of the novices ahead of me swiveled, started circling back, and then changed their minds and went forward again. No one wanted to remark on the situation with the examiner watching us, but a current of unease swept around us all.

I doubted the guy had endeared himself to anyone with his eagerness for a fight, but he'd been one of us. Now he was sprawled unconscious because of a single warning ignored. The Exam had barely started.

Blood was still trickling down his forehead when I reached his body. Where in Hades were the magimedics?

The answer came to me as quickly as the question: The examiners were strategically delaying. They wanted us to look our possible fate in the face, literally. The whole scenario out here had been a setup, hadn't it? They'd never intended to open the door before one of us broke and resorted to casting.

They must do this every year.

Margo's face yesterday swam up in my mind, the tremor in her voice alongside it. *Could you use that weapon on another living being, Finn? Do you really want to become someone who has?*

A chill ran down my back. The rod lay in the pocket of my khakis now, a slim weight against my hip. I'd been prepared for brutally difficult tests but not for brutal callousness from our examiners—from the Confed's own mages. Was this what my sister had tried to warn me of, that I hadn't understood even with her demonstration?

In front of me, Prisha pressed her mouth flat and strode toward the entrance. I jerked my gaze from the fallen body to her back, to the tumble of her glossy black hair against her violet blouse.

I was here now. We'd do whatever we could to protect each other—I knew that much. I couldn't let myself dwell on anything else.

I propelled myself after her. The examiner tipped her head to each of us in turn. I tramped after Prisha several paces down a hall that was as unrelentingly white as the buildings outside. A waft of air conditioning cooled the sweat on my skin. It left a faintly chemical aftertaste in the back of my mouth.

Prisha's arm brushed mine, her baby finger curling around my own. I squeezed hers back. *Pinky swear.* It was a childish gesture, carried over from when we were kids—when all we'd needed to fend off were bullies like Callum or a particularly merciless teacher—but it spoke of a promise all the same.

I'm here with you.

Another mage in a gray examiner uniform started to lead our line down the hall. Someone was sniffling—the guy's girlfriend, I suspected: that waifish girl in a dress like a nightgown. I couldn't imagine how wretched she must feel. At least to the rest of us he was a stranger.

We turned a corner and stepped into a room that held six rows of tall cubicles. The examiner directed us each to one.

The moment I sat down, silence descended over me with a quiver. The slate-gray sides of the cubicle blocked all view of my companions. I might as well have been alone in the room, just me and the staccato beating of my heart.

A stack of ivory paper and a ballpoint pen appeared on my previously bare desk. A flat voice spoke into the bubble of silence. "Write down every detail you can recall about your fellow examinees and the interactions you've had thus far," it said. "When you have recorded everything, tap the wall three times."

I exhaled and picked up the pen. This task I could do without much trouble.

I began with Prisha and the others from our academy, Doria and Paulo. Aside from Callum, we'd all gravitated together on arriving, but our chatter had been rather mindless. The rhythmic rasp of the nib scraping the paper carried me on to the examinees from the other four academics I'd exchanged introductions with, and then to those who'd kept more distance from us—mostly tutorial students, I guessed.

This exercise put them at a disadvantage. We Academy students had the benefit of knowing the others from our own school well, whereas the tutorial classes were so geographically scattered, I doubted any of the new-magic examinees had known each other at all. It truly was unfortunate for the magical community that there was no way to predict where new talents might arise. Newcomers couldn't always simply move to the major centers the way Prisha's family had.

The tutorial students might have an edge of another sort, though. Their inherent abilities might be weaker on average than those in old-magic families, but rumor had it they exchanged methods of twisting magic on the streets that the Confed disdained to acknowledge.

Maybe there was a new-magic technique my teachers had never considered that could strengthen my connection to the magic. I could explore that possibility with my assigned mentor... if I got through this Exam with my talent intact.

When I'd filled several pages with tight scrawl, I tapped the cubicle wall with the end of my pen. A spark lit in the air in front of me. I stood up, and the spark careened toward the doorway like a rolling marble. Some of the desks I passed were vacant, while the others were shielded by a shadow that hid whoever remained.

The spark led me down the hall outside into a larger room with a high ceiling spotted with domed light fixtures. A ring of cubicles surrounded a central platform. There, ten mages in examiner uniforms watched from leather armchairs.

These cubicles had lower sidewalls and, unlike the others, opened in the front as well as the back. As my spark stopped at an empty station, I spotted Prisha standing in a cubicle several over, most of her head visible above the partitions. Her brow creased, but otherwise she looked no worse for wear. A clenching in my chest released.

Callum was still with us as well, five spots to my right, his mouth bent in a characteristic frown as he scratched his russet buzz cut. Doria stood a few more cubicles beyond him, her face even sallower than usual. The boy with the mohawk had taken a station a couple over from Prisha. I didn't see Paulo at all, but a few cubicles still stood empty—or he could be on the other side of the ring, in one of the handful obscured by the examiners' platform. The waifish girl with her lank hair and red-rimmed eyes drifted into her position.

The same flat instructor's voice I'd heard in the other room spoke from somewhere above.

"You will now display basic magical skills for our evaluation. For each concept given, cast a conjuring or 'chantment representing the best of your capabilities. We begin now." A pause. "Send a message."

I sucked in a breath, and my mind went blank. With demonstrations in school, I'd always been able to prepare ahead of time. There were ten mages watching the lot of us. Even as I hesitated, someone across the way shot a conjured paper into one of the examiners' hands, where it bloomed open like a flower. Another was sketching letters in the air with streaks of light.

It wouldn't be enough to appear merely competent. I needed to catch the examiners' notice if I wanted to pass.

I needed to cast *something* before they moved on to the next concept. I groped for an idea, any idea, and grasped at the first that came to me. Go big, literally. With a few intoned words at a brisk tempo, a vibration flowed from my throat into the magic. It formed a sign over my head the width of the cubicle, the word HELLO emblazoned on it.

The examiner nearest me, a woman about Margo's age with a hijab draped loosely over her black hair, flicked her eyes toward my sign and away. I cringed inwardly. That had been *too* big, too gauche, no doubt. The Confed valued subtlety alongside power.

"Transformation," the voice said.

An image popped into my head. I didn't let myself question it, just reached for a poetic phrase of friendly regard. As I pitched my voice to harmonize with the whisper of energy around me, the arm of the mage's chair wriggled—and then stilled again as my tone went flat. I repeated the verse con forza, ignoring the desperate thump of my pulse.

There. The chair arm bent upward, molding into the wrist I was picturing, a slender hand at its end. I trained all my attention on the memory of papery dry skin etched with faint lines of age —oh, it was my grandmother's hand—and rolled out the last few syllables of my casting. The hand offered itself for the examiner to shake.

The mage met my eyes this time and nodded with a quick smile as she released the 'chantment. My arms fell to my sides. That was better.

Keeping up that standard wasn't the easiest undertaking. The boy at my left was fond of flash, and no matter what words the instructor called out, I had something flaring at the edge of my vision. A little to my right, Callum had discovered he could turn the distractive element of the test into a strategy. When we were asked to produce fire, the sparks from his flames leapt over the wall of his cubicle, leaving his neighbor smacking her singed hair. At a request for weather, he sent his cloud sleeting over her.

My jaw tightened as I conjured my own funnel of wind to dance around the examiner—thank the Fates the last text I'd pored over had contained an entire section on air currents—but none of the mages protested.

They hadn't said we needed to keep our castings to ourselves. Evidently good sportsmanship wasn't in the rules.

An examiner appeared behind one of the boys across from me, touched his shoulder, and sent him away. The mage stalked around the circle toward me and then tapped Doria. O gods, she was out already too?

We weren't exactly friends. Doria had barely scraped by all through our Academy years, and she'd compensated for her practical deficiencies by becoming the self-declared expert on every aspect of magical history and theory, which hadn't been a winning quality in social situations. Still, she was one of the few familiar faces here. I couldn't say I believed that she deserved to have even her slight talent wiped away.

The examiner strolled on, continuing my way. My voice broke in the middle of a lyric. The scent I'd been conjuring began to wisp away but returned as I forced the next words out. The mage padded past me.

I trained my gaze in a different direction and found myself regarding the girl who'd tried to stop that boy from breaking the no-magic rule in the courtyard a couple hours ago.

She was what Prisha would have called "cute-pretty," maybe —pleasant enough to look at but far from striking. Average height, average build, plain olive-green T-shirt and faded jeans, a wavy shoulder-length bob as dark a brown as her deep-set eyes and rather pointy features. A sunburst trinket glinted softly below her collarbone. Everything about her was subdued—other than her voice when she'd raised it with the guy outside.

She'd been the only one of us who'd spoken at all when he'd been working himself up to his catastrophe. If he'd listened to her, she'd have saved him from burning out.

Her castings were quick and deliberate, but each contained just enough of a flourish to encourage me to keep watching. For *concealment* she unfurled a swath of shadow over her cubicle with velvet smoothness. For *illumination* she cast out a globe of light with a pearl-like sheen that gleamed brighter when the examiner reached toward it. Most of the time she looked absorbed and serious, but I kept catching a flicker of a smile. She enjoyed performing this medley.

As I watched her in glances between my own conjurings, an ache formed inside me. O muse of magic, what I wouldn't give for skill like that.

The circling examiner was still picking off those who'd failed. The neighbor Callum had worked his machinations on was the next tapped. The mage slowed as he approached Prisha, and my gut lurched before he stopped at the boy beside her.

Finally, the examiners on the platform stood. I let my rough voice fall silent. The instructor overhead spoke. "You will break for a short lunch."

A glass of water, a chicken salad sandwich, and an apple appeared on my desk. I drained half the water in one extended gulp. Fatigue shivered through my joints and pinched the bridge of my nose. I rubbed my eyes as if I could wipe away the momentary dizziness.

I understood magical exhaustion in theory, but I'd never pushed myself far enough to truly experience it. I'd never had to pull off this many castings in so short a time. The energy that reverberated through our bodies wore on our nerves, and extended focus could strain the mind. The effects crept up on you faster the harder you had to work, which meant I was especially fatigued.

We still had half the day left. I needed to pace myself without downplaying my abilities, or I might not make it to the end on my feet.

I'd scarcely set down my apple core when the man who'd sent the failed examinees away announced it was time to move on. He ushered us farther down the hall. I fell back to join Prisha.

"How are you holding up?" I murmured.

"It isn't so bad," she said, but I recognized tension in her voice. She swiped her hand across her face. "Two tests down. I'm managing. You worry about yourself first, okay?"

"On it," I said.

Then we were directed into a room even larger than the last but with a low ceiling that felt instantly oppressive. The rectangular light panels gave off a low buzzing sound. A few rows of gleaming wooden tables stood on the linoleum floor, and the air smelled of a recent polish. One of the stark white walls was covered with framed photographs. Another held a wide steel shelving unit.

I counted the figures around me. We were down to thirty-nine examinees. And Paulo was definitely not among us. He'd always been swift to leap into action but slow on the uptake. I guessed he'd drawn a blank in reporting observations from the courtyard.

Not an impressive showing for the Manhattan Academy so far.

"Until you have completed this task, you will not speak to any other examinee," the voice above instructed.

My lips clamped together.

"As you all know, we and our allies face a number of threats both conventional and magical from hostile parties throughout the world," our invisible instructor continued. "With the inspiration and objects you find here, consider the most deadly foe you can imagine and imbue one item with the magic you believe would best overcome that foe in time to prevent an attack. You must complete this task within four hours."

That seemed a decent length of time. I ambled closer to the wall with the photographs. My gaze tripped over images of violent terrorism: a town burning in a teal-tinged blaze of magic, a passenger train crumpled where it had been blasted off its tracks, and bodies struck by sniper bullets scattered in a city square.

I felt my spine drawing straighter. This was why the magical community had come forward: to defend the rest of the country. Of course the examiners would want to assess our ability to prevent this sort of carnage. If I did one meaningful thing in my entire life, I'd want it to be that.

It wasn't enough to merely pass this test; I had to *ace* it.

"Ah, I remember that bombing," Callum remarked, coming up behind me.

I stared at him, but he didn't look away from the picture of the crumpled train.

"London," he said. "They figured the Russians were behind it but no way to prove it. Totally vicious."

He wasn't technically talking *to* me, only to himself. My hand balled at my side. He'd heard the rule, and naturally his first thought was how he could dupe someone else into breaking it.

I crossed the room to the cluttered shelving unit. Some of the objects scattered on it fit the established theme: a grenade, a pistol, a wooden shield, a warrior's helm that looked vaguely Viking. Others struck me as rather mundane. What use would we make of a fork or a pair of glasses?

Before I settled on an object for my 'chantment, I needed to invent the terrible "foe" it would confront. I found myself picturing dragons and sea serpents.

The girl with the sunburst necklace halted by the next shelf and reached for a woolen scarf. She was going to defend the nation with *that*?

Of course, any item could be imbued with intent. The examiners must have given us this wide selection for a reason. Not every opponent would be best challenged with an obvious weapon.

Our true enemies weren't conjured creatures but the human mages who would wield magic against us, or Dull militants with their penchant for destruction. They were the ones I should target: the people—the sort willing to set off a bomb on a crowded train, to die if it meant taking more of us down with them.

They were dying *for* someone: for the dogmatic organizations behind them, for the hatred those groups stirred up against everyone who held different views. I could work with that.

My eyes caught on an old-fashioned radio, only a little larger than my hand. *Yes.* Coordinating the function of the object with the purpose of the 'chantment would make focusing the casting easier. I scooped it up and headed for one of the tables.

Resting the radio on the polished surface, I closed my eyes and absorbed the lines and ridges of the metal shell against my fingers. One of my few real skills with magic had always been getting it to stick once applied; the tricky part was ensuring the 'chantment did what I intended it to. This idea was going to require a layered casting, one element on top of another, refining as I went to conduct all the components into a harmonious symphony.

I could do this. If I had to use the full four hours, what of it?

Militants controlled their followers through belief and loyalty, so I'd create disbelief and distrust first.

I settled on a few lines about betrayal from a Roman play. The magic in the room was trembling at a slightly erratic frequency, pulled in so many directions at once. As it quivered over me, I pictured shadowy figures on a barbaric mission. Then I rolled the words off my tongue, one after the next, directing the energy from the air into the radio.

When I let my voice fall, the sizzle of 'chanted uncertainty tingled against my hands. I set the radio down and leaned against the tabletop to regain my breath. The pressure in my forehead was sharpening into a dagger.

The first movement was done.

The waifish girl in the overlarge dress hunched over the table ahead of mine. The thin whisper of her voice carried to me: "You have to do this. You can't go back. You *can't*."

Her desperation echoed mine far too closely. I straightened up.

Callum stalked between the tables at my right, jabbing his elbow toward a boy who was constructing a tower out of wooden blocks. The blocks clattered across the table, and the boy whirled. "What the hell are you doing? You—"

An examiner appeared at his side. "But I— But he—" the boy protested.

The examiner said something to him sotto voce as she guided him to the doorway. His face crumpled.

I gave myself the momentary pleasure of imagining socking

Callum's smirk off his face and made a mental note to keep my possessions close. He wandered back over to the table he was sharing with Judith, an amiable girl who'd been with the Seattle Academy novices I'd met this morning. She was frowning at the toy car she'd selected while one hand fidgeted with her purse's spiral pattern of silver beads.

Callum veered to the side at the last second. He banged Judith's shoulder with enough force that she knocked the car to the edge of the table. Her head jerked up, her mouth tightening, but she kept her silence.

At least someone here was wise to his tricks.

I laid my hands on the radio. Stirring up uncertainty wouldn't be a powerful enough defense. To impress the examiners, I had to show I could turn the enemy fully against their own cause. I could provoke paranoia so they'd imagine the worst of their leaders and colleagues, and a sense of urgency to intensify their reactions. Let them commit the violence they intended against each other instead of us.

I chose a lyric, braced myself, and began to weave the new strands of energy into the tremor of magic already intertwined with the radio. Each connection needed to be strengthened, like notes transformed into chords.

One thread of the magic diminished as I sang it forward. I raised my voice, straining to recapture it, and pain spiked through my bones. The thread darted away.

Damn it. I reached out with my voice, ignoring the swell of discomfort all through my body. Stretching the syllables long and cautiously, I inched the 'chantment into place and tested each vibration of magic until I was sure the entire structure was sound. I'd finally finished, with a rough exhalation and a shudder, when Callum started talking again.

"Well, *that's* not going to work," he announced to everyone and no one in particular. "Let me see..."

Judith glared at him. When he fell silent, she lowered her head to intone a verse, but she'd scarcely begun when he interrupted again.

"Yes, that's it," he said in the same belligerent manner. "Maybe if I put this piece with that one. Of course. Excellent."

He was holding a Frisbee. I restrained myself from rolling my eyes. Thank Zeus he hadn't started up earlier.

The strain of my last casting hadn't yet eased. Bracing my hands against the table, I glanced over at Prisha. She'd ended up across from the girl with the sunburst necklace.

Prisha was murmuring a phrase to a bottle of clear liquid. She paused to scan the table, and her brow knit. After a moment, she stepped back to peer underneath.

The starburst-necklace girl raised her eyes from the scarf she was working on as Prisha swiveled to check under the neighboring tables. The girl watched for a few seconds and then smoothed her hands over the woven fabric. She tugged one corner of the scarf back.

The bottle's lid was lying underneath. Without hesitation, the girl nudged it across the table to Prisha's side and returned to her own casting.

At the rattle of the lid's crossing, Prisha turned and made a muted exclamation. The girl didn't look up. Prisha eyed her and then commented to herself, "I'm certainly glad this turned up."

She must be getting tired too, to have been so careless. She was lucky she'd been working next to someone disinclined to take advantage and not, say, Callum.

I inspected my radio. Carelessness—I needed to avoid that too. We hadn't talked a great deal about safeguards in class, because we hadn't generally cast magic intended to have ongoing negative consequences, but the texts I'd studied had expounded on the need for precautions. As soon as you worked a casting on an object, you no longer fully controlled it. With a 'chantment this potentially destructive, the examiners had to appreciate seeing every eventuality considered.

A symbol would do: something that friendly soldiers could wear. Hmmm. Faith protected... A heart in a square? Why not?

I'd have to finely modulate the sensitivity and harmonize it with every thread within the existing 'chantment. Casting this coda was going to be a beast. A splinter of a headache was still jabbing across my temple.

Judith strode past me. She placed her toy car, now stripped of wheels, on a table at the other end of the room and returned to the shelving unit.

Callum picked up one of the wheels she'd abandoned. As he rolled it between his knobby thumb and forefinger, he whispered a few singsong words under his breath. My body tensed.

Leaving his Frisbee, he strolled in the same direction Judith had gone. She was occupied with examining a box she'd retrieved from the shelves. Callum brushed past her new table and dropped the wheel he'd 'chanted into the toy car's seat.

No one but me appeared to have noticed. I lowered my eyes as Callum ambled by. Hades knew what he'd cast the thing to do to her. It didn't require much talent to cudgel someone if that was all that mattered to you. My mind leapt back to the courtyard, to the sprawled body and the blood.

Whatever scheme he was enacting, I needed all my remaining strength to complete my own 'chantment. I barely knew Judith. She'd never expect me to risk my chances for her.

Without intending to, I looked toward Prisha's table again— toward the sunburst-charm girl who'd spoken up this morning. As if she sensed my thoughts, she raised her head. She held my gaze for a second, blinking, and then I yanked it away. A crisply searing sensation was crawling through my chest. Maybe it was only my fatigue, but it brought a suspicion I couldn't shake: she'd know. If Judith came back to her table and something blew up in her face, the girl would know I could have stopped it and hadn't.

Judith was turning from the shelves. My hands clenched around my radio. The idea was absurd; no one here could read minds. Even if she could have, it shouldn't have mattered to me.

Yet it did. My feet were moving.

I strode toward Judith's table. With a flick of my thumb, I extended the radio's antenna to its full length. It could be a simple thing, a swing of my arm...

As I reached the table, I swerved to the side. The antenna caught on the car and sent the toy spinning off the table. A sound of protest broke from Judith's throat as it hit the ground.

The 'chanted wheel popped out of the seat, careened across the floor, and smacked the wall just as Judith snatched my elbow. Then it burst with a bolt of electricity that erupted two feet in the air and thrummed through the floor to my shoes. The smell of ozone flooded my nose.

A cudgel indeed.

Judith gaped at the shattered wheel, and then at me. Before she forgot herself, I rubbed my mouth. She snapped hers shut.

I had to look at Callum then. He glowered at me with a sneer that turned my innards cold.

"I sure am clumsy today," I remarked to myself. "Better get on with this task."

Possibly I'd just hamstrung myself. Still, as I passed Prisha's station, it wasn't the arch of her eyebrows that drew my attention. It was the girl, bent over her scarf, with a little smile curving her thin lips.

CHAPTER SIX

Rocío

The Exam room had no clocks, so we only knew our time was up when an examiner appeared in the doorway. He clapped his hands. "Finish."

I stretched my arms and took a step back from my scarf. The rectangle of rough wool had fit my intent well enough that I'd only added minor tweaks in at least two hours, but I hadn't exactly enjoyed the casting.

"Leave your work on the tables," the examiner said.

My body resisted. I made myself fold the scarf and set it down. The magic reverberating through it sent a sense of constriction creeping up into my hands, amplifying that uneasy pressure. A monster of a 'chantment lurked inside the fabric, cold and horrifying.

Of course we had to leave our work for the mages to test. Considering what they'd asked of us, it'd be awfully dangerous for them to do that testing with us present. I didn't actually *want* to see my 'chantment in action. But it felt somehow irresponsible to walk away from the scarf and the power I'd sent into it.

In the hall, four more mages in gray waited for us. They led us around a corner, down one flight of stairs, and up another, each space as whitewashed as the last. I guessed the flawless surfaces were supposed to give the impression of order and cleanliness. I found them unnerving. Every stretch of unblemished white yelled out how emphatically the Confed was trying to cover up the decades of prison grime and violence.

We came to a stop in another windowless hall, wide and dim enough to give it a cavernous feel. "You will be taken to your dorms now," the first examiner said. "The thirty-five of you remaining have been divided into groups by last name."

As he rattled off the first set, I stared at the novice mages around me. Thirty-five meant nearly half of us gone just one day into the Exam. I hadn't seen Shaleigh since the courtyard.

The second group peeled off, heading to the left, and the third examiner, a large man with a dour, lumpy face, stepped forward. "Lockwood, Lopez, Mathur, Nilsson, Ornstein, Pan, Powell. Follow me." He strode off to the right, and the seven of us fell in step behind.

The boy with the smile ended up a pace ahead of me, the girl with the hennaed hands beside him. He rolled his shoulders as he walked, and the muscles in his back flexed against the thin fabric of his shirt, which had obviously been tailored to fit his lanky frame perfectly.

I jerked my gaze away. This wasn't the time or place for daydreaming. Still, I couldn't help feeling a little pleased that, from what I'd seen today, his good-naturedness was more than just for show.

The rest of our group included the girl with the silver-beaded purse I'd seen on the bridge and Axton's girlfriend, Lacey, her face sallow behind the fall of her mousy hair. I wouldn't have expected her to make it this far based on my first impression, but she must have found strength somewhere inside that billow dress.

The guy with the mohawk tramped along next to her, his hands jammed in the pockets of his baggy jeans. The midnight-blue tint on the 'hawk carried through the speckling of buzzed hair on either side of his scalp. The last of us—a skinny Black guy whose T-shirt featured a faded print of a spaceship—I hadn't noticed before.

The examiner motioned to a row of cubbies beside an open doorway. "Leave any bags or other extraneous belongings here. You'll find what you need for the night inside."

The others filed into the room, but the girl from the bridge hesitated. She clutched her purse. "I'd rather keep this with me."

"Leave any bags here," the examiner repeated without changing his inflection.

The girl let out a sharp breath. With a shake of her head that scattered her sleek black hair, she reached into the purse, drew out an item, and shoved it into a pocket in her chinos. She pushed the bag to the back of one of the cubbies and then headed through the doorway.

It was just me and the dour-faced examiner now. My legs locked. I hadn't found the chance to ask anyone about Javi yet.

I swallowed my nervousness. "Sir," I said, "I've wanted to ask: My brother took the Exam three years ago—Javier Lopez? He... didn't come home. I don't know if you were working here then or if there are records, but it would mean a lot to me to know how he died."

The mage considered me. Maybe asking had been a breach of etiquette after all. Did he think I was trying to get a scoop on the later challenges? I was about to blurt out that if I couldn't know until I'd finished the Exam, I'd accept that, when he opened his mouth.

"Javier Lopez," he said in a cool voice. "Yes. I see the resemblance." He folded his arms over the expanse of his chest. "He wasn't Champion material. I expect you'll end up on the same path soon enough. He went down fighting—I'll give him that—and I suppose you will too. It won't make a difference. We cut the chaff from the wheat. You should have listened to your letter."

He turned on his heel and stalked away without giving me a chance to respond. The chill in his tone seeped through my skin.

It won't make a difference. You should have listened to your letter.

Was he saying they'd already decided my fate? Had they decided about Javi too, before he'd even started their tests? My stomach knotted. Mom hadn't dared to speculate that far, but the examiner had made his implications pretty clear.

Maybe I'd misunderstood. I was still here, wasn't I? They could have pulled me aside at any moment if they'd wanted to.

Unless they weren't going to be content with a mere burning out.

I ventured into the white, windowless dorm room on unsteady feet. My sneakers squeaked on the polished linoleum. Behind me, the door slid shut automatically.

The others had gravitated to the two rows of cots that filled most of the room. The only one left was in the middle of the row beside the door I'd just walked through. Tan blankets, white sheets, everything spotlessly clean. Even the air smelled like over-starched laundry. The dorm was more hospital ward than prison, other than the wooden table at the far side of the room that held stacks of plates and cutlery.

The boy with the smile was sitting on the cot beside mine. The girl with the hennaed hands bent over him, her palm on his forehead. "...push yourself like that," she was muttering.

"I'm fine," he said breezily.

"Maybe now. Keep it that way, all right?"

When she straightened up, her gaze fell on me. "Digging for inside tips?" she asked in a teasing lilt.

It took me a moment to connect that question to my conversation with the examiner. "Didn't get any," I forced out. It was easier if she assumed that was what I'd been doing.

The boy with the smile stood up and rubbed his hands together, looking around at all of us. "So, shall we pretend for the evening that this is just a highly intensive summer camp session and introduce ourselves?"

"What's the point?" Mohawk said with a twitch of his jaw. "Exchanging names isn't going to make us friends."

"*I'd* like to know who I'm sharing a room with." The purse girl held up her hand. "Judith Pan. Seattle Academy, most recently."

"Desmond Powell," said the guy with the spaceship tee, next to her. The sweep of his dark eyes across us was so penetrating I felt as if he'd looked right through me. "Greater Chicago Tutorial. Boldly going where no one back home has gone before." He grinned and tugged at his T-shirt, and I noticed the words "To boldly go" were printed under the spaceship too. A quote from a movie?

The boy with the smile tipped his head. "Finnegan Lockwood, Manhattan Academy. Though we'll have words if you call me anything other than Finn."

"Prisha Mathur," the girl beside me said. "Also Manhattan."

My turn. "Rocío Lopez. Brooklyn-Queens Tutorial."

Lacey pushed her hair back behind her ears. An awed light had come into her face. She blinked, realizing we were waiting for her to speak. "Lacey Nilsson," she mumbled. "Sort of Saskatoon. That's, um, Canada." Then her voice rose a little higher. "Do you think— Are we really done? We made it through the first day?"

"Looks like it," Finn said, his smile widening.

A loud, hoarse laugh burst out of her. A strange reaction, but

I'd take this girl over the beaten-down one I'd seen at Axton's side.

Mohawk let out a huff. "I'm Mark Ornstein from San Diego," he said. "Now I'm going to get to know dinner, thanks."

A creamy, gravy-like smell filled my nose. A spread of platters had appeared on the table while we'd been talking.

The others headed for the table with a murmur of anticipation, and I trailed after them. I picked up one of the steaming mini potpies, a handful of carrot sticks, and a cookie somewhat at random, not sure if I'd manage to swallow even half of what I'd put on my plate. I was turning back to my cot, my thoughts whirling around the examiner's comments again, when Prisha snagged my elbow.

"Come eat with us," she said. "You really saved my hide with the bottle cap—thanks, now that I can say it properly."

I didn't really feel like chatting, especially with the old-magic crowd, but rejecting her gesture felt like a bad strategic move if nothing else. "Sure," I said.

Us was her, Finn, and Judith, who'd spread her cot's blanket on the floor for us to sit on as if we were having a picnic. "So it doesn't actually rain there all the time?" Finn was saying to Judith in his wry tone.

She rolled her eyes. "No. Only, like, ninety percent." Her hand dropped to her side, as if to rest on her purse, and clenched. "I don't see why we had to leave our stuff outside. I wasn't expecting the Exam to be like this."

Prisha raised an eyebrow. "What *were* you expecting?"

"I don't know," Judith said. "I never had much chance to ask anyone about it. I was only at Seattle for two years, and everyone already had their own friends, you know? We were always moving around. My father's a diplomat."

"Well, sorry you had to put up with Callum being a jerk

during that last test. It's definitely him, not you. I've heard him talking with his parents, and I don't think even *they* like him."

"I'm not taking it personally," Judith said. "It's not as if he has any reason to *help* me... But I feel as if I'm so behind everyone else. My whole life, all my dad has ever cared about was me saying the right pleasantries to impress people at the political functions and whatever. I'd like to have the chance to do a little more than that." She jabbed her fork at her pie. "What do you think we'll have to do next?"

"Search me," Finn said. "The Confed doesn't want us to have any clue what's coming—they're too good at holding their cards close."

Not really, unless the examiner in the hall just thought I was a ghetto-girl who was too stupid to infer his meaning.

I reached for my cookie. The buttery dough melted on my tongue with a rich, honey-like sweetness.

It tasted like the last birthday cake Dad had baked me. He'd found the recipe online and been excited to try it out after our traditional birthday weekend excursion to Coney Island, where as always he had eaten too much cotton candy and Mom had hopped onto the rides with me as eagerly as if she were a teenager too. For ten hours we'd been a full family again, like a temporary 'chantment.

There were more days like that waiting on the other side of the Exam. I'd make sure there were.

I gazed at the crumbs on my fingers, wishing I'd at least paid a little more attention to what the cookie had looked like so I could find another the same.

Finn got up to grab more food. Prisha nudged his leg with her shoulder. "Get me an orange?"

"Certainly," he said brightly, but I thought I saw him flinch. Had he hurt himself somehow during one of the tests?

Desmond was contemplating the fruit bowl. Finn made a

comment to him, and after a moment they were both laughing. Finn added something with a goofy expression, and suddenly even Mohawk—Mark, I corrected myself—was grinning despite all his attitude about the bunch of us not being friends.

Clearly the boy with the smile had a silver tongue as well.

Judith leaned toward Prisha. "So how long have you two been—?"

Prisha cut her off with a chuckle. "Oh, no, Finn and I are just friends. He did confess his undying love for me once when we were thirteen. Went down on one knee and everything. I told him I loved him very much too but like a brother—quite a bit better than my actual brothers, to tell you the truth—because I happened to only be interested in kissing girls."

Finn returned in the momentary silence that followed that statement. He took in our combined expressions and glowered at Prisha as he sat down. "Why is it that, without fail, you tell everyone that story within five minutes of meeting them?"

"We obviously like each other too much," Prisha informed him. "People always ask. And it's a good story." She turned back to Judith and me. "See, after I told him that, he asked whether I was completely sure and if maybe I shouldn't give boys a try just to confirm. He must have realized how crass that was from the look I gave him, so he immediately 'chanted his mouth away in contrition. If you've never seen a person without a mouth, I can tell you it's difficult to stay angry when you're laughing that hard. Other than that blip, we've always been good."

She patted Finn on the back, and he side-eyed her as he handed her the requested orange. His cheeks had turned faintly pink. "Yes," he said. "Except for when she insists on telling that story *yet again*. Then I'm forced to question the entire friendship."

I couldn't help trying to picture him mouthless. "How did

you 'chant it back?" I said. "If you didn't have a mouth to speak to the magic..." I trailed off as the three of them stared at me.

Finn recovered with a blink. "I hummed," he said. "It's just the vibrations, the rhythm, that allow you to conduct the magic, right? The words only help us focus intent."

"Don't they teach theory in tutorials?" Prisha said.

My own cheeks flushed hot. "No, they do," I said quickly, remembering back in early elementary when we'd reached the magic by tapping our feet or drumming our fingers. "I just wasn't thinking."

The magic was always there when I reached for it, no long-winded explanations necessary, so I'd focused on practical texts at the library, and it'd been forever since we'd delved into theory in class. What was the point when most of us wouldn't get to use more than a fraction of our original ability?

"It's been a long day," Finn said, but my embarrassment eased only slightly. No one was going to be surprised to see the Exam take me down after that slip. Then he offered me a cookie. I recognized it as the same type I'd grabbed before.

"You looked as if you really enjoyed it," he said when I didn't move. "I thought you might want another."

I met his eyes as I took the cookie, and he smiled just for me. My pulse fluttered.

"Thanks," I said, and yanked myself back to Earth.

"Speaking of stretching one's magic," Prisha said, "you would not believe the conjuring Finn and I saw on Saturday. This amazingly detailed dragon illusion. Considering how high up in the sky it was, the thing must have been at least a quarter mile long."

Finn glanced at her with his forehead furrowed. The second she'd said "dragon," my skin had gone tight. Still embarrassed from my last blunder, I almost kept my mouth shut, but when Judith asked, "Where?" and Prisha started describing it, I knew

I'd only feel worse acting ignorant through a long dissection of my work.

"Ah," I said, and took a bite of the cookie as if it could fortify me. "That was me. Mine. I mean, the dragon was."

Then I did shut up before my *pendeja* of a tongue could stumble more.

"Really?" Finn said. When I made myself look up again, he was outright grinning at me. "It was spectacular."

Both of Prisha's eyebrows had leapt up now. "What was it for?"

I couldn't talk to them about Javi. Not while we were sitting here in the middle of Rikers Island. Not with four more days of the Exam ahead of us.

Not when an examiner had just expressed his anticipation of my impending death.

The knot in my stomach came back. "I just… wanted to see if I could," I said weakly.

"What in Hades's name are you doing here when you can cast like that?" Finn burst out. "You could top every person in our class. And why *weren't* you at the Academy if you live in the city?"

I stared at him, and he looked back at me so earnestly that my careful control started to crack. They were his people, the Confed—it was his world. Did he really have to ask that?

"I wasn't at the Academy," I said, "because the tuition fees would have taken all the money my family needed for food and rent and being able to *survive*. And I'm here because the Confed would rather take half-talent mages with names they know over any level of gutter-magic nobody. What do you *think*?"

I pushed myself to my feet and stalked to my cot. Keeping my back to them, I breathed in and out and willed myself to relax.

Mark had just sat down on his bed. He rubbed his hand along the base of his mohawk. "Confed brats," he said under his breath. "Underneath, they're all the same. I don't know how my brother—"

He cut himself off and looked away. What had the Confed done to *his* brother?

He didn't seem to want to talk about it. Well, like he'd said before, none of us here were going to be friends. I needed to focus on surviving—and surviving in a way the three I'd left on the blanket never had to consider.

I used the little two-stalled bathroom off the side of the room and then lay down on my cot. The time must have been later than I'd have guessed, because after what seemed like only a few minutes, the lights started to dim by increments. By the time their glow had dropped to half its previous brightness, the others were shuffling around me. Lacey tested the door to the hall—it didn't budge. She drifted to her cot.

The light dipped even lower. Prisha crawled under her blanket on the bed next to mine. Fabric whispered behind me. Then Finn's voice reached me, soft and level with my ear.

"I'm sorry," he said, crouched down beside my cot.

I waited for him to offer some explanation, to throw in a joke to break the tension, but he let the apology stand alone. When I didn't answer, he added, "Good night, Dragon-Tamer," and headed for his own cot in the corner.

A lump rose in my throat. *Good night, Silver-Tongue.* My lips pressed tight against the words.

He might not have meant to hurt me. He might be a perfectly wonderful human being. But opening myself up was risking another wound and another hostile response bursting out of me. And that was exactly what the Confed expected from me, wasn't it? Exactly what would justify the examiners culling me like chaff from wheat...

What they *expected*.

The examiner had said, *I expect you'll end up on the same path,* blatant as anything. But what was it Finn had pointed out? That the Confed didn't want us to know what was coming, that they were good at keeping their cards close. He should know, shouldn't he? And it was true that I hadn't heard one hint of what happened here before I'd arrived.

Was it really likely that an examiner would have revealed so much to me out of carelessness?

It might have been a lie, all of it. An extra test just for me, to see how provoking me would affect my performance.

The lights went out completely, and the chill inside me hardened.

The Confed had almost gotten to me. They'd almost shoved me straight into the role I was meant to fill. Whether I was snapping at the others or shunning them, I'd look like the new-magic threat they'd feared enough to throw away whatever good my magical abilities could do.

I didn't want to fight. I didn't want to hurt anyone—I didn't want anyone else getting hurt. Hadn't they seen that when I'd tried to stop Axton, when I'd given Prisha a hand?

It hadn't been enough.

Resolve rose inside me. I'd wanted to use magic to help people see, to give them something they might not have otherwise. Why couldn't I start here, even if it wasn't quite what I'd pictured? I wouldn't just not harm anyone; I'd *help* them.

Let the examiners expect whatever they wanted. I was going to make it through this Exam alive, and so was every other person in this room, no matter what I had to do to protect them. The Confed couldn't watch that and then claim I was any kind of threat.

Tomorrow. Tomorrow I'd accept Finn's apology, and anything else—

My thoughts were cut off by an odd prickle that raced over my scalp. The room around me tumbled away.

* * *

One instant, I was deeply asleep. The next, my eyes were popping open with a jump of my pulse.

I sat up, holding my blanket. The lights were still out, but when I looked around, enough of a glow seeped from somewhere in the distance for me to see that there *was* a distance. The wall that had been at the head of my cot had vanished. A hazy gray space stretched out beyond the dorm room as far as I could see, split here and there by columns of slightly blacker shadow.

A thin peppery smell filled my nose. My heart thudded faster with it.

"What now?" someone—Mark?—grumbled.

Prisha slipped off her cot and waved her hand where the missing wall had been. It really was gone.

"The hall must have been an illusion," she said. "They conjured up those walls temporarily so we couldn't see the whole space."

Someone at my other side—Desmond, I thought—whispered a few lilting words. A square pane of light blinked into existence in the air over our heads, quite a bit higher than the ceiling had been before.

Even with the illumination, the great gray space beyond the alcove of the dorm room didn't appear much less gray. The shadowy columns looked like trees that had lost all their branches, just smooth trunks with flat stumps protruding out at awkward angles. The closest was some thirty feet ahead and to our left, a larger one maybe a hundred feet and a bit to the right. A thick fog drifted around them, obscuring any view of the landscape beyond.

"It would appear Day Two just started," Finn said.

It didn't look like *day* out there, and I wasn't sure we'd slept long enough for it to be light outside. But then again, I hadn't seen sunlight since we'd been brought in from the courtyard. My head felt muddy. They'd 'chanted us to sleep and then yanked us awake, hadn't they?

I pushed myself off the cot and took a few steps into the space beyond the dorm room. When I crossed the boundary where the wall had been, the ground shifted beneath my feet. It had more give there, almost spongy in feel.

A tremor passed through the magic, touching me as if ghostly hands gripped my shoulders. The presence I'd felt in the courtyard was back. I took another step, and it grasped me harder, as if it was trying to hold me back.

"Something's wrong," I said, glancing back at the others. I didn't know what the presence was or what it wanted, but I could tell a warning when I got one.

Judith hugged herself. "I don't like this."

Lacey was gnawing at her lower lip, her arms stiff at her sides. Finn walked past me, studying the fog. His hand hovered by his hip.

A low whirring sound, too crisp to be the warbling of wind, rolled over us. It made my nerves jitter. I recognized that sound. I knew it, because—

A billowing rectangle floated down in front of the nearest amputated tree. Understanding hit me like a fist of ice. No. No, no, *no*.

My voice came out in a croak. "Those deadly enemies we made all those 'chantments for," I said. "*We're* the enemy. The examiners are turning the magic we worked on us."

CHAPTER SEVEN

Finn

O n hearing terror in the tone of a mage infinitely more skilled than I was, the sensible thing would have been for me to run away screaming. Rocío's tan face shone unearthly pale in the hazy magical light, an even starker warning than her tone. But Lockwood dignity kept my feet fixed in place on the rubbery floor—or maybe it was the fact that if I were sensible, I wouldn't have been here to begin with.

"What's coming?" I blurted out. "What did—"

"Lie down, everyone. Close your eyes! Don't move!" Rocío yelled.

I was at least sensible enough to heed her urgency. I dropped onto the foamlike ground and squeezed my eyes shut. My awareness shrank to the hammering of my heart and the rustles of my six dorm-mates following suit.

Whatever the impending danger entailed, it must be the 'chantment Rocío had cast on her scarf. She wouldn't have recognized anyone else's well enough to be that scared.

Hers was the talent I least wanted to be going up against. I'd rather battle a dozen of Callum's blunt cudgels or—

The air stiffened around me, as if a vast sheet of cellophane had snapped tight across my skin. I flinched, and the cellophane turned to steel, slamming my elbow against my side with a lance of pain. When I sucked in a breath, my lip stung against a rigidly rough texture that must have echoed the fibers of the scarf. A drop of blood hit my tongue.

The 'chantment squeezed like a vise against my chest. I exhaled as quickly as I dared. Then I took a slow, shallow sip of air.

The vise eased off a fraction of an inch, and the sharp metallic flavor of blood seeped through my mouth.

Somewhere nearby, Judith cried out. Her voice cut off with a whimper. My eyelids twitched with the urge to see what was happening.

No. I held them shut, stifling a wince at the faint burn even that tiny movement provoked.

O gods, this was vicious. If Rocío had built a failsafe into the 'chantment, she clearly hadn't been able to activate it. The magic's effect would dissipate over time, but how much? Lying there motionless was already excruciating.

The spicy scent of the air tickled my nose. Hades take me, I could *not* afford to sneeze. As I willed the itch away, my bladder pinched. Yes, naturally I'd have to contend with that too.

Even in the midst of my distress, a picture popped into my head of the examiners watching us from afar, snickering at the sight of Eminent Lockwood's grandnephew discovering precisely how deep a pile of excrement he'd stepped into by declaring.

I had to prove I could take it. Still the mind and body. Think clearly. All those meditation exercises could be of some use.

Rocío knew how she'd constructed the 'chantment, so she

must know a way to counteract it. Of course, she'd need to find a way to cast against it while keeping this still.

My mind tripped back to last night, to the conversation that had flowed smoothly enough until I'd made that idiotic comment to her. To the moment after Prisha had related the hash I'd made of my temporary romantic infatuation—suggest to your best friend who's just come out of the closet to you that perhaps you could kiss her straight, just *brilliant*, Finn—and the way I'd atoned for it by 'chanting my mouth away.

Rocío's wary voice carried through my memory: *How did you 'chant it back if you didn't have a mouth to speak the magic?* She hadn't relied on nonverbal techniques often enough for the idea to have been obvious.

Would it be wrong to simply reach out to her? I didn't think she'd fault me for that even if the strategy had already occurred to her.

I drew in a little more air than before, and the pressure on my chest hardened. I focused on the direction where I'd last seen Rocío and drew up a mental image of her. The first one that surfaced wasn't the frightened face I'd glimpsed when she shouted her warning but her little smile yesterday after I'd helped Judith —the smile that had made me feel we were part of something together.

I summoned the rhythm of a Roman poem about searching for lost companions. The whisper of magic trembled in the air around me. I hummed into it, low in my throat. As I sent the vibrations spinning off, I stretched out my awareness through them.

There. Mezzo talent though I might be, I could recognize the pulse of another person's energy. Rocío's flickered with anguish and frustration.

Her distress echoed into me, throwing my own pulse out of

kilter again. I'd be worse than useless if I let her feel my panic and amplified her emotions.

I swallowed hard. My mouth was dry, my lips still parted, but I wasn't keen to discover what would result if I tried to close them. The taste of blood was still fresh on my tongue.

I couldn't mute my discomfort, but I could bury it under a more vivid image.

I pictured myself as I imagined I'd looked when I'd 'chanted my mouth away for Prisha but with my hand held high in a thumbs-up. Shifting the cadence of my hum, I pulled more magic through me, shaped it around the image, and channeled it toward Rocío.

Sweat beaded on my forehead despite the chill in the air. Sustaining a casting without being able to move was exhausting.

A tentative touch reached out to me: a shiver of nerves and a tickle of gratitude. She'd absorbed the magic and the message I'd sent with it. I released my hum. The headache Prisha had helped numb yesterday scrabbled back up my temples.

A faint sound reached my ears. Rocío was humming now. The melody faded in and out. I lay still, listening, narrowing all my attention to the wavering tune to avoid the physical sensations plaguing me.

With a snap, the vise fell away, and someone gasped. My eyelids leapt open of their own accord, but no brutal force seared across them.

As I shoved myself upright, my left arm wobbled and a fresh spear of pain shot up it. My lips prickled when I closed my mouth. I touched them with my other hand, and my fingers came away smeared with scarlet.

The square of light Desmond had conjured beamed over the seven of us in the rough semicircle we'd fallen into between the dorm room and that foggy gray space. Prisha appeared unharmed, though she was flexing her wrist as if testing it. Judith had curled up on her side, one hand over her face, her other arm twisted against her side at an unnatural angle. A muffled sob slipped past her palm.

"I'm sorry," Rocío said, scrambling to her feet. "I'm so, so sorry. Is everyone— Judith, your arm—"

Judith lowered her hand. It wasn't merely her arm she'd injured. Blood flecked the olive skin around her tightly closed eyes, droplets clinging to her lashes. She must have opened them when the 'chantment hit. Cuts blazed across her mouth from when she'd cried out: three of them.

Desmond knelt beside her. "I'm ace at basic healing," he said. "I'll do what I can. Okay?"

She nodded, a small jerk of her chin. Desmond started muttering under his breath.

The rest of us swayed to our feet. At least my arm felt as if it was merely battered, not broken. Rocío looked physically well, though guilt-stricken. If Desmond had been hurt, he was disguising it. Mark was examining one of his hands, but he tucked it close to his chest when he noticed me looking at him.

Lacey backed to the edge of the light. She moved awkwardly, favoring her left ankle. She was clutching the skirt of her dress, the fabric bunched in front of her waifish figure. As she balled it tighter, I realized why. A dark splotch stood out against the pastel fabric. She'd wet herself, in shock or in fear.

Prisha glanced at her, and Lacey's face flushed red.

"Hey," I said quickly, walking over. "I'll take a look at your ankle." I might not have any particular talent for healing, but I'd taken the same magimedical classes as everyone else in the Academy. Who knew what sort of instruction they received in the tutorials in Saska-wherever-she-was-from?

"I—" Lacey's shoulders hunched.

I lowered my voice. "Don't worry about it. It could have been any of us." My own bladder was still heavy. "At this rate, it's likely to be and worse by the time they're finished with us."

She stared at me. A broken chuckle worked its way out of her throat. "Well," she said, "I'm still here." She sank down on the ground with the skirt of her dress collected on her lap and extended her bad leg for me to inspect.

With a few singsong words, I determined that none of the bones were broken. I hadn't a clue how to fix a sprain, but I could make it a tad easier for her to cope. I dredged up a verse for numbing from our lessons in first aid.

The magic oscillated through my nerves as I cast the 'chantment, and my headache sliced across my forehead. I hadn't recovered from yesterday's overexertion yet. I'd have to be sparing in my use of magic after this, but at least I'd contributed in some small way.

"You'll still want to keep your weight off it whenever possible," I said.

Lacey nodded. "Thanks," she mumbled. Her gaze darted to the walls that remained around our dorm room. She scrambled up and limped toward the bathroom doorway, to wash her dress, I supposed.

I heaved myself back to my feet, attempting to hold my head steady to avoid provoking the headache. Desmond was ripping a pillowcase—to make a sling? Judith sat on the ground next to him, her mouth pursed and her cheeks shiny from tears. He'd managed to seal her cuts, though angry pink streaks still marked her lips and eyelids. It'd take a fully trained magimedic to knit bones.

Rocío paced nearby, her hands clenched at her sides. I stepped toward her, and she paused.

"Do you need—" She gestured to my face. "Your mouth."

I tested my split lip. The blood there had gone tacky. It stung only a little now.

I didn't have the energy to take even a rough stab at mending it and didn't see why she should waste hers.

"I'll be all right," I said. "At least you skipped the dragon this time. I'll take a few cuts and bruises over being burned to a crisp any day."

I'd hoped to shake her guilt enough to draw out a smile, but I didn't get one. Her eyes remained serious. "Thank you," she said. "For before—the reminder. I got... off track. You helped me focus."

She looked so disconcerted I had to ask, "Are *you* all right?"

Her gaze dropped. That felt like a no she wasn't willing to explain, at least not to me. Then she inhaled sharply. "When I cast that 'chantment, I drew on my feelings to make it as powerful as possible—how I've felt here in the Exam, and outside too. All the walls, all the restrictions and rules... It wasn't enjoyable experiencing that constriction in condensed form."

She hadn't attended the Academy because, for all intents and purposes, the Confed had shut her out. I didn't even know how much the tuition *was*—I'd just taken it for granted that my parents would cover it, and so had all my classmates. What else of life beyond the boundaries of the Upper East Side had I failed to consider?

Rocío raised her head. "It won't happen again," she said, her expression so fiercely determined that her eyes seemed to spark with light. Something in my chest lit up in response. Had I really looked at that face less than twenty-four hours ago and thought it scarcely pretty? Right then, she might as well have been Helen of Troy.

I might have kept looking at her for longer than was strictly polite, except Judith let out another cry. Standing at the edge of our former room, she flung her good arm toward the open space where the hallway had once been.

"All our things," she said. "They made us leave everything out here in the cubbies, and now they're gone."

"Right," Mark said, tossing his hand in the air. "We were all almost eviscerated, including you, but what's really important is getting your pretty purse." His mohawk was drooping, giving him a peculiarly tilted demeanor.

Judith whirled with more grace than I'd have expected her new sling to allow. "It's not just a purse," she snapped. "It's the last present my mom ever gave me before she left. Not that you'd care, but I can't just go buy a new one of *that*."

"Fine," Mark said. "I'm sorry for your loss. Now can we focus on what's in front of us?"

Rocío frowned. "What's in front of us." She glanced up at me. "We all cast 'chantments. We have to get ready for what's coming next before it's here."

I recalled all the wrenching energy I'd put into my own 'chantment, and a chill washed over me. She was right.

"Hey," I said. "We're all freaked out, but Rocío's right. The examiners must be planning to throw more of our 'chantments at us. If we all share what we cast and any information that might be useful in defending ourselves, we can make it through the rest."

"I agree with Finn," Prisha said immediately, and I shot her a grateful glance.

Desmond rubbed his square chin as Lacey crossed the room to rejoin us. "Mine's more of a mental thing," he said. "I was aiming for distraction. It'll give you the sense that there's something really important that you have to take care of, but you can't find it. Ah, it's sound based. I guess if you make constant noise that should sort of... drown out the effect."

"Good to know," I said. "I built a specific safeguard into mine. If the 'chantment works properly, it will make people paranoid and aggressive, but there's a visual—a square with a heart inside it—that will nullify the magic. We should mark that symbol on ourselves, somewhere it'll be easy for us to see. The back of our hands, maybe? Has anyone seen anything we could draw *with*?"

The others shook their heads. I scuffed my shoe against the spongy surface we were standing on, but it was made out of some sort of smooth artificial substance, no dirt we could smear.

"We could use magic to form the symbol," Judith said, her voice still wavering a little.

"We're going to be racing around disabling other 'chantments for Fates know how long," I said. "It'd be too easy for us to accidentally erase the safeguard mark and not realize until it's too late. Something concrete would be better."

As I scanned the area, Lacey brushed her lank hair from her face and said cautiously, "My 'chantment is shadow creatures. Like wolves. They can attack people, but if you try to physically stop them, your hands will go right through them. A magic shield might work." She began talking faster. "They're quick, though, and sneaky, and the 'chantment is— There was a bag of marbles—"

"We'll manage." Prisha turned to Mark, who'd edged farther back while we'd talked. Why had she cut Lacey off? I raised my hand to catch her attention and paused at the smear of blood on my fingertips.

Oh. That was better than nothing. I touched the tacky spot on my lower lip with my baby finger and quickly sketch the lines of the symbol across the back of my left hand. The ache as I bent my elbow distracted me from the profound grossness of what I was doing.

I looked up, about to suggest the same strategy to the others, and frowned.

Prisha had taken another step toward Mark. Her stance looked oddly aggressive.

"So?" she said. "Aren't you going to tell us yours?"

Mark's gaze darted around the group. His jaw twitched with what was seeming like a habitual tic. "I've got a better idea than this big sharing session," he said, backing away. "I don't like the sound of any of the crazy stuff you all thought up, so I'm just going to jet, and the only 'chantment *I'll* have to deal with is mine. If I'm far enough away from you, they can't use the same 'chanted object on all of us. I'd rather skip yours and take my chances with the one I know."

"I don't think that's a good idea," Rocío said.

My gut had twisted. "Yeah. They arranged us into groups for a reason. If you get into a tight spot on your own—"

"Maybe they put us all together to make it easier for them to hurt us," Mark retorted.

Lacey stepped backward, as if she were considering abandoning the group too.

"You don't know what the range of any of the 'chantments is," I said with a sweep of my arm. I could feel in my bones that his strategy was unsound—and not simply because the last thing I wanted was to navigate this nightmarish place on *my* own. "And you don't know how big this place is. Maybe you *can't* get far enough away. What do you think would have happened if any of us hadn't been near enough to hear Rocío's warning?"

"I'll figure it out," Mark said.

I started toward him, and he raised his hand as if he meant to hit me. "As if you have any idea what it takes to deal with a *real* threat. You worry about saving your own skin, academy boy." A sneer had crept into his rising voice. "I'm here for someone way more important than any of you, and I'm not letting you hold me back."

The sneering was what finally twigged me: something was off. Mark had been standoffish before but not openly hostile. My thumb swiveled over my fingers and drew a dissonant vibration out of the air that felt unnaturally fraught. Another 'chantment was acting on us.

As I strained my senses, a faint hissing reached my ears. Almost like… radio static?

My body stiffened. *My* 'chantment was acting on us. Had it built up in Mark fastest because he'd already had suspicious inclinations?

"Everyone!" I said. "Put that symbol—a heart in a box— somewhere you can see it. Now!"

Mark shook his head and marched off. I glanced at the blood-smear image on my hand—how often did I need to see it to avoid becoming affected by the 'chantment? I hadn't thought to cast my protection in quite that much detail. I hadn't thought I'd need to know.

Rocío murmured something to her thumb. The skin there parted with a beading of blood. In a few quick swipes, she'd copied my strategy. "I'll go after him," she said, starting toward Mark, whose form was fading into the mist beyond a branchless tree. "If I can't convince him, I'll—I'll come right back."

"No!" Prisha said sharply, slicing her hand through the air. O gods, my 'chantment was acting on her too. "All of you just—"

Before she could complete her sentence, a shadowy wolf that could have rivaled Cerberus in monstrousness sprang from the fog behind her.

CHAPTER EIGHT

Rocío

The beast knocked Prisha onto the ground. Her scream split the air, and my body froze.

Lacey's shadow creature. What had she said about them?

Prisha's arm whipped right through the darkly translucent wolf. It sank its flickering teeth into her shoulder, and she cried out again. The blood, red against the violet fabric of her blouse, jolted me into action.

I ran back toward her. Words from one of Javi's favorite rock songs, a line about shoving someone away, leapt to my tongue. Prisha shouted out a quavering verse of what sounded like Greek. Despite her broken voice, the conjuring blasted the creature backward.

The shadow-wolf spun on Finn, who'd been running to Prisha too. It swiped a razor-clawed paw at him, and he stumbled backward. I spat out the lyric I had ready, channeling all my intent into hurling the creature away.

The energy in the air walloped the shadow-wolf several feet back into the mist, sprawled on its side. In an instant, it leapt back to its feet. It blended in and out of the haze as it stalked toward us once more.

I opened my mouth to try a different casting when something small tapped against my shoe. I glanced down. The square of light above us caught on the glossy surface of a marble.

On instinct, I lifted my foot and slammed it down, willing the magic to follow my heel. The marble burst into jagged shards, and the shadow-wolf wisped apart into the fog.

Finn had rushed to Prisha's side, but she backed away, pressing her hand to her wounded shoulder.

"Pree," Finn pleaded. "You're bleeding. There'll be more coming. We have to—"

"I don't *have* to do anything." She glared at him.

Lacey drifted deeper into the mist that filled the great gray room, her watery eyes wide. I looked at the crushed marble again and saw the sketchy image I'd marked on my skin with my nicked thumb. The rest of me turned cold.

It wasn't just Lacey's 'chantment attacking us. We were dealing with Finn's too.

"Wait," I said, hurrying over the spongy ground after Lacey. "We have to stay together."

I turned my hand toward her so she could see the symbol, but either she couldn't see it or I wasn't close enough yet. She spun away and dashed toward the thicker haze—just as three more wolf shapes emerged from it.

She stiffened as they converged on her. This was her nightmare—the most horrible thing she'd been able to imagine. And it was coming for her. I knew how awful that felt.

I dashed after her. The wolves seemed content to draw out the hunt. The muscular confidence of their prowl struck a chord of recognition in me. Their shapes were blurry and artless, but there was a stark honesty to Lacey's conjuring.

The packs of Dull kids who'd sometimes cornered me at

school had given off the same air: nonchalance laced with aggression. They'd worked the same way too, always picking on the tutorial kids when they could catch us alone, focusing on the easiest targets. How many times had I gone still and silent, knowing that raising my voice with the slightest defensive casting was the fastest route to a mandated burnout? How many times had *Lacey*?

"No!" Judith cried somewhere behind me. There was a thump like a body falling. Finn shouted something.

Glass glinted near my foot. I aimed another fracturing jab of magic through my heel as I ran past, and one of the wolves blew apart into the sudden dark. The other two lunged at Lacey from either side.

"We'll have to go *through* them," I sang, and leapt closer to her with magic-enhanced speed. My concentration was shaky. The energy shuddered over my skin. But my groping hand found Lacey's elbow.

I hauled her toward me and gasped out another lyric. A shadow-wolf rebounded off of an invisible wall of magic. Lacey shoved at me with a squeal, but I managed to heave my arm around her so the back of my hand was right before her eyes. At the sight of the symbol, her shoulders sagged against my chest.

Magic reverberated through me as the creatures flung themselves at my shield. It held, and like bullies everywhere, they lost interest quickly in victims who could defend themselves. They stalked away toward the others, who were scattered around the fringes of Desmond's light. Four more shadow-wolves prowled past us out of the fog.

"They're coming your way!" I called out, letting go of Lacey.

She stumbled to the side. "I'm sorry," she said.

"It wasn't your fault. Here." I pressed open the nick on my thumb and sketched the square and heart symbol on her thin hand. Then I tugged her to follow me as I whirled back toward the rest of our group.

Desmond was hustling past the cots in what had been our dorm room. Judith stood directly beneath the glowing square in the mist, clutching her broken arm tight against her slim frame. As the shadow-wolves loped toward her, she brandished a small knife at them.

Finn ran toward her from the opposite direction with Prisha right behind him. Something gleamed on the ground ahead of him.

"Finn!" I called out. "Marble."

He slowed and spat out a quick phrase, shattering the glass. The wolf on the verge of springing at Judith shredded into fragments of shadow. One of the remaining five snapped at her good arm. She sliced the knife at it. Its fang cut a ragged line across the back of her hand, and she gasped, flinching away.

Finn and Prisha charged through the filmy wolf forms from behind. Finn thrust the symbol on his hand in front of Judith's eyes, and Prisha called up a rippling wave of magic that repelled the wolves, sending them back a few feet.

I paused just long enough to stomp on another marble. The remaining four wolves had already turned toward the back of our dorm room, where Desmond was standing braced with a cot in front of him—as if that would provide any protection from Lacey's ghostly creations. His gaze darted back and forth beneath his furrowed brow.

I nudged Lacey toward the other three. "Stay with them," I said. She was so shaky I wasn't sure she'd be much help with Desmond.

"Those things like picking off the strays from the herd, don't they?" Finn observed. "So there's safety in numbers. Shall we go get Desmond?"

I'd meant to go alone, but he had a point. "Right." I turned to Prisha. "Find the marbles?"

She saluted me. "On it."

Finn and I started sprinting for the dorm room. At an exclamation and a crunch behind us, one of the shadow-wolves disintegrated. The other three creatures had just reached the first line of cots, some twenty feet ahead of us.

Desmond crouched behind his cot, his eyes fixed on the prowling forms. His hands felt along the edges of the mattress, but I couldn't tell what he was checking for.

"I'm thinking you zap those things apart, and I'll dive in to get to him," Finn said, managing to sound reassuringly confident while also short-winded. His face was paler than usual, the cut on his lip stark in contrast, but he kept his chin up. "Unless you had something more spectacular in mind, Dragon-Tamer?"

At the teasing note in his voice, I couldn't help saying, "Maybe you can *talk* them into leaving with that silver tongue of yours."

He laughed, a ragged, breathless sound. "Hey, wolves!" he yelled. "I'm sure if we just take a moment to hash things out, we'll discover we're actually on the same side."

In spite of everything, I might have smiled if I hadn't seen Desmond's reaction to Finn's voice. Though the shadow-wolves stalked on without hesitating, his gaze jerked up, as if he hadn't noticed us approaching until then. He stared in our direction so vaguely I felt as if he were looking right past me. Was some other magic acting on him that hadn't touched the rest of us yet?

One of the wolves tensed as if to spring. I threw myself down the left aisle between the cots as Finn raced down the right. Desmond steadied himself with a hand upraised, and a new clawed shadow hurtled through the wall at his back.

"Behind you!" I cried out, losing the lyric I'd been about to cast with.

The wolf smacked against the protective magic Desmond must have conjured around himself earlier, fell onto its feet, and whipped around. Desmond's roving eyes snagged on us, and he snapped out a verse that hurled Finn into the cot beside him.

Two of the wolves leapt at Desmond at once. The air shivered as his shield fractured.

"No!" My lips were already moving with the fastest, surest way I had to protect him. I reached out to the magical barrier I'd built around myself and whipped it toward Desmond, flinging myself after it.

But Desmond, who seemed to see me as just as much of a threat as the wolves, tried to dodge to the side, carrying my barrier with him. I fell on my hands and knees, my joints jarring. One of the wolves slammed into me and pushed me flat into the tiles. Teeth and claws raked my back. Pain seared through my torso. A strangled sound ripped from my throat, but in the haze of panic, I managed to hold onto one thought: I had to get to Desmond. He had my shield.

"Brinca, brinca," I rasped desperately. The slight rhythm to the words gathered the magic beneath me and tossed me forward, dislodging the creature that was still savaging me.

I collided with Desmond, and we both toppled over. With a breath that was more a sob, I yanked my hand up to show him the symbol, but he kept shoving me away as if he couldn't see it.

As if he couldn't *see* it.

My small observations of him across the last half a day clicked together like an interlocking puzzle. Choking down the pain, I muttered a few words to set the dried blood of the mark glowing.

The second the symbol lit up, Desmond's body stilled. He looked at me where I had collapsed beside him on the floor. As horrified as his expression was, his gaze still held that odd distance—the distance I'd noticed earlier but hadn't realized the significance of.

All this time, he'd been hiding his weakness. He clearly had ways of compensating with magic, but needing to focus on those castings distracted from everything else we'd needed to do. And he'd never even hinted he might need a little extra support, let alone asked for it. Because he'd been worried we'd think less of him for it? Or because he'd wanted to show the examiners he could pass without anyone knowing?

It didn't matter. We all had vulnerable spots we didn't want on display. I got it.

The wolves battered the shield that now sheltered both of us, but it held. Gritting my teeth against the agony radiating through my back, I grasped Desmond's hand and turned it over. I hissed the lyrics to shape a line of magic into a matching symbol, glowing bright blue against his dark brown skin. Then a fresh wave of pain rushed through me, and my head dropped to the floor. The floor that was now smeared with my blood.

"I'm sorry," Desmond said roughly. "I didn't— It was like DEFCON 1 blaring in my head."

"Finn's 'chantment," I said. "We're all okay now." I paused, woozy. "It isn't your magic ability they held you back for; it's your sight."

His lips twisted, and his voice dropped. "They didn't give a detailed explanation, but I doubt being legally blind helped my case. I can still see a few things: shapes, movement. Contrast, so light helps a lot. Unless the thing's too far away."

"Hmmm." My head was really spinning now. "My back isn't too far away, is it? Because I could use some of that healing skill, I think."

Desmond shifted closer and swore. So the wound looked bad too. Before I'd had time to register more than that, he was crooning under his breath. A burning sensation spread over my skin so suddenly I bit my tongue in surprise. A numbing chill followed in the wake of the heat.

Rushing feet scraped the floor just behind Desmond. "Don't get up," Finn said quickly. He was panting. Were the others okay? And my shield—the wolves had left us for the moment, but I wasn't sure how stable it still was, or—

The 'chanted chill settled my pulse, and with it my thoughts slowed too. I pushed myself into a sitting position and winced as new aches prickled down my ribs.

"Take it slow," Desmond said. "The cuts were deep. I stopped the bleeding and dulled some of the nerves, but that's as much as I can manage. You're still really hurt."

Finn leaned against the frame of the cot next to us, close enough to Desmond to share my shield. He held his side as he watched the wolves lurking around its edges, but I didn't see any blood on him.

"Are you okay?" I asked.

He smiled crookedly. "I can't say this is the best day of my life, but so far I'm still planning on surviving." His gaze fell on Desmond. "The others are on their way over," he said quietly.

"Thanks," Desmond said.

Finn nodded as if it were nothing. He'd realized Desmond wouldn't necessarily see that, and he was going to keep the secret, no questions asked.

I had the sudden urge to reach out to him. As if he'd sensed it, he offered his hand to me to help me up from the floor. I took it, my fingers curling around his warm, dry palm. My gaze focused on the defined muscles in his arm. Some of that warmth traveled to my face. I levered myself onto my feet with my other hand braced against the cot.

The tatters of my shirt slipped against my newly sealed side and back. I was probably showing a lot more skin than I'd prefer. I'd need to take care of that when I had a chance.

The hum in the air shifted as the others gathered around us.

Their protective shell overlaid ours, and the wolves drew back farther. Only two remained—or remained nearby, at least.

Prisha peered into Finn's face. Before she could say anything, he gave her a firm look. "I'm *fine*. Managed to completely escape getting clawed. Didn't you observe my daring dash?"

She frowned. What did she see that I couldn't?

Judith sank down on the cot beside us, still clutching her blade, which looked like a Swiss Army knife with a pearly handle. She folded it shut against her thigh. Her slim shoulders trembled. "The examiners have only just gotten started. I don't know... I didn't know it was going to be like this."

My throat tightened. Part of me wanted to insist that she should have listened for the stories, she should have paid attention to how ruthless the Confed could be—but I hadn't really known either, had I? I'd known the Exam would be hard, but I hadn't expected this chaos. Another part of me wanted to run for the nearest exit too.

If she broke down and called out to the examiners, maybe they'd come get her and accept her resignation. Or maybe they weren't even watching that closely, and Lacey's wolves would tear her apart.

"We know now," I said. "We're all still here. We can do this together."

I could do this. I could make sure the five people around me made it through.

Judith rubbed her mouth. Then her jaw clenched. "Yes," she said, even though her voice wobbled. "I'm keeping my magic. I *am*."

"So what next?" Lacey said. Her eyes were following the wolves.

"While we're shielded, they can't hurt us," Prisha said.

"As long as they're our only problem," I said. "Who knows what's going to come after this? We've got no idea what Mark's 'chantment even *is*." My back prickled. Was I ready? If I'd been a few seconds slower, if I hadn't made it to Desmond, Lacey's wolves might have torn *me* apart.

But they hadn't, and I was still here. I raised my chin. "Let's find all the marbles and destroy them while we can."

* * *

"It's getting lighter," Desmond said.

I lifted my gaze from the ground and blinked. Sometime in the last few minutes, the fog drifting around us had drawn back. It still lingered in the distance—I couldn't make out the walls of the dorm room we'd left behind—but now we could see about half a mile ahead of us across the flat landscape, and the receding fog had revealed a few scattered buildings and more of those mutilated artificial trees all around.

The narrow buildings all appeared slanted, this one to the left, that one to the right, like cardboard boxes starting to sag under their own weight. When we'd picked up our conversation about our various defensive 'chantments as we'd started our hunt for the rest of the marbles, Prisha had told us hers involved a massive storm that should only affect people outside. I wouldn't count on those buildings for shelter in that.

The buildings, ground, and trees were still gray, but the brighter light above us cast everything with a yellowish tone, as if the landscape were singed. Or going rotten. I breathed in and found the peppery smell had turned sour.

Had we even kept walking away from the dorm room? With that haze all around and the vague sameness of the terrain the examiners had created, we could have been walking in circles for all we knew.

A lone shadow-wolf was still tracking us. It slunk closer to our protective shell, whipping its tail.

Then Lacey called out, "There it is! I've got it," and pointed at the marble she'd spotted.

She shot the wolf a triumphant look before striding away from our cluster. I tensed to run after her, but she was already muttering a phrase, and the marble shattered. The wolf wisped away mid-prowl.

Lacey set her hands on her hips. "Take that, wolves!" she said. "No one's ever been able to beat me down so much I can't get back up."

"I'll toast to that," Desmond said. He raised a fist and intoned, "We'll face our fears, and only we will remain."

"Is that from a movie?" Finn asked.

Desmond's face fell a little. Maybe he'd hoped one of us would recognize it. "Sort of," he said. "Mostly a book. And I was paraphrasing."

"Not that we have any shortage of other things to worry about," Finn said, "but I hope Mark managed to steer clear of the wolves, wherever he is now."

"He seemed to think he could handle anything. I just hope *we* missed his 'chantment, and it's not waiting to spring on—" Judith froze. "Hold on. Is that *food*?"

We all jerked around to look. My stomach pinched before I even saw what she was talking about. We hadn't eaten since last night. We hadn't even had water since we'd left the dorm room with its bathroom behind.

A table had appeared in the open space between us and the distant buildings. It was heaped with shapes that did look as if they could be food. Lacey darted forward first, and the rest of us followed. As soon as we got close enough to identify the shapes as sandwiches, fruit, and bottles of water, Judith and Prisha hurried ahead. An itch crept over my skin as they left the shelter of our shield, but we hadn't seen any other wolves in a long time. Maybe we were safe.

On the other hand, maybe the food wasn't. No one had mentioned a 'chantment that could affect what we ate—Judith had said hers was meant to simply shut out the use of magic, not even to hurt us—but that didn't mean the examiners couldn't add their own tricks to the mix.

I stopped at the table. The smell of fresh bread filled my mouth with saliva.

Lacey grabbed one of the sandwiches.

"Stop!" I said.

She hesitated with it halfway to her mouth. "What?"

Suddenly I wasn't sure what to say. The examiners were probably watching our progress, weren't they? I had to be careful how I talked about them.

Before I could decide on the exact words to express my worry, Finn said, "We should treat *everything* in this place as a possible test, so check before you bite! Simple enough."

He sounded so cheerful in spite of everything that I felt myself relax. He'd understood my fear and taken it in stride, and now all the others were murmuring probing castings over their chosen meals as if that were a standard precaution.

I picked up a sandwich, and Finn tipped his head to me with that smile of his. Yesterday's flutter returned to my chest, headier than before. I tugged my gaze away. Getting caught up in that feeling in the middle of this Exam could be as dangerous as any 'chantment.

Judith dug in to her ham-and-cheese. She swallowed and sighed happily. "I was starting to worry they'd totally abandoned us."

I couldn't stop my eyebrows from rising. "We have no idea how much they're even paying attention to what happens in here," I had to point out. "We just spent the whole morning avoiding being ripped apart by conjured monsters, and the 'chantment before that broke your arm." *The examiners don't give a damn about us.*

"I guess it could be worse." Lacey wiped crumbs from her mouth. "The whole point is to test us. They've got to get intense to really stretch our abilities, right? At least we get a second chance. They could just Damper us, and that'd be the end of it."

Finn shrugged. "Or they could not Damper anyone."

He said it as casually as he usually spoke, but Prisha stiffened. My gaze fixed on him again. He seemed oblivious to us as he directed a probing 'chantment at his roast beef.

Maybe it was easier to say those kinds of things when you were old magic and didn't have to face the same scrutiny.

Desmond cocked his head. "Are there places like that? Where all mages are allowed to keep their full abilities?"

"Dampering was standard policy in all of the countries my family was stationed in," Judith said. "Some places do it younger. My mom grew up in China, and her brother was Dampered when he was ten. It's always been like that, right? To protect us from the Dulls."

"Yeah," I said, remembering the tutorial classes where we'd briefly covered magical history. I could give a show of following the party line. "At least, that was the theory when we were staying hidden, to make sure the only people who had full use of magic were disciplined enough to control it. Get too lax about security, one person messes up in the wrong place, and you end up with the witch trials."

Lacey lowered her sandwich to her chest. "Then... there really isn't a reason to do it anymore, is there?"

¡Ay, no! I hadn't meant to prompt that question, at least not consciously. "They're concerned about... different things now," I said, hoping to deflect her.

"Technically it's the same thing," Finn said. "Avoiding conflict with the Dulls. To be fair, the worry isn't totally unreasonable. It's not as if magicless people stopped being nervous about us after we confirmed we existed, and even a small slip can do a lot of damage. My grandfather was killed in a riot that started after someone accidentally singed a couple of Dulls with an illusion."

"It's two birds with one stone," Prisha said. "Make the Dull hoi polloi feel better knowing the Confed's keeping control over its own, and prevent the older mages from getting careless, because their kids will be judged in part by family history. It's smart, really."

She smiled but so thinly I couldn't tell whether she actually admired that approach or found it as disturbing as I did.

The Confed used Dampering for more than that, I thought but didn't say. If Mom was right—if the Confed Dampered not just the weaker mages but anyone powerful who hadn't been raised on Confed ideology—then they were keeping their own authority safe too. There would never be a group of potential dissidents with enough power to challenge them.

"It makes sense that they have to restrict it," Judith said. "I mean, no one really understands exactly what magic *is* or how it works. What if tons more people started doing crazy things with it, and the government couldn't stop them? Who knows what would happen?"

"We understand it enough to know it follows natural rules," Desmond said. "Anyway, magic is just what we call things we don't have a scientific explanation for yet. You know, 'Any sufficiently advanced technology is indistinguishable from magic.' I bet—"

A thud sounded in the distance. Finn's hand dropped to his pocket, the same gesture I'd seen him make earlier this morning. It was the pocket on his right hip, it occurred to me—where he'd tensed when Prisha had touched him last night.

A memory from five years ago clicked into place: Javier acting edgy, me confronting him, and him pulling a small switchblade from his jeans. *What do you have that for?* I'd demanded.

He'd shrugged, looking unexpectedly ashamed. *It's just in case. Just for show. Some of the guys in the neighborhood were hassling me. I'm not going to have to* use *it, Ro, te doy mi palabra.*

Finn was carrying something like that. Something that made him nervous. Something he thought could cause harm.

I was just opening my mouth to call him on it when the ground pitched beneath us. I stumbled forward—not into the table that had been there a moment ago but into a hard translucent wall that looked as if it were made out of solidified fog.

CHAPTER NINE

Finn

No matter what you're feeling, put on a pleasant face, and you can conquer the world. My mother was fond of giving that advice, and until about five hours ago, I'd considered it sound. Unfortunately, I was discovering several exceptions to her rule. Giant shadowy wolves, for example, were not remotely mollified by friendly banter. Smiling winningly at the strange walls that had shot up around me didn't budge them one bit.

The walls had cut me off from the rest of the group. I tapped the cool surface of the one directly in front of me. It looked like fogged glass—a mottled, pallid gray and faintly translucent—but it was flexible to the touch.

An off-key arpeggio thrummed in the air, setting my pulse out of kilter. The magic was reacting to something—reacting badly. I rubbed my thumb over my fingers, frowned, and murmured a quick testing line. My voice faded without the slightest hitch in the energy around me.

I sang another line. The energy still didn't stir. My chest

tightened. Trying to cast was like groping after a coin submerged in water. I wasn't reaching the magic at all.

I swiped my hand over my face, fighting the cold surge of panic rising through me. We weren't just physically imprisoned; we were cut off from the world as surely as if we'd been sent to Tartarus.

This had to be Judith's 'chantment. She'd said it would stop us from casting.

On the other side of the wall to my left, Prisha muttered a string of curses. I closed my eyes. My headache was merely a faint thudding now. I'd managed to avoid casting during our entire marble search. I could stay calm.

If I couldn't help with magic *or* without, I truly was useless.

"Is everyone all right?" I called out. "Beyond being trapped in a magical blackout box, I mean?"

"As if that isn't bad enough," Prisha remarked flatly.

"I'm alive," Desmond said.

"My arm—" Judith began in a rasp, and halted. "Never mind. I'm sorry about this."

"I *hate* this," Lacey said. "The way it feels..."

"I can't cast anything at all," Rocío said at my right. Her voice was oddly stiff. "Judith, did you put a countermeasure on the 'chantment, like Finn's symbol for his?"

She'd dodged my question about whether she was all right. Desmond had cast a numbing 'chantment on her wounds, and he'd helped Judith too, but if this trap had fragmented not just our connection to the magic but 'chantments in process, both of them would be feeling the full pain of their injuries. And after the mauling Rocío had taken from that wolf...

"No," Judith replied. "I had a hard enough time coming up with the idea in the first place. I'd only just finished the casting when our time was up. Maybe if we'd had more time, I'd have thought of it..." She sucked in a sharp breath. "So I guess this is what it's like being burned out."

That idea only sent my panic spiking higher. "Then let's make sure this is the only time we experience it," I said quickly. "Do we need to worry about anything *else*? Being crushed or stabbed with spikes or fun additions like that?"

Desmond managed to guffaw.

"It's just this," Judith said. "But I don't know how we get out of it."

"There's got to be a way." Unfortunately, everything I'd read about untangling 'chantments required more magic.

There was no use in dwelling on that. Whatever the case, you always started from the same point. To tackle someone else's casting, you had to trace it down to the core of their intent.

"It's an *interesting* idea, anyway," I went on. "I bet the examiners were impressed. What made you think of it?"

"I don't know," Judith said. "I went in a few other directions, but they all seemed too obvious. Then I remembered hearing some foreign security people talking at one of my dad's business parties last year—about how they could keep magic out of rooms they wanted to protect or stop criminals from casting during interrogations or whatever."

Desmond let out a low whistle. "So you've got some swanky government technique going on here."

"I doubt I cast it the same way they would have," Judith said, but she sounded a little less despondent. "They didn't go into detail, but I heard enough to figure out it has to do with the frequencies—you have to make the magic oscillate in a way that scatters any attempt at casting. So I focused on that. Mostly I was thinking of the awful music my brother listens to."

I rested my palm on the wall in front of me. The discomforting thrum penetrated me more deeply, but I held myself still, absorbing it. The magic in the walls was moving at a particular rhythm, then—a rhythm so unnaturally erratic it was disrupting all the energy around us, preventing us from molding it.

If an erratic rhythm could shatter our castings... couldn't the same thing break Judith's? Her attempt could scarcely be as stable as that of a government professional.

"What if we could scatter the scattering 'chantment?" I said. "If we produce a frequency that disrupts the magic forming the walls, we should at least weaken them, right?"

"Except we can't cast," Prisha said.

"No," Desmond said, "but you don't *need* magic to make a rhythm."

"We hit the walls," Rocío said. "The 'chantment can't stop us from affecting it directly."

"Precisely," I said. "I guess... It's all one 'chantment. So if we all come up with different rhythms—something fast and complicated? —and drum them out at the same time... It'll be a cacophony, but maybe that'll be enough to break the 'chantment apart."

"That might work," Judith said slowly.

"It can't hurt to try," Prisha agreed.

There was a pause. They were waiting on me. My voice caught in my throat. What if trying *did* hurt? What if my strategy not only failed but provoked a negative reaction?

A warbling sound drifted through the walls. The hiss and crackle of it tugged on my memory. My Grandma Lockwood had that old transistor radio she used to turn on and tune when we'd visit.

I'd heard that static hiss when my 'chantment had acted on us before. We'd fended off the effect, but we hadn't destroyed it. The examiners must have amplified the radio for us to hear it now. Of course, as long as we had the nullifying symbol still on us, we should be fine—

"Rocío," Desmond said quietly, "when we get out of this, I'll need you to fix my hand right away."

He'd needed his symbol 'chanted for him to see it. That magic would have been shattered too. I clenched my hands.

"One, two, three… go!" Prisha said ahead of me.

Maybe because of Judith's remark about her brother, my mind shot to Margo's favorite band: the screeching guitars and stuttering drums that had filtered into my bedroom from hers years ago. I thrust my hands at the wall, beating out the frenetic melody to the best of my recollection. All around me, the air shuddered with the strikes of my companions' fists.

The impact jolting through my palms was exhilarating—so much better than swiping at shadows. I struck out harder, faster, humming along with the beat.

As the song I remembered wound toward its finale, the wall felt no less solid. "More!" I shouted, resisting the whisper of doubt. "Give it all you've got."

I dredged another discordant song from my memory. A tremor raced through the air, and I thought I might have felt it in the wall too. I threw myself into the seesawing melody of the chorus as fast as my fists could fly. The translucent surface in front of me flexed and swayed. More, more, more—

With a crinkling sound like crushed aluminum foil, the walls fell in on themselves and toppled into the dull gray ground. The whisper of magic steadied around me. I'd have hugged it in my relief if I could.

A few feet ahead of me, Desmond whipped around to glare at Prisha. He lunged at her, but before I could so much as move, Rocío had dashed past me to grab his wrist mid-swing. The bottom of her torn shirt flapped, revealing the smooth brown skin at her waist, and my pulse hitched with a sensation that was very different from relief.

With a few soft words, she set the heart-and-square symbol glowing bright on the back of Desmond's hand.

He let out a rush of breath. "Sorry."

"It's not your fault," Rocío said.

No, technically it was mine.

Judith braced her makeshift sling against her chest. "All right," she said. "We did it."

My radio's static carried on through the air. Had it gotten even louder since I'd first noticed it?

The sound was distant enough that I couldn't determine precisely which direction the radio lay in. If the examiners amplified the 'chantment more, I wasn't certain my safeguard would hold. I'd been exhausted when I'd cast that coda.

A chilly prickle ran down my back. "I have to find my 'chantment and break it," I said. "As long as it's still broadcasting, the examiners can use it against us. You all keep heading for shelter. I'll catch up with you before you miss me."

It felt so natural to speak of them like that now: as the enemy. They'd *made* themselves the enemy when they'd abandoned us to be maimed and tormented in this vast test without a hint of support or even supervision.

"I don't think it's a good idea for any of us to go off alone," Rocío said.

"She's right." Prisha gave me a searching look.

My gut knotted. She was speculating about how drained I was, whether I'd need another of her numbing 'chantments for my head and whether I'd be able to extinguish my own 'chantment without her help.

I'd relied on her more than was fair already. I would *not* let her exhaust her magic to compensate for my weakness. "We haven't faced your storm yet. You need to get everyone to one of the buildings—you said that'd be enough of a defense while we wait it out, right? I'll take care of this and be back in a jiff."

"You have to take *some*one," Prisha protested.

"You're the one who knows your 'chantment best. You need to be focused on that."

"So I'll go with you." Rocío's tense gaze slid from me to the others. "But we should get moving."

A worried shadow had crossed her face, but I could tell she wasn't afraid of what might happen to her without the safety of numbers. She was afraid of what might happen to the others without *her*.

Evidently, she'd decided I needed protection more than they did. Had I already shown my talents to be that feeble?

"Right," I said, suppressing my embarrassment.

"Finn." Prisha grabbed my elbow and dragged me to the side with an abruptness that startled me. She lowered her voice. "I'll come. You don't need to take her. Let's just get this over with."

"I'm pretty sure Rocío can manage to protect me should the need arise," I said.

"Maybe," Prisha muttered. "Maybe not. You came here for me, didn't you? So let me do this for you."

Hadn't she seen what Rocío was capable of? Her concern defied logic. The chaos of the Exam must be wearing on her. It was wearing on all of us.

"I came here for *me*," I said quietly but firmly, and motioned to her shoulder. "And you've already been hurt in part because of my wretched 'chantment. I'll concentrate better on disabling it if I know you're safe. Please?"

Her expression softened. "All right. But you'd better be back fast."

I gave her an obedient salute and turned back to Rocío. The hiss of static beckoned me. "Let's go."

As we set off, I tilted my head for a sharper read on the sound. The wind whistled past us, distorting the crackle. I turned the other way, toward Rocío, and registered the tightening of her mouth as she touched her back where the wolf had ripped into her.

"I'm sorry," she said. "Hold on just a few seconds?"

Desmond had sealed her skin so no blood seeped out into the torn strip of sheet she'd wrapped around her chest, but the lacerated flesh underneath must be total agony. Hades take me— she'd seemed so calm I'd almost forgotten the numbing 'chantments had worn off.

"If you need help—"

She shook her head with a jerk. "I can take care of it."

The flash of her dark eyes before she lowered them reminded me of the way she'd reacted to my blunder last night. I had no idea what she'd endured before this without anyone offering help —and without her needing it.

But I wanted to understand. With every word, every casting she worked, she'd drawn more of my attention. I wanted to know all about her life, about how she'd ended up here, everything.

I wanted her to think me worthy of telling.

Rocío sang a couple lines in a hushed voice—Spanish, from the sound of it. Then she flexed her shoulders and twisted tentatively at the waist. Her sunburst charm slid across the tops of her breasts—and I detached my gaze before she noticed my attention on *them*.

"That's good enough for now," she said, and resumed walking.

"You'll put Desmond out of business," I joked. "Is there any sort of casting you're not brilliant at?"

She let out a laugh—short but genuine enough to warm me. "I'm pretty far from a magimedic," she said. "It was just a standard first aid 'chantment. But... I've worked hard to make sure I'm as strong as possible in every area."

"You wanted to get into the college," I said, and then could have smacked myself for stating the incredibly obvious.

Her voice dipped. "I like learning just to learn—to see what I can do. What's possible. If you keep reaching and reaching, it's amazing how there's always something more. But, yeah, I thought if I covered everything, there wouldn't be any reason for them to doubt I could handle the courses. All I needed was to be Chosen, and there wouldn't even be tuition."

"It'll be the same if you're Champion," I said, but my mind lingered on the rest of her words. She'd given the Circle no reason to exclude her. Prisha they could almost have explained away, played down her marks as more middling than they were, but this girl—this *spectacular* mage of a girl—had done everything right, and they'd still rejected her.

How many great mages had been Dampered because people like my granduncle were afraid of untried lineages?

"It isn't right," I said. "I know you already know that, and *I* should have figured it out a lot sooner than I did, but..." It didn't feel sufficient to call the mages in authority idiots; the problem was larger than that. "That's not how *I'd* decide who's admitted and who isn't."

We continued in silence for a minute or so. Then Rocío said in the same quiet voice, "I appreciate that." She lifted her head. "Do you know where we're going?"

All I'd determined with any certainty was that the radio's static was carrying from a long stretch of branchless trees half-hidden by the mist ahead of us. I hadn't narrowed the direction down more than that yet. She likely expected me to have an approach more refined than hunting aimlessly across the landscape.

Or worse, maybe she didn't.

If I spent the entire Exam depending on other people's skills, the examiners were never going to believe *I* deserved to stay a mage, and Rocío would never see me as anything other than a dolt.

I dredged up a memorized verse about following music and channeled the sense of it over my tongue, grateful now for my extended practice in tracing 'chantments. My nerves jittered and my headache pounded. Ignoring them, I reached my awareness out into the quiver of the magic. A ripple ran through it, guiding me slightly to the right.

"It's over here," I said. My forehead pinched, but I resisted the urge to rub it. In just a few minutes, we'd have the radio, and I'd look decently competent for once.

The breeze rose, ruffling our clothes with a vigor that unnerved me. We *did* still have to worry about Prisha's storm 'chantment. I sped up. Rocío scanned the ground and the trees we were approaching.

"That was Latin you used, wasn't it?" she said. "I've always wondered why the academies are so stuck on dead languages. My tutorial leader never had a clear answer."

"That's just the way magic is done," I said automatically, and bit my tongue. Clearly it wasn't, if she cast in Spanish. "Or not. That's how they teach us. The teachers say it's to get us closer to the roots of magical practice. Drawing on those ancient tongues is supposed to align our minds with all that history. I guess they don't teach it that way in the tutorials."

"The only Latin I know is 'et cetera' and 'carpe diem,'" Rocío said. "Our teacher told us that what's most important is our personal connection to the magic. He said it'd be easier for us to harmonize with it if we're using words we relate to."

I had trouble picturing rows of kids in a dingy public-school room chanting archaic poetry. "Likely for the better," I said. "Why go to the hassle of pushing all that memorization—"

I snapped my mouth shut when I realized what was on the verge of tumbling out.

"With a bunch of novices who are mostly going to end up Dampered anyway?" Rocío suggested tartly.

My unthinking response would have been even more unfortunate. *With a bunch of lesser-talent new-magic kids.* That was how my Academy teachers would have spoken—but I knew better now.

Were the new-magic families lesser in talent at all, or was that a lie the Circle had invented to justify who they admitted to the college?

"I don't think that," I said. "I *wasn't* thinking. Honestly, your theory makes at least as much sense as the one I learned."

Rocío marched on without looking at me.

"Hey," I said. "I mean it. I apologize."

She turned. The wind buffeted us, making her hair billow around her face. She gazed at me so directly I found it hard to breathe.

"Why does it matter to you whether you've offended me?" she said. "No one else seems to care."

I knew without asking for clarification that she didn't merely mean Prisha and Judith. There'd been a long line of slights and insults aimed her way by the Confed-associated mages she'd met before now. I'd heard enough of them, aimed at others like her, from my classmates, my granduncle, some of my father's associates.

I rubbed the back of my neck. "I, ah— Keeping spirits up is one of the few areas where I actually have a little talent. So if I'm failing even at that..." No, don't make this into a joke, Finn. "I have a huge amount of respect for you," I said. "You're an amazing mage. I mean that. The last thing I want is to make you feel otherwise. If I ever say something that sounds like I'm putting you down, or new-magic mages like you... I deserve to be called out."

I must have said something right, because she nodded, and a little of the tension released from her posture.

"So Spanish is the language you feel most comfortable with?"

I said as we hurried on. She didn't have any accent, but neither did Prisha's family, other than the grandmother I'd met once who spoke clipped British English.

"Most of the time, no," she said. "I'm kind of rusty. There weren't any other Latino kids in the tutorial class, and even my parents mostly speak English, so I haven't practiced very much. But when I was a little kid, before I was in school, my abuelo and abuela—my grandparents—babysat me, and they only came here from Mexico after they were married, so they mostly knew kids' songs from there. Something about that part of my life, being so little and unaware of everything else going on, it was so happy and, I don't know, harmonious? I find myself coming back to it when I'm reaching out to the magic."

"And that helps you connect," I said.

"Yeah. Sometimes I feel a little guilty that I'm not more immersed in that part of my family's heritage, but a lot of the time... I like that it's kind of apart. As if that language is something sacred between the magic and me." Her mouth curved with a faint smile.

I'd never experienced that sort of feeling. I knew dozens of classic plays and poems inside and out, but I didn't take joy in them, let alone have a sense of them being *sacred*. The lines and lyrics always swam up through my thoughts with a brittle edge. I could probably blame that discomfort on the stress and sweat with which I'd drilled them into my head.

My tracing 'chantment tugged me out of my distraction. I veered farther to the right.

There, where two trees stood close together, the edge of something rectangular protruded. The static crackled louder as the wind warbled between the trunks. I hurried toward them, glancing at the symbol on my hand to shore up my defenses.

The "trees" bore about as much resemblance to the real thing as the rubbery turf under our feet did to dirt. Their black, stumpy-limbed bodies jutted out of the ground like an overwrought art installation. Their lightly ridged trunks looked more like rippled plastic than bark.

My radio was wedged amid one tree's knobby roots. I bent over it, hesitant to touch it even though I'd handled it plenty yesterday. Up close, the static hiss shrieked hard enough to sting my eardrums. My hand dropped to my pocket, but Margo had said the dissolving rod only worked on organic matter.

"You could just smash it," Rocío suggested, coming up behind me.

I was tempted to, but... "I don't know what sort of rebound effect that might cause," I said. "It'll be safer to unravel the 'chantment."

I pressed my hands to the radio's case. Magic rippled through the metal beneath my palms.

I could do this. It was my responsibility.

The wind blustered through the static, reminding me that I didn't merely need to *do* it—I needed to do it *fast*.

I rolled a few words off my tongue and focused my attention on the vibrations of magic inside the radio. The braided strands of intent I'd composed together shuddered. My headache jabbed deeper. I swiveled my thumb against the metal to ground me and twined my words, larghetto, with the melody.

The threads of the 'chantment sharpened in my awareness. This one, I could snap. I pulled with a sharp accent, and the energy sizzled away through me. The ache expanded through my skull and down my spine.

This thread, I could tease apart. Pain pierced the bridge of my nose as I adjusted my modulation to unwind the measure strand by strand. More magic shimmered away into the air.

My gums were going numb; my tongue prickled. Dolor hic tibi proderit olim, as they said—someday this pain will be useful to you. I sure as hell hoped so. Squaring my shoulders, I called apart two more threads.

The remaining structure collapsed in on itself like a cat's cradle unstrung. The burst of energy clanged through my body, and then it was gone.

I slumped, bracing my hand against the dense gray ground.

"Finn," Rocío said.

My headache thudded in my temples, and the wind whirled around us. Rain had started to fall. As I shoved myself to my feet, tiny droplets sliced across my cheeks. No doubt about it—Prisha's storm was upon us. I fought to orient myself.

The tilted buildings the others had headed for were scarcely visible in the churning mists.

Rocío caught my hand, and my heart stuttered for reasons that had nothing to do with the escalating storm. "Run for it?" she said.

"Good plan, seeing as neither of us thought to bring an umbrella."

A laugh that seemed to startle even her burst from her lips— and was siphoned away into the rising howl of the wind. She squeezed my hand tighter, and we sprinted across the wide gray plain.

The fog thickened around us, stirred by the storm. We plunged through the haze. The buildings had been swallowed from view, but I kept moving forward, holding the image of them in my mind.

The rain turned to hail. It battered our skin, and the shriek of the wind rang in my ears. An abrupt blast wrenched us in opposite directions, jarring the elbow I'd banged in Rocío's vise. I flinched, and her fingers slipped from mine. Another wallop knocked me to my knees.

I scrambled back up, my chest heaving as I attempted to breathe through the rushing air. My vision filled with streaks of hail and crashing fog. I whirled around, searching. My headache prodded my skull with a dozen thick splinters.

I'd lost Rocío. I'd lost all sense of direction. The wind was outright screaming now, pummeling me from all sides, and I hadn't the faintest idea where to turn.

CHAPTER TEN

Rocío

The fog roared around me. I spun, and my wet hair smacked my face. Finn had been right here next to me a second ago. I couldn't leave him in this gale.

I stumbled one way and then another. My groping hand collided with a shoulder. I clutched it, yanking us together. Finn's arm slid across my back to hold us in place. He said something— I heard his voice by my ear—but the screech of the storm stole the words. Hail pelted us, and the wind lashed at us from all sides. I could hardly breathe.

The only solid thing was Finn. I curled my fingers into the damp fabric of his shirt and sang into the stiller space between us. "Como veían que resistía." Magic hummed from the vicious air into me. Maybe I could make a shield strong enough to protect us even against this force, or—

The hum tickled through my mind like the brush of a hand. That presence again? An image swam up of the grate I'd come across in the courtyard, between the buildings. A grate that led to something below.

I knelt down, pulling Finn with me, and pressed my free hand to the spongy ground. The wind tried to steal my next lyrics from my lips, but the magic raced through me all the same—through me and down, down, into an open space I sensed below us like a gasp of fresh air.

I did gasp then, and forced out a verse. I'd never magically transported another person with me before, but I had to. I *had* to.

The magic rushed up around us with the thrust of my words. I clung to Finn, singing the energy around him as tightly as I could. Then I propelled us downward with a lurch.

We surged through rough blackness that rasped over my skin and landed with a feet-jarring thump. I exhaled in a rush, dizzy in the sudden quiet. My eardrums ached from the pounding of the storm we'd escaped and the effort of the conjuring.

We crouched in total darkness. The surface beneath me felt like concrete. Cold dank air hovered around us with a faintly salty flavor that reminded me of the ocean.

My fingers were tangled in Finn's shirt, pressed against the lean muscles I'd admired yesterday. His arm was still around me. In the dark, I was abruptly aware of the rise and fall of his rasping breath, the warmth of his chest, and the answering warmth it sent through me.

He was alive—*we* were alive—and in that moment, it felt like a miracle. I wanted to press even closer.

"Ah," Finn said, his voice distant through the buzz in my ears, "what just happened there?"

"I took us underground," I said. "It's some kind of passage under the buildings. It seemed like the quickest way to get out of the storm."

"I see." He sounded both shaky and amused.

I couldn't see him at all, but I could picture him perfectly:

blond hair slicked back in the wake of the rain, alert green eyes searching for a hint of light, that smile curving his lips even now.

"You know," he said, "the person who was best at teleporting in my entire class—who you can be sure wasn't *me*—needed five full minutes to work up the concentration to get from one end of the school to the other. On her own."

"Maybe she could have done it faster if she'd been about to be torn up by a windstorm?"

"Maybe," he said. "Well, I'm not sure how to say this in a way that's remotely adequate, but—thank you for saving my life."

His head turned toward me, just inches from mine. My skin flushed. "You're welcome," I said, which seemed pretty inadequate too.

I eased back, and he let his arm drop. The loss of that warmth made my throat tighten. As if I didn't have more urgent things to focus on.

Light. We needed to see. I murmured a quick phrase and formed a handful of magic into a small globe in the air above us. It spilled a thin yellow glow over the space.

We'd ended up in a narrow corridor with a blank wall about ten feet to our left and a utilitarian door to our right. Like the Exam buildings we'd started in, the walls, floor, and ceiling were painted stark white, but smudges dulled the gloss on the walls and dust had gathered along the edges of the floor. The Confed had taken over this space, but they hadn't paid much attention to it.

I got up and tried the door's metal handle. Locked. The faint hiss of magic emanating from the door suggested it was sealed in other ways as well. Remembering Axton made me hesitant to test it further. Were the examiners going to find some other way to test *us* while we were down here?

When I turned back, Finn was peering at the ceiling. I

thought his face looked more sallow than usual, but maybe that was an effect of the light.

"Of course Prisha would choose now to put all her effort into a casting," he said in his offhand way. "It's all part of the examiners' evil plan."

"It was actually pretty smart of them—in a horrible way," I said. "They got to test us twice, once in casting the 'chantments and once in defending ourselves. If we'd known about the second part, we'd have held back on the first."

Finn blinked at me. "And now I'm making a mental note to never get on your bad side."

I blushed for the second time in as many minutes, but he'd already shifted his gaze back to the ceiling. His jaw worked. "Given the look of the buildings up there, I suppose the real question is whether they'll have collapsed before or after the others made it to them."

His tone was still light, but there was a strain in his voice. He was worried about Prisha. Probably the others too. Of course he was worried. He was just trying not to show how much.

"Or maybe they didn't collapse," I said. "Whatever happened, Prisha knew her own 'chantment. They had lots of time to prepare. She'll have figured something out."

I hoped that was true. Maybe we should have all stayed together. But then the others wouldn't have had the chance to make it to shelter. I couldn't have transported *everyone* down here in one casting. I hadn't even been sure I could carry Finn.

There'd been no good solution. Which seemed to be just how the examiners liked to play this game.

"Even if she can't find a way to counter it, she said the storm should fade before too long," I said.

"Thank the Fates for that," Finn said. "Should we hold out here or tackle that door?"

"The examiners have some kind of protective spell on it—I'm

not sure it'd be smart to mess with that. At least here we're safe for now. I can cast a conjuring to signal us as soon as the wind has died down. When the storm is over, I'll teleport us back up and we'll go find the others."

I stitched the casting together—a line from a childhood song here, another from an elementary school poem I'd liked there—and tossed the magic up through the ceiling. It quivered into place on the ground several feet above us. The raging of the wind sent a vibration along my spine.

When I looked at Finn, he quickly dropped his hand from his temple, straightened up, and winced.

Crap. "Are you hurt?" I said. I should have asked that earlier.

"No, no." He waved me off, schooling his expression to be calm again and smiling. "Just a headache, from the wind and— Nothing critical. It'll pass."

If I hadn't been looking for it, I wouldn't have noticed the slight tightness in his smile. I remembered Prisha touching his head, checking in on him. Whatever had caused the headache, it hadn't started with the wind. How long had he been in pain and hiding it from the rest of us?

How bad must it be now that he couldn't hide it anymore?

I might not have a special affinity for healing, but I had plenty of practice in this particular area. "My dad gets migraines," I said. "I have a simple 'chantment that helps relieve them. If you're okay with me casting on you."

From the way he drew in his breath, I thought he was going to say no, but he paused, and his smile turned wry. "I've already let you drag me into a secret underground lair. What's a little pain relief after that?"

I knelt beside him, and he closed his eyes, his lashes stark against the sharp pale angles of his cheeks. Between his storm-tousled hair and the smudges of blood on his rumpled clothes, he didn't look much like an old-magic Academy boy anymore.

I touched his forehead gingerly and thought of Dad, of the many evenings he'd come home reeling from all those hours in the noise and heat of the call center. "Arrorró mi sol," I murmured, focusing the hum of magic into a gentle cooling balm to smooth the muscles, settle the nerves, and ease the blood vessels' flow.

Finn's breath shuddered. He must have been in even more pain than I'd guessed. My gaze dropped to his mouth, to the angry cut left by my binding 'chantment, the blood dried and starting to scab now. Instinctively, the words to seal the flesh rose up. I spun them out, willing the skin to stitch itself back together.

A mark still remained when I was finished, but there was no chance of the cut bleeding again. Finn pressed his lips together. Then he met my eyes.

"You didn't have to do that," he said.

My pulse jittered with the awareness of how close we were to each other again. "It was my fault." I shifted back to give him more space and to slow the thump of my heart. "You don't have to pretend you're feeling okay when you're not, you know. The Exam is taking a lot out of all of us."

"I know. That was sort of why— I figured you have enough to worry about already without me adding to the mix."

Oh. He'd been trying to protect *me*.

I didn't know what to do with that knowledge. Restlessness gripped me. I found myself getting to my feet. For some reason, it seemed important that I recheck the door.

"Rocío?" Finn said.

I jiggled the handle again, but it still wouldn't give. I frowned. My alert conjuring hadn't gone off yet. The storm was still active above. This was our only way out.

"We're not safe here," I said. The words spilled out of me. "We have to go. There's got to be a way out."

"You're right," Finn said, his own voice abruptly frantic too. He scrambled up, hurried to the opposite wall, and began rapping on it. "There's something—" He froze, his body going rigid. "Desmond's 'chantment."

Urgency gripped me. "We have to find it. If we don't…" There was something out there, on the other side of this door maybe. Something we *needed*.

"No." Finn was shaking his head. "It's just going to make us — We've got to fight it. How did he say to break it?"

"I have to break the 'chantment on the door!" I said with a rush of resolve.

Finn's eyes widened. In the second it took me to turn toward it, he dashed across the tunnel, belting out in a thin tenor. "The wheels on the bus go round and round, round and round, round and round." He grabbed my elbow, still singing. There was no casting in the words; they didn't catch on the magic around us.

I stared at him. "What are you doing?" I demanded, but he kept going, through that verse and into the next, his fingers tight on my arm. The blare of panic in my head dulled.

Desmond's 'chantment. My thoughts tripped back to the conversation outside the dorm room, what felt like weeks ago. Desmond's defensive 'chantment had to do with distracting— convincing people of some urgent need elsewhere. *It's sound based*, he'd said. *Drown it out…*

Finn paused for air, and I broke in. "It's okay. I'm okay now. It worked."

"Sorry," he said. "It was the first song that popped into my head. We should keep talking, though. The 'chantment can only get to us in the gaps."

"If we could break it…" I frowned. "I guess Desmond's 'chanted object is probably up there in the storm somewhere."

"He'll deal with it, or it'll fade. We just have to give them time."

"Yes." I nodded and found I didn't know what else to say now that I had to. No wonder he'd resorted to kiddie songs. Maybe I could 'chant a general babble of voices?

"Your parents' names," Finn said. "What are they?"

Small talk—that worked. "Ana and Miguel."

"Mine are Jonathan and Laura. Any siblings? Name, age?"

"Older brother. Javier. He—ah—three years older. You?"

"One sister, one brother, both older. Margo's twenty-four and Hugh is twenty-si— No, wait, he had his birthday last month. He's twenty-seven now. Birthdays! When's yours?"

"April twentieth."

"October seventh. Where'd you get that necklace?"

My hand automatically darted to the sunburst charm. "My mom gave it to me… before I left for the Exam."

The flicker of Finn's eyes told me he'd realized that wasn't the best avenue to pursue. He tapped the front of his leg. "Easy questions, easy questions, ah—"

"Maybe we should do longer questions," I said. "I mean, ones that take longer to answer. So we don't keep having to come up with new ones." I hesitated. I had one that'd been nibbling at me since the first moment I'd seen Finn in the courtyard. "How did you and Prisha become friends?"

"What, we don't seem a likely pairing?" Finn replied, but his voice softened. "Okay, the long version but not so long I have to stop talking to think about it: We've been classmates since second year at the Academy. That's when her family moved into the neighborhood. It took her parents that long to figure out that she'd be better off there than in the local tutorial where they were living before." He must have caught my puzzled look, because he added, "They're Dulls. She's the only one with magic so far."

I couldn't help interrupting. "She's *new* magic?" Prisha certainly put on the old-magic airs well.

"There's always a few at the Academy," Finn said. "I hadn't

really thought about why there weren't more. I mean, I assumed it was for practical reasons, but I didn't realize... the tuition— Anyway." He coughed. "We always got along pretty well. We were good at bouncing off each other's jokes, and I liked that she spoke her mind, but we weren't exactly close until— This is a little embarrassing."

"Go on," I said, both to fill the space and because, despite myself, I was twice as interested after that admission.

"We were performing demonstrations in class..." Finn's gaze drifted away from me. "Fifth year. Basic conjured illusions—the beginner version of your dragon. Right as it was my turn to go, one of the Circle mages came into the class. They drop in at the various academies from time to time. He looked at me, and I realized he knew who I was and that if I cast well enough, he might mention it to my granduncle, and then I utterly screwed it up. Couldn't even hold the image long enough for anyone to see what I was trying to cast. I'd done it at least half a dozen times before. I just..."

"It's harder to cast when there's pressure," I offered. "It messes with your concentration. That's normal."

"Yeah. I made a joke about it and acted like it was nothing, but it ate at me the whole rest of the morning, because I knew he'd tell my granduncle all about what had happened, so at lunch hour I snuck off so I could drop the act for a bit. Prisha came looking for me. She told me she hated having to do any type of casting in front of the class, that she was always afraid she was going to screw up, that she felt totally wretched when she did, so did I want some company? And it turned out I did."

The corner of his mouth twitched. "Since then, we've always filled in for each other's weak spots. There were a lot of unspoken old-magic rules she kept tripping over that I could help her with. And I'd test out castings with her, and we'd cover for each other, that sort of thing."

The only close companion I'd ever had besides Javi was a Dull girl from a Dominican family that had moved into the building next door when I was seven. We'd only run around together for a few months before neighborhood talk about just what kind of family *mine* was got to her parents, and after that they'd sent me away when I came by. But telling Finn that felt like a far more pathetic admission than anything he'd just admitted to.

I fumbled for another thread to keep the conversation going. "What do you mean about 'Circle' mages? What are they?"

Finn laughed for the half a second it must have taken him to realize I honestly didn't know. Then his mouth pressed shut. "They're the top tier of the Confed," he said. "The mages who keep all the other departments and divisions running? They're sort of half appointed and half voted on, and then they stay until they decide to bow out or... well, they die. Maybe you don't end up hearing so much about them when your granduncle's not one of them."

His explanation had tickled my memory. "No, I do remember hearing about them. We just... When you're outside the Confed, you tend to see it all as one big mass, I guess. Who exactly is in charge doesn't seem to matter that much. Are they the ones who run the Exam?"

Had his granduncle sent him in here, knowing it'd be like this? Now that was a cabrón I wouldn't want to meet.

"I think they appoint the Exam committee, and then the committee handles everything from there," Finn said. "Now that I've seen what goes on here, I'm pretty sure the Circle doesn't know how far the examiners go. Maybe they don't *want* to know. Plausible deniability and all that." He laughed again, roughly this time. "My granduncle being one of the Circle was enough to guarantee I'd be Chosen, but I still don't think even my dad had the slightest idea it—" He seemed to catch himself, clamping his lips together.

My mouth dropped open. "What did you just say?"

He stayed silent, and then cocked his head. "I'm not feeling the 'chantment working on me. It must have wound down, or else the others came through fast."

"*Finn*," I said.

He averted his eyes. "I was Chosen."

"But…" I couldn't wrap my head around that revelation.

"I was Chosen," Finn said, "because the system is rigged and if your family has enough influence, the Circle just lets you in. But it's rigged the other way, too. Prisha wasn't Chosen, and she should have been, and…" He sat down against the wall and rested his hands on his knees. "I couldn't just accept a spot at the college, knowing that. My choice should have been between being Dampered and declaring. So I declared."

I stood there where he'd left me. He'd been Chosen. He could have walked right into the Confederation college next week without anyone standing in his way, but he was here instead.

I doubted his little stand would make much difference to the Confed. If they'd cared, he wouldn't be here right now. But there was clearly more going on behind that smile than I'd ever assumed.

I sank down next to him. For all he'd told me in the last short while, I'd managed to avoid sharing anything substantial about myself. Maybe that was why I let myself say, "Is that why you were always taking books from the library? You were studying… so you'd deserve being Chosen?"

"Something like that. It didn't quite work out. I mean, I am a better mage than I'd have been without the studying, but there's only so far—" He glanced at me. "How would you know about anything I did in the library?"

"The last three years, I was studying there a lot," I said. "I wanted to learn everything I could, and the library's open to all novices even if the rest of the Academy isn't. It's got all kinds of books I couldn't have found anywhere else."

Finn's eyebrows had risen. "I don't remember seeing you there. I'm usually sharper than that."

"I didn't want people to notice me," I admitted. "The first couple times, I wasn't so cautious, and the other students... weren't exactly friendly. I kept a low profile after that. And you weren't normally there for very long."

Okay, that was enough. I shut up before I started sounding like a stalker.

Finn nodded. "I did my studying at home. Fewer questions that way. You must be overjoyed, spending all this time with us Academy kids here."

I thought of Prisha grabbing me to join her for dinner last night, and the help Finn had offered me this morning, and Judith pushing through her fears. They *were* Academy kids, but here in the Exam, the field felt a little more level.

"It's strange," I said slowly, "but I actually kind of like that part of the Exam. Not specifically Academy kids, just... being surrounded by people who hearken magic and understand how much it matters. My tutorial class was pretty small. I didn't really click with anyone else there, especially after—" No, I wasn't ready to talk about Javi with him.

"The Dull kids either avoided us or harassed us," I went on. "There are some tight-knit groups in my neighborhood, people from the same background sticking together, but the way they feel about magic always overrides anything else we might have in common. Even my extended family—none of them are mages— they'd never shut us out, but they can be kind of weird about it. It's been... I don't know, a little lonely."

For a moment, we sat without speaking. Then Finn reached across the space between us and wrapped his hand around mine. He still didn't say anything, just held on with a gentle pressure.

A weight I hadn't even noticed building in my chest eased. I thought of last night and his apology, so simple and left to stand alone. Maybe Finn's real talent wasn't what he said but knowing when to say nothing at all.

It might have been the uncertain situation we'd been thrown into together, but right then, in the chilly tunnel with the solid warmth of his hand over mine, I felt closer to him than I had anyone since Javi.

Then I shivered. It wasn't just the tunnel that was chilly; my clothes were damp against my skin.

Finn was warm. It would be so easy to shift a little nearer. To learn what it would feel like to have him hold me not out of necessity but because it felt good to be together.

The thought had barely crossed my mind when my body balked. Finn was good-looking and charming and not only old magic but part of one of the most prominent families in the Confed. He probably had girls falling all over him—girls with connections, girls who knew the unspoken rules, girls who wouldn't sound ignorant when they talked about magic.

I'd been drawn to him when I'd seen him in the library for a reason, but *that* was his world: the Academy, the Confed, in among the people who'd looked down their noses at me, who'd seen my abilities as a threat. A world in which he hadn't noticed me and might never have.

I was safe as long as I just sat here and enjoyed the feel of his palm against mine without expecting it to mean anything more.

"I bet the rest of the group isn't having this much fun," Finn said breezily, but I heard the underlying thread of worry. He said what he meant, even when he said it like he didn't mean it.

"They're probably sitting in one of those leaning buildings, watching the rain," I said. "And wondering where we are."

"Is there any way we could send them a message?"

"Through that storm, without knowing where they are, I

don't think so." I had no sense of where those buildings stood relative to here, and the magic propelling those winds would scatter any attempt to send out a seeking spell.

"Right." He let go of my hand to stretch his arms out of front of him. "So do you figure the examiners are cutting us a break down here, or are they lulling us into a false sense of complacency?"

That did seem to be their pattern: giving us a moment to relax and then hitting us when our guards were down. "I don't know. The only things they've thrown at us today have been our own 'chantments, and we've gotten through all of those except Mark's, unless that followed him the way he expected it to. But I have trouble seeing that as a guarantee of anything."

"Maybe they're trying to kill us with cold," he said, pulling his knees in closer.

His clothes would be damp too. "I can cast a shell around us for warmth and protection," I said. "And then... we could try to get some rest, while we have the chance. Who knows the next time they'll give us one."

He nodded, and I called into being a barrier of magic around us, along with a whisper of heat and a protective surface that should deflect an initial attack. Then I dimmed the light I'd conjured.

Finn shifted to lie on the floor, resting his head on his open hand. I eased down onto my back, but even with the numbing 'chantment, my torn muscles throbbed against the hard floor.

I rolled onto my side, facing him, and closed my eyes. My nerves buzzed. How long were we going to be trapped down here before the storm let up?

"Dragon-Tamer?" Finn said after a few minutes.

"Yes?" I replied.

He hesitated so long I thought he'd changed his mind about whatever he'd been going to say. Then he said, low and careful and more serious than I'd ever heard him, "You know, I'd be terrified out of my mind if you weren't here with me."

My eyes popped open. His features were hazy in the muted light, but he was close enough that I could see him looking back at me. His attention and the implied compliment sent a giddy quiver through my body. But at the same time, the self-deprecation in his statement niggled at me. Didn't he know he'd been there for me as much as I'd been there for him today?

"We make a pretty good team," I said.

"Other than the parts where I get blasted away by magic or wind or what have you, and you have to save the day?"

"Yes," I said, unable to keep the dryness from my voice. "Other than that."

He didn't say anything else, but I couldn't close my eyes as long as his were fixed on my face. The silence stretched. Then Finn leaned forward, reaching toward me as if to touch my cheek.

My heart leapt—and I saw him in the midst of the Academy library's glow, where he belonged so well, where I didn't at all. My body went rigid, jerking back from his fingers.

Finn pulled his arm back and rolled over to look at the ceiling. His mouth worked with an embarrassed twitch. A flush too deep for the dim light to hide crept over his face and neck.

My own skin felt as if it were burning. I swallowed thickly.

"Apologies," Finn said. "Very bad timing." His tone slipped into the self-mocking lilt he took on so naturally. "Not that I'm assuming such advances would have gone over well under other circumstances, of course. I understand my ears are a little on the pointy side, and let's not get started on my knees. My fashion sense, well— Also, I may have the tendency to babble on in awkward situations."

A smile tugged at my mouth despite myself. "Finn, I—"

I'd wanted him to do it. A very large part of me was kicking myself right now because I could have been finding out right now what it was like to kiss him.

But...

If we'd met in the library and not here shut away from everything else that matters to you, I wanted to say to him, *would you have looked at me that way even for a second? Do you* mean *this, for real, or is it only an impulse that'll slip away the second we're back in the real world with your parents and granduncle and whoever else looking on? Because I can't do that. I already care too much for it not to hurt when you wake up.*

I didn't know how to say it. I didn't know if he could even tell me the truth and not just what he'd like to believe about himself. How could I trust my old daydreams when they'd come to life in the middle of this nightmare?

But I didn't want him thinking things about me that weren't true either.

"You're not babbling," I said. "I'm not upset. It wasn't— You weren't wrong." I wasn't sure he'd understand, but any other way I could express it might sound like an invitation.

He turned his head. "Clearly I wasn't exactly right," he said tentatively. "You pulled away."

I couldn't exactly deny it. "I did."

"Then... I'm confused."

Emotion squeezed my chest. It seemed to take more effort than I'd expended all day to murmur, "So am I."

Finn's expression relaxed. He shifted onto his side again, keeping a careful distance. "In that case, at least we can be confused together. If you don't mind the company."

A pleased little spark lit up inside me, one I couldn't quite bear to smother. "I don't mind," I said. Then, because I felt I should offer a larger token than that, I scooted toward him. Close enough that when I tipped my head, my forehead could graze his chest.

I closed my eyes again. Finn's breath tickled over me. It *was* warmer like this.

He touched my waist gingerly, and when I didn't move away, he rested his palm there and tucked his head down until his chin settled against my hair. His chest rose and fell. He stayed there, not asking for more, just sharing the moment with me. And in that moment, despite the horrors waiting for us above and perhaps even here, I felt safer than I had since I'd declared for the Exam.

I must have drifted off, because that feeling was the last thing I remembered before I startled awake to the peal of my alert 'chantment.

CHAPTER ELEVEN

Finn

If I'd ever dreamed about waking up next to a girl I was falling for, those imaginings had not included joints turned stiff against a cold concrete floor or a gigantic room of terrors waiting above us. I definitely would have skipped the nerve-scattering blare of magical alarms.

My heart jumped. Rocío was already pulling away from me—there and then gone, the movement leaving me as raw as if she'd scraped my skin.

"The storm's over," she said.

I scrambled to my feet after her. The thin shirt I'd chosen in consideration of the summer heat was now thoroughly wrinkled from the damp and our impromptu sleep. Shoving my fingers through my wayward hair, I felt abruptly, ridiculously self-conscious. Rocío's hair and clothes were rumpled too, but to me that didn't diminish her in the slightest.

She extended her hand with a small smile I couldn't read. The simple gesture was enough to light me up inside.

I'd barely known this girl two days. I'd had attraction spark and fizzle out in that timeline before, but this didn't feel like a spark. It felt like a brilliant aria twining through me from sternum to gut, giddy but bone-deep.

It felt like magic.

Why shouldn't it? Those two days had been long enough for me to know Rocío was awfully magical herself.

After the confidences I'd shared with her down here, she knew things about me that no one else but Prisha did.

Panic jabbed my stomach at the thought of Prisha. We needed to get back to the others—to confirm they were still around for us to get back to. I took Rocío's hand with what I hoped was a casual air. She was already murmuring to the whisper of energy around us, her expression tight with concentration.

It occurred to me that I ought to contribute to the casting. I'd always struggled with even the simplest forms of teleportation, but I could at least—

Magic rushed through me, sending my thoughts soaring away, and we shot back to the vast gray space where the storm had battered us.

Rocío let go of my hand with a shaky breath. My fingers closed around the air.

The sky or ceiling far overhead had returned to its pre-storm pallor, lit with a vague glow. The fog had retreated to a hazy blur beyond the nearest trees and buildings. I couldn't tell whether we were even inside or outside anymore. The terrain all around was that same flat, spongy floor.

The stretch of trees where I'd found my radio stood to my right, their branchless torsos hunched. In the other direction, no more than a five-minute walk away, the precarious-looking buildings were still upright, looking not particularly worse for wear. Relief swept through me.

"Let's hope we catch up with them," I said, setting off toward the buildings. Even if Prisha and the others were unharmed, they'd have no idea what had become of *us*.

A distant thunderclap echoed across the landscape, and my legs stalled, my hand dipping to my pocket. Whatever the noise's source, it was back beyond the trees, not near the buildings. A test one of the other examinee groups was facing? It shouldn't affect us, that far off, Fates willing.

"Finn," Rocío said, "what are you reaching for?"

My fingers jerked away from my hip. "What?" I said with feigned confusion.

She hesitated, studying me with those thoughtful eyes, and my gut twisted. She knew I was lying. After I'd claimed to respect her, after all my gestures of honest admiration, she was going to think it'd all been a charade.

"You're carrying something," she said. "Something that makes you nervous, but you think of it whenever you might have to defend yourself."

Had my movements been that conspicuous? The damned dissolving rod made me twitchy even capped.

"My sister gave me something after I declared. It's a— Well, a weapon," I said. "I wasn't trying to conceal it, exactly. I just... feel odd about it. It must be from the Confed's military division. Having seen what it can do, I find it hard *not* to be nervous having it on me. But at least I have it if circumstances take a particularly bad turn."

"Oh," Rocío said. Her eyes had widened. There was no way she'd have ever had access to a military-grade weapon. That was precisely why Margo had given it to me, right? She'd meant to tip the scales more in my favor—as if they weren't already tipped enough.

An uncomfortable heat crept up under my skin. How could Rocío ever respect *me* when I kept getting by on other people's coattails—including hers? I'd admired her from the moment I'd seen her dragon, before I'd even set eyes on her, and the best she'd seen me cast was a basic communication spell I'd scarcely maintained long enough to convey a single image.

"Is it dangerous just to have it on you?" Rocío asked as we hurried on toward the muted shadows of the buildings.

I shook my head quickly. "No. It'd be impossible to trigger it accidentally. But I'm not exactly in the habit of toting weaponry."

"Okay," she said, and then fell silent. The two feet of space between us might as well have expanded into a gulf. I hadn't a clue how to reach across it.

The buildings loomed in front of us. The closest of the structures was about as big as a couple of brownstones melded into one. I spotted a doorless entrance cut in the side. Prisha's voice traveled out from it. "We have to at least *check*," she was saying.

A grin sprang to my face. I sped up to a jog, loping to the entrance and through. The large room I came into looked as purposefully vague as the rest of this testing space felt. It held no furniture or fixtures, only seamless walls in a white that looked slightly dingy, a set of stairs in the far corner that were a matching shade—and four figures clustered in the middle of the room, who all whirled at the thump of my feet.

A relieved laugh slipped from Prisha's lips. She leapt forward and grabbed me in a hug. I returned the embrace as tightly as I dared, taking care not to bump the makeshift bandage on her shoulder.

She looked fine. They all looked fine. That was the best I could have asked for.

"I assume you all missed us," I teased. Rocío stepped through the entrance behind me. Judith and Desmond were beaming. Lacey's expression was guarded, but after a moment it eased with a smile.

Prisha gave my arm another squeeze. "Don't you dare scare me like that again," she said, a joke and a threat all at once.

"I'm glad to see you too," I said. "Between the storm and Desmond's 'chantment, I was a tiny bit concerned."

"We survived," Judith said with a grimace that suggested it hadn't been the most enjoyable night.

"Where *were* you?" Lacey asked. She stood favoring her sprained ankle. The minor numbing 'chantment I'd put on it yesterday would have been broken in Judith's trap, of course, but one of the others could have cast a new one.

When she noticed my glance, she pulled her posture straighter. Maybe she'd refused to ask.

"We got caught in the storm," Rocío said, "so we had to find shelter somewhere else."

I couldn't help noticing she'd moved farther from me in a manner that felt deliberate. I circled my thumb over my fingertips, and the magic quivered into stillness between us. Purposefully or not, she was setting herself apart from me.

"Do you think—" she began.

With a faint pop, a thin metal table materialized in the middle of the room. It was laid out with a platter of muffins, another of fruit, and a row of water bottles. My stomach flipped as if it meant to jump right out of my body. *Breakfast.*

We dashed toward the food, but everyone glanced at Rocío and muttered a quick testing 'chantment before digging in. For a few minutes, the only sound in the room was the smacking of lips and the gulping of water.

We'd learned our lesson well. There was no guarantee we'd be allowed to enjoy this meal at leisure.

As our stomachs became fuller and no catastrophe descended on us, I started to relax. Apparently the examiners *were* capable of granting us a kindness, however slight. "It's a regular Saturnalia feast!" I remarked. "Nunc est bibendum."

Judith snickered. Prisha elbowed me with a roll of her eyes. The others looked blank. I winced inwardly. I hadn't even considered the reference might not connect outside the Academy set.

Prisha bit into an apple and pulled a face. "Ugh, skin," she said. "Now I remember why I never eat these things." She gave the fruit platter an accusatory stare.

"Allow me?" Desmond said.

Prisha raised her eyebrows and passed the apple to him.

Desmond sang a bluesy lyric and tapped the top of the fruit. The skin sloughed off it in a perfect spiral that settled in a pile on the table. He nudged the naked apple back toward her.

"Wow," Prisha said. "You put my peeling skills to shame."

"It's mathematical," Desmond said with a sliver of a grin. "I hated the skin when I was a kid, but my mom insisted it was healthier to leave it on, so I very quickly figured out a way to get around it by myself. She could hide the peeler, but she wasn't prepared to outmaneuver a mage in the making."

"Are your parents Dull?" Prisha said, perking up. "I love that —they have no clue how to keep up."

"My mom is," Desmond said. "My dad's Dampered. He's still ace at finding things. That's how they met. My mom lost an earring her boyfriend had given her, and my dad saw her looking and offered to help. After two hours of following the trail through the city and getting to know each other, they tracked it down, and she had a new boyfriend." His grin widened.

He was a capable mage, undeniably. Not stunning, but then, how much of his concentration was he expending on whatever castings he must use to supplement his vision? The Circle should have given him credit for that.

There was so much that should have counted with them that clearly didn't.

My gaze slid to Rocío. My eyes caught hers—and then hers darted away. Her mouth was set in a pensive line.

I had the impulse to crack some joke that would bring a smile to *her* face, but my mind went blank. Before I could recover my wit, footsteps thudded outside the doorway. I turned, my fingers dropping to my pocket before I checked myself.

Mark hauled himself through the building's entrance. His mohawk lay limp against the shaved side of his head, and a deep purple bruise ran from just under his eye to the corner of his jaw.

"Hey," he said in a rasp. "I'm back."

The rest of us had tensed. "Now you decide you want to be a joiner?" Judith said, frowning at him. "What, because we've got the food?"

"It was my 'chantment that set him off before," I said, to be fair.

Mark grimaced. "Look, things did get a little... messy. But coming back to the group wasn't my idea. I got a message saying I had to find you all if I was going to pass the next 'assignment.' That's the only reason I'm here."

"I'm sure we'll be incredibly glad for your company," Prisha said dryly.

He glowered at her. "I'll help where I can while we have to work together. I just— I've got different reasons for being here than you do. More reasons. Okay?" His jaw twitched. "So I'd rather depend on myself when I can. It's safer than trusting the rest of you to get the job done for me."

"That sounds reasonable to me," Desmond said quietly.

"Maybe, but he doesn't need to talk about us like that." Lacey stepped forward. "You didn't help us before. Why should we let you back in with us now?"

She looked a little ridiculous staring down our rebel punk in her girlish dress, her nub of a pale chin raised. Still, I had to give her points for speaking her mind.

Mark must have too, because he ducked his head. "Honestly," he said, the rasp coming back into his voice, "I did you a favor. The 'chantment I cast... Let's just say I'd feel a lot worse if you'd all had to deal with it too."

The sentiment sounded genuine. Seeing the way his gaze roved to the table and held there, I wondered if the examiners had provided him with any sustenance while he'd been on his own yesterday. The guy might be starving.

"I expect the examiners won't look kindly on the rest of us going against their orders," I said, "based on past experience and all. If they want us together, we can figure out a way to coexist." I motioned toward the plate of muffins. "Banana, carrot, or bran?"

"Carrot," Mark said with a near-delirious gleam in his eye.

I tossed him the muffin, but my throw went a little wide. He rapped out a quick casting as he extended his hand. The muffin veered toward him—and burst apart with an electric crackle.

Mark eyed the torn pieces that had scattered over the floor while the rest of us stared at him. His jaw twitched again, and he clenched it. "I guess I'd better get one myself," he said. He kicked a chunk of muffin aside and ambled over to the table.

Lacey had blanched. "What was that?"

"Nothing," Mark said. "Nothing any of you need to worry about."

Judith backed away from him as he reached the table.

"Ah," I said, "I think it's understandable for us to be a tad concerned about you detonating random objects."

"I'll second that motion," Prisha said.

Mark sighed. He uncapped a bottle of water, took a long swig, and set it down. "It's not going to affect any of you, because I know better than to try to cast on any of you. All right? I don't always get the best 'reception' with the magic. Sometimes when I cast it's like a phone call breaking up—and the energy doesn't take it well. You can probably thank the Confed. My mom was three months pregnant with me when she failed the Exam and they burned her out. I've gotten better at controlling it. That wouldn't have happened if I'd had a meal in the last day."

He snatched up a muffin and took a bite.

I lowered the one I'd been eating. Could burning out alter a developing child like that? It wasn't inconceivable.

Prisha had crossed her arms over her chest. "So that's your special reason for being here?"

"No," Mark said around his mouthful. "It's not."

There was a moment of silence, and then Rocío said tentatively, "You mentioned your brother before."

He scowled and kept eating.

Judith's skeptical expression softened. "Did *he* get burned out here? Or did... did he die?"

"*No.*" Mark's hand balled against the tabletop. "If it's so important for you to know, I've got a half brother who made Champion two years ago. Since then he's basically disappeared. He barely has time for us anymore, and when he does, the way he talks, it's like the Confed has taken over his brain. All he does is recite the party lines. I can't get him to tell me what's going on, so I'm going to find out on my own."

"I don't think the Confed is *brainwashing* people," Prisha said, a strange edge in her voice.

My gaze jerked to her.

"You wouldn't, Academy girl," Mark replied. "For some of us, it's hard to believe they aren't doing way worse. I'm going to get Tyler away from them too if that's what I need to do to wake him up. But before I can really reach him, I have to make it through this place, so I'm just asking that none of you get in my way."

Prisha's shoulders had stiffened. Why was she so upset? He was just shooting his mouth off—and I could understand his animosity, given his circumstances. "I'm sure we'll—" I began.

A squeal split the air, so shrill it set the hairs on the back of my neck on end. A magic-drawn message started unfurling down the far wall. I squinted at it, but the wan light slipping through the entrance wasn't enough for me to discern the words. We all edged closer.

For your next assignment, the message read, *each group must locate an object of importance inside their designated building. Turn right from the entrance of your current location and walk until you find a structure with a sigil overhead. Make your way into the building, find an object with obvious magical power, and return with it to the place where you saw this message. Only one item is needed for the entire group, but individual contributions will be noted, as will your speed. The building's entrance and interior are guarded by automated sentries that can summon more once alerted. We recommend you destroy them before they have the chance. Congratulations to the 29 of you on making it thus far.*

My throat constricted as I read the last line again.

"Six more gone," Rocío murmured.

"Do you think they were killed by their own 'chantments?" Lacey said, looking horrified but also fascinated.

"The examiners wouldn't let it come to that, would they?" Judith said. "Even if they left it to the last minute to pull them out... It can't be normal for six people to have *died* at this point. It's only the third day!"

I wanted to believe the examiners would have intervened, that the six had simply been taken to be burned out, but I didn't feel sure of it after the callous disregard they'd shown for our safety so far.

"Who knows if they're even watching closely enough to step in?" Mark said. "I didn't get the impression anyone cared what happened to me yesterday."

"It's an *Exam,*" Judith protested. "What's the point in testing us if they're not watching?"

Mark shrugged.

Prisha's lips pursed. "It doesn't matter," she said. "We're all still fine. And this assignment doesn't sound *that* hard. Not as bad as the last section, anyway."

Desmond shifted his weight, contemplating the wall in his overly intent way. Could he read the message at all? "It's probably going to be more complicated than they're suggesting," I said. "We're meant to search a building for magical items and bring back one—how large a building? What sort of 'items' might be there? And how many of these 'sentries' are going to be scanning for us, that we have to destroy before they can summon more?"

Desmond gave me a subtle nod in thanks.

"We can use magic to find other magic, right?" Lacey said. "One of the guys in our tutorial class, he had a casting that would make 'chanted things rattle or light up."

Like a forte version of the casting I'd used to find my radio. I nodded. "That ought to at least help."

"We should take a look at the building," Rocío said. "We can't make plans yet."

"I don't know," Prisha said, tapping her mouth. "The examiners went out of their way to warn us that there'll be sentries outside the building. I'd say we want to be gearing up for a full-on assault before we're even in sight of the place. And I'd guess we'll be counting on you for a lot of that."

Rocío's head snapped toward her. "What?"

"You've obviously got a stronger connection to the magic than anyone else in our group," Prisha said in a careless tone that pricked at me. "You'll be able to take down these 'sentries' the fastest. It only makes sense for you to lead the charge."

"I don't think we should be 'charging' in at all," Rocío said.

"Hold on," I said. "We can at least go outside and determine where this building *is* before making any concrete decisions."

Mark spun on his heel and marched out. The others trailed after him, with Prisha at the rear. I hung back to speak with her apart from the others, but just as we stepped outside, she halted and patted my arm. "I'm going to grab a bottle of water to bring with," she said, and vanished back inside.

I meandered along the side of the building after the others, who were heading to the right toward a pair of tilted dun structures that loomed nearby, as blank on the outside as the one we'd just left. Neither of those boasted any sort of sigil. The building we were supposed to scope out must be farther away. Hopefully closer we'd have a better view. From here, the gray landscape beyond was cloaked with that damned mist.

If the examiners had hoped to establish a general mood of constant uncertainty with these testing grounds, they'd hit the mark. How much of the space was even *real* and not a temporary magical construction?

Of course, it was hard to say which was more unnerving: our surroundings or my best friend's odd behavior. What was Prisha's issue with Rocío? She'd been uncertain the other girl could protect just me yesterday, but now she thought Rocío was the key to us completing this assignment? There'd been something off about the way she'd broached the subject too. It wasn't like her.

Rocío glanced back as we came into the shadows of the buildings. Her gaze caught mine, and she immediately looked away. My chest clenched.

I caught up in a few paces. She stopped when I touched her shoulder. The others continued on.

"Are we okay?" I said quietly. "I don't know what Prisha's thinking. And I'm sorry I didn't tell you about the... the weapon right away."

When Rocío met my eyes, hers were puzzled. "Why are you apologizing for that now?"

"You just— I don't know." Why did I lose my capacity for speech around her so often? "You seem upset," I managed.

Rocío blinked. "Oh. With *you*? No. I— What Prisha is saying is right. It's up to me more than anyone else to get us through this test. I mean, I'm okay with that. It's just a lot of pressure. I don't have room to think about anything else if I'm going to make sure everyone stays okay. So I'm trying to just stay focused on the Exam."

Ah. That explained why she'd drawn back as soon as we'd left our underground hideout. I ought to have been relieved, but the strain in her voice wrenched at me all over again.

Her gaze sharpened. "Is your head all right?"

"Yes," I said. "Yes, it's been fine since last night." I hadn't felt a twinge since she'd melted the ache away—but even if it came back, I wasn't going to amplify the weight of responsibility she already felt. O Zeus, let her never again feel she had to make room amid everything else she was tackling to *fix* me.

"You're not alone," I added. "Remember that. Even if you end up at the front, we've all got your back. I can't speak for the others, but I've become rather fond of... well, all of you, including that back, so I promise it'd require at the very least a broken leg or two to get in the way of me protecting it."

My glibness earned me one of her little smiles. "Thank you," she said, as if she was going to say more, but at that moment Prisha reached us, her bottle of water tucked under her arm.

"Where's this sigil?" she said, tossing back her hair.

The other four had stopped by the far corner of the building up ahead, their faces tilted toward the sky. "Over there, I'd guess," I said.

As we marched over to join them, I shot Rocío a glance behind Prisha's back. She met my eyes without looking away this time, her lips still curved in that slight smile just for me.

I squared my shoulders. It was time to unearth every bit of mage I had in me, because I didn't think I'd ever forgive myself if I broke the vow I'd just made.

CHAPTER TWELVE

Rocío

Floating high overhead in the midst of the gray-brown haze, the sigil shone like a star. Like the silver sunburst on my necklace. My hand rose to the jagged shape and closed around my mother's charm. The sigil's lines faded and brightened in a trembling rhythm.

"They're lighting the way," Lacey said with hushed excitement.

"I don't see a building over there," Judith said. I couldn't either. The mist had drawn back as we'd approached, but nothing stood beneath the sigil except a smooth black wall, maybe fifty feet away. It appeared to be about as long as a Brooklyn block and twice my height, and it stood alone, as if it had risen out of the flat gray ground at random. Thicker fog ate at its edges, hiding whatever might be waiting on the other side.

"We'll have to get closer," I said. "The building must be on the other side of the wall."

"That'll give us some shelter while we come up with our

brilliant strategy," Finn said cheerfully, with a quick glance at Prisha.

I'd been trying to ignore my impulse to stay close to him, but his support both spoken and unspoken warmed me. Maybe I shouldn't ignore it. Maybe his warmth would help me through whatever the Confed had planned for us.

"Let's all get a conjuring or a 'chantment ready to cast in case we have to act quickly," Prisha said. "If even one sentry has time to raise the alarm, we're in trouble."

"How can we be prepared when we don't know anything about them?" Desmond said.

"The examiners said we should *destroy* them," Lacey pointed out, bouncing on her feet. "I say we blast them apart like we did those marbles."

"I guess that's a good starting point," I said, even though my skin crawled at the idea of carrying an offensive casting on the tip of my tongue. Was that how Finn felt with that weapon in his pocket?

But we wouldn't be destroying anything *real*. The message had also said the sentries were "automated." Conjured, I guessed.

I drew up the words I'd used to shatter Lacey's marbles and held them in the back of my throat as we started forward. Dale, no pierdas el tino.

The wall loomed over us as we reached it. The sigil overhead faded out. No sound penetrated our hush. Since the wall was too high to see over, we crept along it, searching for a way past. I trailed my fingers across the glossy black surface and found it cold and hard as glass. The shiver of energy against my hand told me it was conjured, magic condensed into substance.

Lacey copied my gesture, swirling her fingertips over the glazed black. "It's like oil," she murmured. "Or what I think oil would look like. I've never actually seen it for real—only in the oil-company commercials back home." Then her face tensed.

"Axton always said magic meant he'd never have to work like that."

Axton who'd now be waiting back home, burned out. I got the feeling she wasn't looking forward to a reunion.

I slowed coming up on the corner of the wall and realized it wasn't a corner at all. The black surface simply ended, revealing another stretch of flat gray terrain beyond it. I peeked around the open edge.

The fog had drawn back farther at our approach. In the thinner haze, a short jog from where we stood, lay a black cube of a building about as big as my library branch. Its face was as smooth as the wall other than the faint protrusion of a doorway, and like the wall it rose straight from the ground as if it'd been placed there without any connection to its surroundings.

Something was moving outside it.

Prisha set down her bottle of water at the base of the wall and leaned to peer past me. "So those are our sentries," she said in a low voice.

There was an air of unreality about the scene in front of me— a sensation in my eyes as if I should have been able to see right through it. The conjuring didn't look as if it were so complex the examiners would have struggled to maintain it. If anything, the shapes were oddly vague and artless, more like Lacey's shadow creatures than the work of several established mages. Was there more to them that we *couldn't* see?

Three boxy almost-human figures were staked out around the building, partly blending into its dark face. They might as well have been people thrown together out of chunks of glossy black stone. One was nearly as tall as the doorway and spindly thin. Another was a bulky giant. The third was shorter and squat.

A block that amounted to a head sat on each sentry's torso, but I couldn't make out any features: no eyes, nose, or mouth. Their faces were as smooth as the building behind them. A muted light flickered in each of their "chests," nearly swallowed by the black. That pulse, like the beat of a heart, sent an uneasy tremor through my own chest.

"What do you think the glowing spot is for?" Judith whispered, crouching beside me.

"A target, maybe?" Finn suggested.

"It's not like the examiners to give us an easy solution," I said. I didn't like that. I didn't like the way the sentries lumbered by the building, pausing and speeding up and turning here and there without any pattern I could follow. Even the one that mostly stayed beside the door wasn't completely still. It shifted in increments, straightening up taller, adjusting its jointed limbs.

"I don't know," Judith said. "It's a pretty small spot. If that's the only way to stop them, it'll be hard enough even with the target."

"Blow them up—that'll take care of everything," Lacey said.

Prisha glanced at her with a smile that looked faintly patronizing. "You have a lot of faith in your ability to blast your way through your problems. Those things are bigger than marbles."

"So?" Lacey said with a shrug. "I can handle one. I know I can."

"What if we all try to aim for the light," I said, "with as much force as we can manage in case they're shielded against strong blasts? If two of us each aim at one sentry, we'll double our chances of taking them down."

"You should take the one to the right of the door," Prisha said. "It's the biggest and the farthest away."

"Right," I said, managing to keep an edge out of my voice. She was following the same line of reasoning as before: I was the strongest mage here, so I should do the hardest part of the fighting. I still didn't enjoy the feeling of being set up as the group's attack dog. That wasn't how I wanted the Confed to see me. That wasn't who I *was*.

As the others decided in hushed conversation who would aim at which sentry, I ran my lyric through my mind, collecting my sense of intent, imagining the conjured blow slamming into the blocky figure's chest and shattering its "heart."

Lacey rubbed her hands together eagerly, and Mark rolled his shoulders. Judith tucked her broken arm tight against her chest and hummed a faint melody. Her lips pressed tight together.

Finn edged slightly closer to the end of the wall. "All at the same time, then," he whispered. "Three, two, one—"

"Engage!" Desmond said.

We leapt around the wall as one. The lyric dropped from my lips, thrusting a wave of power through the vibrations of the magic toward the glowing spot on the sentry by the door.

My blow struck it straight on the light, and the crackling bolt of energy Judith had conjured hit right beside mine. Just as I'd pictured, the figure rocked backward. Then its body crumbled into a heap of rubble that melted into the ground.

The tall, spindly sentry burst with an explosion of dark shards. The short one stumbled backward as if punched, hit the ground, and cracked open.

"Yeah!" Lacey cried with a pump of her fist.

Prisha stepped forward as if to run for the building, but at the same moment the air jittered around me.

"Wait!" I said.

The invisible presence I'd felt before pulled around my shoulders. Its trembling made the hum of the magic quaver. In that instant, it gripped me so tightly I could hardly breathe.

What? I thought at it. *What are you? What do you want?*

It didn't respond, only wrapped itself more solidly around me. It was something… something in the magic that rejected what we'd done or were about to do?

A memory slipped through my head, as if drawn up by the magic's grip: I was eight, in my grandparents' living room. Abuelito had stumbled and bumped his elbow against Abuelita's figurine of a man and woman dancing, the one she'd had since childhood and brought with her from Mexico. It had cracked into at least twenty pieces on the floor, and Abuelita's expression had cracked in dismay along with it.

She'd looked so upset that even though she stiffened up whenever I cast in front of her, I'd dared to ask, *Can I fix it?* When she'd hesitantly nodded, I'd used one of her old songs to bring the shards swirling around each other in their own beautiful dance as they found their places and reconnected. I'd wanted her to see the music in the magic. And she had. She'd laughed and hugged me, and she'd never tensed again when I worked with magic in her presence.

That was what casting was supposed to be like—what felt right to me. What we were doing here, smashing through these things, was the *opposite* of that. Was my discomfort making the magic behave oddly?

"Come on," Prisha said in my silence. "The examiners said to be fast. We've got to get going."

I didn't know how to explain the sensation stopping me. The presence was loosening—still with me, still clinging but less forcefully. A false alarm? A problem averted? One more trick from the examiners' sleeves? The tenor of the magic didn't feel directed by outside intent, but I'd never felt anything like that presence before to compare.

We didn't have time for me to puzzle the problem out. I shook my head. "Never mind."

No other sentries had emerged outside the building. Prisha set off toward the building's door, and the rest of us ran at her heels. Our heads jerked this way and that as we scanned for any threat, but nothing came at us.

Prisha reached the door and pushed it. When it didn't budge, she muttered something at it, and the lock clicked. She nudged it open gingerly. A long dark hallway stretched out on the other side.

The interior was the same impenetrable black as the outside but without the glossy shine. The inner walls seemed to absorb the light that slipped through the open door before it traveled more than a few feet inside. Staring into the space made me dizzy, as if my mind were slightly removed from my body—as if I were there and yet not.

"I don't like this place," Judith said. "It feels... weird."

"Well, the point of the Exam isn't to make us comfortable," Prisha said. "I don't see any sentries in there, at least."

"Not yet," Mark said grimly.

We eased inside onto the harder floor, staying close. The presence in the magic continued nagging at me with little tweaks of my skin. The actual air around me lay still, not a draft or a shift in pressure as we moved, as if it weren't air at all. As if it were nothing. Our feet barely made a sound against the hard floor. I shivered, keeping my lyric ready.

"I'll cast a search charm," Desmond said. "I've got some practice at those. I'll target it to any strong weaving of magic."

There was a strange muffled quality to his voice, as if he were speaking through a thick scarf. Something about the walls—did they absorb sound the way they did light?

He stepped a little ahead of us and rolled out a short verse. The hum of magic twisted in my ears. We stood still, waiting for him to say when the casting had hit its mark.

He was just turning back toward us when two sentries burst straight through the wall in front of him.

My shattering spell burst from my lips automatically. I slashed out with my hand, hurtling lances of magic toward both.

The energy in the air clenched and surged, and the sentries exploded into bursts of pebbles.

The presence wrenched at me. I coughed, fighting the urge to wheeze. My elbows twinged with the aftershock of the casting.

Desmond had ducked low. He straightened up with a sharp exhale. His gaze found my face without quite meeting my eyes. "Thanks," he said.

A hand grasped my shoulder—Finn. The others were staring at me.

"Nice casting," Prisha said, her voice similarly muffled. "Two of them, just like that." She snapped her fingers. Her tone had sounded impressed, but I saw something wary in the set of her mouth.

Judith rubbed her arms. "Do you think those ones alerted any others?"

I swallowed hard. "I guess we'll find out."

"I definitely don't think I should try that again," Desmond said. "It's like the casting drew them. But I did get a sense... There's something upstairs, to the right. We should hearken it when we get close enough, if we get there before my 'chantment wears off. I didn't have time to make it really stick."

"Upstairs?" Lacey said, peering around us.

I couldn't make out any doorways in the walls, not even a bend in the hall. Although... had the sentries come *through* the wall or had it just looked that way?

I stepped closer to the wall just past Desmond. My reaching hand sank into the black surface as if it were nothing but mist. A cool tingle ran over my fingers. I tensed, ready to defend myself, and walked right into the wall.

An empty black room spilled out into my vision on the other side, lit hazily by a small window.

Mark poked his head in after me. "Now *that* is creepy."

"I'll check in here," I said. "Maybe the rest of you could see if there are any other rooms?"

I felt along the walls until I'd circled the whole space but found no other opening. When I emerged back into the hall, the others had spread in pairs, checking the walls all the way down.

"Here!" Lacey called out, half-immersed in the wavering wall at the end. "There's stairs here."

We followed her through into a small landing with the same flat black walls. Only a thin streak of light from somewhere above outlined the shape of a straight, narrow staircase ahead of us, leading up.

"I'll go first," Lacey announced, starting forward.

"We don't know what other traps might be set," Prisha warned, but Lacey didn't slow down.

I hurried after her. For all her newfound confidence, her castings hadn't been the most precise. Maybe I didn't want to be an attack dog, but I wasn't sending someone else off to be a sacrificial lamb either.

The others tramped up behind us. We were just a few steps from the top when a sentry poked its "head" into the space above us and thrust out its arm. Lacey yelped as the magic it flung at us glittered into a netlike grid. The melody reverberating through it gave me the same dampened impression as our voices. I snapped out my casting, and the lines broke apart with more of a gasp than a crackle.

The sentry peeked out for another attack. Lacey sputtered a quick line. Her conjured burst of flame had enough power that the air thrummed, but it hit the blocky figure in the legs, missing the glowing spot completely. The sentry stumbled and reached for the wall to steady itself in a gesture so human the sight sent a sliver of ice through my stomach.

Before I could form a second casting, Mark barked out a few words by my shoulder. His tiny glowing meteor whined past me with a vibration so erratic it made me cringe—but it smacked the sentry on target. The figure split in two and then into a dozen tumbling pieces.

"What was it trying to do to us?" Judith said quietly.

"Capture us, it looked like," I said, remembering the conjured maybe-net.

Prisha motioned us upward. "Let's move."

Nothing else confronted us as we gathered in the second-floor hall, which was as unnervingly blank and dark as the one we'd left below. Desmond shuffled a little ahead of the rest of us.

"I can hearken it over here. There's got to be a doorway..." His fingers sank into the wall, and he grinned. "There you are."

Mark leaned in beside him. "All clear," he called back.

The rest of us filed into the room, eyeing the seamless black walls.

"This is a little anticlimactic," Finn remarked, though he sounded not at all disappointed by that fact. "I don't see any item, though."

Through the magic's hum, a faint hiss reached my ears. I turned toward the seemingly bare space along the wall and lowered my hands. At knee height, my fingers caught on a metallic surface. I grasped it, and suddenly there was a thin silver box in my hands. The threads of a 'chantment tingled against my skin.

Lacey giggled. "This place is crazy," she said. "Can I see it?"

I handed the box to her and watched carefully as she turned it over. It had no obvious lid or latch, but the examiners hadn't asked us to open it. I wasn't sure I'd want to find out what was inside.

"Great," Judith said with a shudder. "Now let's get out of here already."

I turned, and a strange heat wafted over me from the direction in which Mark was standing. I jerked around to see what he was casting, but he wasn't speaking or even moving, just studying the box as I had. He looked completely unaware that anything unusual might be going on, and yet magic had condensed around him with a vibration so piercing I could almost hear it as well as hearken it.

A chill raced down my back. "Mark," I said, "are you—"

"Everyone get back!" Prisha shouted.

A blaze of even deeper heat washed over us, and a squad of sentries burst from the far wall where there'd been no door before; I'd checked. My mind stalled in shock. Then I threw myself forward. The sentries were already lashing out with magic. Laser-sharp streaks riding on a sizzling wave whipped through the air toward Mark. He screamed.

"Como veían que resistía!" I yelled, pushing every ounce of force I could summon into each word. We needed a shield.

The barrier slammed up, knocking the sentries to the ground, but a sliver of their slashing magic slipped through. I batted it away from my face on instinct, and it sliced straight through the base of the smallest finger on my right hand.

Pain lanced through my hand as I clutched the bleeding stump to my chest. Mark was groaning on the floor, his clothes scorched and his face mottled red and black. Even as I dropped down beside him, the sentries were righting themselves on the other side of my shield. I didn't know if it'd be strong enough.

Any lingering doubts I'd had about destroying those *things* fell away. I snapped out my shattering lyric. Behind me, other voices called out in simultaneous castings, and the sentries shuddered and crumbled in the wake of our intent.

"Let's go, let's go!" Prisha shouted.

Finn and Desmond crouched with me beside Mark. He'd curled up on his side, his breath ragged. His arm trembled where it was pressed against the burnt tatters of his shirt.

"The casting went right through him," Desmond said. "I can't fix this."

Of course he couldn't. Every inch of Mark's body looked scalded or burnt.

My eyes turned watery. I'd felt something was going wrong. I should have spoken up sooner, gotten to him faster. I was supposed to be the one protecting us all.

"You're bleeding," Finn said, so close I felt his breath.

He grasped my right hand with its severed stump of a baby finger. My mind tipped as I looked at the stream of blood down my forearm. That last casting had left my nerves jangling. Suddenly the floor didn't feel so solid.

Desmond shifted closer, and Finn's grip tightened.

"Do what you can for him," Finn said, his voice strangely harsh as he nodded to Mark. "I'll help her."

"Finn," I said, but he was already rasping out a verse in some dead language. His jaw clenched, and his hand trembled. The wound on mine sealed over.

The color had seeped from his face, and when he smiled at me, it looked almost sickly. But I wasn't bleeding anymore.

"There," he said.

I didn't have time to make sure *he* was okay or to gather myself to help Desmond or anything else, because two more sentries popped into the room with a crackle.

Lacey belted out two castings, one that went wild and one that smashed its target, but more sentries were arriving. My shield shuddered with their attack. Desmond grabbed Mark's legs, and I lunged for his shoulders. Mark groaned.

He was dying. And if we didn't get him out of here soon, the rest of us would join him.

CHAPTER THIRTEEN

Finn

Apparently it was possible to drain your magical abilities so thoroughly you went through the pain and emerged into something more like numbness. My headache had erupted the second I'd joined the group in fending off the charge of sentries, but when I'd pushed all my intent into sealing Rocío's finger, it had ballooned until the sharper edges fell away beyond my consciousness. The world around me was warped and blurred, as if I were moving underwater.

Judith and Lacey pushed around me to help Rocío and Desmond lift Mark's body, and Prisha was waving frantically from the doorway. The sentries battered at Rocío's wall with flares and crackles of magic.

I staggered upright, swaying away from them. The floor felt perfectly flat, but my damned feet couldn't seem to find purchase. I stumbled out of the room as quickly as I could manage without tipping over.

My gaze fell on Mark, carried along by the others beside me, and my stomach lurched. His spectacular mohawk was blackened to a crisp. Blisters had transformed the wan skin of his face into a riot of angry pink and crackled brown. His lips were contorted with agony, and his eyelids were clenched tight, red around the rims as if weeping blood.

He needed help. He needed everything we could give him. *I* should be helping him.

I reached toward him, and my feet tangled beneath me. I groped at the wall, staggering as I caught my balance.

I couldn't even help carry him without risking dropping him.

As we rushed down the hall, a thought crept through my daze like a stream of frigid air. Everyone around me had used more magic in the last hour than I had all day, and they were still steady on their feet, still casting. I was the only one hollowed out. Even Judith, with one arm out of commission, was doing more than I was capable of to support Mark.

I wasn't just a middling mage who'd never found his footing. Gnôthi seautón. I was the weakest one here, by a significant margin. By what incredible luck had I scraped through the first few tests to make it this far?

Had I even scraped through? The chill cut deeper. Every mediocre grade I'd received in class—every mild compliment a teacher had offered me, even—must have been skewed in my favor in recognition of my family. Otherwise I'd have known I had no business declaring for the Exam. I'd have known how far below standard I measured. Were the examiners following the same line: bump me along at a bare pass, make me Champion as heedlessly as they'd named me Chosen before, and shuffle me off to a tutor who'd direct me straight into the spot that had been delegated to me from the start?

A screech reverberated through the air from behind us, and we all flinched. My heart beat wildly.

Maybe not. Maybe next year I'd be a cautionary tale like Shasti's brother, and someone like me would look back on my reported death and think, *I'd have expected him to know better than to try.*

Fates help me, I couldn't let that happen. I couldn't fall here and take the others down with me. If Mark or anyone else died here, it would be my fault.

"Rocío!" Prisha yelled.

My head jerked up. There was no bossiness in Prisha's voice now, only the same shrill terror clawing through me. She'd reached the top of the stairs we'd come up and then pressed herself against the wall as if to jerk out of range of something below. Just ahead of me, Rocío hesitated, her gaze on Prisha, her knuckles white where she clutched Mark.

No. I couldn't let her hold herself back. We needed her casting more than we needed her carrying.

I grabbed ahold of Mark's shoulder as securely as I could and nudged Rocío to go on. She dashed toward the stairwell the second my arm touched hers.

I could manage this. One foot. The next foot. Across from me, Judith emitted a strangled squeaking sound as she shifted her grasp on Mark's arm. I couldn't think any less of her for it when it was taking all my concentration just to stay upright.

Rocío and Prisha ducked in and out of the stairwell. The air shuddered with their expelled castings. As Judith, Desmond, and I hauled Mark over to them, Lacey darted ahead of us with an unnervingly exhilarated gasp. "I can smash some too!" she said.

Mark squirmed, and my hold faltered. I grappled to balance both of us without inflicting more pain.

A groan broke from his mouth. "You're useless," he mumbled without opening his eyes. "All of you. Useless."

My scrambling fingers must have pressed on a particularly raw spot, because he cried out. My whole body had gone as hot as if I'd been the one burned.

"We're trying!" Judith cried.

"I know," Mark said, his voice scarcely audible between the oddly dampening walls. "Please..."

I shoved most of my arm under his back, teetered, and found a brief equilibrium.

"Come on!" Prisha hollered. "The stairs are clear!"

We squeezed down the flight of stairs in one solid mass, the bodies around me holding me in place. Rocío sang out a casting. The air glinted around us, but my numbed senses didn't hearken even a whisper of the magic she'd conducted. Some sort of shield, I guessed.

We were almost at the bottom when Judith glanced back and yelped. Lacey whirled, snapping out a lyric, and the bulky figure at the top of the stairs toppled. The bolt of magic it had conjured twanged across our shield.

Rocío sang out again to fortify her casting. Her forehead was slick with sweat, her bangs plastered to her skin.

The sight jarred me like a kick to the gut. She'd put in more effort than the rest of us from the start, had felt the weight of all our expectations as she blazed the way forward, and now even she was fatiguing.

We might not make it out of this building alive—any of us.

We burst into the first-floor hallway. Our exit was lost in the blackness at the other end, but it was there. We had only to cross that distance.

With my pulse pounding in my ears, I threw myself forward alongside the others, not letting myself care how much I jostled Mark. Getting him out of here was the greatest kindness I could offer.

We'd made it three steps when a squad of sentries barreled out of the wall ahead of us.

Rocío and Prisha barked out their destructive castings in ragged voices, and Lacey belted out hers. One, two, three sentries shattered or crumbled as the varying conjurings struck the pulsing glows on their chests.

There were more. The air shook with the magic the sentries hurled at us in turn, so violent that even I could hearken it now.

Sweat streaked down my back. Our bubble of protection was heating up. Rocío paused to reinforce the shield. Her legs wobbled for a second before she braced herself against the wall.

I opened my mouth, but all that came out was a hoarse sputter. Hades take me, I didn't know what to tell her, what I could possibly suggest that might save us, how I might make the slightest contribution.

I'd come into the Exam like Phaeton commandeering his father's chariot, believing my family's magical talent had to be hiding within me somewhere. Now I was watching the world set ablaze by my conceit.

Mark's muscles seized up in my hands, stiffening against my fingers. Then his body went as slack as a wet rug.

"Set him down!" Desmond said.

Judith sobbed. I crouched with them, my eyes fixed on Mark's chest, the seared skin beneath the charred rags of his shirt. It didn't move.

I pressed my palm to his ribs. "He's not breathing."

As Desmond groped for Mark's wrist, Rocío dropped down beside me. She touched Mark's neck, and her face tensed. "His heart's stopped."

She moved to bend over his chest, and I scrambled to the side to make way. Setting her hands on his sternum, she murmured something in Spanish.

Mark's body twitched and stilled. Rocío grimaced and tried again.

I recognized the pose from our magimedical emergency first-aid seminars, which the tutorial classes must have received too.

She was trying to jumpstart his heart with magic the way a Dull doctor would with electric paddles.

As Desmond hunched to take a turn, Prisha called out in a quavering voice, "Can someone help, please?"

I swiveled and fell, banging my knees on the floor. Prisha and Lacey had backed up almost to Mark's prone body, and the shield was still contracting. More blocklike figures were charging at us through the hall, hurtling magic in thrashing whips and sizzling bolts of energy. Lacey yelled a few words that seemed to slow the sentries, but they were almost on us.

The warbling in my head rose like a wave about to crash, wrenching all the air from my lungs.

No. We were not falling here. I had to do *something*— something that would make a difference, for once in my sorry lie of a life.

I pitched myself onto my feet. My body felt like a blank wash of panic, but through that terror rose a single goal: the door. A spear of adrenaline spiked through me.

The thunder of the sentries' onslaught rattled through the barrier and into my bones. They were a hair from smashing our shield.

No. Push it back. I *had* to.

A verse popped into my mouth. A throbbing ache seared even deeper into my head, but I pulled magic to me with every shred of my being. "Sustulit et magnum magno conamine misit." In, in, in, swelling around my joints, jangling under my teeth and down my spine, into every hollow I could gather it in. Into every mistake, into every failure, into every place found wanting.

Bile shot up my throat, and I almost choked. But I propelled myself forward, shouting the verse once more, and hurled all that power out of me toward the hulking shapes descending on us.

It likely wouldn't have been sufficient if I'd tried to simply pummel them. I couldn't have orchestrated that much magic to my will even in my blaze of desperation. But my mind had fixated on shoving their attacks back at them, and that was precisely what my conjuring did, without my fully comprehending the design of my frantic casting.

The amplifying wave of magic I'd called up slammed into the sentries' battery of conjurings and repelled all of that energy backward with twice as much force. The power of their own attacks exploded back through the sentries with a resounding *boom* and a spray of crushed rock.

My desperate lob had given it no focus, though. The energy blared on in all directions, echoing off the walls and ceiling. The building shook.

A chunk of black stone plummeted to the floor in front of us. A crack opened in the wall next to me, an even deeper black than the darkest I'd thought possible. My tongue tangled for an instant before I found my voice again. It seemed to come from a long, tenuous distance beyond me: "Out! Get out now! The building's coming down."

Prisha snatched the back of my shirt to haul me with her, and I grasped Mark's arm. I registered that he was breathing again, that this was a good thing, but otherwise the world had narrowed down to a hash of fractured gasps and stumbling limbs. I hurled myself forward with the others.

Another slab of ceiling fell, clipping me on the shoulder. Powder coated my nose and mouth. We ran and ran as the darkness collapsed in on us. I couldn't tell which shapes were real and which were caused by my failing vision. Every thump of rock reverberated through my body.

Prisha shoved open the door to thin gray-brown light. The doorframe crumpled as we tumbled through to sprawl onto the spongy ground outside. "There's more coming!" Desmond shouted. I tried to raise my head, but I no longer had a solid sense of which way was up or down.

Rocío's voice carried through the chaos, clear in the open air. "The wall! Get to the wall where we started. We need shelter."

I clasped Mark's shoulders and heaved him along with the panting figures around me. Follow them, follow them. It didn't matter if I could see where I was going as long as I stayed with them.

Wordless bellows rang out from behind us. Light flared around us. Prisha yelped. Mark shuddered in our grasp, but we couldn't do anything for him here.

"Almost there," Judith said. It sounded as much like a plea as encouragement.

My feet tripped over themselves and rediscovered the ground. An electric clap rattled my skin. Then the glossy black surface of the wall was looming over me.

We charged around the edge and dove behind it, and the air abruptly stilled.

My legs buckled. I sagged against the wall, scarcely managing to lower Mark's body rather than drop him.

Rocío gazed back the way we'd come. My view, rapidly narrowing into a pinhole, caught on the silver sunburst charm dangling below her collarbone. Somewhere in the mad battle, a bit of magic had touched it, melting two of the tiny points toward each other and faintly blackening the metal. As I stared at it, the shape doubled before my eyes.

"It's all gone," Rocío said. The hiss in my head all but drowned out her words. "The building, the sentries—they just disappeared."

"Thank the Fates for that," Prisha muttered. "I'd had enough of that test."

Judith drew in a shaky breath. "What are we going to do for Mark?"

Rocío swiveled back toward him, her charm swinging. "Is he still breathing? Can we—"

The hiss heightened, and the air around us shimmered. A melodic voice vibrated through it.

"Examinee Ornstein forfeits the Exam."

With a rush of energy, Mark's body disappeared.

"Wait!" Rocío yelled, crouching over the spot where he'd been. "You could at least have given us a chance..."

To what—to heal him? I wasn't certain that even a fully trained magimedic could repair the damage done to him. The thought of us novices restoring that ruined body suddenly struck me as so absurd I might have laughed if I could have found my lungs, my throat.

Rocío leapt to her feet, the charm snapping to the side, and my vision blurred to nothing. The last thing I felt was the give of my knees as my mind fell away into the void.

CHAPTER FOURTEEN

Rocío

"F inn!" Prisha cried out.

I spun around, my legs wobbly from all the adrenaline that had been coursing through me. Finn sprawled on the ground at the base of the wall, his face ashen and his body limp.

¡Dios mío! I dropped to my knees beside him. A piercing chill gripped my chest.

Not him too.

Prisha knelt by his other side and set her hand on his forehead. I touched his wrist. His skin was clammy, but a pulse fluttered against my searching fingers. His chest rose with a halting breath.

He was alive. Alive and not dying, just fainted, I guessed from the strain. I sat back, trying to gather myself. How could I help him?

He needed me. But it was suddenly hard to think as I looked at him lying there. I'd hardly noticed it happening, but Finn's smiles and jokes and the honesty behind them had opened up a hopeful space in me that now felt painfully empty.

"He shouldn't have done that," Prisha muttered, looking sick. "Trying to take them all out at once—that was insane. He could have killed himself."

"He could have killed all of us," Judith said, but she sounded more frightened than accusing.

The ache that had spread through my joints with my repeated castings condensed into a sharp pang behind my ribs. Finn had done it because I'd been busy reviving Mark, as well as I could. And now Mark was gone. To be burned out or to die?

Was the Confed going to take Finn too? Every second he stayed unconscious, fear clutched me tighter.

I grasped his hand, even though the movement hurt the stump of my little finger—the stump he'd sealed. If I could just find the words that would wake him up—

His eyelids jittered and then blinked fully open. He gazed at us staring down at him.

"I'd better not be dead," he said, his voice rough, "because the two of you are definitely not allowed to be."

Tears sprang into my eyes. I had the urge to throw my arms around him and hold on until he couldn't doubt how much I wanted him here, making those jokes, smiling his smile—until I'd made up for every moment I'd shut him down or pushed him away.

"You're perfectly alive," Prisha said. "No thanks to you. How about you hold off on any more building-shaking castings for another year or two?"

Then her gaze darted up and caught mine. For just an instant her face darkened. That twitch of a frown held enough animosity that I rocked backward on my heels, my fingers slipping from Finn's.

He didn't belong with me. He didn't even belong in my vicinity, outside of the Exam. She knew that as well as I did.

"I got you all out, didn't I?" Finn said, wincing as he tried to push himself into a sitting position.

Prisha caught his shoulder to help him up. He pressed the heel of his hand to his temple. She set her palm over his and murmured a numbing 'chantment.

His headache was back. So it came from magical rather than physical exhaustion? How dry had Finn run himself even before our frantic dash through the building? Before he'd put everything he had left into that casting? He'd nearly broken himself to save the rest of us.

He turned and smiled at me, a little sheepishly. Of course he would smile even now. And of course my pulse would leap, as if I'd been waiting just for that.

I glanced back at the others. Desmond was standing with one hand against the wall, watching our movements. Judith was hovering behind me. Her makeshift sling and her designer clothes were smudged with ash—from Mark's body. Tear tracks ran down her cheeks. Lacey hung back, clutching the silver box under her arm.

We'd failed Mark—failed him epically. If I'd been faster to react, faster to recognize the danger...

I wasn't going to let myself forget that failure for a second. The rest of us had survived, and I had to make sure we continued to do so.

"We should head back to the building where we got the message," I said. "Get the rest of this test over with."

"Yes," Prisha said. "Of course." The quick smile she flashed me made me wonder if I'd imagined her hostility.

She motioned for me to help her lift Finn onto his feet. He made a noise of protest, but he let us haul him up, which I knew meant he probably couldn't have stood on his own no matter how much he might have wanted to.

"Let's go, compadre," I said, and he gave me another wobbly grin.

He swayed but held his balance between us as we all trudged across the flat gray landscape. Yesterday's haze had closed in around us again, blocking all view of anything except our path to the row of lopsided structures. Lacey walked with something between a limp and a skip in her step, her chin held high. Judith had folded her good arm across her sling. Her breath was still raspy.

When we stepped over the threshold of the building where we'd had our last meal, Judith halted with a sharp exhale and spun around. "What the *hell* was that? People getting cut up, burned to death! That's not a trial. That's… that's torture. What are they testing us for with that?"

Cut up. My thumb reached for the stump where my little finger had been. It took me a moment to realize I wasn't surprised. Why *wouldn't* the Confed torture us? Why wouldn't they run us ragged every way they could? This was our punishment for not accepting their judgment.

Even the Champions mustn't feel very triumphant after they made it through two more days like this. And that was just how the Confed would like it, wasn't it? To have even the victors beaten down.

I didn't say any of that, though. Caution held my tongue.

Mark had been standing in almost the same spot that Judith was now when he'd accused the Confed of brainwashing and worse. Less than an hour later, our next test had nearly killed him. Just a coincidence?

"They must have their reasons," Prisha said, but her voice wavered a bit.

"They want to make sure we actually deserve the chance to keep our magic," Finn said, sounding bleaker than I'd expected. He let go of us and immediately sank onto the floor, though he managed to make it look as if there was nothing he'd rather do more.

"There have to be better ways to make sure of that than what we just went through," Judith said.

My throat tightened. If the Confed had heard Mark, they could hear her too. He'd lit up with magic before the sentries charged at him. Maybe he'd cast something earlier that had made him their target... or maybe the Confed had interfered.

Had they heard Javi make similar comments three years ago? Had they painted a target on his back in return?

We cut the chaff from the wheat, the examiner had said to me. They'd cut Mark away so easily. It could have been me if I'd spoken more freely.

"We made it," I said, wishing I had Finn's way with words to calm Judith down. "We did the best we could. That's all we can focus on for now."

"We blasted them back even harder than they blasted us," Lacey said with a short laugh. "I wish the people back home could have seen me."

Her enthusiasm rankled me. "It'd be better if we hadn't needed to 'blast' at all."

Her shoulders tensed, but then her posture deflated. With her overlarge dress drifting around her, right then she looked like the hesitant girl I'd met in the courtyard again.

Before I could add anything that might have softened my implied criticism, Judith said, "Do you think Mark will be okay? I mean, he obviously *wasn't*, but they must have magimedics on the island, right?"

"Even if they could heal him, he failed the Exam." Desmond scratched his elbow, his tone vacant. "They'll burn him out. That's how it works."

"If they were going to take him anyway, they could have transported him from the hallway instead of waiting until we got out," Judith said. "It wasn't as if we were going to be able to help him either way."

But that would have made the test easier for the rest of us. I bit my lip.

"Hey!" Lacey pointed to a faint glow that was creeping across the wall where the message had been. It resolved into the outline of a door, growing more defined until a knob protruded from its surface.

She hurried forward while the rest of us hung back. Finn scrambled up before anyone could offer a hand and managed to hobble over on his own.

As Lacey pushed on the door and it opened, I braced for the start of another test, but nothing came through the doorway except a thin wash of heat.

Lacey beamed, peering through the doorway. "They're bringing us back."

She stepped right inside. When I reached the door, I saw what she'd meant. It opened into a white-walled room like the ones we'd spent most of the first day of the Exam in, filled with bright light. Savory smells reached my nose from tables along the far wall, where a bunch of examinees was already clustered. A few examiners stood around the fringes, keeping an eye on them— and now us.

One by one, we headed in. From its size, I thought the room might have been the one where we'd constructed our defensive 'chantments, although photos and the shelves and half the tables were gone. The remaining tables were covered with platters of food: roast chicken, pasta casserole, heaps of hamburgers, assorted salads and fruit, and bottles of juice and pop. The other examinees were already digging in, silent except for the smacking of their lips. Lacey and the rest of my group joined them.

Hunger and queasiness twisted together inside me. I hadn't eaten a full meal since that first night in the dorm room, but images of blistered skin and severed flesh were still too fresh in my mind. My right hand ached.

I had to keep my strength. I had to take every opportunity the examiners gave us to fortify myself. Even if the last thing I wanted to be doing right now was enjoying a meal. I forced myself to walk over to the table, pick up a hamburger, and murmur a quick casting to check for 'chantments or toxins. One bite and then another, the meaty juices turning sour in my mouth.

Another group, this one of five, stumbled through the doorway. They caught sight of the food, and all five fell on it like starved animals.

Had the examiners not given their group any food at all, or had they somehow lost it? One girl brushed past me to grab some of the pasta. I wanted to ask them, but the question stuck in my throat. I didn't know her at all, and I felt too overwhelmed to navigate a conversation with a stranger. Especially one who looked that desperate.

Judith, Lacey, and Desmond must have been feeling similarly wary, because they stuck close to each other as they grazed from the platters. Desmond's lips moved briefly with a casting too quiet for me to make out. Something to help him navigate the room with so many people close together?

Prisha had stopped by the gangly guy with dark red hair who'd hassled Judith before. Callum, she'd said his name was.

"So your group survived," she remarked a little tersely.

He gave her a flat grin. "Two of us, anyway."

What had happened to the others with him around? I suppressed a shudder.

Finn had retreated into the corner to lean against the wall. He drained the last of a bottle of orange juice and then lowered his hand to let it dangle from his fingers. Despite his banter when he'd first recovered, he looked uncertain now.

I remembered the story he'd told me in the underground passage about his failed demonstration for his granduncle's colleague and his shame afterward. Suddenly I could see that crushed boy in the young man in front of me. Was he embarrassed that he'd fainted? My heart squeezed.

I slipped out of the crowd around the tables to join him.

He lifted his head as I reached him. "Hey," he said with a lopsided smile. "How are you doing?"

"I— You know..." I didn't have the words to adequately express the jumble inside me, at least not any I wanted to say out loud.

"Yeah," he said. "That's about the size of it." He laughed, but there was an edge to it that bothered me. "Sorry," he added. "I'm a little spacey still."

"That casting you pulled to get us out was kind of stupid," I said, "but you know, it was also pretty spectacular."

The light I'd wanted to see came back into his eyes. "You think so?" he said with closer to his usual breezy tone. "All part of my devious plan to impress you. If I've managed that, then the rest is just icing."

"Maybe try a little less hard next time?" I suggested, and he laughed for real. His hand edged toward me, and without thinking I took the unspoken invitation, twining my fingers with his.

This was stupid. It couldn't mean anything. But all I wanted was to rest my head against his chest the way I had in the tunnel and let him talk my fears away, if only for a moment.

"Rocío," Finn said, "I—"

A crinkling sound quivered through the air, and three more examiners appeared in the empty area at the other end of the room, startling us. My hand jerked from Finn's, and one of the other examinees in the room dropped a bottle that thumped on the floor. Another's back jarred the table.

A couple days ago, we might have turned toward unexpected

arrivals with only curiosity. Instincts could be reprogrammed so quickly.

The examiner in the middle stepped ahead of the two men flanking her. Her tall, elegant bearing and pale gray hair made me think *swan*.

"Hello, examinees," she said in a voice that rang through the room. "I'm Examiner Lancaster, and I'm pleased to welcome you to this way station at the midpoint of your Exam. Congratulations to you four groups—or parts of groups, at least—on successfully completing your most recent trial. Please note that you are not to use magic again until you enter the next stage of the Exam."

Only four? So one group hadn't reached their objective at all? My stomach sank as I glanced around the room, taking a quick count.

Eighteen. Eighteen of us were left of the thirty-five who'd been sent off to the dorm rooms the other night.

How many of the missing seventeen had simply failed to complete a task and been whisked away for burning out, and how many had fallen like Mark?

How many had died?

"Please gather together so we can discuss exactly what you have accomplished," Examiner Lancaster went on.

I didn't know what she meant by that, but her eager tone jarred my nerves. What we'd "accomplished" was seeing one of us tortured nearly to death.

I glanced at Finn, and he shrugged before peeling himself off the wall. We headed past the tables to rejoin the others. He walked with carefully steady steps. I wanted to offer him my arm for support, but I didn't think he'd take it.

We stopped at the fringes of the group. "You should be the one to give them the box," he said in a low voice. "You're the one who found it."

"Desmond got us most of the way there," I pointed out. "And Lacey carried it through the mess while we were getting out. We all contributed."

"Let's just hope the individual assessments aren't public, right?" he said with a grimace toward the waiting examiners.

Prisha came up on Finn's other side and slid her hand around his forearm with a confidence I envied. He leaned toward her just a fraction. "Still alive."

She rapped him in the side with her elbow. "Stay that way."

When everyone was standing still and silent, Examiner Lancaster clapped her hands. "Let me begin," she said, "by showing you where your last test took each of you."

The two men brought out a contraption like an overlarge easel mounted with a sheet of white canvas. Lancaster held out her hand to us. "Which group will be first to share what they brought home?"

"Here!" Lacey said where she was standing at the front of our small crowd. She brandished the silver box.

Lancaster accepted it and waved her back. "Excellent," she said. "Group Three, here is the building you were exploring a little more than an hour ago."

She gestured to the canvas with a melodic murmur. Her casting conjured an image onto its broad surface: a house—a large one, with stucco walls and an arched roof covered in dark red tiles.

"Isfahan, Iran," she said. "A home identified by our local allies as that of a member of the Middle Eastern Magical Alliance, the extremist faction that is one of our most zealous enemies. Thanks to the risks taken by those friendly Iranians and your efforts after your partial transfer there, the MEMA no longer has access to this one tool." She sang another soft word, and the box snapped open. A 'chanted holographic map popped up from within.

I couldn't wrap my head around what she'd said. I'd never

seen the house in her picture before. "What do you mean by 'partial transfer'?" I said. "We weren't actually *there*, so how could we have taken anything from there? We were in the Exam area the entire time."

"Oh," Lancaster said, "you *were* there. The 'chantment required is a complicated one, but it allows us to temporarily superimpose a small area anywhere in the world into our Exam building. As soon as you passed the dividing wall, you were half here and half over there."

A murmur of surprise passed through the examinees around me. My eyes widened. I'd read about small-scale superimposing —of internal organs onto a model, for example, to allow operations without having to cut open the patient—but not an entire building that people could literally walk around in. How many mages had it taken to pull that off? No wonder it had felt so indistinct and unreal.

"So we were in the Exam room... and somewhere else at the same time?" someone said, sounding puzzled.

Lancaster motioned toward the image of the house. "In a way. Your physical presence was mainly here. You would have appeared to anyone who saw you there as nothing more than a vague figure, as unrecognizable as our 'chantment made the guards appear to you. But it wouldn't be as valid a test if we weren't putting you in an at least partly real-world scenario."

The guards. The sentries? All those figures we'd blasted apart?

"Wait," Judith said in a thin voice. "The sentries were *real*? The message said they were automated. I thought..."

Lancaster shook her head sharply. The bottom dropped out of my gut. Finn squeezed my shoulder. He looked straight at the examiner, his mouth pressed flat, but he held on to me, keeping me from swaying.

The sentries had been people. *That* was what had felt off about them to me. They'd moved like human beings, too subtle to be programmed conjurings. How could she talk about this so calmly?

"We have to be a little obscure in the earlier stages of the Exam," Lancaster was saying. "We can't reveal the full truth of the matter until you've passed far enough to have earned it. Now—"

"What happened to the... sentries we destroyed?" Desmond broke in.

Lancaster pursed her lips. "Your magic affected their true bodies, just as theirs affected yours. But we were able to include a target in our 'chantment to help you guide your castings effectively. They had no such advantage."

A target. That pulse. It'd looked like the beat of a heart because that was what it *had* been. Then we'd...

"We *killed* them," I said, too shocked to hold my tongue, and an anxious muttering rippled between the examinees around me. "We thought it was only a test, but you had us *kill* people—real people."

How many of those blocklike forms had I struck down on the way to retrieving the box? Five? Six? And how many more on the way out? A wave of nausea flipped my stomach. I clamped my teeth together to hold down the hamburger I'd forced myself to eat.

"They were enemy combatants," Lancaster replied with an odd gentleness. "They do the same to our people every chance they have. You should be proud of how you helped the entire nation today. This is the job you've been working toward."

"Job?" Finn said hoarsely. "What are you talking about?"

Lancaster folded her hands in front of her. "I was getting to that," she said. "With this test, with the abilities you've shown in making it through, you've taken your first true step toward becoming the Confederation's most valuable soldiers."

Soldiers?

"Excuse me?" someone said, and someone else spat out a

startled, "*What?*" Beside me, Finn sucked in a breath.

I wouldn't have thought I could reel any more than I already was, but my knees wobbled.

Lancaster gave us a small smile that was knowing in a way I didn't like at all. "You're all aware that we've faced numerous threats from mages and Dull societies abroad," she said. "The Unveiling happened so that we could better protect everyone within this nation, magical or otherwise. But to hold on to our advantage, we must take risks.

"Every day, military campaigns are run covertly around the world in collaboration with our many allies. We do our best to keep the upper hand against those who would undermine our security and who would escalate any successful breach into a full-out war. Those of you who make Champion will serve on the front lines of those efforts as part of the Confederation's Special Operations team."

No. That wasn't right. We were fighting to keep our magic, to get our spot in the college, to have our studies assisted—whether we needed it or not—by a respected tutor. Not to actually *fight*.

But we'd already fought. We'd fought and killed, like the soldiers she was saying we were going to become.

The sentries had attacked us too, of course, but why wouldn't they have? We'd charged at them throwing spells, broken into their employer's home... I didn't know what those people had done in the past, but in that moment they'd only been defending themselves. From us.

"If you make Champion," Lancaster went on, "when you are fully in the field, most missions will allow for more... subtlety than that test. Less combat and more reconnaissance. Unfortunately, the protections that enemy mages keep on their residences and workplaces make it difficult to create a precise experience through the partial transfer. Nonetheless, you have proven yourselves."

We'd proven ourselves. *The Confederation's most valuable soldiers. You should be proud.*

I shivered. What was there to be proud of? If they'd wanted *value*, they'd have picked the cream of the crop from the academies, from the college. But no, they were testing the novices they'd already deemed not quite good enough, the ones desperate enough to risk unknown trials just to keep their magical ability. Old-magic disappointments. New-magic street trash no one had expected much from anyway.

Of course they were. No one would be paying that much attention to what the Champions did after they left the Exam. Our families would just be glad we were employed somewhere, somehow.

Our "value" to the Confed was how expendable we were.

I remembered Mark talking about his brother—the one who'd been made Champion, the one who'd all but disappeared on him. No wonder. How could you talk about your life when it was made up of secret military missions to steal, to kill? The thought of telling my parents what *I'd* done here, even unknowingly, made me queasy all over again.

Had Javi made it this far? Had he heard the same announcement? I could almost hear his horrified mutter. *Of course. Why wouldn't these cabrones trick us into doing their dirty work?*

The actual muttering around me grew louder. "That's not how this is supposed to work!" a boy across the room from me protested, and another said, "No one told us! I thought..." And behind me a girl was chattering under her breath so rapidly the words blurred together.

Finn stood motionless at my side, his hand clamped on my shoulder. I wasn't sure anymore which of us was holding the other up.

Examiner Lancaster raised her graceful arm and snapped her fingers. All of us fell silent.

"We realize not everyone can stomach this sort of work," she said. "We have pushed you to your limits specifically to determine what each of you is made of, whether you could withstand whatever brutality the enemy may deal out if a mission takes a turn for the worse. The Champion's role comes with many pressures and, yes, horrors. Anyone lacking the necessary strength —magical, mental, and physical—would be a liability in the field."

She paused. "You should know that there are two more stages of the Exam you will have to pass if you're to make Champion. Stages that will stretch your endurance even further."

Someone on the other side of the room let out a laugh that sounded almost hysterical. Beside Desmond, Judith had twisted her fingers into the fabric of her sling.

"You will have a short time to rest and think before the Exam continues," Lancaster said. "I can tell you right now that fewer than half of you should expect to receive the honor of being named Champion. Any who wish to forfeit their chance and accept burning out may come to us with that request during the next several hours. The last thing we want is to force anyone to proceed unwillingly. But first, why don't you hear what else your amateur operations have accomplished? Which group will bring their finding forward next?"

The gangly red-haired boy—Callum—strode over. Lancaster brought up an image of another building on her canvas, in Moscow she said, but I shut my eyes. My mind was spinning too fast for me to follow more of her words.

They didn't want to force anyone unwilling? Then they hadn't given us the freedom to make that choice properly. The only roads that lay ahead of me were giving up all magic, accepting death, or becoming a murderer however many times over.

CHAPTER FIFTEEN

Finn

I f I'd ever been a champion at anything, it was sleeping. When I was a kid, Margo had teased me about how I could nod off no matter what family chaos was transpiring around me. Even that first night in the Exam's dorm room, despite all our uncertainty about what awaited us in the morning, I'd been exhausted enough to drift off within a few minutes.

Tonight, I wasn't so lucky. Lying on a mat amid the restless breathing of the other remaining examinees, I couldn't settle my mind.

I was exhausted, make no mistake. In the hours since I'd collapsed after my massive casting, my bones had gradually become less rubbery and my muscles less jellified, but a dull ache lingered in the spaces between them. A sharper pain prodded the backs of my eyes now that Prisha's last numbing 'chantment had worn off.

What wrenched at me the most, though, was the memory of my conjured force sending the sentries' magic crashing through that pitch-black hall.

What had become of the elegant house Examiner Lancaster had presented to us after I'd ravaged it? What remained of the bodies I'd... ripped apart? Had I wrought devastation as horrifying as the photos the examiners had shown us for inspiration two days ago?

Margo had killed a rat. I'd slaughtered at least half a dozen human beings.

I rolled over, and the dissolving rod jabbed my hip. Had my sister known this was what the Exam entailed? Had my father? He'd mentioned the responsibilities of being made Champion...

No, I didn't think he'd been conscious of the full picture. If he had, I couldn't conceive of him backing down on the matter of my rescinding my declaration. He'd just had an inkling that there were unknown elements—elements he'd consider unsavory.

Maybe I should have listened to them. My being Chosen could scarcely seem more a farce now. I certainly didn't feel like a *Champion* in any way, let alone the sort Lancaster had spoken of.

At a rustling beside me, I half opened my eyes. Prisha was getting up. She padded around the other prone figures to the doorway. Going to the bathroom, presumably.

The relative brightness of the dim hall lights sliced into the darkness of our room. Several minutes passed. Prisha didn't reappear.

A girl from group five had gone to the examiners as soon as our debriefing was finished and hadn't returned. But Prisha wouldn't forfeit without even talking to me. Still, I found myself waiting, watching the doorway. A restless itch passed through me. We'd had time to shower before lights out, but my two-days-worn clothes felt worse against my freshly clean skin than they had before.

My heartbeat counted the seconds until I couldn't stand to lie there any longer. I eased upright and slipped into the hall.

The examiners had instructed us not to leave this area, and I suspected if I tried to turn the corner at either end of the short white-walled hallway, I'd have encountered a magical barrier. There was no sign of Prisha.

Trying to ignore the twist of apprehension inside me, I meandered into the men's bathroom. I made use of the facilities and studied my bleary face in the mirror as if it would offer some sort of answer. No such luck. With a scowl at my reflection, I shoved myself back toward the hall.

Prisha was standing near the other end of the hallway, leaning against the wall with her arms folded tight. She startled at the sound of the door thudding shut behind me, and then stilled when she caught sight of me.

Relief flooded me. She was still here.

I ambled over and propped myself beside her. "You couldn't sleep either?"

"It's a lot to take in," she said.

"Yeah." She'd barely been able to speak of Examiner Lancaster's revelations as we'd prepared for bed. She'd blasted through at least a few of the sentries herself.

All the frustrations and doubts that had been churning inside me bubbled up, threatening to spill out. How long ago had she realized the vastness of my ineptitude as I only just had, as she'd watched me in comparison to our classmates, seen the teachers favor me with so many more considerations than they would ever have extended to her? She'd known just how little I'd deserve my Chosen spot and how much more she did.

To lay that guilt on her now, to ask her to *comfort* me about it, would be rubbing it in her face. My throat constricted, and my mouth stayed shut.

She must have been thinking along the same line anyway. "You should get out of here while you have the chance," she said, an unfamiliar edge hardening her voice. "With your granduncle and all, they'd probably even let you skip the burning out."

"I wouldn't want to skip it." My voice came out louder than I'd intended. I reined in my emotions. "I wouldn't accept that. If I forfeit, I'm burned out. That's how it works."

"Not always. Not for everyone."

"You don't know that. Besides, would *you* want a free pass you hadn't earned, just for—"

"I didn't want to be here at all!" she burst out. "I didn't want any of this. Even if you are burned out, Finn, your parents will find something worthwhile you can do. You have an easy way out. You're probably the only one here who does. So why can't you take it? Why couldn't you have taken it in the first place?"

I stared at her. "It wasn't right. I couldn't just— It wasn't *right*."

"Well, you being here doesn't make things any more right for the rest of us. It just means something awful happens to you that wouldn't have happened otherwise. How is that better?"

Her eyes were fierce but shining with unshed tears, and I felt more hopeless than I had in my entire life. I reached for her, and she let me pull her into an embrace. I hugged her tight.

"I'm sorry," I said. "I didn't mean... If I'd known it seemed that way to you..."

"I don't know how much it does," she said thickly. "I shouldn't be so angry with you. There's just so much— I had no idea— *Killing* people..." She shivered. "I hate this. I hate it so much. Of course coming here wasn't going to be enough to get me into the college. Nothing I do, with *my* family, with *my* name, is ever going to be enough for them."

There was nothing I could say to that. I closed my eyes against the heat building in them and held on to her until she shifted away. She turned away from me and ran her hands through her hair, wincing as she must have pulled at some hurt from yesterday's trials.

"What are you going to do?" I said.

"I'll keep going," she said, her jaw set. "I have to. The alternatives... But I won't think any less of you if you don't. I promise."

Because she'd never expected very much of me to begin with.

"I haven't decided yet," I said, "but, Pree, you have to know that whatever happens to me, it was my choice, okay? I came here for me. If I stay, it'll be for me. And I promise I won't lean on you anymore. I won't weigh you down."

"Finn, I didn't mean—"

"No, you did. And it's fine. I just... have to figure out the best way I can live with myself, all right? I'm trying."

"I know you are," she said. "You always do."

The examiners must have been honest in their declaration about us choosing to proceed freely, because I woke up to the same room, with all its walls intact and a morning-like light streaming down from a stripe across the ceiling. My head felt foggy but no longer outright painful. I stretched, and the smell of fresh baking filled my nose.

The tables along the wall were now laid with platters of fruit and turnovers and trays holding sausages and scrambled eggs. My mouth watered despite the knot of guilt still filling my stomach.

My fellow examinees were stirring. I pushed myself to my feet. I had to eat something. My abilities were feeble enough even when I was well-fed.

I'd just spooned some eggs onto a plate and moved to the sausages when Callum leaned over beside me. He cleared his throat and spat a glob of saliva into the tray of eggs.

"What are you *doing*?" I said, forgetting my policies about speaking to him.

Callum lobbed another splatter of spit into the tray. Then he offered me a grin so off-kilter it set the hair on the back of my neck on end. He'd always been an ass, but he'd usually been at least somewhat serious about it. Now he looked as though he was having fun.

"Maybe people don't eat as much, or maybe I make them sick," he said. "Either way, it weakens the competition. You have a problem with that strategy, Lockwood?"

Three days ago, I might have backed down or laughed it off to avoid discovering how he'd respond if I admitted that I did, in fact, have a problem with it—but it had been a long three days, during which I'd faced adversaries much more frightening than Callum. What could he inflict on me that was any worse than what was waiting for me afterward, no matter what I chose next?

"You don't get a spot by enacting Medea on people," I said, my voice low and calm. "If the only person left standing is a screwup, there'll be no Champions this year."

"Hmm," Callum said. "Pot, kettle, et cetera. Anyway, the fewer losers in my way, the better. So maybe you should steer clear."

He aimed an ironic salute at me and sauntered off.

Was that what the examiners wanted to see: total ruthlessness? I supposed brutality could be a useful quality for a soldier, but I wasn't sure Callum had any others.

I hadn't realized Rocío had come up behind me until she spoke. "Only one other person from his group made it this far," she said. "I hope the last guy stays on his guard."

"Yeah," I said. "Assuming the experience of partnering with Callum hasn't traumatized him into leaving."

My gaze slid to Prisha, who was sitting on her mat with Judith. The other girl's presence was a bit of a surprise. From the way she was cradling her broken arm, the examiners clearly hadn't tended even to it.

Maybe Judith was, like me, still in the process of deciding

whether to stay. As I watched, she fished her pearl-handled Swiss Army knife from her pocket and handed it to Prisha, who set about carving the peel off an apple in a much clumsier fashion than Desmond's casting yesterday. I would have joined them, but after last night's conversation, I felt suddenly uncertain of my welcome.

One of the other examinees pushed past Rocío to grab a turnover, and the corner of the sheet still wrapped around her chest drifted down her side. She groped after it, mumbling a curse in Spanish. Her fingers caught the corner, but her arm bent awkwardly as she tried and failed to tuck it back into place.

"I would be pleased to offer you my assistance," I said with a mock bow.

The corner of her lips twitched up. "I seem to need it. But let's get out of the way first."

We retreated to the corner near the door. I set my plate on the ground and took the end of the torn strip of sheet from her. As I lifted it, the slashes in her still faintly bloodstained T-shirt gaped open, revealing tan skin mottled by paler marks where Desmond had sealed her wounds—and a sliver of the band of her bra.

Heat crept through my body. I schooled my gaze to the cotton fabric of the sheet, wrapped the ends around her back, and tucked them in as tightly as I could, careful to avoid brushing my fingers over her bare skin.

"Thanks," she said when I'd finished. Was her voice the slightest bit rougher than before?

She turned, tugging lightly at the strip to test it, and appeared to deem my efforts satisfactory. "I rinsed everything out last night, but I guess tying that back up without magic was more than I could manage."

"We all have our flaws," I deadpanned. "I'll try not to let it color my opinion of you."

She rolled her eyes, but she was smiling. I missed the warmth of her body close to my hands.

"How do you do it?" she said. "It's not really that what's going on doesn't bother you, but you make it sound like there's nothing at all we should be worrying about. How can you keep that up?"

"Loads of practice," I said automatically, with more honesty than I might have preferred if I'd thought my answer through. "I don't know. When life hands you lemons, juggle them and see how many people will laugh, even if it's only you. I find thumbing my nose at the worrying makes me feel better and makes the hard parts easier, even if I'm still worried."

She hummed to herself. "These are some lemons we've got now."

"You can say that again." I drew in a breath to ask her what she was going to do, but I didn't need to ask. I knew her at least that well.

"You're staying in," I said. "You're going for Champion."

She bent to pick up her plate and poked at a ring of pineapple. "I made a kind of promise to myself, the first night here, that I wasn't going to let anyone with me get hurt. That we were all going to make it through to the end, whatever the Confed does with us after that. I can't protect anyone if I give up. I already failed with Mark. Even with what they want us to do..." She jabbed her fork into the pineapple.

"They want *us* to hurt people." Thinking about it sent my skin crawling.

"They already thought I might hurt people, somehow or other, just because I'm new magic," she said. "If I'd known what was really going on in that test... If I could go back and do it over, find a way that didn't prove them right... But the only good thing I can do now is keep going. As long as I have magic, I have choices. Burn me out and I'm just another ghetto-trash Dull girl."

I couldn't imagine there ever being anything *just* about her. Her words, and the confidence with which she spoke them, called a pang into my chest that recalled my first sight of her dragon.

She was so certain she had the power to save people, to make a difference.

She was right, about that and about how holding on to our talent meant holding on to possibility. No matter what the examiners said, no matter what I'd have to grapple with in the future, I'd never truly wanted to abandon that.

No. My hesitation was about what I already lacked.

"And you?" she said, in a careful enough tone that I couldn't tell if she had hopes one way or the other.

"I'm not sure," I admitted. "I want to go on. I want to keep my magic, and I want to find out how far I can make it, but..."

"But?"

The answer had been dangling in the back of my mind the entire time. Why was it so hard to force it out? "I don't want to drag anyone else down with me if I go down." *Which I likely will.*

"Finn—" Rocío began, but I motioned her silent.

"I know how much trouble I've already caused for the rest of you. I know I haven't held my own. I'd be essentially useless without Prisha—and you—handling my headaches. You could have died rescuing me from that storm, and I almost massacred all of us trying to save us yesterday. And what would you all have done if I'd fainted *before* we reached the wall?"

Rocío's eyes had widened. "Okay," she said. "Everything you said might be true, but all of us needed help some of the time. *You* helped *me* right at the start, getting me on track to break my 'chantment. You figured out how to break Judith's too. And if you hadn't blasted the building yesterday, would we have gotten out at all? I don't know."

"You would have," I said. "You'd have found a way. That's what you do."

"That's not my point." She shook her head with a fractured laugh. "Don't you have any idea what *you* do? Magic isn't the only thing that matters. The way you pay attention to people. The way you talk. The—" She waved her hand vaguely. "What you just said about lemons. I know I can survive the Exam, but it's easier with you here. Okay?"

A blush colored her cheeks. She snatched a grape off her plate and started chewing it with intense concentration. My own face had warmed, but it was a pleasant heat, one that tingled down to my chest. "So what you're saying is I'm the comic relief?"

She laughed properly then, hard enough that she clapped her hand over her mouth and I thought I'd made her choke. "No, I'm all right," she said when I touched her shoulder. She coughed a few times and met my eyes again. "That's not how I'd put it, but if you'd rather look at it that way... We all have our flaws? I'm pretty sure we all have our strengths too."

"What is it with the throwing my words back at me today?" I protested, and she smiled. O gods—all of them—let nothing ever destroy that smile, because decades from now I'd still want to be basking in it.

A knot of doubt remained in my gut. "Fine," I said. "But can you promise me something? I want us all to survive to the end of the Exam as much as anyone, but if I get in trouble, if you can't get me out of it without being hurt yourself... Promise you won't let me drag you down."

Her expression turned serious again. "Finn, I can't promise that."

"I'll almost certainly be safe," I said with assurance I didn't feel. "Chances are that if it looked as though I were actually going to *die*, they'd pull me out rather than risk my granduncle's wrath." That was assuming Granduncle Raymond cared much about whether I lived or died after I'd defied the Circle by coming here, but Rocío didn't need to take that factor into consideration.

"I hope that's true," she said. "But whether it is or not, you have to trust me to know what risks I can take and which I can't. If anything happens to *me*, it'll be because *I* messed up. It won't be your fault. Got it?"

"All right," I said. Her declaration wasn't everything I wanted, but it'd have to suffice. I retrieved my plate and scraped up a forkful of eggs.

Rocío ate a couple more grapes. Then she said, hesitantly, "If your family is so high up in the Confed, had you heard about any of this before: the Champions working as soldiers, or special missions overseas? I knew that the Dull government has all kinds of operations going on, counterterrorism and that kind of thing, but not that the Confed was so wrapped up in it."

"No one in my family is directly employed by the military divisions," I said. "Although even if they were, they wouldn't have been allowed to mention confidential information to me. But... protecting the country is the main reason people like my dad campaigned for the Unveiling, you know? I realize they all look like jerks from your position, but many of the established mages felt incredibly guilty that they hadn't exerted more influence in the world wars and natural disasters and all sorts of other conflicts. They knew that mages in other countries were starting to reach out to the Dull leaders of factions that oppose us. There were more wars brewing. My dad says at the time it seemed almost everyone had weapons that could destroy entire continents..."

"So the Confed came forward and offered their help," Rocío said. "I've heard that story. I just figured the real reasons were more selfish than that."

I made a face. "For some people they might have been, but

my parents genuinely believe in the cause. And I think the Circle feels we *have* to continue assisting with national security as much as we're able. Really, it's the only activity that lets us keep peace with the magicless. If they felt we were more of a threat to them than a defensive presence... We are more powerful, but there are a lot more of them than there are of us."

"So we're stuck doing their dirty work."

"Until we can shut down all the people scheming to attack us, I suppose so."

"What are you two discussing over here?" Prisha said, strolling over with Judith and Desmond in tow. I took the teasing arch of her eyebrows as a peace offering.

"The same subject as everyone else," I replied more easily than I would have without that gesture, and then to Judith and Desmond, I said, "I take it you two are staying in."

Judith shrugged a tad stiffly. "È tẳn è epì tâs. If this is the way I can contribute as a mage, then that's what I've got to do. I did make it this far, after all." Her mouth slanted into a crooked smile. "My dad would probably like it. He's always said we should be doing more to neutralize hostile mage groups."

"I don't know," Desmond said. "I feel like I've ended up in a movie. If the Confed wants to turn me into a super soldier, who am I to say no?" He didn't sound entirely convinced. I supposed he didn't like his alternatives either.

"What about you?" Judith said, and it occurred to me that I hadn't said it out loud yet. I could still decide anything.

I had decided, though, somewhere during that conversation with Rocío, even if I hadn't spoken the words.

"I'm staying," I said, avoiding Prisha's watchful gaze. "I can't let you bunch have all the fun."

"Group Three, together to the end," Desmond said with a nervous chuckle. "Fantastic!"

Not all of Group Three was here. Lacey was loitering near the doorway. Based on the smudges under her eyes, it appeared she'd slept worse than I had, but her expression was firm and her head high. She caught me considering her, took in the whole group of us, and jerked her eyes away. Did she assume we were purposefully excluding her?

"Let me round up the straggler," I said.

Lacey pretended not to notice me approaching until I was a few feet away, but her shoulders tensed. I halted, drawing up the right words.

"It's a tough decision," I said.

She smiled thinly. "Not really. I can't go home burned out. So I'm staying here."

I can't go home. I'd overheard her saying something like that to herself during one of the earlier tests.

"The guy you were with," I hazarded, recalling our first morning in the courtyard. "He pushed you around a lot, didn't he?"

"A lot of people did," Lacey said. "But when I'm the only one with magic, they won't dare. Not for a second. No one's going to treat me like I'm nothing again."

She stared at me, all defiance, as if she suspected I might try to diminish her.

I shifted back on my heels. "We're all going on too," I said, motioning to the others. "It seemed to work out well before, all of us sticking together."

"Maybe," she said. "Not everyone liked how I cast."

I didn't follow what she meant. Had I missed something when I'd passed out?

"I'm sure we'd be glad to have you on our side all the same," I said.

She didn't answer, but when I turned to head back, she drifted along behind me. I'd scarcely reached the rest of the group when silence snapped through the room.

"The next stage begins now," a piercingly clear voice announced. Examiner Lancaster, her hair glinting silver above her examiner robes, had materialized in the middle of the room. "I assume everyone remaining wishes to be here?"

When no one spoke or moved, she nodded. A door appeared in the wall behind her.

"You will enter the next stage in your original groups," she said. "Group One, come forward."

We *all* moved forward then. Could we catch a glimpse of what lay beyond that door before we had to go through?

Desmond ambled closest, his gaze fixed on the interplay of glowing light and shadow around the door's outline. As the four members of Group One marched over, Callum sauntered past me too, flipping his fork in his hand.

"You said there's no magic allowed before we go in there," he said to Lancaster. "Are there any other rules we're supposed to be following right now?"

The examiner gave him a measured look. "As long as you follow the rules that have been spoken, you'll face no punishment."

He nodded in such a serene manner that my back stiffened. I peered past the first group as they filed through the doorway, but all I made out around them was darkness.

Lancaster paused for a beat after the door closed, and then said, "Group Two."

A boy I didn't know, so bulky with muscle he looked as though he'd barely fit through the doorway, started forward. Callum's sole remaining companion, apparently. My former classmate trailed behind the bulky guy, his narrowed eyes sliding over the gathered crowd. They settled on Desmond, who was still studying the door.

Hades, no. I wasn't certain what I needed to warn Desmond of, only that I needed to. "Des—"

Callum had already lunged, ducking and lashing out with the fork. Desmond didn't catch the movement at his periphery until it was too late. The other boy slammed the metal tines into his calf. They punctured the thin fabric of Desmond's slacks and burrowed into his flesh.

CHAPTER SIXTEEN

Rocío

I threw myself forward, catching Desmond's arm as he stumbled, and Callum pushed away to bolt through the open doorway.

Desmond steadied himself, his lips pressed tight, and glanced down at his leg. The fork protruded from his calf. He braced himself and batted it off him. Blood soaked through his pant leg.

I was about to check the wound when Examiner Lancaster said, without missing a beat, "Group Three." The door that had closed behind Callum opened again.

Desmond limped forward, and the rest of us hurried after him into whatever waited for us in the second-last stage of the Exam.

The moment we stepped through the doorway, all signs of the room behind us vanished. Thick hedges loomed on either side of us and behind, where the door should have been. The dark green brambles climbed nearly ten feet toward the hazy gray sky. A narrow passage stretched out ahead.

We were alone. The door must have taken the other groups someplace else.

"Hold on just a second," Desmond said. He hunkered down on the ground, which was the same gray spongy stuff as the Exam area before.

I knelt beside him.

"Leave it," he said sharply but quietly. "I can handle this, Rocío."

My face heated. He was the one with the most healing practice, after all. I eased back a step. "I'm sorry."

He didn't look at me as he pulled up his pant leg. "Don't treat me like I can't take care myself, all right? I've been hurt worse than this. I get by just as well as any of you."

He murmured a few words over the pricks of red that shone wetly against his dark skin, and the wounds closed over. It didn't look like Callum had stabbed the fork in deep enough to do any major damage.

Desmond straightened up a little tentatively and turned to survey our surroundings. I would have missed the additional subtle rhythm he tapped out on his thigh if I hadn't watched for it. He'd been compensating for his sight all along with no help from me.

"I apologize on behalf of the Manhattan Academy," Finn said. "The Confed should have burned Callum out to begin with."

A lump formed in my throat. "Why would they?" I said. "That kind of guy is what they want here. They want people who can be cutthroat and calculating."

"But working *for* them," Judith said. "You can't be a good soldier unless you can follow orders. He's only looking out for himself."

"He managed to stay inside the rules while he was doing it," Desmond said. He reached toward the hedge and yanked his fingers back with a wince.

I peered at the brambles. They weren't real plant life but barbs of greenish metal, twisted to mimic thorns. A thick coppery smell wafted off of them.

"Well, let's get moving," Prisha said.

There wasn't anything else to do, so we set off down the passage.

"You know, it can't have always been like this," Finn said after a minute. "The Exam, I mean. They tested people before the Unveiling too. There wouldn't have been any magical special ops division back then."

The path widened by a couple feet, and Prisha drew up beside me. "It was convenient," she said with a breeziness that felt forced. "There was a history of letting people opt to be tested rather than go for Dampering. After the Unveiling, it would have been easy to adapt it for a purpose like this."

"I guess they *had* to keep it a secret," Lacey said. "Making people into magical assassins or whatever—that's got to be against some law."

But the Confed did it anyway. Because they wanted to be so involved in responding to threats from other countries? Or, as Finn had suggested, because they were afraid that if they weren't, the Dulls would decide we were too much of a threat to live alongside them?

"I wonder how long they've been using the Exam this way even after the Unveiling," I said. "Was it always like this, starting from when they took over Rikers Island, or did it... I don't know, evolve as things got worse internationally?"

No one answered. None of us knew.

The path split off to the left, a tighter passage rambling away from us. Judith craned her neck to look down it.

"Which way do we go?" she said.

"Let's keep straight," Prisha said. "Follow the main path as long as we can."

"I don't know why the Confed didn't just round up all the bright talents into a special program when we were kids," Desmond remarked. "Call it the School for Gifted Youngsters. I'd have been jumping to sign up."

"They don't want the bright talents," Prisha said. "They send the Champions off into situations where some get killed. And if they were training a whole bunch of kids for years and years, people would start asking questions. It's easier to make the best of what they get when people declare, I'd guess."

The desperate novices, the families who no longer hoped for better, like I'd thought last night.

"They're looking for a lot of *different* talents," Judith put in. "They want people who are strong physically—able to endure a lot. Páthei máthos." Her right hand brushed over her sling. "They want us to be good with offensive and defensive castings."

"Observational skills," Finn added. "The first test. They were checking how alert we are to our surroundings."

"And how well we follow the rules," Desmond said. "You break one, you get burned."

That was what they'd be watching for with me, I guessed. They'd already known I had power, and I'd proven beyond a doubt I could use it destructively. My skin twitched at the memory of smashing through the sentries.

I'd meant what I'd said to Finn at breakfast. I was going to find a way to get us through the rest of this Exam without *any*one getting hurt. The examiners couldn't fault me for that—but they also couldn't think I was any kind of danger to them.

I had to balance the scales after what I'd done to those unknown guards, after I'd let Mark almost die on my watch.

"Hmm," Finn said, and I looked up to see the walls ahead of us had converged into another hedge-like barrier. "It's a hedge maze." He addressed the sky. "This test could do with a little more originality!"

Prisha elbowed him, and he gave her his crooked grin. "Since they didn't supply us with a ball of thread to chart our travels," she said, "we'll have to mark the paths we've tried so we don't go in circles."

We made our way back to the last branch. Prisha tried to etch an X on the ground with a lilted verse, but the gray surface only quivered and stilled, remaining as blank as before. She frowned.

"Maybe you're thinking too small." Lacey rubbed her hands together. "Why are we letting some walls get in our way?"

She rattled off a casting and thrust her hands toward the hedge beside her. A blast of energy, invisible but powerful enough that it crackled in the air, walloped the brambles. They hardly trembled. The metallic smell in the air thickened.

Lacey raised her hands again.

"Stop," I said. "That's enough."

She gave me a flat look. "There's no rule against breaking the walls."

"It's not working," I said with a wave toward the hedge. "Anyway, we shouldn't just... throw magic around trying to destroy things, not like that. We've got to be smart about it."

She didn't answer, just stared back at me. Something about her expression reminded me abruptly of Axton, or like when she'd laughed that first night in the dorm, as if she were a little loca herself.

How many years of intent had she pent up while she tried to avoid provoking him?

A whirring rustle trickled over the top of the hedge, and all our heads jerked up. The sound rose and ebbed, leaving my skin jittering.

"Well, that's not at all ominous," Finn said. "I feel it would be a good idea to keep going. Isn't there some other trick to mazes, like you always turn right and eventually you'll get to the end? Or maybe it's left?"

"Either should work as long as you stick to the same rule," Desmond said.

Prisha nodded. "Then onward!"

Our new path split into three after less than a minute, so we took the left again. After a couple turns, we hit another dead end.

The creepy-crawly sound continued to drift over the walls, and a tremor shook the ground. I braced my feet, trying not to wonder how much it would hurt to fall into the brambles beside me.

Lacey walked a little ahead of me as we hurried on to the next branch. She rubbed her forearm, where her bruises had faded to a faint greenish brown. Finn would have known what to say, how to smooth over the awkwardness I'd created.

I pushed myself faster to catch up. "You've been helping us a lot," I said. "I'm sure the examiners have been impressed." I doubted they'd expected much from her at first glance either.

She lifted her head higher. "It wasn't my idea to come," she said. "But I'm glad I did. I didn't really want to lose my magic. And now I can do this my way."

The ground shuddered again, and Desmond grabbed Judith before she could stumble into the hedge.

"Thanks," she said, looking a bit flushed. Then her brow knit. "This might be a weird question, but does anyone else think the magic feels a little... off?"

When I focused on the hum in the air, I did feel a twitching in it that I hadn't noticed before. Maybe echoing my nerves, twitching with apprehension?

As if noticing me noticing it, the now-familiar presence in the magic slid around me, embracing me gently but firmly.

"I haven't felt anything strange," Finn said, and Prisha shook her head.

"Same as usual to me," Desmond said, looking thoughtful.

The thought of trying to explain the presence and the times it had come to me before made me tense up. I'd be the one sounding loca.

"It's probably just me being oversensitive," Judith said before I could decide whether to mention it. "My teachers were always saying I tune in too close."

"That sounds like it should be a good thing," Desmond said.

"Not so much if any little shift in the energy distracts you from what you're casting," Judith replied.

What I felt was more than just a little shift, though. During that test yesterday, it had been nearly constricting. Surely the examiners wouldn't allow the magic to act like this if it wasn't some type of clue?

Or a trick to distract us from what we really needed to see.

The rustling heightened in pitch with an erratic series of clicks, and the six of us drew closer together without speaking. As we walked on, the ground started to rock, as if the entire maze were being carried on the waves of the ocean.

Maybe it was. We could have walked beyond Rikers Island by now.

We turned another corner, taking another left-hand branch. Lacey drifted to the front of the group again, her arms rigid at her sides. I flexed my shoulders, trying to release the tension building inside me. An eerie creaking rose up, like ice on the verge of cracking. It softened again. Silence fell.

The hedge ahead of us burst open in a shower of shards.

We all ducked backward, our arms flying up to shield our faces. Sharp little shreds of bramble tore at my skin from hand to elbow.

A roar echoed through the maze, and a stench rolled over me, putrid as bagged garbage left to bake in the sun. I stared past my bleeding arm at the mountain of a creature, taller even than the hedges, that was lurching through the opening it had smashed.

In that first glimpse, my eyes caught on heels, wrists, knees, and torsos, all jumbled together in one giant humanoid form. *Was* it just one being, or was it a mass of figures charging through the maze together?

The thing swung to face us. Dios mío, it *was* all one creature. One creature made up of dozens of pieces of others melded together along rippled pink seams. The thing's fingers were twisted legs, its limbs were built out of thighs and shoulders with joints of battered heads. A mishmash of body parts melted into one another across its heaving chest. Its eyes were hands opening and closing as if clapping in a horrible heap of a face. Broken bones protruded like teeth from its raw red "mouth."

Judith screamed, and the magic contracted around me, trembling against my skin with a horror that matched mine. We scrambled backward down the passage.

The thing swiped at Lacey. She leapt out of the way, and its mess of a hand only grazed her hair. My mouth opened, but the words to speak a casting caught in my throat with that stench.

Was that the only option we had? Just smash this thing apart?

The creature bellowed, barreling toward us. The magic clutched me tighter. A lyric slipped from my lips—to push it back, or get it away from us at least. I had to protect *us*, whatever I did.

The magic shuddered with my shove, as if sticking against my intent. The thing hardly stumbled. My gaze fixed on a head with blank staring eyes that looked almost like Mark's, fused into the middle of the creature's nightmarish chest. My breath stuttered. No, no, this was all wrong.

Beside me, other voices were shouting out castings. Lacey glanced back at me. Whatever she saw in me in that instant made her spin back toward the monster with a hoarse chuckle and belt out a lyric. Her voice seared through the air, and the magic rippled with it.

A shudder passed through the creature. Then it split open with a ball of fire that seemed to eat it from the inside out.

Its immense corpse crashed to the ground, flaming. Lacey swiveled back toward us. The emotion in her face, so stark and wild, made my breath stop. She was looking at the rest of us as if we were as much of a threat as the monster she'd just toppled. A threat she meant to destroy.

"Light them up! Light them up!" she hollered, and threw a surge of crackling energy toward us.

CHAPTER SEVENTEEN

Finn

The notion that your life flashed before your eyes right before you died was a total crock. As the conjured wave of electricity blazed through the passage, I understood with complete certainty that it would slaughter us, and in that frozen moment of panic, my vision narrowed down to the most arbitrary detail: Lacey's feet as she darted past the jumbled monster she'd just felled, her bad ankle wobbling. She'd been walking on it all this time, even though it was still sprained. She could have asked Desmond or Rocío—or any of us, honestly—to help with the pain, but she hadn't.

Rocío choked out a casting, and the searing energy slammed into an invisible wall scarcely a foot from my face. The impact was so forceful that even with the protective shield, the air shuddered and walloped me backward. My ears popped. I stumbled and caught my balance, sucking in a breath saturated with the monster's burning stink.

If not for Rocío's wits, we'd all have been fried to a crisp.

"Lacey!" she shouted.

The other girl had already vanished behind the heap of mangled flesh. I didn't think she'd even glanced back to see what damage she'd wrought on us.

Rocío pushed forward through the shield. I snapped out of my shock and dashed after her. As she tried to pick her way between the gigantic corpse and the debris of the shattered hedge, I caught her arm.

"Let her go," I said.

She whirled toward me. "She can't run off *alone*. She won't have anyone to help if... if..."

"I don't think she wants our help," I said. My ears were still ringing. "She tried to kill us, Rocío."

"I said I'd get us all through this."

"You can only protect the people who decide to stay with the group. If it matters so much to her to go it alone, we should let her. What do you expect she'll do to you if you try to stop her?"

Rocío's shoulders sagged. She looked so wretched I wanted to wrap my arms around her, but I didn't know if the gesture would be welcome. I settled for letting my hand drop to hers to squeeze her fingers. She'd said I made getting through this easier for her. Even if I wasn't of much use otherwise, I had to keep giving her that.

"It was my fault," she said. "I should have been more careful how I talked to her. I pushed her away."

"You were right to speak up," Prisha said. "*She* should have been more careful with her castings."

"Why did she attack us?" Judith asked, her voice muffled. She was holding her hand over her face to ward off the monster's stench. Blood dribbled down her forearm from the little scratches from the hedge blast. The sting of my own wounds crept back into my consciousness.

"Who knows what she was thinking?" Prisha said with a briskness that suggested she wasn't merely nervous but outright scared. "I guess she decided she liked Callum's approach. Good riddance, in that case. Now can we get out of here already?"

"It's shrinking," Desmond said abruptly.

All our gazes jerked to the monster's corpse. It was contracting in on itself, the odor fading as we watched. In a matter of seconds, all that remained was a dark stain on the gray ground and the wreckage of the hedge it had smashed through.

Rocío exhaled. "It was just conjured," she said. "I wondered... The parts looked so real."

"Some mage was having too much fun playing Dr. Frankenstein," Desmond said with a grimace. He gestured to the new passage the monster had opened up. "Anything interesting down that other way?"

I peered through the smashed opening. "It looks the same as all the other paths to me."

"It's on the right," Judith said, toeing one of the glossy green shards. "We were keeping to the left. I think we should stick to that. Otherwise we could end up looping around through places we've already been."

"There you go," I said, my hand still clasped around Rocío's. "We have a plan: left to the end. Might I suggest that if anyone else is considering parting ways, they do it now and peacefully? As much as I appreciate the extra challenge."

"I'm good," Desmond said.

Judith laughed. "You know I'm not going anywhere."

Prisha merely snorted.

"It looks as though we're not getting rid of these ones," I said to Rocío.

She didn't smile, but her expression had softened. "All right," she said. "We'll keep moving. But let's heal any injuries as well as we can while we have the time."

She leaned into me, a sudden heat against my chest, letting me take her weight for one brief instant. My pulse skipped with giddiness that was utterly inappropriate for our current circumstances. Then she pulled away. I relinquished her hand.

Desmond murmured a sealing casting over his arms. The scratches transformed into spidery tan lines against the deeper brown skin. He winced as he swiped his hand across them. How deeply had they cut into the muscle? My own scratches prickled pain down through my flesh, stark red against my general paleness.

Desmond turned to Judith. Prisha had managed to attend to her own cuts, though they looked more scabbed than sealed.

Rocío finished healing herself and glanced at me in question.

I loathed having to rely on her or anyone else, but my connection to the whisper of magic around us had worn far too thin. If the others needed me, if one major casting could swing the balance between us surviving and not, then I'd be ready—that was, as long as I didn't freeze up again in the moment when it counted. Otherwise, I refused to turn myself into a liability simply to make a point.

I extended my arm to Rocío. "Just enough to stop the bleeding," I said. "That's all that matters. Anything else can wait. And thank you."

We walked on as a group, our ears perked and eyes wary. Rocío's casting tingled over my forearm. As we took another left, she let go of my wrist. Her head lifted and her forehead furrowed.

"What is it?" I said.

"Judith was right," she said. "There was something strange about the magic before that... thing appeared. The energy felt too tense and scattered to hold a casting easily." She paused. "But now it's calmed down. It feels steady again. I don't know what's affecting it."

I didn't want to admit that the quiver of magic felt the same to me as it always did, like a distant breeze. "The shifts might give us some warning next time."

She nodded, still pensive.

The skittering sounds that had dogged us earlier rose again. The back of my neck itched. Was another of those monsters stalking us? Nil admirari. Whatever came, we had to be more prepared this time.

Lacey's fire had dispatched the last creature well. I sorted through the lines I had memorized that referred to flames and burning.

If Rocío could cast with childhood songs, and the other new-magic examinees drew on everything from rap to rock, I didn't need to stick to the classics the Academy had drilled into us, did I? Maybe I'd connect to the magic better using a language that came more naturally to mind.

The first song that popped into my head was a Christmas carol about roasting chestnuts. Hmmm. That wasn't quite the tone I required.

Judith was humming quietly to herself, a tune that I thought I'd heard her fall into before. "What song is that?" I asked when she stopped.

Her cheeks pinked as if she hadn't realized anyone would notice. "It's just from a movie I liked a lot as a kid," she said. "The words are in Mandarin, but there's a line about 'staying strong as woven threads.' It helps me focus."

The path took another turn then, and we found ourselves faced with a wall of hedge broken only by a round opening so small we'd have to crawl to enter it. Inside, the sharp barbs of the "thorns" had fused together to form a smooth surface.

"They probably wouldn't have included a tunnel if they didn't want us to go through," Prisha said.

"It could be a trap," Judith said, pulling her sling closer to her chest.

"I'd bet good money it is," I said. "Any thoughts on the least potentially painful method of springing it?"

There was no satisfactory answer to that question. We couldn't know how to avoid trouble when we had no idea what the examiners might want to test us for next.

"We'll go through one at a time," Rocío said. "I'll go first, with a shield in case I set anything off. All right?"

The urge to volunteer myself in her place filled me, but I caught the words before I said them. The unavoidable truth was that I stood a much higher chance of getting us all killed than she did. I settled for saying, "Be careful, Dragon-Tamer."

She gifted me with a flicker of a smile before crouching down and crawling into the tunnel.

We stood waiting with the skittering sound carrying around us. Judith hugged herself. The ground jiggled under our feet, and I teetered.

When the tremor stilled, I leaned toward the opening. Shadows draped the other end of the tunnel. There was no sign of Rocío. I cleared my throat. "Rocío?"

"Maybe there's a 'chantment muting sound from the other side," Prisha said.

In that case, anything at all could be transpiring over there. Dread trickled through my chest.

Before any of the others could speak up, I hunched down and crawled in. The roasting-chestnuts tune hovered on my tongue. The tunnel's floor was slick and cool under my hands and knees. I scuttled through and out into the darkness at its end.

In the hazy space into which I emerged, the shadows twisted close around me like echoes of the hedge's thorns. They didn't touch me, but they were so thick my hands vanished into their depths when I reached in front of me. I could scarcely see a foot in any direction.

"Rocío?" I said. "Anyone? Can you hear me?"

I turned back to the tunnel, planning to stay near it until the others arrived, but the brambly shadows had swallowed the opening up too. They swayed as if in a low wind.

I took a tentative step out into the space, and another, wading through the shadows, but no wall met my outstretched hands. This space was bigger than the passage I'd left.

Several more steps got me nowhere. I swiveled, trying an alternate angle. There was nothing but shadows as far as I walked that way too. A cold sweat formed on my skin.

"Rocío! Prisha! Hello?" I yelled. The shadows brushed my mouth and coated it with a mildew flavor.

I spun around again, and this time the darkness parted in front of me. I perceived a figure up ahead, her back to me, light brown hair spilling past her shoulders. She was too fair to be any of the other girls in our group but Lacey, only Lacey was waifish and this girl was tall and large-boned. I eased toward her cautiously. The shadows pulled farther back, and she turned to face me.

It was Margo. She stood with her blue eyes fixed on me, her bangs rumpled and the tails of a characteristic fitted plaid shirt hanging loose over her jeans.

"Finn," she said in a voice raw as if from crying.

O Hades, what had the examiners brought on us now? I'd only heard my sister sound that wretched once or twice before, when I'd been a kid and she a teenager.

"What are you doing here?" I said.

"You can't be Champion," she said. "I came to tell you to stop. Say you're done with this. Say you don't want it anymore."

She reached into the shadows and broke off a piece that turned solid in her fingers. Her freckled hand clutched the dark green thorn, which curved dagger-sharp.

Was this real or just an illusion? I wasn't certain the examiners would have gone to the hassle of bringing Margo here to confront me, and I couldn't imagine my sister turning that makeshift knife on me.

"I'm not going to stop," I said. "I'm seeing the Exam through to the end, or at least as far as I can get."

"Please," she said, and raised the thorn-dagger.

I braced myself, ready to dodge. Whether she was real or not was of no consequence; the examiners' conjurings could deal plenty of damage.

She didn't strike out at me, though. She pressed the tip of the thorn to her cheek.

"Margo!" I cried out, and leapt at her, but she slipped backward, just beyond my reach. Her hand dragged the sharpened edge down, splitting her skin from cheekbone to jaw.

Blood bubbled in a stream down her face and neck, soaking into her shirt. The wound gaped angrily when she opened her mouth. My stomach lurched.

"Stop," she said. "You're forcing me to do this. I can't stop until you stop. Please."

It wasn't her, I told myself, my heart hammering. It couldn't be her. The examiners wouldn't dare 'chant a real Lockwood into carving herself up. My family's outcry, the Circle's backlash, would ruin every mage on the Exam committee.

Nevertheless, a cold wave of nausea washed over me when the fake Margo set the knife against her other cheek.

"This is just a trick!" I shouted as she etched a matching red line through her skin. "Do whatever you want. I'm not quitting!"

Please believe me. Please let this end before I change my mind.

Margo brought the thorn-dagger to her sternum above the open neck of her shirt. "Please," she said, sounding even more desolate than before. "It hurts. I don't want to do this. Please let the Exam go so they'll let me go too."

I clamped my mouth shut against the nausea still surging

inside me. Then she plunged the blade into her chest just below her collarbone.

I turned away, unable to bear the sight, but I heard it. I heard the wet rattle of her breath around a moan, the rasp of metal against bone, the patter of blood spilling onto the ground. Acid seared up my throat.

"My heart," she said in a gurgle of a voice. "I have to cut out my heart to make you see."

"No!" I protested, and staggered away from her into the shadows.

I made it several steps before knifing over. The remains of my breakfast spattered from my mouth.

I couldn't hear my sister anymore. Tentatively, one hand on my gut, I swiped at my chin and straightened up.

The shadowy brambles had converged around me. There was no sign of Margo.

There was still no sign of any escape either.

All of this was just an illusion—even the shadows. I might be wandering in circles on one of those paths between the hedges, oblivious to everything real around me.

I wobbled on. After another few steps, Prisha's purple blouse shone out brightly between the shadows ahead of me.

Thank the Fates! I hurried toward her.

"Pree!"

She swiveled to reveal a length of vine coiled around her neck.

"Finn," she croaked. "Please. They said if you forfeit now, they'll let me go."

I didn't have the chance to respond this time. I'd emitted no more than a strangled noise when the end of the vine wrenched up into the great wall of shadows above us, yanking Prisha's body with it. Her chin snapped up; her limbs flailed.

"No!" I snatched at her, and Rocío shoved between us. She

held a thorn as long and narrow as an ice pick. I froze as she stabbed it into her abdomen. A red circle of blood bloomed on her shirt. She jerked the thorn out with a pained grunt.

"Leave the Exam," she said in a whimper. "Please, Finn."

I sprang after her, after Prisha, but an invisible force tugged them just beyond my frantic hands. I lunged again, faster, to no avail. My breath rattled in my chest.

I had no guarantee *they* were illusions. They'd been in the maze. I didn't doubt for an instant that the examiners would manipulate those of us in here however they pleased. No one questioned the deaths reported from the Exam.

"Stop it!" I pleaded.

"I can't unless you give up," Rocío said.

Prisha clawed at her noose with a gurgle that made me want to vomit all over again. Rocío rammed the pick into her side a few inches above the first wound. Her shoulders buckled, but she lifted the thorn again, higher.

If it was them, if the examiners were compelling them, I couldn't conceive of the agony they were in.

I couldn't let this horror continue. I couldn't take the chance. "Okay," I said. "Okay! I—"

The acquiescence caught in my throat as my gaze snagged on Rocío's sunburst charm—on every perfect point around its untarnished circle.

It wasn't her. The real Rocío's necklace had been warped by the sentries' assault yesterday.

The examiners must have missed that detail. I might have too, if she hadn't been drawing so much of my attention. These were illusions after all, as Margo had been.

I covered my face with my hands, fighting to steady my breath through the fleshy smack of Rocío driving in the pick, through Prisha's gasps. Then, queasy but with my jaw set tight, I drew myself up and strode forward with firm but unhurried strides.

The illusions didn't pull away this time. As I made to march between them, they dispelled into the shadows as if they'd never existed. I wiped the sweat from my brow and forced myself to keep walking.

Please, O gods of Olympus, let that be the last of it. If there was a Tartarus, it had nothing on this place.

I tensed up at the sight of another figure ahead of me. The shadows crept back, withdrawing into the more solid brambles of familiar hedges on either side of me, where they'd been all along, undoubtedly.

Desmond—the real Desmond—startled at the rasp of my footsteps. His intent yet distant gaze tripped over me. He relaxed and offered me a tip of his head.

He'd escaped ahead of me even though I'd gone in earlier. Had his limited vision made seeing through the illusions easier?

I halted beside him and glanced back the way I'd come. Roiling shadows choked the other end of the path.

"Just us, so far?" I asked.

"I haven't seen anyone," Desmond said. "I mean, no one real."

The hollowness of his voice, the way it broke on the last word, told me more than any description could have. Whatever he'd faced, it had cost him.

"I thought I should wait for the rest of you," he added. "Or... however many make it out."

I crossed my arms, attempting not to consider how close I'd come to *not* making it. "Of course," I said. "We'll wait."

Rocío had entered ahead of all of us. What did it mean that even she hadn't emerged yet?

CHAPTER EIGHTEEN

Rocío

T he shadows that had grown out of the hedges stretched on and on until I started to think I might end up crossing all of Manhattan before I found my way out. The slow but unsteady rhythm of my pulse kept time with my steps.

It hadn't been hard to figure out that the people the examiners had shown me here were conjured. The friends and families of kids who went into the Exam never just disappeared. My parents were probably working right now, worrying about me but completely safe. Abuelito and Abuelita might be taking their midday stroll through Prospect Park. And there was no way the Confed was going to sacrifice a prominent old-magic examinee like Finn just to test a gutter-girl.

It had still been painful watching those illusions torture themselves and hearing their pleas. I had a feeling I'd be seeing those images all over again the next time I tried to sleep. Maybe for the rest of my life.

I paused to look around, rubbing my arms. Was that part of the test done, and now I just had to find my way out?

Then a tall trim figure ambled out of the darkness toward me. My heart stopped.

Javi halted a couple feet away, his hands slung in his pockets in a familiar pose. His dark hair hung in the same shaggy hairstyle he'd always liked. But he looked different too. A shadow darkened the bronze skin along his jaw, as if he'd missed a morning shave and was now growing enough of a beard for that to matter. His lips were chapped and his cheeks slightly sunken in a way that reminded me of Sean.

And his eyes. Those deep brown eyes, holding mine, contained more helplessness and loss than I'd ever seen in the brother I'd known—from before the Exam.

He looked *older*. A chill raced down my back. He looked as if he'd really aged three years, as if he were a young man of nineteen standing before me.

I hadn't believed the examiners would have taken my parents or grandparents or that they'd hurt Finn, but I could accept, without hesitation, that they might have kept Javi from us all this time, held him for some purpose or another.

He didn't appear to be carrying any weapon. That was different from the others too.

"Ro," he said in a croak of a voice. In Javi's voice, echoing through my memories. "Ro, I want to come home."

A lump rose in my throat, but I managed to speak. "I want you to come home too. Are you— Is this really you, Javi?"

He frowned. "Don't you know me? Is three years all it takes to forget?"

"I never forgot *anything*," I said, tearing up.

"They said if you'd come with me, I could finally go home. We can go. Right now. They promised me."

Oh. Of course. The examiners had made this step in the test about a completely different kind of hurting. "I'd have to leave the Exam?"

"What does the Exam matter if we have each other again?" he asked.

The magic mattered. He'd only come here so I could keep my talent. He might have sacrificed even more for that than I had.

"And if I don't leave now?"

His expression turned so puzzled it wrenched at me. "Then I'm stuck here," he said, "for whatever other uses those cabrones decide to put me to. Rocío, please. You have no idea. The last three years..." He dragged in a breath, the way he always had when he'd been trying to avoid saying something he knew would upset me. "Don't make me go back to that. Let's leave. Please."

A small portion of awe tickled through me even as I shuddered. The skill it must have taken to conjure such a perfect replica... The examiners were so horribly, magnificently cruel.

Or he might be real. Could the Confed have broken Javi, reduced him to a boy who wanted nothing but to go home? Part of me even wanted to believe that, if that was the only way he could still be alive.

I closed my eyes, and a different memory swam up. Finn's crooked smile, the teasing lilt of his voice, the squeeze of his hand around mine. And Prisha and Desmond and Judith, standing around us, agreeing that we'd all go on together.

I'd promised I'd be there for *them*. I'd committed to seeing all five of us through this maze and through the rest of the Exam unharmed.

The Javi I grew up with, the Javi I'd made other promises to, had wanted me to get into the Confed's college no matter what. He'd risked his life for that. A ripping sensation ran through my gut as I made my decision, but I couldn't betray that Javi or the four other lives that might depend on me.

I forced myself to meet his gaze again. "I have to keep going. I'm sorry, but I need to. But I *will* make Champion, for you. And then, if you're here, I'll get you out. Te doy mi palabra." I ducked my head and hurried past him. "I'm sorry."

"Rocío!" Javi called after me. "If we don't go now, they'll never let you see me again! They'll say this was all a trick. Please, don't leave me. This is all your fault!"

I almost stopped, almost turned back. Then I gritted my teeth.

Yes, it was my fault. And it would be my fault too if I gave up and if everything Javi had been through before was for nothing.

My eyes were so watery I didn't notice the shadows had faded until someone called my name. Finn ran to me, reaching for my hand. My last thread of self-control snapped. I clutched his shirt and pressed my forehead to his chest, holding on as tight as I could as I choked on the air.

"Hey," he said gently. "Hey." His arms circled me with warmth. Even after three days, his shirt held a lingering sweetness —some fancy fabric softener, I guessed. Breathing it in, feeling his solid body against mine, pulled me away from the memory of Javi. But not completely.

"It's over now," Finn said. "It's finished."

"They took my brother," I said.

"It wasn't real. None of it was real." A quaver ran through his voice, and I wondered what he'd been through.

He didn't know what I meant. How could he? I hadn't told any of them. I'd hidden that truth all this time, and I didn't even know why.

"No." I swiped at my tears. "They really did. He died here three years ago." Saying it made my eyes heat up again.

Finn's arms tightened around me. He bent his head close to mine, his breath tickling over my hair. "Then they can't do him any more harm," he said quietly. "Whatever they showed you, it means nothing. They can't touch who he truly was. They can't touch anything that's in our heads and our hearts, not if we don't let them."

Those last words rang with anger. I eased back far enough to look at him properly. He stared at me with a strange intensity, and then he jerked his gaze away, a blush staining his pale cheeks.

Oh. I shouldn't have been surprised—I'd seen him, hadn't I? —but a flutter passed through me all the same. "They showed you me?"

"Yeah," he said.

The examiners had thought I was important enough to Finn that out of everyone he'd ever known, they'd used me to get at him. And they'd been right to, from the way he'd been looking at me a moment ago.

"But I knew it wasn't you," he added, meeting my eyes again with a smile more like the cheerful boy I was used to. "It'd take more mages than they have on staff to make a facsimile that lives up to the real thing."

My lips twitched upward even though my throat was still tight. I wanted to tell him that I'd seen him too, but just then someone else came swaying out of the shadows at the other end of the path.

Prisha was wiping her eyes with short, brisk motions, more like she was trying to get dust out than to dry tears, but it was obvious from the wobble of her jaw that she'd been crying. She combed her fingers back through the dark waves of her hair as she came to a stop. That was the first time I noticed Desmond was there too, hanging back from my little moment with Finn.

Finn's smile had fallen. He hurried over to her. "Pree, are you all right?"

She nodded. "I'll live."

He must have recognized something in her bearing, because he set his hand on her shoulder, leaned in, and said, "You know if your brothers and sister were here, they'd be taking bets on which one caused you the longest hesitation."

A startled laugh burst out of Prisha, and Finn grinned, if a little grimly. As I watched him, any part of me that might have been uneasy about how I'd clung to him disintegrated.

He liked being there for people. He was good at it—because he actually cared.

He cared about me. For the first time, I let that knowledge sink in without any *buts* about his family, his background, his prospects in contrast with mine. The truth of it wrapped around me the way his arms had just a moment ago.

Desmond stirred. "Not that I'm suggesting we take off right now," he said, "but how long do you think we should give Judith?"

He spoke from an understanding I suspected we all shared: Judith was the one least likely to make it out. She'd been on the verge of giving up before, and this time none of us had been with her to talk her through it. The muscles in my legs tensed with the urge to walk back into those shadows to search for her. I would have if I'd thought there were any chance the examiners would let me find her.

"What order did the rest of you go in?" I asked.

"Finn, then Desmond, and then Judith," Prisha said. "I went last."

"Then she hasn't been in there *that* long," I said. "We—"

Footsteps padded over the spongy ground, and the girl in question marched out of the thicket of shadows, her face tight and drained of color.

She was clutching her pearl-handled knife at her side. The thin blade was streaked red. Her other hand, bound to her by the sling, dripped blood onto her shirt. She looked at each of us defiantly, a wet gleam in her eyes.

"I'm here. I made it." Her gaze shifted to Desmond, and her mouth twisted. "I made more work for you. Sorry."

Desmond had already started forward. As he touched her broken arm gingerly, the rest of us gathered around her.

"What happened?" I asked.

She hesitated. None of us had mentioned what we'd seen in the shadows, only *who*. It had seemed better to leave those awful images unspoken.

Judith must have felt the same way. "I almost told them to take me out," she said. "I almost did, but I was trying— I bumped my arm." She nodded to the sling. "And it hurt. And then... the people wavered a little. I could tell they were only conjured. Just for a second. So I used that. The pain helped. My arm was still partly numbed, though, so I needed more."

Her fingers clenched around the palm Desmond had just sealed. She wiped the knife on her jeans and folded it back into the base. Her knuckles were white.

"I guess I cheated," she added. "I wasn't really strong enough."

"You made it out," I said. "That's all that matters."

"They're not just testing us for magic," Finn put in. "You said that. You showed them... that you could pay attention to what worked. You figured out how to use the tools you had. That's valuable too."

"Well, now that we're all out, let's get going," Prisha said. "I'm ready to be done with this place."

Desmond made a face. "I think we've got a long way to go still."

As we headed onward, the hedges around us revealed nothing except the vague impression of a sky above. The crawling noises had stopped, and the ground stayed still. I'd have appreciated that change if the silence hadn't felt even more ominous now.

"Do you think Lacey made it through those shadows?" Judith said.

"I've gotten the impression there are a lot of people in her life she'd be *happy* to see get hurt as payback," Prisha said dryly.

"Those aren't the people the examiners would have shown her," I said. What kind of torture had they conjured up for her?

Judith shivered. "It's *sick*," she said. She left it at that so long I thought she was done. Then she blurted out, "There are countries where they don't go in for Dampering, you know. A few of them. Places where everyone just keeps the abilities they have. No big tests so you have to fight to stay a mage."

"I've heard that's only in places where they hardly have any magical culture to begin with," Prisha said.

"Maybe," Judith said. "But I heard people talking a couple times at the embassy functions with my dad. They'd say that Dampering isn't really about protecting us or maintaining the peace. That it's just about the leaderships keeping control, pushing us around. I thought they just didn't understand. But there's no *reason* to put people through something like... like that back there. There's no reason to make everything so *horrible* just to see..."

Her voice had gone ragged. She swiped her hand across her mouth. "Maybe they were right," she said. "The people who criticized the Confed and the other coalitions like it. Everything the examiners are doing to us, it gets worse and worse. Is this really just a test? Or are they trying to get 'payback' from us because we didn't go along with being Dampered the way they wanted?"

A prickle ran over my skin. The examiners might be listening to her saying these things right now. "The job they want the Champions to do could be as bad as this," I said, hating that I was defending the Confed when I agreed with everything she said. "It does make sense that they'd want to watch us and see how far they can push us, *right?*"

Say "That's true." Take back what you said, Judith. Just for now, just out loud. Remember where we are.

But Judith was shaking her head. "That's part of the problem," she said. "Even if we 'win,' we don't get any more choice than if we'd let ourselves be Dampered. We get less! At least if we were Dampered, we'd be able to pick something to do with the magic we had left. We'd have options. Options that don't involve killing people or risk being killed. Even if they need people to fight, even if there are huge threats we have to worry about... I *hate* them."

Before any of us could figure out how to answer that, we turned a corner and found ourselves facing a wide space in the middle of the maze. It was divided into five lanes, each separated by hedges only a couple of feet high. Beyond the lanes, the taller hedges converged into another narrow path.

"I've got a bad feeling about this," Desmond said.

"You don't imagine they're generously offering us a little breathing room?" Finn said, his eyes fixed on the lanes.

"Well, we have to go through it either way," Prisha said.

We filed in tentatively. I'd only taken one step into the wider space when a 'chantment caught me. The unseen force tugged me to the right. I tried to pull against it, but my legs jarred.

My feet locked in place in front of one of the lanes. When I tried to lift my sneakers, they resisted. Judith had come to a halt at my right, Prisha at my left.

"What—" My voice died as five figures slipped into the room from the narrow passage across from us.

I stiffened automatically, but the two men and three women who spread out opposite us didn't look the slightest bit threatening. They were all adults, not fellow examinees: one quite young, one who looked as old as my abuela, the others somewhere in between. The only thing odd about them was that they all looked panicked, and all wore pale blue tunics that ended around their knees.

Hospital gowns. They had on hospital gowns.

The woman directly across from me stood with an artificially straight posture. Her chubby arms hugged her torso, and her eyes were stark with terror within their frame of chestnut curls. She was trembling.

A light flared into being on her chest and those of the other four at the same time: an angry scarlet light that seemed to churn as it pulsed. Like the pulsing lights on the sentries in what we hadn't known was Iran. A vise squeezed around my heart.

No.

The presence in the magic condensed around me with an iron grip, digging into my scalp and shoulders. I winced. This time I wasn't surprised to feel it. The magic always contracted like this when something or someone was going to die, as if it wanted to resist as much as I did.

A low female voice began speaking, seemingly from right in front of us. "Each of the people you see before you carries a detonation 'chantment," it said with clinical calmness. "If they reach your end of the room, it will explode with enough force to kill you, them, and all your companions. But it is tied to the host's life. Strike them where the light pulses, and they will die. Then the 'chantment will dissolve."

As the last word faded in the air, the figures in the hospital gowns moved. They slid slowly but steadily toward us as if on invisible conveyer belts, their feet coasting across the smooth ground. The red lights on their chests blazed brighter.

"No!" I said, out loud this time. The woman in my lane flailed as if trying to reel backward, but her legs were locked in place like mine. She gasped.

Where had she come from? How had the Confed just... taken her for this horrific purpose?

Or maybe she and the others weren't real at all. They could be more illusions.

She didn't feel like an illusion, though. There was a quality to her, like the sentries in yesterday's test, that I only now realized had been missing from the conjured figures in the shadows. A subtle irregularity to her movements that no automation could quite duplicate. And why wouldn't the examiners want to see if we could kill real people when the targets actually looked human?

I couldn't do it. They'd made me a murderer unknowingly, but I *couldn't* strike down another human being. A human being who was looking me in the face, unarmed and petrified. ¡Ni madres!

She swayed closer. The scarlet light of the detonation 'chantment pulsed harsher. But murdering her couldn't be the only answer.

My tongue tripped. "Cuando tienen frío," I sang out, to cool and to calm. I propelled the energy through the shivering clench of magic around me and into the woman.

The light didn't dim. Her forward motion didn't slow. Not good enough.

I snapped out a line that should have frozen her in place, but the magic pressing her forward tore through my intent, leaving my chest aching from the effort. She inched another foot closer, and another. Halfway to me. Tears trickled from her eyes.

I was vaguely aware of Judith beside me, her breath stuttering as she tried to hum, voice breaking when she tried to cast, and of Prisha muttering to herself. But they felt far, far away from the woman who slid closer to me with every thud of my pulse—far from the red light glaring at me from her chest. I wanted to glance toward Finn, to see how he was coping, but I didn't dare shift my focus from my intended victim.

"Please don't," the woman whimpered. "Please. Help me."

I rolled out another line and another—to unwind, to disperse, anything I could think of that might defuse the bomb within her or release her from the pull toward me. Nothing sank in. Every effort wisped away as if I were a toddler attempting my first castings. I scrambled for something else to try, fighting the rising mass of panic inside me. Fifteen seconds, maybe twenty, before she'd reach me.

I couldn't let that happen. I couldn't kill her. Please, God, if I never conjured up a vision of beauty for Dulls again, lend me the art to save this one woman.

"Help me!" the woman wailed. She leaned away from me, but only a couple feet remained between us now. There was a thump somewhere down the line. A choked gasp. My stomach tightened into a ball as I threw out one more verse.

The 'chantment on the woman didn't so much as waver. The squeeze of the magic around me jittered.

I pushed my awareness through those tremors toward the scorching hot threads of the 'chantment. There. I could hearken it, the rhythm of it. I sucked in a breath. Maybe I could unravel it if I just—

Prisha's voice rang in my left ear, shouting a line in Greek.

A gleaming bolt hit the woman where the detonation 'chantment glowed. Instantly, she seized up. Her limbs went rigid and her eyes rolled. The red light blinked out. I knew she was dead before she hit the ground at my feet.

I whirled around, my vision blurring. Prisha stood beside me like before, her mouth terse but her eyes wide. Another body sprawled between the low hedges in front of her, just a few paces away. Maybe she'd also tried to find another solution before following the examiner's instructions, but—

"Why did you *do* that?" I said. "I was going to— I could have—"

"You were going to get us all killed," Prisha broke in. "Didn't you listen to the instructions? Another few seconds and that woman would have blown *all* of us up. If you want to commit suicide, do it some way that doesn't take the rest of us down with you."

"You killed her," I said.

"She was already dead from the moment the examiners put that 'chantment on her. *They* killed her. I just made sure she didn't kill anyone else in the process." Her voice was harsh, but she couldn't quite control the tremor in it. How much was she justifying the action to me and how much to herself?

A sob burst out behind me. Judith was crouched on the ground, her face pressed to her knees. The man she'd killed slumped just beyond her. Her pearl-handled knife lay beside him, not even unfolded. She'd jabbed him in the chest with that, I thought distantly. She hadn't been able to pull a casting together, so she'd struck the pulsing light whatever way she could. A tap with the handle had been enough.

Past Prisha, two other bodies in hospital gowns sprawled limply. Desmond had sat down at the end of his lane, his head bowed. Finn had turned toward the hedge behind us with his hands clenched tight and his face ashen. His throat worked. Then he pushed himself away, spinning toward us.

"Pree," he began, so rough and wretched it broke my heart.

"I had a little more time," I said. This was my fight, not his. "I might have found a way to defuse it. I almost did."

"And if you hadn't?" Prisha said. "You were cutting it too close. You didn't have the guts to do it. You would have let us all die."

"I don't want *anyone* to die!" I protested.

But that wasn't all there was to it, was there? I hadn't wanted to be a killer. So now someone else was two times over.

"Then you shouldn't have come into the Exam," Prisha snapped.

Finn grasped her shoulder. "Pree, I'm sure Rocío would have done what she had to in the end, if it came to that. But it's done now anyway."

"Because *I* did it!" Prisha said. She looked from my strained face to Finn's sickly one and let out a strangled sound. "I need a minute. I need... I just need a minute." She whirled and stalked off down the path we'd emerged from.

"I—I'm sorry," I said to Finn, not totally sure what I was apologizing for. For not coming up with a better answer in time? For not killing that poor woman?

Maybe I *wouldn't* have acted in time if my last try had failed. Maybe I'd have resisted the role the examiners were forcing me into so stubbornly that I'd have lost the last second and become a murderer in a totally different way. I swallowed hard. There were no easy answers here.

"I know," Finn said softly. His hand grasped at vacant air. He stared after Prisha. "She shouldn't be off on her own. I'll—I'll get her."

He propelled himself away from the rest of us and hurried down the passage after her.

CHAPTER NINETEEN

Finn

There were some matters in life no person should ever have to question, such as: Would you have received utterly different grades if the teachers hadn't known who your family was? Had your best friend only pretended to respect you to spare your feelings?

Did you have the capacity to kill an innocent human being?

Even as I hurried after Prisha, my mind remained stuck. Nothing shifted in my head except a single gear spinning and spinning without catching on anything. I barely felt my body other than the cramping of my gut with each thud of my feet.

He'd looked so distraught, the man. The man I'd had to— So bewildered. From the moment that cool voice had recited our instructions, I'd known no casting I could produce would undo the ones the examiners had set. I'd scarcely had the strength to pick apart my own on the radio.

I'd still tried. I'd tried with shaking voice and shakier hands while the man's skin turned waxier and his eyes bulged with fear, until I'd given in.

I'd let myself look at nothing but that burning red light as I tossed the slightest conjuring at it, and just like that, he'd fallen—fallen and lain there, sprawled, not absorbing into the floor as the creature before had.

He'd been real. He'd been alive.

And then not.

My stomach flipped again, but there was nothing left for me to vomit. I'd already emptied what little remained in it as I'd retched and spat at the base of the hedge right after.

Think about Prisha. Think only of finding her and bringing her back to the group, so we can go on, so we can escape this place—so we can be *finished*, Fates willing.

I heard her before I saw her. Her voice, so low and thready I couldn't make out the words, traveled from around the first bend in the passage. I assumed she was murmuring to herself. It was only as I came around the corner that the sounds composed themselves into sentences.

"...isn't anything else I can tell you. Answer me! I—"

My legs stalled. Prisha cut herself off, and her hand jerked away from her mouth. We stared at each other. The gear in my head spun and spun and—

"Who were you talking to?"

Prisha straightened up. Her cheeks were dry but the rims of her eyes red. "No one. I was just thinking out loud." She kept her gaze a hair averted.

My hands balled. "You were asking someone to answer you—"

A tremor tossed the ground beneath us. I stumbled to the side and threw myself down to avoid crashing into the serrated hedge wall. Prisha dropped to her knees next to me. The ground pitched and rumbled, and a crackling sound tore through the air ahead of us. Where Rocío and the others were waiting.

Before the ground had fully stilled, I scrambled up. I delayed only long enough to help Prisha to her feet, and then I ran for the killing lanes.

I halted partway down the path. The wider space and the lanes were gone. Nothing remained in front of us but a straight, narrow path stretching off into the near distance. The hedges had shifted, cutting us off from the rest of the group.

"Rocío?" I shouted. "Desmond? Judith?"

My voice bounced thinly off the glossy thorns. No one replied. Either they couldn't hear us, or they could but were incapable of answering.

"If they're still around, we're not going to get back to them standing here," Prisha said. "Come on. We should keep moving."

"We can't just— We don't even know what happened to them!" I said.

"And we can't chop through that hedge to find out," Prisha said. "Look, everything—*everything*—the examiners have done to us…" Her voice quavered, and she paused to swallow audibly. "They wouldn't just wipe out three of us in a snap. That wouldn't test anything. So the others have got to be here somewhere. We'll just— Judith and Rocío were on the right side of the room, weren't they? So we'll take every right turn. And Judith will insist on taking the lefts. If the paths connect again, we'll find them."

I despised all the uncertainties in that plan. We didn't know that Rocío and Judith had stayed where they'd been in the minute or two after I'd departed. We didn't know where Desmond might have been. We didn't know any of them could even walk right now.

Nonetheless, it was something—something my mind could latch on to apart from the memories I'd already relived too many times.

If Rocío *could* go forward, she would.

"Finn?" Prisha's expression was wary.

My thoughts shot back to the moment when I'd discovered her, the questions she hadn't yet answered.

"We'll talk," she said. "But not now, okay? Let's just— One thing at a time. We find the others first. All right?"

It wasn't all right. Nothing that had transpired in the last half hour was remotely all right. The burn of stomach acid lingered on my tongue—the tongue that had cast the conjuring to…

I pressed my hand to my face. Breathe in. Breathe out. Take it one step at a time. Get through this.

We had to get back to the others. I'd already wasted too much time standing there.

"All right," I said.

We started forward, Prisha keeping close to my side. "It wasn't your fault," she said. "You had to do it. We all had to do it. It's what the examiners wanted."

"I had a choice… I *made* a choice."

"They're the ones who gave us those choices. Your only other option was letting all of us die."

I'd almost forgotten she'd made the same choice twice over. I glanced sideways at her. Her jaw was clenched.

It felt imperative to say this much: "I don't blame you for what you did. With Rocío. I don't think she'd have let us be hurt, but I understand why you stepped in. I—I'm sorry you felt you had to."

"*You* shouldn't be apologizing for that," she muttered, but her shoulders eased down a fraction.

The path turned, forcing us to the left. We walked on. Several minutes later, it split in two, and we took the right branch as we'd agreed.

A voice carried to my ears—faint, but it sounded like Rocío's. My spirits leapt. I made to dash forward, and Prisha grabbed my arm.

"Wait!" she said. "There's... I think there's a 'chantment on the path."

I studied the stretch of gray ground and dark green hedges before us, which looked no different from the paths we'd encountered before. The magic whispered around me in the same faint harmony. I'd never been able to hearken subtler castings, but then, neither had Prisha.

"What?" I said. "Why?"

"It's just a feeling," Prisha said. "Let's go back and take the other branch."

"Our plan was to stay to the right. We could lose the others completely."

"Will you just trust me on this?"

If it had been the first day of the Exam, I would have immediately said yes. It wasn't, though, and Prisha had been behaving rather strangely for longer than I'd wanted to admit. I'd put her pushiness and odd moods down to stress, but suddenly I wasn't so sure.

Prisha grimaced at my hesitation. "Look," she said. "I'll test it out, and we'll see."

She murmured to her hand and conjured a wooden ball. It looked too small to be sure of triggering any possible trap, but she lobbed it down the path as if she knew precisely where it needed to strike.

The ball bounced twice on the rubbery ground and then hit a patch where it stuck. The gray surface rippled around it, swallowing it down.

"See?" Prisha said. "Now let's go."

No mark remained on the ground where the ball had disappeared, not even a dimple—nothing at all to indicate where the sinkhole began or ended or that it existed at all.

A prickle ran down my spine. "Prisha, how did you know?"

"The floor just felt off. Can we go now? I thought you were in a hurry to find the others."

I was, but I couldn't let this subject drop.

Prisha hadn't merely prodded us onward at each new challenge with increasing insistence, had she? She'd never appeared all that fazed by the tests. She'd taken each of them in stride... as if she'd had some prior knowledge. She'd *defended* the examiners when the rest of us had complained.

The words spilled out of me before the revelation had even quite dawned. "You've been talking to them. The examiners have been telling you things, letting you know what to watch for? How—"

"You don't want to know," she broke in. "I promise you, Finn, you don't. Can you please just drop it?"

My thoughts were already whirling too fast. She'd slipped apart from the rest of us last night before I'd found her in the hall. Had she gone to consult with the examiners? She'd ducked away right before the Iran test too. To grab a bottle of water, she'd said, but she'd taken at least a couple minutes coming back.

That had been immediately after she'd questioned Mark about his distrust of the Confed, and less than an hour later, a squadron of sentries had come charging straight at him, as if someone had pointed him out as a target.

Every inch of my skin went cold. What had I heard her say when I'd caught her back there in the maze? *There isn't anything else I can tell you.*

"Did you make some sort of *deal* with them?" I burst out. "You tell them things about us, and they help you make it through the Exam? I can't just ignore this, Pree. What in Hades's name is going on?"

"It's not like that," Prisha said.

She'd fixated on Rocío too. The chill ran down to my bones. Prisha had brought up the conjured dragon out of nowhere, even though she'd barely cared about it when we saw it. She'd badgered Rocío about whether she'd be quick enough to fight—not just today but before as well.

She folded her arms tight across her chest. "Gods, Finn, as if you could understand."

"Of course I can't understand! You've been hiding it from me, *lying* to me—"

"What was I supposed to say?" she snapped, her voice so pained and yet furious that my throat closed up. "'By the way, Finn, a representative from the Exam committee came by to inform me that I've got a spot at the college if I report for them during the Exam, and if I say no, I'll be Dampered. So obviously I'm going to let them buy me'? Should I have mentioned that before or after you got completely caught up in your crusade to prove you wouldn't accept any injustice?"

"Pree…" My hands fumbled at my sides. I didn't know what to do with them. I scarcely knew what to do with my mouth.

"What would you have said to me? How would you have looked at me? As if it's so easy to take a stand when you don't already have the higher ground. No one in the Confed would ever have forced *you* to choose between playing snitch and losing everything."

"So… from the beginning… before we even went in, you were working for them?"

"They told me it was the only way. That they'd guarantee I'd make Champion as long as I did what they asked." She laughed roughly. "Of course, I'm not even sure of that now, but what was I supposed to do? Say no and spend the rest of my life as an errand girl ten steps behind the rest of my family? It was the only real choice I had."

"What exactly did the Exam committee tell you?"

"Only that they'd ensure I got through. And they gave me some methods of identifying the traps, at least the smaller ones, like that." She nodded to the sinkhole. "I wasn't supposed to say anything to anyone else. I shouldn't even have stopped you."

I rubbed my forehead. "And in exchange, you were 'reporting' on us."

"There must be circumstances where they can't fully monitor us," she said. "All they asked was that I let them know if I heard anyone speaking against the Confed or if another situation arose that I thought they'd want to be informed of. They mentioned a couple of people they wanted me to keep a particular eye on, topics I should bring up with them. That's it."

I tried to imagine being approached with the same ultimatum. How would I have responded if I'd felt my only chance at a life in which I could be happy meant betraying a bunch of other mages who hadn't deserved their misfortune any more than I had?

Prisha was right: I couldn't place myself entirely in that perspective. I *could* accept how she'd made the choice at the start, when the betrayals had been theoretical, the people strangers.

They hadn't remained theoretical, though.

"A couple of people," I repeated. "Mark and Rocío. That's why you made a point of hanging around her at the beginning."

Prisha lowered her head enough for the motion to serve as an answer.

"Mark almost died, Pree! Maybe he *did* die. You told them that nonsense he was saying about his brother, didn't you? And then they sent those guards right at him. They must have prompted that attack."

It hadn't been nonsense either, had it? The brainwashing part, maybe, but if Mark's half brother had made Champion, then he could be overseas running missions right now. Of course he'd have withdrawn from his family.

"I know!" Prisha said. "I didn't realize... I didn't *want* to go behind everyone's backs, but the sorts of things he was saying were exactly what the examiners wanted me to watch for. I had no idea how much they could hear right then. They might have known he'd said something and I hadn't reported it, and that would have ruined the deal. It never occurred to me they'd set him up like that."

Her voice broke. She dragged in a breath. "I went to try to talk to them last night, but they wouldn't listen to me. They just told me to follow our agreement or accept burning out, and then sent me away."

I swallowed thickly. "Who else have you reported on? Did you— *I've* criticized the Confed."

"I know," she said darkly. At my expression, her mouth twisted. "Fates help me, Finn, do you really have to ask? I didn't want you here in the first place. Of course I didn't say anything that would hurt you."

I supposed I hadn't made any truly seditious remarks— nothing close to Mark's rant. Still...

Her gaze remained on me, both despairing and accusing. I found myself wrenched between two ends of anger, toward her and toward myself.

No wonder she'd pleaded with me to leave the Exam last night. She'd already given me another advantage I hadn't earned. If I *had* said anything she couldn't just ignore, she'd have been forced to decide between throwing me to the examiners and risking the future she'd sacrificed so much for already.

"If you'd told me—"

"What would you have said? What would you have done? It'd only take one slip for the examiners to realize I'd revealed the secret."

What had I told her when she'd announced that she'd declared? That she should have appealed the Dampering decision instead. I'd believed all the ruling bodies within the Confed were reasonable at heart. It hadn't crossed my mind that the Exam committee could be so scheming as to plant spies among us.

If she'd told me, I wouldn't have understood how vital it was that I held my tongue. I might even have protested on her behalf. Where would that have gotten her? No doubt I would have emerged unscathed, while she...

"So now you know," she said. "I don't care if they see I've told you. I'm pretty sure if I hadn't stepped in with Rocío back there, I'd have been blown to bits with the rest of you, so *their* end of the deal clearly counts for nothing." She sighed. "You can think whatever you want about me, but can we at least keep moving?"

The conversation didn't feel complete, but I didn't know where I'd have it go. An ache was spreading through my forehead to my temples. I'd worn down my limited endurance, attempting to save the man in that last test.

"I think we should stay to the right." It was the sole certainty I still held. "Is there anything to worry about other than that sinkhole?"

"I can't be sure," Prisha said. "The bigger things... I didn't have any more warning of when they'd come or what they'd be than the rest of you did. They're testing me too."

"Conjure me a stick or a pole, several feet long?"

She cast without questioning me and handed me the long slender tube she'd conducted the magic into. The material felt as flimsy as cardboard, but it would serve for my purposes.

I tapped the ground ahead of us and, when the gray surface held, walked forward, pushing the end of the tube along in front of me. After a few steps, the tip sank into the ground, just as the ball had before. I yanked the tube back up and swung it as far as I could reach. The ground a few feet on the other side of that spot was solid.

Not so difficult then. I backed up for a running start and

jumped the sinkhole. Prisha leapt after me. I grabbed her hand to steady her, and then dropped it as if her touch had stung me.

"I'll take the lead from here," she said, pretending she hadn't noticed. "At least I have a better chance of noticing if there's a snare we need to avoid."

She stepped ahead of me. At the next branch, she turned right without protest.

I trudged on, grappling with the twist of horror and guilt inside me. Then one thought pierced through the turmoil.

"Rocío?" I said. "Did you report anything about her?"

"There hasn't been anything to report," Prisha said. "That girl keeps a close council." She peered back at me. "Though not always with you."

My back tensed. Rocío hadn't spoken overtly against the Confed to me. The worst was likely her snarky remark about which novices they chose for the college the first night, which Prisha had witnessed too. She'd even tried to talk Lacey and Judith down when they'd—

My feet stumbled as the recognition hit me. She *knew*. Rocío had known the examiners would be paying attention to what we said, by whatever means. I'd bet there were innumerable thoughts she'd felt it wisest to keep to herself. Her brother had died here, she'd said. How could she not hate the examiners, if not the whole Confed?

I certainly wasn't sharing that observation with Prisha after what she'd just revealed to me.

"You like her a lot," Prisha said after a moment. It wasn't a question.

"I do."

Prisha was silent for several paces. Then she said, "Be careful, all right? The Circle has their eye on her, and not with approval."

That cautioning sounded so absurd from someone who'd

admitted she might very well have gotten one of us killed that I scarcely caught a laugh before it jolted out of me.

My eye caught on a flicker of movement far off down the path: a figure emerging from a side branch. Hope raced through me.

"Rocío?" I called, speeding up. "Hey!"

Rocío stepped fully into view, froze, and then relaxed at the sight of us. Desmond and Judith joined her. They all looked well enough—as weary and beaten down as I felt, but alive. After everything, I'd count that as a miracle.

Rocío's gaze skimmed over Prisha before settling on me. If she was still upset about Prisha's interference during the last test, she must have decided to set aside her feelings. The small smile she offered me was a light flickering on amid the shadowy clash of emotions inside me.

"It looks like we might finally be getting somewhere," she said, motioning toward one of the walls.

Not far beyond the hedge, an ivory spire pointed up past the brambles toward the gray of the faux sky above. Did it mark the exit to this labyrinth? Were we nearly there?

"The maze could twist us around for another ten miles before we get there," Desmond said, but his tone was hopeful. We hurried forward, maybe lacking quite our usual caution.

When we took the next bend, a hiss split the air. The hedge to our right erupted into dozens of thick vines, the same metallic dark green as the brambles. They lashed out in every direction.

I flinched backward, but a clump of the vines caught me around the arms and legs. As I struggled against them, more and more spiraled around me. Some snatched at my body, their jointed surface rasping against my bare arms and neck, as rough as sandpaper. Others arched around me like a cage.

The vines heaved me up, clinging tight. For an instant, I flashed back to a friend's lakeside cottage, to the feel of seaweed tangling around my ankle when I'd accidentally swum into a patch—that sensation as if I were about to be pulled into the suffocating darkness of the water. A gasp slipped from my lips. I flailed harder, managing to wrench my ankles and one of my hands free from the grasping strands.

The vines circled me until I was completely encased in a pocket of air. They overlapped so tightly only a sliver of light seeped in through a tiny gap down near my feet. No sound reached me from the outside. Had the others all been caged like this too?

I lay there on my back, panting and staring at that gap, taking stock. I was trapped, but only one vine held me directly now—a tight loop around my left wrist, pinning it to the wall of my cage like a shackle.

Well, the goal of this test was clear. I had to get out.

I tugged at my wrist, and the vine pulled tighter into the wall, scraping my skin. Okay, simply wriggling my hand out was not an option.

I groped for words and found a lyric that provoked a sense of loosening, expanding. I murmured it, focusing my intent on the cord.

My headache pulsed with the tingling of the magic—and the vine clenched even tighter. My tendons pinched so painfully I choked. The entire cage contracted at the same moment, forcing me to press my head against the surface behind me to prevent the strands from scratching my nose.

O gods, this was a tough one. My casting provoked the vines. If the loop around my arm yanked more, it was going to break my wrist. The trap would crush my entire body at this rate.

My breath had sped up again, harsh in my chest. That slit of light by my feet was still open, giving me a direction to the world outside. It was the closest thing I had to an escape route. Was there a way to get through that? I'd have to get down there if I wanted to test it.

I steadied the heaving of my lungs. First things first. Start with what you do know.

Before anything else, I needed my arm free.

I tipped my head to the side to inspect my wrist. The skin on either side of the vine's shackle was flushed an angry red. A persistent, splintering pain radiated through the muscles. I closed my eyes.

I couldn't wrestle myself free, and any attempt at magic would only worsen the situation. What other options did I have?

Rocío's words from this morning returned to me. *Magic isn't the only thing that matters.* I'd stayed in the Exam because I'd believed I could contribute somehow, even if not with powerful castings. I'd survived that test of illusions without any magic at all, simply by paying attention and noticing the details.

I'd told Judith that counted—that it wasn't how you made it out that mattered, only that you found a way. If the way I had to beat the Exam was by puzzling my way through it, finding the loopholes in their traps, instead of by any real power, well... so be it. I might not be proud, but at least I'd be alive.

Where were the loopholes here? What did I have that I could use? A small range of motion in all of my body except my left hand. The clothes I'd chosen for comfort rather than any sort of utility. Margo's dissolving rod in my pocket, which would have been spectacular if I couldn't feel that the vines around me were no more organic matter than the metallic barbs of the hedges.

Organic matter. I paused. In my mind's eye, I saw Judith emerging from the shadows with blood dripping from her palm, the knife in her other hand. We used the tools we had.

If I couldn't widen the loop around my wrist, then I had to narrow my hand.

The thought made my stomach turn. I forced myself to slide

my fingers into my pocket and draw out the rod. At that small movement, the cage contracted. I cringed. Then, even more slowly, I eased my arm across my chest until I held the rod level with my left hand.

Bile rose in the back of my mouth. I gritted my teeth.

What was a thumb? What was it *really*, compared to everything everyone around me had sacrificed to make it this far —in the Exam and in their lives before that?

Margo had urged me not to hesitate if the rod could save my life. Better that it was myself I hurt than someone else.

I flicked open the lid and set the tip against the curve of flesh below my thumb. My muscles tensed, and my heart thumped faster in anticipation of more than just the pain. I was going to need to move swiftly as soon as my hand was free.

Bracing myself, I pressed the base of the rod and jabbed the point in.

The rod's 'chantment ripped through my flesh with a searing burn, and every nerve in my hand screamed. A cry broke from my throat. I jerked the rod back, and my left hand slipped too, the side of it bloody and useless. It popped from the restraint with a sucking sound that made me even queasier. A stream of blood gushed down my arm, the pain blaring on and on.

The vines shuddered around me. Threads popped on my shirt as I shoved myself toward the opening with a moan. I thrust my good hand through, dropped the dissolving rod, and shoved up with all the leverage I could wrench from my elbow. The strands resisted, but for a mere instant the space gaped wider—wide enough for me to haul my head and shoulders through.

Writhing, kicking, gasping as the vines snapped around my ribs, I shoved again. Something cracked in my side, and my body fell through. I hit the ground beside the dissolving rod with my mutilated hand clutched against my belly, soaking my shirt with the warm flow of blood.

CHAPTER TWENTY

Rocío

When the hedge's tendrils whipped around me, my first instinct was to struggle. I jerked my arm, and the presence in the magic gripped me from head to toe, so urgently that I went still. I lay motionless as the dark strands wrapped over and under me in a ribbed cocoon, cringing as their rough surface scratched my skin.

A tendril slid around each of my wrists and ankles. The presence held on, and I held with it, clamping down on my frustration. *Wait*, it seemed to be telling me. *Wait.* It had helped me before.

I breathed shallowly within the shrinking space. Every other sound faded away. My mind drifted back to the hallways at Brooklyn United Collegiate, to moments when I'd frozen by a locker or a doorway as kids who'd harassed me before ambled past, when I'd willed them with my stillness to overlook me.

The last of the strands settled into place. The conjured trap stopped moving, its walls solid except for a tiny gap by my feet.

About a foot of space remained above me and along my sides. The presence eased off in the silence. I stayed still.

Panic gnawed at me, but the tendrils hadn't hurt me while I'd lain there. Maybe getting out of this trap required a slow and careful touch.

I turned one wrist, my right, ever so slightly. The stump of my little finger stung as it brushed the tendrils beneath it, but the loop didn't shift. That strand was loose enough that it barely grazed my skin.

Gingerly, like casting a delicate spell, I pressed my remaining fingers together in as narrow a point as I could form and drew my hand through the loop. At the bump of my knuckles, the strand contracted. But I was already out. I tugged my hand away as the loop snapped tight.

The knobby wall around me clenched a little closer. My heart stuttered. Oh. So there was that to worry about too.

Retrieving my left hand was easier. I adjusted my balance incrementally and slid it out using the same tentative process. Again, my knuckles bumped, but I was ready this time. The space around me shrank, but I didn't flinch. I'd only lost an inch or two. I still had room to work with.

I peered down at my feet. My sneakers were going to be a problem. I had to get them off, and that meant I had to untie them.

I opened my mouth to 'chant the knot loose, but the presence smacked across my face as if clapping a hand over it. I pressed my lips together, and the sensation receded.

I couldn't cast? Okay, okay, I could deal. I'd just have to do this the Dull way.

The ceiling of my enclosure was too low for me to sit up, but I doubted that would have been a good idea anyway. Instead, I bent at the waist inch by inch, rolling onto my side at the same time.

My shoulder knocked a ridge in the "floor," and the walls closed in by another inch. I moved even more slowly after that. Finally, my fingertips hit the tops of my sneakers.

I wiggled apart the knotted laces and loosened them as much as I dared. I didn't think I could pull the shoes off without more squirming than seemed smart, but all I needed was for them to fall off when I tugged out my feet.

Reaching a little farther, my stomach muscles straining, I repeated the process with the other sneaker. Then I let myself sag back for a moment. Sweat coated my forehead and trickled down my neck.

Even as I lay there motionless, the tendrils contracted another inch. I was running out of time.

I made my left foot go limp and dragged on it as intently as I was willing to risk. My heel slipped out of the sneaker. The shoe thumped against the loop, and the strand clamped tight around the ball of my foot for an instant before I yanked my toes free. My foot throbbed as I slumped down.

Just one more to go. Easy-peasy. Ha!

After all the 'chantments and conjurings I'd cast in the last four days, of course pulling myself free of a few vines was the thing to really wear me out. I imagined telling Finn that—imagined him laughing and teasing me about how I needed to work on my plant-taming.

A tight smile crossed my face, but the ache in my chest grew. He and the others had to be stuck in this trap too. I couldn't help them until I got myself out.

I pulled at my other leg. This time I managed to slip my foot out of the shoe gently enough that it only settled against the loop, but by then, the whole space around me had clenched by another couple inches. The top of my enclosure nearly brushed my forehead now. I swallowed thickly.

At least the little slice of daylight hadn't squeezed smaller, though it was tiny enough to worry me. Sliding my legs out of the way, I reached toward the opening. Every nerve urged me to throw myself at it, but slow and careful had worked well for me so far.

I edged one hand through the opening and tested the flexibility of the edge with the faintest press of my palm. It gave just a little, enough that I dared to continue pressing as I slid my head out into the open air.

The gray sky above had never looked so welcoming. I maneuvered an arm all the way out and used it to pull at the rest of my body—and the strands around me shivered and started to clench. A bolt of terror shot through me. I shoved myself forward with all my strength, leaning into gravity, and hurtled down. The opening snapped shut just in time to graze my toes.

My spine jarred against the ground. I rolled over and scrambled away.

When I turned, my jaw went slack. A mass of artificial vines loomed over the path higher than the hedge it had sprouted from and at least another ten feet wide, like a lumpy, overblown tree. Cocoons of twisted tendrils jutted out here and there from the denser tangles, dangling like ghastly fruit.

At the sound of a ragged breath, my gaze jerked down—to the only other figure outside the trap.

Finn hunched over several feet farther down the path, his face sallow and his shoulders rigid. He'd cut some khaki fabric from the leg of his pants and was pulling the cloth tight around his hand. A reddish splotch was already seeping through the fabric, and the front of his shirt was drenched with blood.

Horror choked me. I ran to him, my feet stumbling over each other. His head jerked up after my first few steps, his eyes hazed with pain, and I could tell he hadn't even heard the thud of my escape. My own eyes filled with a rush of heat that wasn't just tears but anger.

What had they done to him? What had the Confed done to my brilliant boy with the smile?

"I'm all right," he rasped, and lurched to his feet.

I blinked hard. Of course he'd say that even if there was more blood on his clothes than still in his body. "No, you're not. You—"

Finn cut me off with a wave toward the monstrous tree, keeping his other hand cradled against his abdomen. "We have to get everyone else out. I don't know how much time they have."

He was right. He looked like death itself, but he was alive and out and standing by his own power. As soon as we'd freed the others, I'd do what I could to heal him, whether he liked it or not.

Amid the tendrils, I hadn't heard anyone but myself. Now, I could make out faint noises of discomfort: an indrawn breath, a grunt, a whimper.

"Desmond?" I shouted. "Judith?"

No one answered my call. Maybe sound only traveled out but not in. Letting us hear their struggles but denying them the hope they might have gotten knowing we were working to save them. The examiners were cabrones, all right.

A muttered curse filtered from one of the cocoons of vines that dangled near us. The strands shifted as if in response. We dashed beneath it.

A small gap showed between the tendrils at the lowest point of the cocoon, a few feet above my head.

"Pree!" Finn yelled.

I raised my hands toward the opening, but it was far beyond my grasp.

"Las nubes se levantan," I murmured at the ground to boost me upward—and before the lyric had even finished leaving my lips, a couple vines from the massive trunk beside me lashed out. One clung to my calf, but I heaved myself backward just fast enough to break its grip. Finn dodged to the side.

"They didn't like it when I tried casting either," he said.

The stray strands whipped back and forth and then, when they caught on nothing, retracted into the giant mass.

Finn stepped forward again. "Here," he said. "Use me."

He knelt down, bracing himself against the ground with his good hand, and motioned for me to clamber onto his back. Blood dripped from his rough bandage.

My resolve wavered. "Are you sure—"

"I can handle it," he said, repeating the gesture. "We need to get them out *now.*"

I hadn't climbed on anyone's back since Dad had given me piggyback rides as a little kid. I set my feet as gently as possible just below Finn's shoulders and tried to ignore his wince as he took my weight. The faster I did this, the faster I could get off him.

"Prisha?" I said, trying to peer through the gap in the vines. The space inside the cocoon was too dark for me to make her out, but I could hear her breath coming in short bursts.

Cautiously, I eased my hand through the opening without touching the surface and gave a little wave.

"Hey," Prisha said softly. The bunch around her contracted an inch, but then her fingers squeezed mine. "I don't know how to get through. Every time I move..."

"It'll give you room if you push," I said. "You just have to be fast. Are you completely free?"

"Yes," she said. "It—it's pretty tight in here, though. I don't think I can do 'fast.'"

I lifted my other hand. "I'll help. It's only going to get tighter. Ready?"

She clasped my hands in answer. Together, we shoved at the opening. It gave, and I hauled on her arms as hard as I could.

Prisha tumbled out, toppling me with her. We fell to the ground beside Finn. My elbow jarred, but I pushed myself up right away. I didn't want to think about what additional damage I might be doing to those numbed muscles in my back.

Finn caught Prisha staring at his hand as he straightened up, and his expression went strangely flat. "It's fine!" he said. "We still have two more people to help."

Someone was crying openly now, a thready sobbing I knew was Judith. "We're coming!" I said, pacing under the remaining cocoons. There were far more of them than could hold the rest of our group. "We just have to find you."

She didn't answer. She couldn't hear us. God, with a broken arm, she'd have no chance of working herself free. None of us could have managed that.

Prisha pointed to a spot at our right, where Desmond's arm had protruded from a clump of vines just a few feet off the ground. He was already squirming out. The three of us ran to him, and he tumbled into our arms with a groan that his gritted teeth couldn't contain. The skin of his arms and face were mottled with dark abrasions. The clenching opening caught around his left ankle.

Desmond kicked at the tendril and yelped when it dug in even tighter. His foot was trapped just below the knob of his anklebone. The strands twisted tighter, and his ankle made a horrible cracking sound.

Finn yanked the other boy's shoulders, and Desmond fell the rest of the way out. We lowered him so he could sit on the ground with his legs sprawled. His foot jutted at an angle so unnatural it sent a shudder down my spine.

"Sorry," Finn said raggedly as Desmond hunched over, both of them shaking. "Another second and it would've crushed your foot too."

Desmond only nodded, his lips clamped shut.

"Don't cast!" I warned him, even though he looked as if he was in too much pain to consider trying.

A shriek split the air. "No!" Judith cried out. "No, please, stop it. No!" Her voice broke into sobs.

I leapt up from where I'd knelt next to Desmond. Where was she? Higher, to the left? I sidestepped, trying to tune out the sharp yet heavy thud of my pulse. "Judith!" I called, even though I knew she wouldn't hear me.

"Help me!" she gasped out. "Please, I give up. Burn me out! I don't care. Just *make it stop*."

Her last word was cut off by a crack like the sound Desmond's broken ankle had made, and then a desperate moan carried down.

"Stay still!" I yelled, my throat raw. "Stay quiet! We're trying to get to you!"

There. That clump near the top of the mass... too high to reach even if I stood on someone's shoulders.

Judith shrieked again. I rushed to the corded trunk of the "tree." My fingers found purchase on the ridges of vine, but only for a few fleeting seconds before the tendrils split off and swiped out at me. One spiraled around my elbow, and another smacked my waist. A ream of them unfurled as Finn and Prisha wrenched me away.

The vines kept sweeping forward this time. Prisha and I heaved Desmond up and braced his arms against us. Then we ran down the path with Finn. Over the hiss of the lashing tendrils and the thump of our frantic feet, I could still hear Judith. She wasn't speaking in words anymore, only incoherent sounds of pain.

"We have to help her," I said. I'd promised. I couldn't fail again. I couldn't let the examiners win.

But when I let go of Desmond to turn back, the whole mass of tendrils was shifting, surging along the hedge after us. A bunch of tendrils whipped at us so close that the tip of one scraped my cheek.

We staggered backward, Finn grasping my shoulder. Prisha kept her arm around Desmond's back, holding him off his broken ankle.

"Didn't you hear her?" I hollered at the sky—at the examiners, wherever they were. "She wants out! She quit! You can't just—"

Another jab from the vines caught me in the chest. I reeled backward, colliding with Finn. He pulled me to him, wrapping his arm around my waist.

Judith's next shriek turned into a gurgle.

My muscles tensed with the urge to race back to her, and Finn's hold tightened. His face bent close to mine, his heart thumping in his chest against my back.

"We have to help her," I said. My voice sounded very small. What was the *point* of all the studying I'd done, all the skill I had, if I couldn't manage this one thing?

"I know," Finn said with a hitch of breath. "I trust you. Tell me there's still a chance, tell me you see a way, and I'll be right there with you."

He would be. I believed him then with total certainty. He saw just how warped and wrong his Confed must be to have brought us here with their ruthless, brutal magic. Maybe we'd grown up at opposite ends of the city, on opposite sides of that invisible divide between old magic and new, but in that moment we were feeling the exact same horror, and he would go every bit as far as I would to overcome it.

Except as I stared at the writhing vines with fresh tears in my eyes, I also knew I didn't really believe we had a hope in hell of saving Judith now. I wasn't even sure there was anything left of her to save.

I sagged against him, and the wave of vines swelled as if to crash over us.

"Finn!" Prisha cried.

He grabbed my hand, but he didn't have to pull me. With my conscience tearing at my heels, I ran.

CHAPTER TWENTY-ONE

Finn

I f I'd ever thought the examiners lacked a sense of humor, that impression was corrected when we barreled around the first corner away from the lashing vines and the girl we'd abandoned to them—and discovered the end of the maze had been waiting for us fewer than thirty feet away. The hedges fell back to reveal a wide-open stretch of ground free of any visible threat.

We'd been a mere minute from safety—a mere minute from Judith walking out alive.

It was a sick, sadistic joke. I pictured Examiner Lancaster watching us on a distant screen, sweeping back her silver hair as she smirked to herself, and wanted to both punch someone and to keel over helplessly at the same time.

I did neither. Sharp shards of agony stabbed up my arm from my mutilated hand, and a duller ache in my side turned into a jab if I inhaled too deeply, but even through the haze of pain, I knew that whatever safety we'd attained was only relative. The Exam wasn't over yet.

The space we'd emerged into was a huge circle maybe a mile

across, bordered by a dark hedge all the way around. The ground had shifted from the previous gray to a yellow-brown hue, with a gritty texture under my shoes that fit its sandy color. The faux sky above us emitted a coordinating pallid yellow light. Small dunes rose and fell in ripples to our left. A dozen or so narrow spires of an ivory rock-like material were scattered across the rest of the clearing. Smooth platforms of the same color jutted from their tops and sides like embedded discs.

The tallest of those spires stood in the middle of the clearing, with a single huge platform at its peak that gave it the look of a gigantic gaunt mushroom. Its stalk rose at least thirty feet from the ground. A fountain cascaded from the side into a glinting pool at its foot.

A pang ran down my throat. How many hours had passed since I'd last tasted water?

Desmond sank to the ground. He set his hands on his broken ankle with a wince.

"Is there anything I can do?" Rocío asked. The longing for him to say yes, to give her the chance to fix *something*, radiated from every tensed inch of her body. Judith's shrieks echoed in my head.

"Do you have professional medical training?" Desmond inquired. At the droop of her head, he added more gently, "I think I'd better just freeze it. I can manage that. Hopefully they'll have some magimedics waiting for us when we're finally through." He spoke without betraying any concern that he wouldn't be among those who made it, but his gaze was more vague than usual. How much pain was he suffering from?

He leaned over to cast his 'chantment, and I looked down at my most visible injury. Thank the Fates I'd chosen pants with a natural fabric that the dissolving rod could cut through. The strip of cloth I'd wrapped around my hand had slowed the gush of blood until I'd managed to stammer out a 'chantment to close the pulsing artery.

I hadn't found the wherewithal to deal with the smaller vessels, though. The bandage was tacky with blood only half-dried. Gods only knew whether my work on the artery would hold, considering the state I'd been in.

The thought of attempting to seal it more thoroughly brought back my headache with a vicious thump. Maybe keeling over wasn't such a horrible idea. The ground was looking more and more welcoming.

"Finn," Prisha said.

The worry in her voice woke me up. I was swaying.

Rocío reached me first and grasped my forearm. She examined my hand, her fingers tightening.

"Your thumb," she said. "The trap did this to you?"

I managed a shaky laugh. "*I* did it to me to get out of the trap. It seemed my best option at the time." I nodded to her right hand, to the fused stump where her little finger had been. "Now we match. In an opposite sort of way."

She shook her head at my joke. Her thumb tested the edge of the makeshift bandage, and my body stiffened at the thought of her glimpsing the mess underneath.

"I don't think we should take the cloth off," I said. "I tried to seal the worst of it, but… I had a bit of trouble concentrating. It might not hold. And I've lost a little more blood than I'd prefer already."

The back of Rocío's shirt and the tied strip of sheet around her chest were streaked with that blood from when I'd pulled her away from the vines—from the front of *my* shirt, which was sticking to my chest in a gruesome fashion. A metallic butcher-shop scent tinged the air. I swallowed hard.

"I can 'chant the cloth," Rocío said. "That'll be easier than trying to tackle the wound directly anyway. Maybe I can fuse the fabric with the skin and harden it so it blocks off the blood flow completely..."

Her brow furrowed. The distress in her face receded, focus taking its place. She rolled out a few singsong lines.

The rag tingled against my hand. A searing pain shot through my wrist, and I flinched. A cool balm washed over me an instant later, reminding me of the 'chantment she'd applied to my headache two days ago.

She let go. My hand still throbbed, but the sensation was distant and contained now.

"Are you hurt anywhere else?" Prisha asked.

My head and my chest still hurt, but not so much I couldn't function. "Nothing major," I said, and, to Rocío, "Thank you."

Prisha pursed her lips as if she didn't believe me, but she was scarcely in a position to accuse *me* of lying.

I pointed to the fountain with my good hand. "I could really use a drink."

"Count me in," Desmond said. He levered himself to his feet.

Rocío offered him her shoulder for support, and he hobbled alongside the rest of us toward the central spire.

"We're not the only ones here," Prisha observed.

I followed her gaze. A couple figures were stalking over the low dunes. A moment later, I spotted a girl limping from one of the smaller spires to a black structure beside it. The structure was little more than a few walls leaning together, and so low she had to crouch to enter.

"I wonder how many others made it this far," Rocío said quietly.

As we approached the central spire, shadowy dimples came into view down its stalk. Handholds? But my attention was more drawn to the low jet of water that streamed into the pool, which was wide enough that I could have lain down in it if a swim had appealed. Two taps near shoulder height protruded from the stalk a short distance from the pool.

The moment we reached the spire, I walked up to the nearest one and waved my hand beneath it. Water spurted out, splattering the already damp ground and trickling into a channel that led to the pool.

I gulped from my cupped hand until the parched sensation in my mouth eased, and then stepped aside to give Prisha a turn.

She took a drink, wiped her mouth with her sleeve, and peered upward. "What do you imagine is in those bags?"

A ring of sacks dangled along the edge of the platform thirty feet above us. They looked lumpy, as if stuffed full. The platform was too wide for anyone to reach them from the side of the stalk, but there were square openings at the tops of the columns of handholds.

"We should at least check. Carefully." Rocío prodded one of the notches in the side of the spire, judged it secure, and started clambering up.

Desmond, who had no chance of climbing with that ankle, hunkered down beside the pool. I considered making the attempt, but the continuing ache of my ribs kept me in place.

"Just wait here," Prisha said to me briskly. "You're not going to be any use to us if you fall and crack your head open."

It was the right thing for her to say, such a Prisha thing to say, but I still couldn't look her in the face without unease twisting inside me.

"Be careful," I said. "And if there's anything good up there, save some for the rest of us."

She scrambled up the spire after Rocío. I sat down near Desmond and scanned the desertlike landscape.

"'In the land of Mordor, where the shadows lie,'" Desmond intoned gloomily. "I wouldn't mind having a 'chanted ring right now, cursed or not."

Rocío and then Prisha disappeared through the platform's trapdoors. One of the sacks above us lurched out of view as the girls heaved it up over the edge. A pleased exclamation followed.

"Watch out below!" Prisha hollered, and tossed a sack down toward us. I leapt up as it landed at my right, scattering some of its contents on impact: granola bars, pears, and a wrapped sandwich.

A different sort of pang wrenched through my abdomen. I snatched up the food and hauled the bag over to Desmond.

The next few minutes passed in a blur of groping hands and crinkling wrappers. I'd inhaled a ham-and-cheese sandwich and plowed halfway through a pear before the gnawing hunger inside me subsided enough for me to think about anything other than sating it. My head felt a bit clearer, the jabbing in my forehead duller.

The raw, bloody smell of my ruined shirt filled my nose as I inhaled, and I almost vomited up everything I'd just eaten. I should probably take care of that.

As I stood, Prisha slid through an opening above me to descend the stalk. Rocío appeared at another a second later. They both carried sacks slung over their shoulders by cords.

I shuffled to the tap and held my shirt out under it. The rush of water slicked right over the 'chanted bandage on my hand, but it soaked through the shirt's fabric, chilly where it smacked my skin. Scarlet eddies swirled in the stream that careened across the ground to the pool.

By the time both of the girls had reached us, I looked less like a horror-film victim. A stain remained in the pale blue fabric, but it could have been from tomato juice for all you could tell now. I splashed a little water onto my face to further revive myself and stepped back. We gathered around Desmond, and the girls dropped their sacks.

"They feed us, they give us a chance to relax, and then they hit us harder," Rocío said. "That's how it's always gone so far." She eyed the spires, the black hovels spaced between them, and the dark line of the hedge beyond.

"They've always given us at least part of a night between stages," Prisha said. "But who knows, for this last one?"

"I wouldn't put anything past them now," Desmond said. "They proved Judith right, didn't they?"

My gaze snapped to him. "What do you mean?"

"What she was saying before," he said with a jerk of his hand that belied his nonchalant tone. "The part about them liking to see how far they can push us."

Horror swelled inside me. I'd forgotten what Judith had said just before the test in which we'd been forced to murder those people. She'd disparaged the Exam committee and the Confed...

And a couple hours later, the Exam had killed her, even more quickly and efficiently than it had assaulted Mark.

When I'd overheard Prisha, she'd been protesting that she couldn't tell them anything more. Anything more than what? She might have repeated every one of Judith's incriminating remarks before I'd interrupted.

Prisha went rigid when my gaze caught hers.

"What had you already said?" I forced out. "Before I found you. What did you *say*?"

"Finn," she said, "we were *all* in that trap."

Judith's cage had been the farthest out of reach, and hers might have closed even faster than ours too. The examiners could easily have made it seem as though she'd simply failed when they'd never intended her to survive.

Rocío frowned at me and then Prisha. "What's going on?"

I couldn't bring myself to drag out Prisha's horrible secret in front of the others. I shouldn't have to be the one to say it. It had been her choice.

She hadn't denied she'd spoken about Judith. She'd told them something.

I couldn't accuse her outright, but I couldn't stand to look at her right now either. I couldn't stand her *being* here, talking with Rocío as if she wasn't waiting for her to let the wrong comment slip. We were all too emotionally raw to be perfectly cautious.

"You should go," I blurted out. "For tonight. Find someplace else to wait it out. That'll be better for everyone."

"What?" Rocío said. "No! We have to stay together."

Prisha inclined her head. "It's okay," she said. "Finn has a point."

"If we're splitting up, shouldn't we at least stay in pairs?" Desmond said, his eyebrows drawing together.

"Maybe," Prisha said. "You want to find a spot to stake out with me? You've just got to swear you'll keep the conversation light."

She glanced at me, like a promise and a plea.

O gods, of course I didn't really want her off on her own in the midst of... whatever wretched tests this place concealed.

The examiners hadn't asked her to press Desmond. She'd told him to stick to lighter subjects of conversation. It was Rocío she was most likely to hurt.

I knew she didn't *want* to hurt anyone—but I also knew that even after what had happened with Mark, she'd gambled on Judith's life to protect her "deal."

"All right," I said. Rocío made a noise of protest, so I added, "We'll stay within sight of each other. We'll be able to keep a wider eye on things if we spread out a little. If you see anything concerning, just shout."

Prisha helped Desmond to his feet, and they set off in the direction of one of the black hovels. I didn't want to stay by the central spire either. It felt like too blatant a target.

"We can take that spire," I said, pointing to one about fifty feet to the right of Prisha and Desmond's destination. It boasted two platforms, one near the middle and another at the top: a bit of shelter and a higher vantage point from which to keep watch. "If that's okay with you?"

Rocío was still frowning. "What's going on with you and Prisha? And don't tell me 'nothing.' You think she said something to Judith that threw her off?"

"Not like that," I said. "Not precisely. I—" Could the examiners hear us now? There was no way of discerning where their surveillance might begin and end. The thought of spilling the whole story still sent a ripple of uneasiness through me. "It's complicated. Just be careful what you say around her, all right?"

Behind her, a couple of new arrivals were heading toward the pool. Callum might be lurking, or Lacey. I extended my hand to Rocío. "Trust me?"

For a second, she looked ready to refuse. Then she hefted the remaining sack and joined me.

We slunk across the gritty ground to the spire I'd selected. The lower platform jutted only a couple feet above my head. Rocío slung the sack back over her shoulder and scrambled up a set of handholds. She reached down to help me haul myself up. I winced as I sat down hard.

Rocío paced across the platform. "I haven't seen Lacey, even though she went ahead of us."

"She might have taken a different route through the maze," I said. There was no need to mention the other possibility: that the maze had consumed her as it had Judith.

Rocío sat down, letting her legs dangle over the platform's edge. Her head bowed.

"Are you all right?" I asked.

"Yes," she said, "and no. Not at all. Too many people died today."

I swiped my hand across my lips, my mouth suddenly dry. "Any is too many."

"Yeah." She let out a choked little laugh. "I thought if I just tried hard enough, I could get all of us through this without anyone getting hurt. I guess that was stupid."

"No. It isn't on you. It's on them." I knew I didn't need to state which 'them' I was referring to.

"I just... I don't want to be the kind of mage they're trying to shape us into," Rocío said. "I don't want to be the kind of *person* they're trying to make me be. But it seems like no matter what, I lose."

"As long as you're still you, you haven't lost," I said. "I think... I think it's spectacular that you tried to find another way. They didn't offer us any good choices, and you tried to make your own. That's more spectacular than your dragon."

She glanced at me, her expression unreadable. "Do you really believe that?"

"I do."

She turned back toward the view. A breeze whisked over us, chilling my wet shirt. The drenched fabric had gone clammy against my skin, which didn't feel any more comfortable than the blood had. It was seeping water into my pants. I shivered.

No one was nearby. Even Prisha and Desmond had disappeared from view into the hovel they'd chosen.

"I'm going to wring out my shirt," I said. "Please keep your eyes averted to avoid being blinded by my shockingly impressive physique."

Between my useless left hand and the jagged pain in my side when I lifted that arm, maneuvering the damned shirt off me was more difficult than I expected. I managed to yank it over my head and scooted to sit at the side of the platform. The surface was smooth, almost silky, as if it were constructed out of real ivory.

Wringing the fabric, I squeezed out at least a couple cups of water. Afterward, the shirt wasn't *dry*, but I'd take damp over soaked through. I instinctively swung it flat and hissed as pain splintered through my chest.

Behind me, Rocío sucked in a startled breath. "What *happened* to you?" she said.

I looked down. Yeah, it was bad. Bruises blackened my skin from my left armpit to just below my ribcage.

I tried to chuckle, but the effort only sent the pain deeper. "Some crazy vines trying to crush me to smithereens happened," I said, keeping my tone as light as possible. "They decided to bash a few ribs while I was on my way out."

"You didn't say anything."

"My hand was the more immediate problem."

"Finn..." She stopped at my shoulder. Her voice dipped. "May I?"

If I hadn't been dizzy with agony, I might have appreciated having a girl I quite liked asking permission to touch my half-naked body. As it was, the best I could accomplish was to nudge myself back from the edge so I wouldn't go toppling off. "Be my guest."

Rocío knelt at my back. Her hands hovered over the bruises. Then, so gingerly I barely felt it, she set one against the skin. She whispered a casting.

"I don't think they're broken," she said. "Just cracked."

"That's something."

"Peor es nada," she muttered. "Yes."

She spoke again with the soft, lilting tone she'd used when calming my headache and when numbing my hand. It rolled over me like a lullaby, singing the nerves to sleep. The pain crawled away. I filled my lungs with air and felt only a mild pinching.

When Rocío leaned back, the atmosphere shifted. I gripped my shirt, suspecting that if I attempted to put it back on, she'd insist on helping. What would be more embarrassing: submitting to that or continuing to sit here shirtless? I didn't think the sight of my body was unpleasant, per se. The Academy curriculum included regular phys ed under the principle that a limber body encouraged a limber mind, but...

Her fingers grazed my back to the right of my spine and traced down over the unbruised muscles there. My breath hitched at the sudden flush of warmth her touch provoked. Then it was gone.

"I'm sorry," she said. "I didn't mean to—"

"No, you didn't hurt me," I said quickly. "It felt good." My face flared as I heard the last words spill from my mouth. I fumbled for something else to say, afraid to turn around and witness her expression.

Then her hand settled onto my back again, below my shoulder blade. She let it rest there, just the gentle weight of her palm and fingers. My heart thumped so hard she must have felt it through my skin.

"Are there any other injuries you've been keeping quiet about?" she asked, as if this were a normal conversation.

I shook my head. "You discovered them all."

"You had me *stand* on you to get to Prisha when you had multiple cracked ribs. You pulled Desmond out of that trap."

"So what you're saying is, maybe I don't make the wisest decisions ever."

"No. I'm saying you're definitely spectacular too."

Her words echoed through me with a rush of a different sort of warmth, one that fortified me to ask, "So does that mean you'll give me the time of day when we're back in the real world?"

"I think I'm the one who's supposed to be asking that question."

"What?" I said, blinking. "Why?"

Her hand twitched against my back. "Really? How much

room is there usually for ghetto-trash street-magic girls in your kind of life?"

I swiveled, not caring that the movement meant her touch fell away. I had to see her face. "Don't call yourself that."

She gazed back at me steadily, not looking angry or distraught, merely resigned. In a way, seeing that pricked at me more than if she'd been upset.

"They're not my words. That's what people would see if I turned up at your front door, isn't it? What your family, your friends, your neighbors would think?"

"*No,*" I said. "My dad— My sister—"

I halted. I longed to tell her how my dad had fought the old Circle so that mages like her could have a chance at a magical future, how my sister had abandoned our old-magic enclave to mingle with the Dulls, and how they would have respected Rocío for her abilities at the very least. Yet of all the friends my parents had invited to their dinner parties, I wasn't certain even one of them had been new magic, though Dad had mentioned new-magic colleagues. The only people I'd seen Margo socializing with were old-magic kids, just the more rebellious sorts.

I didn't want to say it if I wasn't sure.

"I don't know," I finished weakly. "I don't think so, not everyone, but I don't know."

Rocío shrugged as if to say, *There you go,* and started to turn away. Whatever moment we'd been sharing tipped, ready to shatter apart if I didn't catch it.

I gripped her wrist. "Rocío." She glanced back, and I barreled onward. "I may be a joke of a half-talent mage who puts his foot in it far too often, but what you said isn't what *I* see. It was never what I saw."

The ache in my side started to pinch deeper from the twist of my torso, but I held her gaze. Her mouth slanted as if it wasn't sure whether to curve up or down.

"And I don't see a joke," she said. "All right?"

"All right," I said, my voice abruptly rough.

Rocío moved to stand, and I let go of her arm. She tipped her head upward. The faux sky overhead was dimming from yellow to burnt orange. Long shadows sprawled away from the spires in an intermittent ring.

"I guess we're meant to rest," she said. "I'll cast a shield to alert us if anyone approaches. Who knows how long the examiners will leave us before they start up the tests again."

I stood up too and pulled my shirt over my head with a careful tug. Easing my arms into the sleeves, I watched Rocío sing her casting.

Focus tensed her features. Her fingers wove through the air in precise motions as she conducted her intent into being. The quiver in the air around me heightened slightly. Her expression relaxing, she lowered her hands. The breeze tossed her hair, and all I could see was how beautiful she was.

She turned and caught me staring. "What?"

"You work like an artist," I said honestly. "It's beautiful."

Her cheeks flushed. She dropped her gaze to consider her clasped hands.

"I'm not confused anymore," she said.

My pulse stuttered. For an instant, I couldn't recall how to move. Then I was crossing the short distance between us, reaching to touch her cheek the way I'd tried to before. This time, Rocío leaned in to meet me. It was the most natural act in the world to lower my mouth to hers.

She kissed the way she cast, with a focused certainty, as if she were conjuring me into being with the press of her lips against mine. My hand slid up into her smooth hair. She shifted closer, and if I could have drowned in the feel of her right then, I likely would have happily. It was heaven simply losing myself temporarily in the heat of her breath, the sparks tickling over my skin as her fingers trailed down my chest, the little sigh that escaped her when I kissed her again.

When we came up for air, she leaned her head against my shoulder. I wrapped my arms around her, reveling in that beautiful, fragile moment. The landscape around us was still and silent, but we both knew it wouldn't stay that way. Likely it was that sense of fragility that loosened my tongue.

"I'm falling in love with you," I said.

"Finn—"

I interrupted before she could argue. "I know it hasn't been very long and this situation is so far from either of our real lives, but… I know what I feel. I know I'll still feel it when we're out of this place. *If* I get out of this place. So I wanted to say it now, before I could lose the chance. That's all."

Rocío was silent for a time, peering across the darkening clearing. "Okay," she said. "I'm not going to say anything like that back, but I can say that nothing is going to happen to you as long as I'm here to stand in the way."

I was gratified for the second it took me to remember: "It seems to me you've made that commitment to everyone in our group."

The corner of her mouth curved upward. "I'm going to do everything in my power to protect everyone here," she said. "That's true. But… with you, it seems like there's a lot more 'everything.'"

My breath caught. I held myself still, afraid whatever I said in answer might make her regret that admission. Finally, in the most casual tone I could summon, I managed to say, "So you do like me, then."

Rocío made a scoffing noise. "Shut up."

"Why don't you make me, Dragon-Tamer?" I said with a grin.

She did, exactly as I'd hoped, with another kiss.

* * *

What was the proper etiquette for waking up next to one's lover of sorts the morning after you'd first exchanged kisses? I hadn't done all that much kissing in general, and I expected that being in the middle of the Exam altered expectations regardless.

I looked down at Rocío, curled against me with her head on her arm in the warm light that was starting to glow across the faux sky, and an ache filled my chest. We had one more day of the Exam before us: the day that might rip this girl away from me.

Rocío snuggled closer and raised her head to brush her lips across mine, then sat up to survey the clearing as if there were nothing all that complicated about the situation. Maybe there wasn't.

More of our fellow examinees had turned up overnight. A few figures were scavenging on the central spire's platform, and others had scattered along the fringes of the clearing. Prisha and Desmond, who was favoring his wounded foot, stood outside the hovel where they'd taken shelter. I counted twelve of us examinees altogether, though more might have been lurking beyond my view.

None of the structures appeared to have shifted, and no new terrors had emerged to meet us—but it was only a matter of time.

After the meal and the rest, my headache had retreated. Rocío's 'chantments held steady on my hand and side. Whatever the examiners threw at us, I had to be ready.

Rocío prodded our food sack and made a face when nothing but a fine dust spilled from the opening. "It all disintegrated," she said.

A pang shot through my stomach. Several more bags hung

around the edge of the tall platform. They looked as lumpy and full as before.

"They're making it harder for us," I said. "Forcing us to put in an effort to get more."

"We'd better go do that before they launch whatever else they've got planned at us."

"Wait." The second we left this platform, it wouldn't be just the two of us anymore. We might never have this intimacy again.

I tugged her to me and kissed her until I had to stop to breathe. She stayed there with me, cheek to cheek.

"Let's make it through," I said. "All the way to the end."

She smiled a little tightly. "I will if you will."

We climbed down, and Prisha and Desmond walked over to join us. I hesitated, but I couldn't just turn Prisha away. She was my best friend. We could discover whether our friendship had survived after the Exam was over.

Desmond was carrying a white box about the size of a textbook. "We found a prize," he said with half a smile. "There was a first aid kit in that shed." A blue bandage swathed his foot and ankle: a 'chanted numbing wrap.

"I guess we've got another climb ahead of us," Prisha said with a nod to the central spire.

"Looks that way," I agreed. "Come on, before everyone else has the same bright idea."

Desmond sat by the pool in the same place he had yesterday, but I eyeballed the spire and decided I was sound enough now to make it. I wanted the chance to survey the entire clearing from up there to get a stronger sense of what tricks I might rely on in a pinch.

Rocío shot me a concerned look, but my expression must have been unyielding enough that she opted against protesting.

I hauled myself up after her, bracing my left wrist against the holds instead of my numb, mangled hand. I was sweating when I heaved myself through the rectangular opening onto the platform, but I felt a certain sense of accomplishment.

The feeling lasted until I caught sight of Callum bent over a sack several feet away.

He offered me a sharkish grin that held about as much warmth as a sheet of ice. Then he went back to tearing into the sandwich he'd grabbed.

Prisha ignored him and strode to the edge, where the sacks dangled. She moved over when the first hook she checked proved empty. Rocío headed in the opposite direction.

Callum eyed her and then Prisha. "You know," he said to me as he straightened up, jerking the drawstring of his bag tight, "there are still too many of us. The examiner before said they'd be picking fewer than half."

My skin crawled, but I kept my voice even. "I'm sure they'll find some method of further narrowing us down."

He kicked aside the sandwich's plastic wrapper. "I think we're better off speeding up the process," he said, and barged toward Prisha without another word.

"Pree!" I wrenched out.

Callum hurled his sack at her before she could straighten up from grasping the bag she'd found. His projectile hit her square in the back, and with a gasp, she tumbled over the platform's edge.

CHAPTER TWENTY-TWO

Rocío

The wind hissed as Prisha disappeared over the side of the platform. I was already running. Words tumbled over my lips: a cradlesong, a cradling song.

The magic rippled with me as I dropped to my knees, whipping my intent down over the rim.

Prisha smacked into a cushion of air a couple feet from the ground. The impact sounded painful but less so than the ground would have been. She coughed as she rolled over, but she was alive.

As I pulled back from the edge, a thump sounded behind me. I spun. Callum sprawled a few feet from me with Finn on top of him, struggling to pin him down. Callum elbowed him in the face.

A wordless cry escaped my lips. Finn's hand. His ribs. Why was he fighting? He was going to hurt himself worse.

Then it hit me. Callum had been going to shove me off after Prisha. Would have, if Finn hadn't stopped him.

I scrambled away from the treacherous edge. "Stop it!" I shouted.

Callum rammed his fist at Finn's eye, but Finn jerked his head to the side, and then flinched as the other boy kneed him in the gut.

I circled them, my hands clenched, trying to figure out how to intervene without accidentally giving Callum an opening. Finn wasn't much of a fighter to begin with, but now he was working around major injuries.

Callum kicked out, sending Finn tumbling backward. I dashed over and grabbed Finn's arms as Callum heaved himself to his feet. With a rough laugh, he charged at us.

The lyric that had transported me from my living room to the shoreline nearly a week ago slipped to the front of my mind. I sang it out and pulled Finn closer, wrapping the strands of magic around us with the cadence of the words, picturing the spot near the fountain below us where Desmond was waiting. Energy whipped through the air around us.

My last glimpse of the platform before I squeezed my eyes shut was Callum staggering backward. The magic grabbed us with a lurch and a drop. We hit the ground I'd been picturing still on our feet.

Finn was breathing so harshly I suspected he was suppressing a sob. "Prisha," he said, clutching my shoulder. "He tossed her right over."

"Prisha's okay. I caught her."

He raised his head to see Prisha walking over to us. Relief flashed across his face, followed by another shudder. His gaze slid back to me. "He was going to— He was coming at *you*—"

"It's okay." I hugged him tight, as much for my reassurance as his, burying my face in his shoulder. Callum hadn't hurt him. I'd gotten him out of there. "I'm okay. You made sure of that."

"For now," Prisha said, coming to a stop beside Desmond.

A shriek carried from the platform high above us, and my back tensed. Prisha grimaced. "Fates only know what havoc Callum's wreaking on the rest of them up there."

As Finn let me go, the hum of magic condensed around me. It clung to me even more urgently than before. Almost... desperately. As if it were a small child begging for help.

The impression unnerved me, but I didn't have time to puzzle it out. We had to help ourselves.

"This seems like a good time to head for cover," Desmond said.

"Right," Finn said. He rubbed his hand over his face as if to ground himself. "Let's go."

We'd just started for the nearest of the small black shacks when another cry rang out behind us. I whirled to see a girl falling from the platform. She flung out a strand of magic to catch herself. It smacked into the side of the stone spire and brought her swinging after it, and she slammed into the stalk hard enough that I heard bone crack. I winced.

"Come on," Prisha said.

We ran the rest of the way, as fast as we could with Desmond hobbling at Prisha's side. I peered into the shadowy interior of the shed. It was empty except for a long, flat object lying near the back. The light in the sky was intensifying with a sunlike glare, and I could already feel heat wafting from the black walls.

"I don't think we'd want to hide out in here," I said. It didn't even look big enough to hold all four of us, at least not if we wanted room to maneuver.

But that object might be something useful. I ducked in and grabbed it. As I held it up in the light, my stomach sank.

It was a slim, curved knife in a leather sheath.

"Is it 'chanted?" Finn asked.

"I don't think so." I couldn't hearken any whisper of magic in its surface.

A thud carried to our ears, and we all looked to the central spire. The girl who'd fallen partway had jumped to the ground. She didn't glance our way, just limped off toward one of the other shacks. Then the air shuddered.

With a sizzle, a line of magical fire seared across the ground and smashed into the girl. She screamed, dropping and rolling, and the flames immediately sputtered out. A familiar pale figure stepped out from behind one of the smaller spires.

Lacey had made it here after all. She was holding a dark rope in her hand. She swung it, casting a flame along its length, and I recognized it as a whip.

When had she gotten herself a *whip*?

"What in Hades's name is she doing now?" Finn said, with a wince as the flame sizzled toward its target. "I'd say I'm glad she's here, but... I guess they'll be distracted from fighting when the next stage starts. The examiners know how to occupy us well."

My fingers clenched the sheath of the knife. A cold certainty settled over me.

"I think this *is* the next stage," I said.

"What do you mean?" Desmond said, scanning the clearing. His fingers jittered softly against his thigh. I guessed he hadn't hearkened anything that told him more than I could see.

I raised the knife. "The examiners are giving us weapons," I said. "They've left us here with no instructions, just the knowledge that they're taking no more than nine of us. They *want* us to fight each other. They want to see who's willing to go the farthest to make Champion."

Finn went rigid beside me. Prisha's expression was dark, but she didn't look surprised by my suggestion. I wondered again what had passed between the two of them so that Finn hadn't felt safe staying with her last night.

"The last test," she said, her voice hollow. "Why wouldn't it be that? Total chaos."

The memory of Sean swam up in my mind: his gaunt face and haunted eyes, the tremor that had passed through him when he'd talked about the Exam. He might have failed during one of the early tests, but suddenly I had the feeling he'd lived through this final stage. Lived through it and still been discarded.

I was so close...

The girl Lacey had blasted was struggling onto her hands and knees. Lacey walked a few steps closer. She spoke words too low for me to hear and raised the whip.

"No!" I couldn't help yelling.

Lacey snapped the whip with a *crack* against the other girl's head. The girl slumped limply on the ground.

Lacey looked up, and her cool eyes fixed on us.

We braced ourselves instinctively, and Prisha stepped closer to the shack. I murmured a shield into being around us. The presence in the magic was still wrenching at me, but with a sense of helplessness that was new. The energy around us felt almost limp as I pulled strands of it into my barrier.

I frowned, singing the words again, reaching more firmly. Why was the magic so weak? The hum was faltering, dipping here and there to a quaver.

"Rocío," Finn said, grasping my forearm.

Lacey took a step toward us. A guy sprang from behind a shack to her left and charged at her, another boy racing at her from the right at the same moment. I thought I remembered both of them from Group One. The wiry one with black hair and brown skin appeared mostly unharmed, but his taller, fairer companion wore a vicious red welt across his face where his right eye had once been. An image flashed through my mind of one of those vines squeezing around his head, and I shivered.

Lacey darted back to her spire, and both of the boys hollered castings after her. She managed to shatter a surge of crackling energy with a swing of her whip, but the ground bucked under her, and she tripped onto her knees. The one-eyed boy stalked forward, hefting what looked like a medieval mace.

Even though I hated what Lacey had done to the other girl, I didn't want to see her battered to a pulp. The urge to act gripped me, but uncertainty glued me in place. Attacking the boys instead wouldn't be any better.

Finn's words from last night about making my own choices came back to me. But carving my own path didn't work. I hadn't been able to save Mark or Judith. The examiners had gotten what they wanted in the end anyway.

Finn's fingers slid down to squeeze my hand. I glanced at him, and the ache around my heart softened. I'd saved him more than once, and Prisha, just now.

If this test was to see how vicious we could be to each other, then we *could* beat it. We had another choice. If we all refused to play—

Finn read the shift in me before I'd finished putting it into words in my own head. "No more deaths?" he said.

"Not if I can help it." I pushed away from the shack.

"Stop!" I raised my voice, hoping everyone across the whole clearing could hear me. "We all need to stop attacking each other! Is that really how you want to make Champion? If we just wait, we'll all be alive, and the examiners can choose the people who've proven themselves already."

"Says someone who's not afraid she won't be picked," the wiry boy snapped, and slashed his hand toward Lacey.

She dodged a slap of energy that left a dent in the ground and rattled off a verse right back at him, fumbling with her whip.

The bolt she cast flew wild, but the boy managed to smack it toward his supposed ally. The one-eyed boy yelped as it caught him in the belly.

"Whoa!" Finn said. "We could at least come up with a contest that's less fatal. Long jump? Capture the flag?"

The three ignored us. Lacey scrambled behind her spire. The wiry boy glanced between her and his companion, who was doubled over with an arm around his belly. He hesitated for a second—only a second—and then he strode toward the one-eyed boy, his lips forming another casting as he narrowed in on the easier target.

Every nerve in my body resisted the sight. I called out the same words I'd used to summon our shield and cast it toward the one-eyed boy.

The wiry boy's slice of magic bounced off the magical barrier. He swore. His former ally swayed upright and fled for a nearby shack.

The wiry boy turned with a glare so sharp, I flinched. "If you want attention that badly, you can have it," he said.

Finn pulled me around the side of the shack with the others. The boy's voice rang through the air, and a wind filled with razor edges blasted around us. My shield shuddered and cracked, and Prisha yelped. We all ducked down, Prisha clutching her shoulder. Blood bubbled up beneath her fingers.

"I'm not sure I want to keep playing the pacifist," she said.

The boy was rapping out another casting. I conjured a new shield, my tongue tripping over the words. Then there was a sizzle and a gasp and a thudding of receding footsteps. Lacey must have gone after him while he was distracted, or the one-eyed boy had.

This was the wheat the examiners had cut us down to over the last four days: a few of us who'd supported each other and everyone daring and brutal enough to make it through all the tests alone.

"Do you want help with that?" Desmond motioned to the red seeping down the sleeve of Prisha's shirt.

"Thanks," Prisha said.

As Desmond muttered a verse to seal the cut, the magic in the air vibrated. The presence loosened its hold on my shoulders.

I could almost picture it drawing in a breath of relief. What *was* that?

"If they want to see who survives and *how* we survive, why don't we just get out?" Desmond looked at me. "Could you teleport us the way you did with Finn from the platform, to... someplace other than here?"

My body stiffened. The thought of leaving the rest of our fellow examinees to slaughter each other made me feel sick. Maybe a few of them, like Callum, were enjoying throwing around their power, but the rest were probably just desperate.

Prisha shook her head. "It won't work," she said. "There's a... a shell, I suppose you could say, around the arena. It doesn't let any magic in or out. The examiners would never risk anything we do here leaking out and being noticed."

She meant by the Dulls and the unknowing mages in the vast city that surrounded Rikers Island. I'd forgotten how close we were to civilization. A big enough blast of magic, uncontained, could easily raise questions the Confed's leaders wouldn't want to answer.

"How do you know?" I said. Her phrasing—the way she'd called this space an "arena"—rubbed me oddly.

Finn's jaw clenched.

Prisha looked at her feet. "I'd rather not get into it right now," she said, but in that instant I had enough of an idea that I no longer needed her answer.

She'd gotten information from the examiners somehow. She knew more than the rest of us. And Finn had found out. He thought she could have prevented Judith's death.

No wonder he'd been upset.

Something twisted in my chest, but I couldn't let my horror distract me. I closed my eyes and extended my awareness out through the hum around us.

Yes. There. I hearkened it, faintly but clearly, along the circle of the walls: an arched barrier I couldn't penetrate with the press of my intent. The magic tremored against it, crawling along its surface as if searching for a crack.

As if it were as desperate to escape as we were.

"She's right," I said. "I can't do it. But maybe—"

I pressed my hand to the ground, hearkening downward now. If the tunnels like the one where Finn and I had waited out the storm extended this far...

No. All I felt below was a cold mass of rock.

I peeked around our shack. Lacey and the wiry boy were taking shots at each other. He was warding her off, but he'd ended up slouched on the ground. His hand shook as he held it in front of him. He'd had the power for a few big castings, but he was draining himself.

To their left, the one-eyed boy was racing toward *us*. I scrambled for words for a protective casting.

Lacey spotted him too. She slashed her whip toward him with a lyric more shrieked than sung.

The force she channeled through the weapon walloped the boy so hard he toppled head over heels. His body crashed to the ground and stayed there, motionless.

I swallowed a sound of protest. The magical presence contracted around me with a frantic but worryingly thin quivering.

What? I thought at it. *What's* wrong *with you?* Or was it something wrong with me? Had I drained myself without realizing it, and it was my hearkening that had weakened, not the magic itself? I didn't feel that tired.

Across the clearing—the arena?—a few of the other examinees were facing off. One girl stopped her casting with a shake of her head and simply threw herself at her opponent, fingers clawing and knees jabbing. Queasiness filled me.

Was this what the examiners really wanted? What would

make them happier: if I danced to their tune and threw myself into the fighting like the ghetto-magic upstart they'd pegged me as or if I refused their test altogether?

I didn't give a damn. Al carajo with their tests and their judgments. All that mattered was whether *I* could live with myself after today.

"We're fine for now while they're ignoring us," Desmond pointed out, "but this isn't the most strategic standoff spot. I like the feel of the hills over that way."

He motioned with his thumb toward the slopes molded like dunes on the other side of the central spire.

"I'm all for strategic," Finn said. "Shall we run for it?"

That would be faster than me trying to teleport them one at a time, if the magic could even support that many major castings right now. "Stay close to me," I said. "Get ready to help me hold up our shield if someone decides to come at us."

Finn nodded.

The sheathed knife was starting to feel uncomfortably heavy in my hand. I didn't want to use it, but I didn't want to leave it for someone else either. I settled for shoving it between my shoulder blades under the strip of torn sheet that was holding my shirt together.

We all dragged in a breath, and then we took off.

A faint smoky smell had started to saturate the air amid the crackles and cries. The false sun overhead beat down, baking my dark hair. I sprinted toward the first rise beyond the central spire, maybe two hundred feet away, my hand on Desmond's elbow. Prisha gripped his other arm.

We'd just passed the spire when a girl with tear-streaked cheeks and a stream of burgundy dreadlocks leapt after us. She held no weapons, and her eyes were wide. "Please," she said, panting. "Can I join you?"

Prisha frowned, but Finn made an unfamiliar gesture with his fingers and nodded. "She's okay."

I motioned the girl over. The more of us stayed together, the more protection we could provide each other. And the more likely some of the others would change their minds and join us too.

We clambered over the slope and slid down the other side.

I turned, surveying our surroundings. The trench was steep in front of us but more gradually slanted at our backs, giving us a solid wall to hide behind and an easy escape route if we needed to retreat. Although there was nothing to retreat *to* other than the next trench.

Desmond nodded with apparent satisfaction. The girl with the dreadlocks stood a little apart from us, as if she wasn't ready to completely let down her guard. Then she edged closer.

"Hi," she said with a soft, rounded accent. "I'm Leonie. Thanks for—for not blasting me to Hades and back."

Desmond cocked his head. "Do I hear a little New Orleans?"

Her eyebrows rose. "New Orleans by way of Houston, thanks to the Academy. Good ears."

"I've got cousins down there."

Finn cleared his throat and pointed over the rise. "Here comes trouble."

Callum was climbing down the central spire, his red hair stark against the ivory even in the platform's shadow. His head swiveled. He'd seen us.

But he must have spotted someone else that seemed a better target, because he stopped partway down and pressed himself against the stalk, peering in a different direction. He pulled an object I couldn't make out from his pocket and hurled his arm forward as if sending an army into a charge.

The air shrieked and shimmered. Something crashed;

someone squealed. And the magical presence around me didn't just contract but shrank.

It was almost as if the castings aimed to destroy were hurting the magic itself.

I went still. What if it *was* that? The magic in here was just as trapped as we were, and I could feel it as solidly as I could feel any of the people beside me. It had shown intent. It had helped me—in the windstorm and the trap of vines. Like a conscious thing.

Judith had said that no one knew exactly what the world's magic was or why we could use it the way we did. Maybe that was because all this time, we'd simply failed to recognize a very different but no less real living creature.

"The castings," I said. "Every 'chantment and conjuring that's breaking things, hurting people... I think they're killing the *magic* too."

CHAPTER TWENTY-THREE

Finn

If someone had suggested that I'd murdered every drop of water I'd ever drunk, I'd have found that only marginally harder to accept than the proposition that magic was something we could kill.

"Killing the *magic?*" Prisha's tone conveyed similar disbelief. "What are you talking about?"

Rocío's gaze was distant. "I told you before I could feel something strange in it," she said. "The feeling has kept getting stronger. Something in the magic doesn't like what's happening here in the Exam. I think it was trying to tell me, to get me to notice it, from the first morning, but I didn't understand until now. The more we cast destructive spells, the weaker it gets, and the more... shaky, I guess. Scared."

The whisper of magic around me didn't feel much different from how it usually did, but Rocío had to be infinitely more attuned to it than I was. Still...

"Wouldn't someone else have noticed before now?" I said.

"The magic in the arena is cut off from the rest of the world,"

Rocío said. "Right? There's just a tiny portion of it in here. Out in the world, the impact would be so spread out it'd be hard to pick up on the change. But here, anything that hurts that energy hurts it badly."

"You're talking about magic as if it's *alive*," Prisha said.

"I think maybe it is." Rocío's voice dropped. "I know how crazy that sounds, but it seems to... to want things, to care about things. It's warned me, helped me. I'm not saying it's, like, some huge creature wrapped around the planet. But maybe it's millions of little bits of life that are all connected? Isn't that possible?"

"'Any sufficiently advanced technology is indistinguishable from magic,'" Desmond murmured. "Any sufficiently advanced life form could be too." He laughed. "I never thought— Wow. If that's true, we'd have to rethink everything."

"Even if it's only obvious here," I said, "the Confed must know. The Exam committee would observe the effect, and—"

I cut myself off. And what? I wasn't certain even the Circle was aware of half of the Exam committee's undertakings.

"Maybe the examiners do know," Rocío said, echoing my thoughts. "Maybe it's one more thing they decided to keep secret from everyone else."

The new girl, Leonie, scratched at a broad burn mark that marred the olive-brown skin of her forearm. I recalled speaking with her briefly in the courtyard, but so much had transpired since that morning four days ago that I couldn't dredge up anything about her other than what she'd just told us.

"When it's just us family, my grandmother talks that way about the magic," she offered. "As if it has a mind of its own. MawMaw always says to think of casting more as bargaining than creating."

The sun was blazing now like Helios himself. The dunes were too low to provide much shade. I swiped my damp hair from my forehead and registered the quiet around us. Not a single grunt, cry, thump, or crackle carried in the air.

It didn't much matter whether the magic were alive if we didn't stay the same.

"Something's up," I said. "They've stopped fighting. And I'm going to guess it's not because peace has suddenly come into everyone's hearts."

We eased up, leaning against the gritty surface of the slope that sheltered us, to peer over the top. There was no one in view across the arena except the bodies of the two examinees Lacey had felled. Then I spotted the flash of Callum's red hair. He was ducking out of one of the hovels, clutching a slingshot.

Another boy, the one with dark curls who'd been battling Lacey, emerged from a different hovel. He'd retrieved a box that looked like the first aid kit Desmond had found. After he'd tucked it into an emptied food sack slung over his narrow shoulder, he and Callum exchanged a glance. Callum headed left, and the curly-haired boy went right, toward the next of the small black structures.

I did not at all care for the looks of that. "They're gathering the supplies the examiners left for us," I said.

"That doesn't bode well," Prisha muttered. "Are there any we can get to first?"

"The shacks are all pretty far from the dunes," Rocío said. "And we don't know which ones they've already emptied. I'm not sure it's worth the risk of going out there and making ourselves a target."

"I'd vote for no," Desmond said. "Weapons can't beat magic. We'll stay rested while they wear themselves out fighting each other."

Rocío nodded, but her mouth was tight. She'd rather they didn't fight each other either, I knew.

Of course, they weren't fighting each other at the moment. I'd gotten the distinct impression that Callum and the other boy were working *together*.

We waited, watching, as the artificial sun beat down on us. After several minutes it became clear that two other examinees were searching the hovels too: the tall, bulky guy who'd apparently survived being in Callum's group all the way to the end and a girl with raggedly chopped brown hair who carried a hatchet shoved under her belt. I was pretty sure the guy had been on the new-magic side that first morning, but the girl had been with the San Francisco Academy group. She'd had a long, sleek ponytail then.

They stalked methodically across the arena, not talking to each other but offering occasional gestures of acknowledgement. My spirits sank. We had five and they four, but those four subscribed to Callum's brutal methodology.

Sweat slicked down my neck and back. The edge of the pool shimmered faintly beneath the central spire. I swallowed against the dryness in my mouth. Áriston mèn hýdōr. We'd never retrieved our breakfast, but if the heat didn't let up, it was thirst that would spell our doom first.

The girl with the hatchet finished her rounds. She hauled her sack over to the central spire, clambered up it with a speed that made me tense, and dropped a few more bags over the edge of the platform. When she'd climbed back down, she sat with her back against the stalk on the opposite side from the fountain. She pawed through one of the food sacks and started peeling open a wrapper.

A different figure slipped into view just then. A boy so slight he looked scarcely thirteen darted across the open ground to the fountain. I recognized him from the first morning too—even remembered his name: Jamie, from the Seattle Academy. He'd been flushed with a giddy mix of nerves and anticipation.

His face was pallid now, his steps wobbly. He must have

believed the coast was clear, as he didn't even glance over at the girl sitting in the spire's shadow. I suspected he'd held out as long as he could bear. He didn't bother with the taps but simply collapsed at the edge of the pool and began scooping water into his mouth.

The girl with the hatchet raised her head. Beside me, Rocío stiffened. Her lips moved to shape a casting, but I doubted any of us anticipated how swiftly the girl would move. She whipped onto her feet and around the spire's stalk, snatching her hatchet from her waist.

Jamie didn't have the chance to so much as look up. The girl screeched out a conjuring that slammed him forward into the pool. Then she rammed the flat of the hatchet's blade down on the back of his head.

Nausea shot through me, and a strangled sound escaped Rocío's lips. She leapt up but caught herself on the crest of the slope, her fingers gripping the yellow-brown surface. Hades knew there was no helping the poor kid now.

The girl with the hatchet straightened up. Jamie's body bobbed on the ripples still stirring where he'd hit the water. Her shoulders shuddered. She clenched her hands and dipped the head of the hatchet into the water to rinse off the blood. Then she strode around the spire, hefted her sack of supplies and the others of food, and disappeared from sight.

"Goddamn," Leonie said.

No words I had seemed adequate. Rocío slid lower on the slope again. I took her hand, twining my fingers with hers. She leaned into me, but her gaze was still trained on the rest of the arena.

Callum and his other companions had headed off too. The back of my neck prickled. They knew where we were holed up. They were carrying out some activity they didn't want us to see.

Time ticked away from us, and they didn't reemerge. "I don't like this," I said. "They're planning something, and I wouldn't be surprised if it's to do with us." There weren't many other people left besides those four and Lacey, wherever she'd absconded to. Actually, there might not be *any* others left.

Prisha anxiously twisted a strand of her hair around her finger. "Should we spread out a bit and see if we can spot them?"

Rocío sucked in her lower lip. "All right. But let's keep each other in sight. We've gotten this far by having each other's backs. I don't want to lose that advantage."

"With my ankle, I think I'd better man the fort here," Desmond said. He looked toward Leonie. "Stick around so we can keep two sets of eyes on watch?"

"I can handle that," she said, tossing back her dreadlocked hair.

Rocío's grip tightened on my hand for long enough to make my heart squeeze with it. Then she slipped away to the right. Prisha followed her, peering over the rolling landscape behind us. So I headed left.

Rocío had been wrong. There were hovels near the dunes—or at least there was one. It stood just beyond the nearest spire, which had hidden it from our original position. The structure would make a good observation point without taking me too far from the others.

My dragon-tamer had been right that working together made us stronger, though. The whisper of energy in the air shifted around my movements, and I wondered if that wasn't the way all magic operated as well, whether it was alive or not. It let us work with it, let us conduct its energy to our intent when we matched the rhythms of its flow.

What Rocío had said about the magic actually made a lot of sense when I thought of it that way. Taking something so harmonious and making it destroy parts of the world that sustained it—why wouldn't that harm the magic in turn or weaken the power it could channel?

A symphony could suffer for a single off-key note. It would be stranger if the magic remained unaffected by how we used it.

I came up parallel with the hovel, hesitated, and scrambled over the slope. When I glanced back, I could still see Desmond's dark head and Leonie's mass of dreads where I'd left them, but as I crept toward the hovel, the spire concealed them. They'd hear me if I hollered, though. Desmond might even be following our movements in his surreptitious ways. I doubted he was using his literal eyes to monitor our surroundings.

The hovel's doorway faced the dunes. I peeked inside. Evidently, Callum's group had either missed this one or been too cautious to venture so close to our hideout. A metal mallet little larger than my hand lay on the ground amid the sweltering heat inside.

I scooted in, grabbed the tool, and yanked myself back out before I had to inhale that heavy air. Wedging the mallet's handle into my empty pocket, I edged to the side of the hovel to peer around it.

My legs locked. The four we'd observed earlier were gathered beside one of the shorter spires, obscured by the shadow of its platform. They'd all fashioned belts from strips of the sack fabric, which now held their extra weapons at their waists. The boy with the dark curly hair had wrapped a numbing bandage around his right bicep and elbow.

As I watched, the bulky guy's mouth moved and Callum waved his hand. They were too distant for their voices to be audible, but the ground between them and me offered no cover.

I was still a mage, wasn't I? Uncovering their schemes was worth expending a little of the limited energy I had left.

I recited a poetic line sotto voce, focusing my attention on the air near my ears. It took more concentration than I'd expected to modulate my melody and shift the magic into an amplifying cone.

My headache woke up, piercing the back of my skull. Then Callum's brusque voice reached me.

"What's there to agree on? Taking out the wimps is simple. I've already done half of the job for you."

"You can't know for sure they'll make us all Champion even with everyone else gone," the girl with the hatchet said.

"If we get rid of that last bunch, it leaves the four of us and what's-her-face," Callum said. I assumed he meant Lacey. "The Confed *wants* their special soldiers. Do you really think they're going to cull more of us after all this?"

"We can decide how we deal with each other after," the bulky guy said. "I don't care, as long as the freaks who can't even be bothered to fight don't get our places."

"It'll be even easier taking them down with them all clinging so close together," Callum said. "We surround them, and they're not going to be able to defend against all of us at the same time."

"Are you sure you can hold up *your* end?" the curly-haired boy said in a nasal sneer. "I saw your last castings. You're almost out of juice."

Callum snorted. "I just don't put in more effort than I need to. Maybe you should consider the same approach. And I've got more of those 'chanted cracklers too."

I didn't know what a "crackler" was, but knowing Callum, it couldn't be anything pleasant.

"All right," the girl said, shifting from foot to foot. "Let's get on with it, then. What's the plan?"

"Move fast," Callum said. "Just keep enough distance that they don't see you coming. I'll go over there and distract them while you're getting into place—pretend I'm too hurt to fight, beg for mercy." He laughed harshly. "I know a couple of those dopes. They'll buy it for long enough. I'll hit them first, hard, and the rest of you jump in then. Agreed?"

The others nodded. The group fanned out. Callum sauntered straight ahead, toward me.

I jerked back behind the hovel. Resolve settled like a stone in my gut.

He was alone now—and he wasn't aware I was here. He was the trigger in their plan. If I incapacitated him and then ran to warn the others, we could escape before his allies agreed to launch their attack. I could eliminate our most dangerous enemy: the figure who'd sparked the violence here, who'd united the four of them and aimed them at us.

I'd have to disable him quickly enough to avoid retaliation and hard enough to prevent him recovering before the Exam ended. Even without a headache pulsing between my temples, I wouldn't have counted on myself to accomplish that much with a casting in one try.

The answer wasn't magic, then. I needed another trick... or the same one. My hand fell to the solid line of the dissolving rod at my hip.

This was why Margo had given it to me: so that if it came down to my life or someone else's, I could save mine.

It was *more* than just my life now. The memory of Callum heaving his sack at Prisha flashed through my mind, and my stomach twisted. The way he'd run at Rocío next—I had bruises on top of my bruises from where he'd hammered me after I'd tackled him. He meant to kill all five of us, using whatever means he could. Attacking him first was merely self-defense.

I drew out the rod, my fingers curling around it. At the press of my thumb, its lid flipped open. The ache in my head expanded a little farther as I cast a quick 'chantment to thicken the shadows beside the hovel. Then I leaned out just enough to set eyes on Callum.

He was only twenty feet away, clutching his side and limping toward the hovel, putting on his act now that he was in view of the dunes. I supposed he meant to use the structure for the same purpose I had, as a defensive position from which to scout out his enemies before he made his final approach. A short metal baton bobbed on his belt.

When he turned his head with a wary glance toward the other end of the arena, he allowed himself a smile—that hard, narrow smile that had always served as a warning to run for cover.

A rush of heat coursed through me. Abruptly, I imagined myself jamming the dissolving rod right into the center of his chest, watching that smile falter with a bloody gurgle as his heart disintegrated and his eyes fogged. My lungs clenched at the image, but a tickle of anticipation followed.

He deserved it. He'd *earned* it. It would pay him back for everyone he'd hurt, everyone he meant to hurt, now and ever.

That last thought caught me with a chill that washed the anger right out of me. What was I thinking? Since when was I aiming to act as executioner? If I had to, if Callum gave me no choice, I'd do it, but I didn't want to. I didn't want to become someone who wanted to.

Callum scanned the area around him again. Then he pressed the heel of his hand to his forehead and closed his eyes with a wince that looked… genuine.

Was his head bothering him too? Had the other boy guessed right that Callum had drained himself?

How could he not have? Even *I* had been able to cast with more strength than he had in our classes. That had to be why most of his assaults had been physical, not magical. He was rationing his energy, attempting to work around his weakness.

Like me.

For one peculiar moment, through the ache in my own head,

I felt as though I stood in two places: where I crouched and where he walked. *I don't think even* they *like him*, Prisha had said of Callum's parents, and it was true. They'd known from the start he lacked the talent to be Chosen. Everyone had been able to observe how his family's favor lay with his sister.

How crushing would it have been to feel Granduncle Raymond's cutting disdain every day from the people who'd raised me? Would I be the one raging at the "wimps" and grasping for every vicious advantage?

I had no time to ponder the possibilities. Callum was nearly on me. I gripped the rod.

I wouldn't kill him, but if I was to ensure he didn't kill *us*, I had to hurt him badly enough that he'd need to focus whatever energy he had left on keeping himself alive.

My gaze settled on his upper leg. If I hit him in the thigh, he wouldn't be able to walk again without proper medical treatment, but he should be capable of containing the bleeding, especially if he was carrying one of those first aid kits in his sack. That seemed like the fairest compromise.

I pulled back against the hovel. Callum's halting footsteps scraped across the ground. I flexed my shoulders, bracing myself. All at once I felt like vomiting, as if I hadn't already purged enough in the last two days. Maybe I didn't have the will to commit even this much violence…

I had to—if not for me, then for Rocío, for Prisha, for everyone.

Callum slowed near the hovel. He started to step around it. My pulse lurched, and I threw myself around the corner at him.

He flinched at my charge but not fast enough to avoid me. Ducking beneath the swing of his arm, I jabbed the rod's point into the side of his thigh.

His exclamation broke off in a hiss of pain, and we both toppled, me stumbling over him. He pummeled me with his fist and the baton he'd wrenched from his belt. It must have been 'chanted, because every strike sent an unnatural sting lancing through my body. One of his knuckles ricocheted off my forehead, but I held on to the dissolving rod.

I heaved myself backward, dodging his sprawled feet. A red gush soaked through his cargo pants down to the knee. There was no need for him to pretend injury now.

Callum bent over his leg, his breath ragged as he choked out a verse over the ruined hollow where a chunk of his thigh muscle had ceased to be. Skin, muscle, and bone had melted in the gash. I gagged at the sight.

As I reeled back toward the hovel, Callum reached into a pocket by his knee. His face was yellowing. He broke from his casting with a hoarse shout.

"Get them!" he said, fixing me with a glare that would have burned me to a crisp if he'd had the power to. "Kill them all!" He whipped the stone he'd grabbed from his pocket at me.

I heaved myself out of the way, and it struck the hollow on the far side of the dune with an earth-shaking *boom*.

CHAPTER TWENTY-FOUR

Rocío

"Finn's not back yet?" Prisha said when we returned to our stakeout spot.

Before the worry in my gut had time to reach my thoughts, a shout rang out. A thunderclap reverberated through the air and the ground, tossing me backward into the others. Leonie caught my arm.

A thin whine from above made my head jerk up. Tiny blades of energy were raining down on us.

I managed to blurt out a shielding lyric. Desmond and Prisha's voices rose to join mine, but we weren't quite fast enough. One of the blades sliced across my shoulder; another caught the edge of my ear. Pain burst through my skin. Voices hollered all around us.

Finn stumbled down the trench toward us, his face flushed and his eyes wild. Fresh blood splattered his shirt. My heart stopped.

"Sorry," he said, panting. "I thought I could prevent this without—"

A rush of flame seared over our shield. The surface shook, enough heat seeping through to singe my scalp. The magic was cringing around me, cowering against my shoulders, and the barrier protecting us trembled with it.

With the magic weakening, our opponents were going to have trouble drawing power to conjure their attacks too, but that wouldn't help us if our shield broke first.

With a hiss, a rush of clear liquid cascaded down the floor of the trench toward us. From the way it was steaming, I didn't think we wanted it touching us. Our "strategic" position wasn't so strategic anymore.

"Run for it!" I shouted.

No one needed additional convincing. We scrambled up the slope and charged down the other side. Desmond pointed across the arena, and I veered to follow him.

The air warbled with a conjured force, but the blur of energy streaked by us, hardly touching our shield. We raced around the spire where Finn and I had slept and on toward another that stood just a few feet from the hedge. If we had shelter in front and the hedge wall at our backs, our enemies would have fewer directions to assault us from.

Except the spire was barely wide enough to shield three of us effectively, let alone five. We clustered behind it, our breaths ragged. Finn bent to snatch up a mallet he'd dropped—when had he gotten that?—and Leonie held out her hand.

"Would you give me that?" she said. "I should be able to— I can arrange us a better barricade."

He passed the mallet to her and rubbed his forehead. His headache was back, it seemed, but he didn't seem physically injured, at least no more than he'd been when I last saw him.

The blood on his shirt wasn't his.

He saw me looking. "Callum," he said roughly. "I didn't—

He's alive. He's just going to be... distracted until this is over. But the other three are fixated on taking us down."

"And Lacey's here somewhere," I said. "Unless they—"

He shook his head. "They mentioned her. I think we all have to keep an eye out for her."

Leonie had slipped around the side of the spire. She raised the mallet, its head hardly wider than her fist, and sang out a short, rolling line in Latin as she swung it against the spire.

The ivory rock cracked. The split raced through the stalk as the spire above wobbled. Leonie smacked it with her palm, and it tipped with her shove. Ten feet of rock careened to the ground like a chopped tree.

"Come on," Leonie said, dropping down behind it.

"Where'd you learn to do *that*?" Desmond asked as we spread out along the fallen spire.

"I've got a knack for stone," Leonie said. "Not something that came up at the Academy a whole lot, granted. I've never worked on anything quite that big before." She let out a shaky laugh. Then she glanced toward the rest of us. "So there's just three of them after us? How're we going to strike back?"

"We're not going to," I said. My chest clenched at the thought, the magic clenching around me in turn.

"Why not?" she demanded. "The way you can cast, you could probably deal with all of them on your own!"

"It doesn't matter," I said. "If we start hurling those kinds of castings around too, we'll just drain the magic even faster. And... I don't want to make Champion if I have to hurt people—*kill* people—to do it. Do you?"

She stared at me, and I braced myself. She might decide we were obstacles rather than on her side. She wiped a hand across her mouth, and her hazel eyes shadowed.

"We have to do *something* other than hiding," she said. "They were already finding ways to get around our shield. They almost broke it. I don't want to kill anyone—that goes without saying—but I would like to leave here alive."

"We don't have much choice," Prisha said. "We *could* take them down. She's right. We haven't fought back yet, so they won't be expecting it. If we hit them hard and fast enough—"

"*No*," Finn said. "We're finding another way."

Another way. Something other than the avenues the examiners had left for us: killing or being killed.

I inhaled slowly. "We can't keep running and hiding all day." That was pretty clear.

"As long as they can maneuver around us, we can't keep them off us," Finn said. "Could we box them up somehow?"

"No," I said. "They'd break a cage just like they're breaking our shields. No matter what we cast, they could cast something to counteract it."

"Judith's boxes *stopped* us from casting," Desmond pointed out.

Hope sparked inside me but only for a second. "We couldn't build something that complex quickly enough. They'd feel it coming." And shatter it before it took effect. Judith had needed four hours to cast her 'chantment. I might be able to do it faster but not fast enough.

But that idea felt like a step in the right direction. I hadn't wanted to use magic for anything other than helping or healing, but as long as I wasn't *hurting* anyone, I could still pass this test on my terms.

"What if," I said, testing the idea as I put it into words, "instead of trying to build something to stop them from conducting the magic, we just stopped the parts of them that they use to conduct it, directly?"

"Without killing them?" Prisha said.

"It'd be tricky to pull off," I said. "But if we manage it, we'll *all* get through this alive."

"I'm listening," Desmond said, propping his elbow against the side of the spire. "But we should figure it out fast. They're coming."

I peeked over the top of the fallen spire. The three figures had gathered together again. They were stalking from one far-off spire to a closer shack. The obscuring 'chantment they'd cast on themselves turned their bodies into blurs that, at a glance, could almost have been shadows.

They weren't going to make carrying out my plan easy for us, and in a couple minutes they'd be close enough to start up their assault again.

The dark blurring of their forms stirred up my memory of the sentries in Iran—the guards we'd ripped through unknowingly. My throat tightened.

I was *not* going to let that happen here. Not again. That was not who I was, no matter what the Confed thought of new-magic families and our street-grown talents.

I dropped back down. If I'd had the training, I'd have hit them with the magimedical equivalent of a general anesthesia, but the brain was far too delicate an organ for me to want to risk experimenting. I wouldn't know where to start. But we did have other, less sophisticated options.

"Okay," I said. "If we can stop them from moving—their arms and legs, their mouths, their vocal chords too, I guess, and anything else they could use to make sound, to cast—then they're stuck. They can't do anything to us. And we just wait down the clock."

Prisha frowned. "We'll have to focus carefully if we don't want to accidentally stop them from *breathing*, which I assume is not what you're going for."

"It's better than planning to stop them from breathing in the first place, isn't it?" I said.

And hopefully it wouldn't hurt the magic either. It would just be a... rearranging of states rather than blatant destruction.

"I have to be honest," Finn said. "I don't think I'm capable of handling even one of them on my own, but I'll give everything I have to support the rest of you."

"You and I could take on one of them together," Desmond suggested. He pushed himself up onto his knees.

"Then the two of you could focus on another," I said to Prisha and Leonie. "And I'll take the last one."

I could handle that to start with, at least. For how long, I didn't know. How many more hours were left before the examiners would call this test to an end?

"So what about—" Leonie started, but Desmond made a silencing jerk of his hand.

We all straightened up to look over the side of our barricade.

The shadowy figures had reached the next spire over: a short, spindly one with a single platform near the top of its stalk. They'd have to cross open ground to get at us now.

"They're climbing it," Finn said. "Going for a higher vantage point."

Maybe they *could* reach us from that distance. I watched them as they scrambled up, one after the other, staying on the far side of the spire. "We need to be ready as soon as we have a good view of them," I said. "I'll focus on the one closest to the right."

"We'll do the left?" Finn said to Desmond.

"Works for me."

"So middle for us it is," Prisha said.

I drew a lyric onto my tongue: an old lullaby. *Arru arru.* The air around the platform shimmered with the start of an opposing conjuring. I choked out the command: "Now!"

I aimed all my attention at the hazy figure to the right of the trio. As I sang out the lyric, I propelled my awareness toward his hulking body, hearkening the shapes of elbows and hips and feet, the movement of lips, the vibration of a membrane in a throat.

The magic stretched and quivered but held my intent. I clamped it around the boy.

The 'chantment he'd woven around himself dissolved to reveal a startled face, arms partly raised, mouth half-open. The strain of his muscles pushing against my 'chantment echoed through the magic into me, but I could ignore that. In the first few seconds, the casting felt almost easy.

Then a blaze of light slashed across my vision, rocking the fallen spire I was leaning against. Desmond swore, and my concentration snapped. As I lost my grip on the boy across from me, I felt him whipping into action.

No.

The impact had knocked Leonie onto her back, her shoulder twisted at an unnatural angle. She groaned as she tried to sit up.

"Desmond!" I said.

He was already spinning to help her. I threw my focus back at our attackers' platform. I could see all three of them clearly now; we'd dispelled their disguises.

The wiry boy hurled another of his bladelike assaults at us. Prisha shouted out a poetic line that solidified a new shield in front of us. The streaks of energy bounced off it into the ground, leaving a line of gouges in the gritty surface.

"Arru arru," I cooed again, trying to toss my intent around all three of our opponents. I caught two, the hulking boy and the girl beside him, who I thought had cast the blaze. Limbs. Mouths. Throats. Still, still.

The effort dragged at me. An ache spread down my spine, and my fingernails prickled. Prisha called out another line, Finn's voice twining with hers, and the wiry guy stiffened too.

Desmond finished murmuring over Leonie. As she gasped in apparent relief, a different kind of tremor tickled through the magic. A sense of eagerness or reviving. It wound around me, strengthening my focus.

Wait. I'd felt that rejuvenation in it before. When we'd cast healing 'chantments at other times. Maybe the effects of our castings didn't just work one way. If forcing the magic to destroy weakened it, then being used to heal and create *should* restore it.

We couldn't use that knowledge now, but it meant something for the world outside the arena. It meant that no matter how much damage any mage did, we had hope of compensating.

I pinned the hulking guy and the girl with the hatchet even more firmly in place. Our current castings didn't seem to be affecting the magic we were using one way or another, neither strengthening nor weakening it, but they affected *us*. The ache was creeping across my back.

A tremor ran through Finn's body beside mine. All the others must be getting tired too. Even if Desmond and Leonie took over one of my two, I wasn't sure I could make it a full hour, let alone the entire day, keeping my focus that exact.

The cut on my shoulder throbbed. With each blink, my eyes felt hotter. Sooner or later—probably sooner—one of us was going to crack again, and our opponents had to be forming the most horrific castings they could think of as they stood locked there.

I'd gotten us into this mess. I needed to find a better solution than this, one we could hold until evening fell. Somehow.

CHAPTER TWENTY-FIVE

Finn

No doubt there were many lessons the examiners hoped we novices would learn over the course of the Exam: lessons about our capabilities and our limitations, about how ruthless an enemy could be, about where we truly stood in the world, about the Confed's absolute authority. The biggest lesson I'd come away with, though, was to always assume that even an utterly wretched situation would get worse.

The fabricated sun was scorching my face, searing across my forehead to combine forces with my headache. My ribs were throbbing again. The strain of my casting gnawed at me like a thorn digging under every fingernail. My voice rasped even at a murmur.

I drew out the verse, keeping as stable and slow a tempo as I could manage. My eyes stayed trained on the curly-haired boy's limbs, while Prisha focused her intent on the more delicate work around his face and throat.

Stop him moving and hold him in place—that was my sole responsibility.

The quiver of magic twitched by my ears, and the boy's hand slipped away from me. He clapped it against his hip, launching into a wordless casting.

My lungs clenched. I blurted out the Greek verse louder and caught him before more than a spark glinted in the air around him. The ache in my head pierced straight through the center of my brain. My dry lips prickled against each other as I continued chanting.

Prisha was mumbling to herself where she knelt beside me. A tremor ran down her back. How fatigued was she?

"I've got her, Rocío," Desmond said.

The girl at my other side let out a sigh. She'd been holding two—*two*—of our attackers, utterly on her own.

"I suppose I'm backup, then," Leonie said behind us.

I couldn't tell how much Desmond had been able to do for her shoulder, but she sounded steady enough. If we'd had three or four of her, I might have felt more hopeful. Rocío might be able to hang in there, but the rest of us were going to need to tap out soon.

The boy's murderous fury thrummed through the tension in his muscles. Rocío was trying to save the three of them, and yet their deepest desire was to murder us.

The thought had scarcely passed through my head when an explosive *boom* shook the air, and the ground beneath us pitched. Rocío clutched the spire, her chin knocking the ivory stone. I fell back on my rear, and Prisha toppled over next to me. With a startled grunt, Desmond stumbled to the side, into Leonie. All our castings shattered.

A cry echoed across the open ground from the spire where our would-be assailants had stationed themselves. Their platform perch had split. One half tipped and plummeted to the ground, the hatchet girl and the curly-haired boy falling with it. The hulking guy stumbled to the side and nearly fell over the opposite edge, but he managed to grab on to the stalk. The ground gave another lurch and sent him tumbling into a heap by the others.

"Quick!" Rocío said, rubbing her banged chin with a wince. "We have to stop them before they get back up."

Prisha and Leonie were already springing to the fallen spire. "I can take one on my own for a while," Prisha said to me. "You rest while you can."

"Just stay ready to jump back in, you hear?" Leonie added.

Desmond righted himself as the quakes subsided. He massaged his temple. How was *his* head faring? The sharpest shards of my headache had smoothed as soon as I'd ceased casting, but my nerves still blazed all across my skull. My empty stomach listed queasily.

"Was that your classmate?" Desmond said. "The explosion? Is he still running around?"

"Not *running*, I wouldn't think," I said. "He did have these rocks... They must have been 'chanted. But the other ones didn't have quite that wide an impact."

"It'd take a lot of power to conjure an earthquake."

"Yeah. I don't know if that was him. He's never been a stellar talent." I glanced toward the edge of the dunes where I'd left Callum. "It might have been Lacey. She's still around."

"It might be both of them," Desmond pointed out. "We can always hope they keep each other busy the rest of the day."

The ground hiccupped, and I braced my hands against it. A terrible idea occurred to me. "It might not be any of us. It might be another part of this test. The examiners quite enjoy mixing things up to throw us off, I've noticed."

Desmond grimaced, and Prisha shifted her weight. Yesterday's confession came back to me like a punch in the gut. In our struggle to stay alive, I'd almost forgotten: She knew the examiners' modus operandi better than any of us. I guessed she didn't have anything useful to contribute now. We were on our own, as always.

I eased onto my wobbly feet and walked to the stump of the spire Leonie had cracked open. The section still standing was as tall as my shoulder at some of its jagged points. Across the way, our trio of opponents sprawled near the chunks of their broken platform, motionless. On our side, Rocío's face appeared placid for now, but Prisha's shone with sweat. Leonie's rounded jaw clenched around each word she rolled out.

There was no sign of Callum or Lacey by the dunes, but that only made me more wary. If I'd seen them, at least I'd have known where they were.

Our greatest enemy was time passing far too sluggishly as our castings wore us down. Tempus edax rerum. I didn't think it could be more than midday. We might have hours to go. Why would the examiners cut this day short?

"Desmond," Prisha said through gritted teeth. "Switch?"

He leaned against the spire next to her. After a few seconds, she sagged backward. "Thank you."

A shiver rippled through the ground, as if to remind us that we might have even bigger problems in the next several hours than simply maintaining status quo. I set my hands against the spire's stump, recalling how simply Leonie had broken it with that mallet and her talent.

I couldn't depend on my magical ability in the slightest, but could I find another tool? A couple of hovels stood nearby.

"They'll have checked all the shacks on this side," Prisha said, noticing my look. "I'm sure of it, Finn. We need you here."

Did they? Hades only knew what for. I pushed away from the spire, heading toward one of the slanted black shapes. I had to at least attempt to help.

When I hunched to peer through the hovel's doorway, I found the interior empty, as Prisha had predicted.

As I walked back, splinters of pain tingled up my left arm. The numbing 'chantment on my hand was deteriorating.

O gods, how laughable was it that I'd once imagined I might take a role in the Confed's defensive division, protecting the entire nation? I could barely hold myself together. Even Callum, with his leg mangled and his magic drained, was making more of an impact in the battle than I was.

I'd had a real impact in that muffled, shadowy hall of the house in Iran, when I'd dug in as deep as I could and hurled every particle in me into the magic.

I halted at the spire's jagged stump. My gaze shot back to the trio on the ground. I'd summoned that much power once. It had been for a mere moment and at great mental and physical expense, but I'd found it. I didn't need a wallop quite that expansive to win the day here.

I could still make Champion. If I cast a wave of fire or electricity at our enemies, if I destroyed three more lives, I'd prove myself exactly the sort of soldier the Exam committee appeared to be seeking. I might even end the Exam. Only seven of us would remain. The examiners would step in and call a halt then, surely?

Whatever else might be said about him, Callum's logic was sound: They wouldn't want to lose *all* of their prospective special ops team.

The solution felt so clear and simple—and as if it weighed a thousand pounds. I swallowed thickly.

Maybe if our three opponents had been charging at us in an attack, if I were saving our lives in a more immediate manner, I could have pulled it off. But while they lay there helpless? No. I was looking at three defenseless novices no older than I was, novices who'd stood in the courtyard four days ago as unknowing and unprepared as I'd been. They'd likely ended up here not because they had some fondness for ghastly trials but because it had seemed like the best of bad choices.

The magic wouldn't bend to an intent I couldn't commit to.

I *wasn't* the sort of soldier the examiners wanted. I never had been, and I never would be. Even if I'd appreciated the prospect of spending the rest of my life in that type of service, I wasn't meant to be Champion.

Leonie exhaled sharply, and the curly-haired boy kicked out a leg. I stiffened, groping for a casting, but he stilled again.

She shook her head. "I'm all right," she said. "I can keep at it a little while longer."

Prisha scanned the ruin we'd made of the arena. "No wonder the Dulls are afraid of mages," she muttered. "If we're capable of doing this to each other..."

"True," I said with a hoarse laugh. If the magicless ever caught an inkling that the Confed encouraged their own kids to slaughter each other, they'd never trust any mage again. The examiners would never have set up a test like this without that shield over the arena to eliminate any risk of the truth seeping out—

I froze, my good hand closing so tightly around one of the stump's sharp points that the stone stung my palm.

If the shield were no longer over the arena, they'd stop the Exam. A conjuring that immense, that powerful, must have required hours to build. If it were demolished, there'd be no hasty reconstruction.

It'd take more of a mage than I was to break their conjuring, of course... but I didn't actually need to break it, did I? I merely needed them to *believe* I was going to. I had my tools: I had tricks and my "silver" tongue. I had my words.

I had exactly the right person to say them to.

I drew myself tall and sucked in a breath. "That's it," I said as if to the entire rest of the group. "I think I can end the Exam now —at least, I'm going to attempt to. I'll break the shield they built around the arena, and then I'll project what's happening here up over the island, so everyone in the city can see what the examiners are making us do. They'll have to put a stop to this madness then."

Desmond's eyebrows rose. Rocío gave me a little nod without removing her focus from her target, as if she had faith I could pull all that off if I said I could. My throat constricted at that gesture, but it was Prisha's reaction I was most interested in.

She stared at me, her shoulders rigid. "Finn," she said, "they'll burn you out."

"I know." Suggesting insurrection on this scale wouldn't go unpunished regardless of my success. "They probably will anyway."

She pushed herself upright and pulled me toward the hedge. "You *can't*," she said, pitching her voice low. "They'll see it as an act of rebellion."

"It *is* an act of rebellion," I said. "It's what I need to do."

"There has to be something else we can try," Prisha protested. "You can't just throw your chances away."

I'm not, I thought. *I'm taking a chance.*

"This is the best strategy I can think of. I have to contribute somehow. But don't worry about me. They'll find out what I'm up to as soon as the shield is down anyway. So you do what *you* have to do too."

They must have given her some way to communicate with them even in here, one that didn't require magic passing through the barrier. Why else would they have informed her of that detail in the first place?

I hadn't anticipated the lift of her chin and the flash of her eyes.

"No," she said with a quaver. "I can't turn you in. I won't. I shouldn't have reported on anyone before, and I'm done with it."

It turned out it was possible for one's heart to swell and sink at the same time. Any other moment, I'd have loved my best friend for that conviction, but it was the opposite of what I needed right now. I wasn't going to break the shield. I doubted I'd make even enough of a dent for the examiners to notice I was trying to unless she tipped them off.

"Pree..." I said, my voice thick. Maybe it hadn't been fair anyway, to trick her, to leave whatever became of me on her conscience. She'd never turned her back on me. I set my hand on her arm, leaning close. "I want you to tell them," I said quickly. "I *need* you to. That's the only way this plan works."

Prisha held my gaze, her brow knitting—and then relaxing. I'd been afraid she might still argue, but all she said was, "Are you sure about this?"

"One hundred percent."

"I hope you know what you're doing." She twisted her hand to squeeze my arm in turn, and I knew I'd been right to count on her. Maybe the chasm that had opened between us wasn't as insurmountable as it had seemed last night.

She hurried off and ducked into one of the hovels.

I approached the hedge wall. I had to make my performance convincing if the examiners were going to believe I posed a real threat.

I rested my hands against the warm metal brambles, avoiding the razor edges. Then I shut my eyes and extended my awareness upward to hearken the hiss of the massive conjured shield.

My reflex was to turn to my memorized Classical verses for one that matched my intent. The vast spread of the barrier loomed above me, and my headache stabbed through my skull. No, I needed more. I needed words as close to the core of me as I could delve.

A casting didn't require ancient Greek or Latin. It merely needed to speak to me so I could speak to the magic through it.

A tune swam up from my memory, from one of my mother's favorite albums when I'd been little. She'd mostly played it when Margo and Hugh were out with friends for the evening and Dad was working late. I'd learned the lyrics to every song so I could sing along with it—with her. It had been one bond I'd shared with her that the rest of the family hadn't, and when I was six years old and my world much smaller, it had never occurred to me I'd want more.

"And the walls will bend, and the walls will break," I began. I channeled all my intent into the melody and into propelling the magic up toward the shield with it. My voice rose. Let the whole arena hear it. "And when we look up, there'll be no mistake."

The energy I was conducting vibrated through me, into the hedge and up to the tightly woven barrier. The shield held firm against my faint pressure, but like Patroclus donning Achilles's armor, the semblance of greatness was all that mattered.

I called illusions from the magic, one after another: sparks shooting, fissures gleaming. The examiners had to look down and see their shield cracking. They had to come.

They didn't. The throbbing of my headache burrowed down the back of my head to my neck. Sparks danced not only on the shield but behind my eyes. I belted out the lyric again. The shield even trembled as my illusion swam across it. That was the most impact I could manage.

Where were they? If they didn't show up soon, I wouldn't be able to hold even the illusion of power. They'd see through my bluff.

I'd have failed yet again.

My hands clenched the brambles. Maybe I had to stop bluffing. I reached down and thrust all the will I had in me upward. "And the walls will bend, and the walls will break," I sang, my voice shaking with the effort. Every shred of emotion I had in me, I pressed into the shield.

O Spirit, hear my plea. Let me do this one small thing. Just break. Just break and be *done*.

The headache pierced straight down my spine. I swayed on my feet. My next inhale shuddered into my lungs.

I couldn't penetrate it.

A touch tingled across my back, one I hearkened more than felt. Even in my foggy state, I read Rocío in it, her intent like a solid stream of light beaming through the scattered energies around us. She extended herself to me in a question, an offering.

My entire body balked. *No.* How could I take more from the girl who'd sacrificed too much for me already? I'd thought I could see through this one act by myself—

But I couldn't. I *knew* I couldn't.

She was offering because she believed in me, in my plan— and because I needed her. I wasn't going to be the real hero here. If the best I could contribute was to become a tool to direct *her* power, at least I could trust I was in good hands.

I opened myself up and let her in.

A torrent of the magic she'd channeled burst into me and through me. It jerked away my breath. Radiating up through my ribcage and behind my eyes, it burned away my headache and every other sensation beyond the energy Rocío was conducting through herself and into me.

I urged the vast wave of it up toward the shield. The more energy I cast out, the more that poured in, so swiftly I thought I might float off the ground on it.

The magic battered the conjured barrier like a caged animal frantic to escape. I barely needed to direct it. The shield groaned, silent but echoing into my bones.

Images wavered through my mind with the rush of magic. Maybe Rocío didn't have quite enough focus left to fully control what she passed to me, or maybe this was how it always worked when mages conducted magic together—I'd never accepted anywhere near this much from anyone else.

Some of my impressions came from the present moment: I experienced the balling of her hands as she stared at the bulky guy she'd transfixed in place, the knots in her gut at the sight of the corpses strewn in the arena and her drive to ensure she didn't add to that number... and the urgent clutching of the magic around her—like a living creature, just as she'd said.

Other glimpses were different. Others were of me.

Through her eyes, from within her remembered body, I saw myself in the Academy's library grinning at the library assistant and felt a tickle of warm curiosity. I watched me interrupting Callum's trick on Judith during the defensive test and chatting up Desmond and Mark during dinner not long after. I absorbed her loneliness in the underground passage and its release when I'd taken her hand, the comfort she'd drawn from that touch... and her fear that it wouldn't last.

A lump lodged in my throat. I wouldn't have guessed there was much that scared Rocío, but she'd been afraid of me— because she cared. She cared so much it filled me like a soaring wind: her terror witnessing my collapse after our raid on the Iranian house and her pain confronting an illusion of me scraping a blade across my neck amid the deceptive shadows in the maze. I rode out the surge of panic that had flooded her when she'd discovered me slumped and blood-drenched outside the vines' trap, the wave of relief mingled with sorrow when I'd offered to follow her back into the fray for Judith.

Woven through every memory, every other emotion, was the tender yet wrenching mix of protectiveness and affection coursing through her right now, her support for what I was trying to accomplish—for who I was.

In her mind, I had never been found wanting.

I could recall the opposite sensation so sharply in contrast:

the day I'd declared, the day a shield of my own making had crumbled apart along with my father's hopes for me. I could *taste* it, the way the strands of magic had stretched until they'd snapped.

As if latching on to that image in my head, the torrent of magic Rocío was directing to me heaved through me even more swiftly. It focused into a point, pressing into one small spot on the shield's curve. Up, up, up it pushed, stretching the surface, thinning it.

Every quiver of energy whipped through my nerves as I threw my intent after it with my fading voice, until the boundaries between me and the magic blurred. I was nothing but its vessel. In that moment when I no longer had a sense of where I began or ended, the surrender felt like something sacred.

The shield cracked. It gaped apart along one widening seam, and all the magic outside crashed in to embrace the parts we'd drained. With a sigh I hearkened through every cell, the conjured barrier above us shattered into a shower of gauzy shards.

As they rained down on us, my knees gave, and I fell too. My vision, the world, and Rocío slipped from my grasp.

CHAPTER TWENTY-SIX

Rocío

The cracking of the enormous shield overhead sent a giddy tremor into the energy coursing through my body—into the strands of intent aimed ahead of me at our opponents on the ground and into the wide-open stream I'd channeled toward Finn behind me without any directive other than that it follow his will.

Then the magic slammed down on us.

The deluge whirled around me in a breath-stealing embrace. It splintered my vision and left every nerve jittering. My tie to Finn broke off, and my conjured hold on the other boy faltered too. I leaned against the broken stone in front of me, reached out to the magic whipping around me, and threw a mass of it at the hulking boy again.

Thankfully, the sudden wave of power had startled our opponents too. They'd hardly moved. Desmond swayed with a trembling laugh, but he clamped his hold back in place too. Leonie swore, and Prisha said, "I'm here! I'm here!" The wiry boy who'd been shoving himself upright froze too.

The magic that had streamed through the broken shield was

settling over us, its hum as full and vibrant as magic was meant to be. The limited portion that had been trapped inside the arena had weakened so gradually during the fighting that I hadn't realized just how depleted it had become until now, feeling it set right.

My nerves settled with the sensation. Our conjured bonds holding the trio across from us in place felt suddenly airy. I could have held all three of them if I'd needed to. Since I had only one at the moment, I dared for the first time to look behind me, to make sure that Finn was okay.

As I turned my head, a blur of motion hurtled toward me.

Lacey rammed into me, knocking me to the ground with her fingers jamming around my throat. My concentration broke. Leonie gave a little cry, and I knew the hulking guy must have shaken off my casting. I kicked and shoved at Lacey, bizarrely grateful for the childhood ambushes of Dull bullies that had taught me how to fend off the worst of a beatdown.

Lacey had dealt with bullies too—of course she had—but she wasn't used to being on the offensive. She matched me squirm for squirm, jabbing me with her knee, her head knocking against mine, but her grip on my neck loosened.

I thrust my hand backward to tap out a stuttered rhythm on the ground. My casting heaved me up, rolling us over with me on top. I jerked one of Lacey's hands to the ground and smacked the other away. My throat burned, but I managed to swallow.

Lacey spat a casting into my face. I thrust my arm up. My skin seared with a conjuring that would have blinded me if I'd been any slower. She mashed her elbow into my ribs, and I fell off her.

Something hard wrenched against my back. As I scrambled around, Lacey spun away from me as if to make for the others by the fallen spire. A blast of conjured hail pelted down at us, battering my head in the second before I managed to gasp out a shield. The others were shouting—the trio must have gotten free.

I had to stop them, all of them, now. I had to stop *this* before anyone else died.

Lacey veered in the opposite direction, a knife flashing in her hand. She'd yanked it from the sheath still wedged against my spine. Then I saw where she was headed now.

Finn was lying limp on the ground beside the hedge, his head lolling, his lips nearly as pale as the rest of his face. Completely defenseless.

Panic ripped through me. I dashed after Lacey, shouting out a lyric that tangled her feet. She tripped and sprawled. As I came up on her, she hurled the knife at me with a shrieked casting.

The blade barely nicked my shoulder. Her aim was still shaky.

"Stop!" I said. "I don't want to hurt you. I don't want anyone getting hurt. Can't you just stop?"

"My whole life, I've been *stopping* to keep other people happy," Lacey rasped. "You think that didn't hurt me? I'm never—"

Her fingers were moving to beat out another casting. I grasped for the words I'd used before to still, to quiet. "Arru arru."

Lacey's arms and legs pressed flat to the ground. Her mouth clamped shut, her pale hair strewn on the ground around her head. She glared at me standing over her.

Desmond and Prisha hollered to each other. The shield I'd thrown over me shuddered with some casting from behind me. The freed magic twined through my body, cringing at the rage that echoed up from Lacey through my hold.

I had to get back, had to stop our other attackers, but I could feel to my bones that the instant I shifted my focus from Lacey, she'd be at me—or Finn—again. We could all die because of her. Because she wouldn't *listen*.

My pulse thudded, and all at once I saw a glimmer in Lacey's head. As I stared at it, the magic between us hummed louder. Her desire to cast trembled through its wavering glow. I could hearken the strands of magic, delicate and beautiful, weaving in and out of her thoughts from that spot—the spot *she* hearkened from.

Certainty that I could crush that glimmer unfurled inside me —from me or the magic, I couldn't be sure. If I directed all my intent at it, I could sever those strands and cut Lacey off from the magic just as completely as the Confed's mages had burned out Sean and so many other mages across the country in the last thirty-five years.

I could break her. I could stop her from breaking anyone else.

Instinctively, I trained my attention on the shimmering strands. Lacey's eyes widened. Even as my stomach flipped, some part of me reveled in the understanding. I had the power to decide whether she would ever cast again. I didn't have to ask her to stop; I could *make* her.

Lacey shuddered, and I caught myself. Tears were streaking down the sides of her face. I stared at her, my awareness shrinking back.

"Rocío?" Finn said faintly, somewhere to my right. My thoughts hazed with a wash of cold horror.

The Confed had been right to be afraid of my talent. I wasn't a dragon-tamer, or at least not just that.

I was also a dragon.

An ear-splitting roar blasted through the arena, knocking me off my feet. I tried to push myself back up and found I couldn't move.

"All of you stand down," said Examiner Lancaster's dry voice. "Your Exam is now concluded."

* * *

I'd been sitting alone in the small windowless room for at least half an hour when the three examiners finally came in. One was Examiner Lancaster, another the man who'd sent us off to our dorms on the first night, and the third was a younger woman I thought had been in the ring of chairs during our group casting session. They sat across the table from me as if I were a suspect in a police interrogation.

"Rocío Lopez," Lancaster said. "These are my colleagues, Examiner Welch and Examiner Khalil. We will be conducting your final evaluation together. How are you?"

I looked down at my arms and flexed my hands. We'd all been teleported from the arena separately by the mages. The first person I'd seen after that had been a magimedical specialist who'd wiped the burns from my skin and repaired the welts in various muscles while I gulped down an offered snack and a bottle of water. He'd insisted on reconstructing my little finger too, even though I'd protested that I could manage without it.

I couldn't manage if I forgot what the Exam—what the Confed—had put me through. But I suspected that was exactly why the examiners healed us: so our bodies gave no evidence of how harshly they'd treated us.

They'd even given me new clothes: jeans and a T-shirt that looked much like my old ones, but I still had Mom's sunburst necklace. Its points nipped my fingers as I fidgeted with it.

"How's Finn?" I asked instead of answering Lancaster's question. "Is he all right?" He'd been conscious but still slumped on the ground when the mages had transported us out. I hadn't seen any of the other examinees since.

"Mr. Lockwood is recovering well," Examiner Welch replied, clasping his thick hands, which were as ruddy as his round face, on the table.

"I want to see him." I wanted to be sure that what they meant by "recovering" fit my definition. And he'd be worried about me too.

Or would he? With the urgency of our situation gripping me, I hadn't worried about what else he might see when I'd pulled all that magic through me and sent it on to him. All the thoughts and feelings, all the memories I'd felt flowing with it, were so much more than I'd have wanted to say to him yet. They might have overwhelmed him. Especially now that he was out, safe and sound, the urgency fading with every minute that separated us from each other and from the Exam.

We'd gotten out. That was what mattered. I'd done everything I could, and at least five of the seven in our group had made it through the Exam alive. And five other examinees were alive as well, at least partly because we hadn't fought back.

"There will be time for you to speak with him later," Lancaster said.

"And everyone else?" Other than Finn, mostly what I'd been thinking about in the last few hours had been the moment when I'd almost ripped Lacey's magic from her.

I could have done it. I might have done it. How would that have been any better than ripping off a limb?

No matter how the Confed wanted to frame it, I knew the violence I'd almost committed had nothing to do with my new-magic roots. All they'd done was prove that anyone with power, old magic or new, was dangerous when pushed to their limits. What did they think of the horrors Callum and the others had carried out since entering the Exam?

Even Finn—gentle, honorable *Finn*—had left the arena with Callum's blood smeared across his shirt. The memory wrenched at me.

I didn't think the examiners knew what I'd almost done. As long as I didn't let anyone push me that far ever again, they never needed to know.

Lancaster pursed her lips. "First we need to discuss your performance in the Exam."

I wanted to not care, but I couldn't stop myself from tensing. Were they going to tell me it hadn't been good enough? That despite everything I'd survived and everyone I'd helped, they were burning me out?

"It was really quite impressive." Examiner Khalil shot me a flash of a smile that brought a deeper dimple into her cheeks, which were faintly flecked with acne scars. Her slim fingers fidgeted with the edge of the gray hijab draped over her hair and across her shoulders.

"I agree." Welch rested his piercing gaze on me. "I'm not sure I've seen anything quite like it before."

Was that a good assessment or bad? "Thank you?" I ventured, and this time Lancaster smiled, slow and sharp.

"You don't need to worry, Miss Lopez," she said. "We're pleased to declare you one of this year's Champions."

I was probably supposed to experience some rush of triumphant relief. Instead, my body tensed further. "What?"

"We're naming six Champions," Welch put in. "And you are one of them. If you'll accept the position. Of course, the alternative is a voluntary forfeit."

"You mean I'd be burned out."

Khalil's mouth twitched. "Yes," she said softly.

They were watching me intently now. Under the table, my hands closed into fists.

Accept the position? Become one of their secret soldiers? I'd wanted to keep my magic. I'd wanted to win... but not for that "reward."

Not to work for people who'd thought nothing of putting fifty-seven teenagers—and others too—through hell.

"You said we'd be sent on missions against our country's enemies," I said. "That if we had to kill, it would be 'enemy combatants.' But those people you sent at us in the hospital gowns... How can you justify that?"

How do I know you won't ask me to do that again?

The examiners didn't look fazed by the question. Lancaster leaned forward with a strangely maternal air.

"Rocío," she said, "I know it may seem this way after the ordeals you've just been through, but we're not monsters. The people you encountered volunteered to be used in our test in exchange for financial compensation. They are all alive and well. Striking the target spot merely put their bodies into stasis. It didn't actually kill them."

I blinked at her. Her words didn't quite sink in. The woman's terrified face flashed through my memory. "They looked so scared," I said.

"They hadn't been told the exact nature of the test," Khalil said, her expression earnest. "They believed the announcement in that moment, just as you did. But they don't even remember it now. We 'chanted away those memories."

"It was a cruel scenario to put you all in," Lancaster said, "but the real enemies you'll face will be much more ruthless, and sometimes you may have to decide between one life and many. We must be cruel to ensure our Champions are up to the task, but we believe the thousands you may save in that role more than justifies the cost."

That was easy for her to decide when she wasn't the one paying that cost. I was still struggling to believe her. "What if we hadn't 'killed' them? What if— *I* didn't kill anyone in that test."

"There would have been no explosions," Welch said briskly. "They would have reached each of you simultaneously, and any examinee who hadn't complied would have been removed from the Exam. As to your own completion of the test, you were interrupted, but in light of your behavior before and after, we are satisfied that you would have carried through when you'd exhausted your other options."

I might not have exhausted them. I might have broken your horrible lie of a 'chantment. But I knew better than to say that out loud.

I supposed this would be their answer to any complaint I could make about what had happened to Mark and Judith, about the carnage they'd allowed if not encouraged in the arena, about *all* the Exam's horrors: The brutality was worth it if it revealed which of us was most equipped to fight in turn for our country.

Every complaint except one.

"There's something else we need to talk about," I said.

Welch gave me a thin smile. "What is that?"

"Whatever military operations the Confed is involved with— they're not good for the magic," I said. "They're... The castings that hurt and destroy people or things weaken the magic too."

The three examiners exchanged a glance. I wanted to think someone in the Confed already knew about this, but maybe they didn't after all. The other examinees hadn't felt it. The magic had reached out only to me. Maybe it had sensed I could hearken it well and that I'd be willing to listen.

"I could only feel the effect for sure in the arena, because of how contained the magic was with us," I went on. "But it must be happening everywhere else in the world too, even if the damage isn't as obvious. We have to find ways of dealing with our enemies that don't harm the magic, or else..."

I hadn't let myself think that far before. What would happen to the world if we were using more magic to kill than to create? Was the planet's magic already fading? Could it *die*?

I felt more responsibility to it than to any of the mages in front of me.

"We caught part of your conversation with your fellow examinees on that matter," Lancaster said. "And we were able to register some of that effect for ourselves. It certainly is a concern —one you showed yourself to be impressively able to adapt to. In fact, we anticipate that as Champion, your skills will enable us to find more effective methods with which to approach our national defense."

For a second time in the conversation, I was struck dumb. I stopped myself just short of blurting out, *Really?*

"I—I'm glad to hear that," I managed.

How much did they really care? I couldn't tell whether they believed me or were just humoring me. But they had listened… They had accepted without arguing and opened a door, if only a crack.

And now they were waiting—to hear whether I would accept their offer. I wet my lips.

I didn't trust the examiners or their version of Champions, but I wasn't going to help anyone or anything if they burned me out. I'd helped keep nine people alive despite the Exam's best efforts. How many more could I protect *with* the Confed's backing behind me?

The hum of magic sang around me and through me: the power they wanted to use and that I'd tried to hold back. The power that did make me dangerous.

I didn't want them taking it and aiming it at others the way Lacey had used my knife. If I wielded that power myself, held it firm with my convictions, and didn't let myself be pushed, maybe I could break the shroud of secrecy that allowed the Exam committee to carry out their awful trials like I'd broken the shield over their arena. Maybe I could stop the Confed from using the soldiers those trials produced and from approving the castings that weakened the magic.

Let them think they'd tamed this dragon. Let them think there was no threat to fear here. I could play the role they wanted me to if it meant I had a chance to make a difference, to make up for Mark and Judith and Javi—and for everyone else who'd ever fallen. For all the wrongs the Confed had done here and elsewhere, now and for so long before.

For *Javi*. There was one answer I couldn't leave here without.

"I have to ask," I said. "My brother, Javier Lopez—we were told he died in the Exam three years ago. He appeared in one of my tests…" Did I want to admit how much that trick had managed to affect me—if it had been a trick? "I'd just like to know for sure what happened to him."

Welch exhaled with a dismissive sound, but Khalil looked at Lancaster, raising her eyebrows in question. Lancaster nodded. The younger examiner turned back to me.

"Your brother was lost on the second day of his Exam, during the final challenge. I'm sorry."

Lost. As if he could still be found. They couldn't bring themselves to say they'd killed him?

My whole body went hot, but the wash of grief faded as quickly as it'd swept over me. I'd already done plenty of mourning in the last three years. At least Javi hadn't been forced into the brutality of that final arena. I could take a little comfort in that and in knowing for sure that the agony of the boy I'd met in the shadows had been completely conjured.

"Thank you for telling me," I said.

I'd made it, like he'd always wanted. And he'd have wanted me to keep fighting.

I could do it. I could be a champion for what the magic was meant to be, like I'd always wanted, except on an even larger scale.

All I had to do was pretend I'd chosen from the paths the Confed had offered me—accept or be burned out—and then find my own to follow. Oh, I was a threat all right. They could thank themselves for showing me that. A threat to their lies, a threat to their awful secrets. I'd be their Champion and follow their rules… until I didn't need to anymore.

"Have you made your decision?" Lancaster asked.

"Yes," I said, offering a smile that was only partly forced. "I'd be honored to be named Champion."

"Excellent." Lancaster held out her hand. "We'll assign you a mentor and a spot at the college as expected, though naturally you won't spend much time there. I believe this will be a productive partnership for both of us."

Her hand was firm and dry when I shook it.

The three of them stood up, and Welch cleared his throat. "We'll conduct a final debriefing shortly. In the meantime, you'll find a meal at the end of the hall."

"You'll be able to see your parents tonight, before you take your new position," Khalil added.

I pushed myself to my feet, a little dizzy. That was it? The conversation was over? Lancaster motioned me out of the room, and I went.

My thoughts were buzzing as I walked down the hall, but they stilled when I stepped into the dining room and saw Finn by the food-laden table.

He was just straightening up; he'd heard me coming. He looked at me with those bright green eyes as if I was exactly who he'd wanted to see walking through that doorway. The last of my lingering grief fell away under a giddy rush of joy.

"So we made it, Dragon-Tamer," he said in a wry tone that didn't quite fit the intensity of his gaze.

"Looks that way," I replied automatically. I didn't know what else to say. A few hours ago, I'd spilled the contents of my heart into his head. My own gaze skittered away.

His left hand was healed, the thumb reconstructed as neatly as my little finger had been. So we still matched, in our opposite ways.

"They couldn't send me home in pieces," he said, noticing me noticing. He clasped his hands together in front of him, the old right thumb rubbing over the new left. "It looks the same as ever, doesn't it? But there's a bit of a twinge if I bend it too quickly. It didn't come out of the Exam quite right, for all the magimedic tried to fix it. Funny how well I relate to that notion in general right now. As the great Horace once said, 'I am not such as I was.'"

"Yeah," I said quietly. Then I dared to meet his eyes again. "What did they decide for you?"

He smiled crookedly. "What do you think? Apparently while my strategy 'demonstrated a certain creativity,' it also showed 'a concerning disregard for the security of the Confed and its institutions.' I'll be burned out before I leave. That's all right. I knew what I was doing."

"It's not fair," I had to say.

"Actually?" he said. "Just this once, I think it is. They told me you made Champion. Prisha and Desmond too. That's fair enough for me."

My heart tugged at me to go to him, to wrap my arms around him, as if I could hold him away from his fate. But here in the stark white room, healed and freshly clothed, already halfway back to the life that had been so distant from mine, he looked almost like a stranger.

"Rocío," he said, "I— It was—" He paused and let out a noise of frustration. His throat worked. Then he lifted his head and spread his hands. "Come here? I want to show you something."

My legs balked before I walked forward. But as soon as I stood right in front of him, as soon as his arms came around me and the warm, sweet smell of him filled my nose, my hesitation fell away. I leaned my head against his shoulder, hugging him back. My eyes welled up.

Finn pressed a kiss to my forehead. Then, with his breath tickling over my bangs, he murmured a lilting verse.

Magic washed through his embrace and into me with a cool tingle. I closed my eyes, and images sprang up behind them.

A glimpse of my conjured dragon from over the rooftops of stately brownstones, along with a pang of startled awe. An irresistible draw pulling his gaze back to me around the circle of cubicles during one of our first tests. The spark of conviction provoked by my little smile as I leaned over the scarf I'd cast my defensive 'chantment into.

More memories, and more, flooded me with admiration and desire, until my mind spun with it.

Finn dipped his head, and I raised mine instinctively, still caught up in the feeling of him from the inside out. He kissed me hard. Even as my own delight shivered through me, his joy and wonder in that moment—that I was here at all, that I wanted him—reverberated through me alongside it.

A different kind of tremor ran through his shoulders beneath my palms. What he was offering me was carried by a casting. He must be tired still; he'd only had a few hours to recover. This might be the last magic he ever cast in his life.

And he was casting it for me, to give me what I'd given him.

I eased back, opening my eyes, and looped my hands behind his neck as the images fell away. "You can stop," I said, gently so he'd know it wasn't a rejection. "That— Thank you."

"I don't care where I end up or what Dull job they stick me in or any of the rest," Finn said. "I'll want you with me, whenever you can be, however you can be. As long as you want to be with me too."

I nodded, my throat tight.

He lowered his voice, pulling me closer again. "None of this is over," he said beside my ear. "The Exam, the Damperings, the way the Circle cuts down new magic... *I'm* not done. There has to be something I can do to start setting things right, and I'm going to find it."

I pressed my cheek to his. "Good," I said, "because so am I, and I still think we're a good team. Whatever we end up having to do."

He let out a rough chuckle. "I suspect there's going to be a lot of 'whatever' in our future, then. But we've made it this far."

"We have," I said. The path ahead of me looked as uncertain as ever, but my dread loosened just slightly.

I wasn't alone.

For the first time since the examiners had transported us out of the arena, a real smile crossed my face. "Just let them try to stop us now."

ACKNOWLEDGMENTS

This book's magic would not exist without the help of a whole lot of people along the way. I offer many thanks to:

Deva Fagan, Amanda Coppedge, and the members of the Toronto Speculative Fiction Writers Group, who offered invaluable feedback on the early drafts.

Linda Nieves Perez, Elsa Viviana Munoz, Sunshine McGillis, Felicia Thorn, and Rania Barazi for evaluating the book from a cultural perspective.

My awesome editor, Marissa van Uden, who untangled my prose where I went astray.

Jennifer Munswami, for designing a cover so gorgeous it makes people gasp.

My husband, Chris, for being there for me from the original idea he encouraged me to pursue all the way through to celebrating the release day.

And last but never least, all the amazing readers who've stuck with my books. It's because of you I get to make a life out of making magic.

ABOUT THE AUTHOR

USA Today bestselling author Megan Crewe lives in Toronto, Canada with her husband and son. She's been making up stories about magic and supernatural conspiracies and other what ifs since before she knew how to write words on paper. These days the stories are just a lot longer. Her other YA novels include the paranormal *Give Up the Ghost*, post-apocalyptic the Fallen World series, the sci fi Earth & Sky trilogy, the contemporary fantasy *A Mortal Song*, and the supernatural thriller *Beast*.

Connect with Megan online:
www.megancrewe.com

CPSIA information can be obtained
at www.ICGtesting.com
Printed in the USA
LVHW04s1630260618
581952LV00003B/751/P